NIGHT FLOWER

SHIRL HENKE

S0-AFI-426

WARNER BOOKS

A Warner Communications Company

In love and gratitude to Matthew C. Henke, who has
always been understanding about "not disturbing
Mom when she's writing."

WARNER BOOKS EDITION

Copyright © 1990 by Shirl Henke
All rights reserved.

Cover illustration by Max Ginsburg

Warner Books, Inc.
666 Fifth Avenue
New York, N.Y. 10103

 A Warner Communications Company

Printed in the United States of America

First Printing: May, 1990

10 9 8 7 6 5 4 3 2 1

ACKNOWLEDGMENT

My associate Carol J. Reynard originally came up with the titles for our Gone to Texas Trilogy. A floral designer for many years, she had the background for research into the three flowers that symbolized our Texas heroines. The cactus flower and the moon flower proved to be no problem. Not so the night flower of this third book. The night blooming cereus (which grows indigenously only in South America) obviously was not appropriate. After much digging, Carol discovered the lovely evening primrose, whose delicate golden blooms are native to Texas soil and ideal symbols for the hardy loveliness of Melanie.

We are indebted to a number of people for their kindness and technical expertise in the preparation of this manuscript. Once again the Public Library of Youngstown and Mahoning County and the Maag Library of Youngstown State University were key resources. Mrs. Hildegard Schnuttgen, head of reference for Maag Library, proved an invaluable and tireless worker in locating the odd volumes we always seem to need for our research. J. Myler, Librarian of the San Antonio Public Library, furnished us with our first leads about local newspapers in that city. We owe particular thanks to Dr. Taylor Alderman, Ph.D., bibliophile, and former newspaper reporter, whose expertise unlocked the mysteries of the Washington Hand Press and gave us a job description of that jack-of-all-trades, the small-town newsman who served as editor, reporter, and compositor.

When we first conceived the idea for Lee and Melanie's story, it was painted in bold, albeit shaky, brush strokes as a brief synopsis, which we turned in to our editor, Mary Elizabeth Allen. From a long and productive roundtable session in New York with her, the motivations of our protagonists were refined and Father Gus was born. For the leads that furnished the young priest's background and the reasons he had "gone to Texas," we owe thanks to Father Daniel Venglarik, Ph.D., and the Diocese of Youngstown.

The action of *Night Flower* moves from Texas and the Apachería during the 1840s back to San Antonio in 1852. For Lee's guns, as well as those of a large and diverse cast of characters, Carol and I are once more indebted to our friend and weapons expert, Dr. Carmine V. DelliQuadri, Jr., D.O.

Prologue

The South Texas Plains, 1830

Smoke burned his eyes though he squeezed them tightly shut, trying in vain to staunch the acid tears. He could hear the shrieks of the Comanche raiders as they rode furiously around the smoldering ruins.

Six-year-old Leandro Velásquez lay huddled beneath a musty hemp sack in a corner of the root cellar. When the Comanches had come, his mother had raced into the ranch house and scooped him up as he watched the savages approach from the front window. They were fierce-looking warriors with fearful bison-horn helmets on their heads and black paint smeared across their faces. Their small wiry horses were adorned with feathers and encumbered only by small rawhide "saddles." As one warrior whooped and shot, he slung himself over the side of his horse, holding on to the rawhide band around its belly with one leg. Using the horse as his shield, he rained arrows from beneath its neck. The *vaqueros* returned the fire until the last of the defenders had been cut down. No one had been expecting an attack, especially by such a large, well-armed band.

Dolores Velásquez had instructed her son to stay very still and remain hidden no matter what happened. Then she vanished up the steep steps in search of Tomás and Josefina, his older brother and sister.

Lee was frightened. Where was his father? He wanted to follow his mother's instructions, but the smoke was choking him in the dark cellar. Then he heard Josefina's sharp, piercing shriek, followed by a series of whimpering cries.

1

Desperate beyond fear, he climbed the rickety stairs, coughing and sobbing, stumbling as he raised the trapdoor to the root cellar.

All around him, thick smoke enveloped the room. Because it had rained for days and the roof was soaked, the fire smoldered instead of flaming. He crawled across the floor until his hands touched a body—his fifteen-year-old brother, Tomás, who lay with his head at a grotesquely twisted angle. The dead youth had been shot and scalped. Mercifully, the smoke obscured the body's hideous condition from the crying child.

Unable to rouse Tomás, Lee crawled toward a window, drawn by the piteous moans of Josefina. As the Comanche horses pounded into the distance, he rubbed at his burning eyes with two grimy little fists and tried to see. The painted warriors now were vanishing over the hill, leaving carnage in their wake.

The boy stumbled from the house in a daze, ignoring the fallen bodies of two of his father's *vaqueros*. He ran to Josefina, but when he crumpled by her side, she was dead. Her gleaming raven hair had been cruelly sheared off to adorn some warrior's scalp pole.

Turning from the unbearable sight, he was assaulted by one even more fearsome. His mother was sprawled protectively across the body of his father, clutching it tightly in death. His father's throat had been pierced by an arrow and both his parents had been scalped and mutilated. Lee threw himself on their contorted bodies, screaming until his raw throat could emit no more sound. He lay still, faint with exhaustion and terror. That was how Will Slade and the militia found him the following morning.

St. Louis, 1838

The attic was dusty and filled with cobwebs, but that made the child feel even more certain the trunks and boxes piled beneath the accumulated grime must contain hidden treasures. Impatiently brushing a sticky web from her hair, she knelt before an ornate leather chest. It looked very old. It must have been the prized possession of a great lady, she was sure.

She struggled with the straps that bound it, then threw back the lid. With a small gasp of delight, she lifted the buckskin garment that lay inside. It was primitive and beautiful, elaborately fringed and worked with thousands of brightly colored beads. As she held it up for inspection, a leather-bound book tumbled free of the dress folds and slid to the dusty floorboards at her feet.

When she draped the dress across the chest and reached to open the book, its yellowed pages crackled in protest. The handwriting was neat, but cribbed and small. She took it over to a dormer window behind a pile of boxes. Bright morning sunlight illuminated the pages of the diary. The first entry was dated 1750.

The light was growing dim when she heard *Grandmère's* voice. "Where are you, child?" Melanie could hear the woman's footfalls in the hallway as she searched from room to room on the second floor of their brownstone. With her heart pounding, half afraid she had done something that was forbidden, Melanie sat very still.

"Melanie, are you up in that filthy attic? However did you get the door open?" The steps creaked as Marie Duval ascended into the attic.

"I—I'm here, *Grandmère*," Melanie replied from where she stood at the window, silhouetted in the fading light.

Marie sighed with relief. "I told Hattie to watch out for you while I was out, but she said you refused lunch and I thought—" Her voice froze as she spied the opened chest with its buckskin treasure spilling over the edge. Then she looked back at the pretty eight-year-old and the diary clutched in her hands. "What have you been doing, Melanie?"

"Reading about your *grandmère* and *grandpère* and how they met," Melanie said. "Are you angry with me?"

Smiling, Marie Duval held out her arms, and Melanie slipped around the piles of crates and boxes to run into her embrace.

"So now you know one piece in the patchwork quilt that

is our life.'' Marie sighed as she stroked the child's lustrous black hair. "I had hoped to save this conversation for a few years, until you were older, but now you have taken that decision from my hands. Come, let's have Hattie brew some tea and I'll tell you all about Sweet Rain and Simon Duval.''

Melanie sat perched on the edge of her chair in the parlor, sipping tea and listening as her grandmother told her the story of how Marie's grandfather, a French fur trapper, had met and married the daughter of a Cherokee tribal leader in Georgia. "Is our Cherokee blood the reason we can't live with Papa in New Orleans?'' Melanie asked.

Marie shook her head. "No, *petite*. Your papa's family does not even know of our Indian blood.'' She added sadly, ''Men of your father's class do not ever marry women from our backgrounds.'' Marie hesitated, uncertain of how to explain. "You understand Hattie is full-blooded African, *non*?''

"*Oui, Grandmère*, but Hattie is a servant, a slave. What has that to do with Papa, or with us?''

"We too have African blood in our veins, *petite*. Oh, a very much smaller amount, to be certain. My great-grandmère was African.''

"But we're not slaves!''

"*Non*, of course not, *petite*. We are Free People of Color,'' Marie said proudly. "My *Grandmère* Sophie was a black slave who earned her manumission papers. Now we live in a lovely home and have servants of our own.''

"Then it is our African blood that keeps us from living with Papa in New Orleans,'' Melanie said softly.

Watching the child digest this cruel fact of life, Marie Duval felt her heart might break, but the girl's next words truly shocked her.

"Now I understand about the silver-haired lady at *Mère*'s house. *Mère* argued with her until Papa came in and carried the lady away. Papa was very angry. If he couldn't marry *Mère* because of her African blood, he must have chosen the white lady to be his wife. *She* doesn't want us there,'' Melanie said forlornly.

Marie Duval herself had been a *placèe*, as had her

mother. Now Lily, Marie's daughter, was the mistress of a rich Creole gentleman, Melanie's father, Rafael Flamenco. Melanie would be fortunate when her time came to find a lover as generous.

Marie took the fourth-generation Duval daughter in her arms and let her cry.

Chapter 1

Mexico City, December 1845

The tall, slim man stood silhouetted against the library's leaded-glass windowpanes. Deep in concentration as he read a letter, he was as oblivious to the beautiful fuchsias and lavenders of the sunset as he was to the worn comfort of the masculine room. On all four walls, books that had been precisely catalogued by his Uncle Alfonso were shelved floor to ceiling. A dark leather sofa faced the large fireplace on the north wall and several soft, upholstered chairs invited a reader to enjoy his book in their comfort. Massive stained-oak tables were littered with manuscripts and writing utensils.

Leandro Angel Velásquez had spent over three years of his life in this genteel atmosphere of scholarship and refinement since his father's elder brother had invited him to attend the university in Mexico City. *If Uncle Alfonso's wife and son hadn't died, I'd never have left San Antonio*, he mused to himself.

Now he was being beckoned back to Texas. His mind conjured up the wide rolling hills and burbling springs around his birthplace. The austere windswept plains of south central Texas were so different from cosmopolitan Mexico City on its high, temperate yet tropical plateau.

I would never have met Dulcia, either. Lee could still

picture the exact moment he had first laid eyes on her. She had come home from school for the Christmas season, an ethereal girl with an inner beauty that illuminated her fragile prettiness. Her chestnut hair had gleamed lustrously dark, spilling down her back in a cascade of thick honey-brown waves. She was just fifteen, still a schoolgirl not allowed to pile her hair high in elaborate coiffures set with combs. Clear blue eyes and a small bowed mouth smiled up at him as she had shyly watched him approach.

"You must be Dulcia." He had given her his most engaging smile. "A sweet name for a lovely miss."

She had replied, "And you must be Uncle Alejandro's son from Texas. Uncle Alfonso speaks highly of you." Her soft eyes never dared to rise to his.

As he bowed, he noted with approval that her innocent shyness was genuine. She had been as guileless and refreshing as spring rain.

"I—I should not be alone with you. My *dueña* is in chapel and I came out only for some fresh air," she had said hesitantly, embarrassed to even mention the proprieties.

Lee had smiled again, gravely this time. "Never fear. We are both Uncle Alfonso's wards, and so related. I'm sure it's proper."

Dulcia had shaken her head, "You are his nephew, while I am but the daughter of a distant cousin. I fear our relationship is not all that close." A second after she had said the words, she flushed at their unintentional implication.

Lee had not been able to resist reaching gently for her hand and bestowing a brief, chaste kiss on the back of it. "Then may I be so bold as to hope we may become closer—friends, perhaps?" He had left the rest unspoken, but, nonetheless, she had fled inside the house to her *dueña*.

Lee had watched her grow from a budding adolescent into a serene and lovely young woman of seventeen. When she was at last home from the sisters, her course of study complete, his own tenure at the university was drawing near to its conclusion. He was afire with dreams and ambitions, eager to begin fulfilling his role in life. Lee wanted the love of his youth beside him.

From the first Dulcia had been shyly receptive to his courtship, listening with wide, adoring eyes to his stories about the rich, wild land of his birth. They had been married last summer with Uncle Alfonso's blessing, and had returned from their honeymoon in time for Lee to complete his final examinations with his professors at the university. Now he was looking forward to a year or so during which their marriage could cement itself. He had not expected the sudden intrusion of the outside world into his own realm of contentment. But events were outstripping his plans. Texas and his friends there called him.

"Homesick?" His uncle entered the room quietly, asking the question, although he already knew the answer. Over the years, his nephew had corresponded with his friends in Texas regularly.

"Charlee asks if I'll be home for little Will's birthday in June. He'll be three years old and I've never even seen him," he replied, still deep in thought.

The frail gray head nodded. "And Texas is still home? I had hoped after your marriage to Dulcia, that you would begin to consider this your home," he said sadly.

Lee placed his letter on the scarred oak table and walked across the large room to take his uncle's pale, veiny hand in his firm dark one. Ushering the old man to a chair, he pulled up another across from him. "Texas will always be home," he replied. Then he added gently, "But a part of me will always remember and treasure my years here, too. You've been so good to me, taught me so much. I can never repay your kindness."

The old blue eyes twinkled. "And I introduced you to a second cousin's granddaughter—the greatest gift I could bestow. Just think, if you had not come to Mexico, you would never have met my ward, and found such a paragon for a wife."

Lee smiled broadly. "Most of all, I'm grateful for that. And you're right, for all your teasing. She is a paragon."

Alfonso's expression turned grave. "Do you think a convent-reared, delicate young lady such as Dulcia will be happy in your wild Texas?"

Lee sighed and stood up, starting to pace restlessly. "I don't know if she will or not, Uncle."

"Have you discussed your plans with her?" Alfonso prodded.

"Yes. Before we ever married, I told her I was bound to return to San Antonio, that Jim and Charlee and Asa, all the people I grew up with, were there. Will Slade raised me when my parents . . ."

"Died violently," his uncle finished the difficult sentence for Lee. "Did you ever explain to Dulcia the reasons you were orphaned and raised by an Anglo family?"

"That's not fair. Comanche raids around San Antonio are growing increasingly rare. And Will Slade's wife was a Sandoval. Jim is half *Tejano*. I'm *Tejano*, not truly Mexican, no matter how much I love you or how much I honor my Mexican heritage. Your own brother chose to become a *Tejano* when he emigrated. I was born one."

"Alejandro was young and idealistic," Alfonso said sadly, his gentle scholar's soul still appalled by the savage deaths of his younger brother and his wife. "And now you wish to carry on his dreams of carving a cattle empire out of the wilderness," he added with a wistful smile. "Remember, your father went to a state of the Mexican republic. You grew up to see a revolution make it an Anglo republic. Soon it will be a state in the American union. I've seen this coming for a long time, Leandro.

"President Polk's Minister Plenipotentiary, John Slidell, has been refused recognition by that imbecile President Herrera. The war party in the Yankee Congress already cries for troops to be mustered at our northern borders. Last summer the Americans sent their General Taylor to Corpus Christi with an army. Our leaders and the Yankee leaders will get their wish. There will be a war, Leandro. A war Mexico cannot win. When Mexican and Yankee fight, where will that leave the *Tejanos*?"

"Caught in the middle," Lee conceded unhappily. "But that's all the more reason for me to be there. Jim Slade and a lot of other *Tejano* ranchers like him are in the same position. We have to band together and defend our land—Texas is where I must build my life, Uncle Alfonso.''

The old man stood up and put his thin arms around the youth's broad shoulders. "Then you must prepare your bride to leave very shortly, while you can still do so unmolested. Once war breaks out, travel will be very dangerous, especially with an American navy in gulf waters."

Lee nodded in agreement, saddened as he was by his disagreement with his uncle, who was far more than a kinsman. He was a teacher and a friend. Lee hated to desert the frail man, who was alone now that the rest of his family had died in a yellow fever epidemic four years before. Since he had married Alfonso's ward, he was even taking her away from the old man.

"I did not want to go this soon, Uncle. We can wait another season. Perhaps . . ."

"No. I, too, was once young. Even now I still am not too old to recall the impatience of youth. If you stay with me and the war prevents you from leaving, it may be years before it's over. I know we will lose to your Yankees."

"They're not *my* Yankees just because I have some Yankee friends. Was Santa Anna *your* president just because you're Mexican?" Lee rejoined. "I see things in both countries to admire."

"You can be a bridge between the two, eh? Well, perhaps you can at that, my son, perhaps you can," Alfonso said, with animation and warmth once more infusing his thin face. "But for now, you must speak with Dulcia."

"What are you doing, Dulcia, daydreaming about Leandro?" Luz Rodrigues's dark eyes flashed with mirth at her friend's pinkening cheeks. The two young women had just completed a shopping expedition and were riding back to the Velásquez house in Juan Rodrigues's carriage.

"If I had a husband as young and handsome as yours, I'd daydream, too," Luz said in an attempt to ease Dulcia's discomfiture. If only she weren't so shy!

"Do you really think he is handsome? I—I mean, more

handsome than Juan?'' Dulcia's delicate porcelain complexion was still flushed.

Luz's laughter rang like a silver bell. "Of course he is! Juan is forty years old. Oh, he is distinguished, I suppose, if a bit thick about the middle, but he is rich and my parents were ecstatic about the marriage settlement. How I wish I had been like you—able to choose whom I married. Your guardian has been more doting than any father I know.''

"And generous, taking in an orphaned girl of such distant kinship and providing her the best education.''

At that, Luz made an indelicate harumph of disgust. "That convent school may be highly rated by strict parents, but I hated every minute of it! Being married, even to Juan, is better than living with the sisters.''

"I liked living with the sisters. Sometimes . . . oh, Luz, sometimes I'm not sure I like being married at all." Dulcia averted her eyes, her desire to confide in her older and more experienced friend warring with her embarrassment at bringing up such an indelicate topic.

Luz's face softened, and she took Dulcia's hand in hers and squeezed it. "You agreed to marry Leandro. He is handsome and young, from a fine family, a gentleman. Even if the Velásquezes aren't rich, they are comfortable, and Leandro gives you anything you want. You just ordered three new gowns today."

"Oh, no, it's not that he isn't kind to me or generous or anything like that. I had just thought, perhaps with an older husband that you might not have to . . . you know, submit so often." She burrowed her face in the folds of her hooded fur cloak.

Luz nodded, finally understanding the nature of her friend's problem. "Your *Tejano* is a wild stallion in bed. A quick plunge in and then out satisfies them, but never for long. With practice, he'll learn to go slower for you."

Dulcia seemed to cringe. "Oh, Mother of God, I hope not! I mean . . . he takes forever now, undressing me and touching me all over. I've tried to do what the good sisters said—I try to please him. He is my husband and I do love him. It's my duty, but I pray I'll conceive quickly. Then I can ask him not to . . ."

Watching her seventeen-year-old friend's shuddering misery, Luz could have wept for them both. Dulcia had a young, virile lover who apparently wanted to please his wife, and she had a fat, selfish old man whose interest in making love was secondary to finishing quickly so he could go to sleep! *Too bad we cannot trade places, little one*, she thought sadly as the carriage clattered through the deserted streets at dusk.

"What do you mean, leave now! How can we do such a thing? Uncle Alfonso is not well. We cannot leave him. We cannot leave here. Oh, Leandro, these past few months since leaving the sisters I've learned to love my home here." Dulcia's slender hands were clasped in supplication.

Lee looked at her pale, distraught face. Damn, he had dreaded this, knowing how hard it would be for her. Taking her in his arms, he said softly, "We'll build a new home in Texas, Dulcia. Remember, I told you how beautiful the land is. My parents' land is waiting for us. It's where my roots are, where I belong."

She stiffened and sobbed, "Your roots are in Mexico where your parents were born, not in some foreign land overrun by Yankees."

Lee continued stroking her gleaming chestnut curls. "Oh, Dulcia, we talked of this before we were married. You knew I must return to Texas, that I own land there. With the funds Uncle Alfonso has given us, we can build a prosperous ranch."

"But you never said we'd have to leave so soon," she hiccuped.

"I would have waited if the choice were mine. I know Uncle Alfonso is frail and lonely. He'll miss you, his beautiful little princess." He smiled down at her cherubic face, so vulnerable and sweet. *She's just a child, fresh from convent school*, he thought, willing himself to be patient with her fears. "But we can't wait much longer to leave, darling. Uncle Alfonso himself urges us to go now while we can still get a ship.''

''What do you mean, 'while we can still get a ship'?'' she asked, looking up at him with wide, tear-filled eyes.

Lee put his arm around her shoulder and led her to the big bed in their spacious sleeping quarters. A warm fire crackled in the grate, and he went over to stoke it. As he knelt and turned the logs on the andiron, he explained carefully to her, ''I know this may shock you, princess, but Mexico and the United States may go to war. If that happens, the gulf will be under siege and travel by ship will be restricted. Even if we took a neutral French or English vessel, it might be fired upon.'' He stood up at her small gasp of horror and walked quickly over to her.

''It'll be all right. If we leave now, no one will be shooting, princess. And deep in the interior of Texas, where my ranch is, the war won't touch us. But if we stay here too long, we may not be able to leave for years. I just received another letter from Charlee Slade today. She's so eager to meet you, and she wants us to be there for her son's third birthday.''

Dulcia wrinkled her nose. ''I still think that is a dreadful name for a lady—Charlee. But I do want to meet your friends—the people who raised you,'' she added quickly.

''You'll like Charlee and Jim and Asa. Even Weevils grows on you after a while,'' he said. His black eyes sparkled as he envisioned the beloved faces of the only family he had known until Uncle Alfonso had located him.

Sighing in resignation, Dulcia said timidly, ''Well, I can begin to pack tomorrow if both you and Uncle Alfonso feel it is the only thing to do.''

''Oh, beloved, it will be a whole new adventure for us. Like a second honeymoon.'' He sat down on the bed and took her hands in his, raising them to his lips and kissing them as he said, ''Speaking of honeymoon, it seems to me we're still on ours. . . .''

He kissed her lips softly, then trailed warm, moist kisses down her throat and across her collarbone. When he slipped her blue satin dressing gown open, baring a pale ivory shoulder, he could see her pert young breast beneath the thin silk of her night rail. His hand cupped the small peak and his thumb worked delicately over the nipple. Although Dulcia did not resist, neither did she respond. As he peeled off her robe, revealing the slim curves beneath the sheer night rail, she sat very quietly, moving her arms in response to his unspoken directions, letting him slide the sleeves off, untie the sash. When he returned his attention to her breasts, caressing them and working the nipples, they remained unaroused.

Sighing, he slowly raised his hands to run his fingers through her gleaming chestnut hair, holding her head gently as he kissed her, willing her to open her mouth to him. *I must go slowly. She's straight from the convent, shy, modest, a lady.* With a muffled groan, he laid her back on the bed, then stood up and walked over to the candelabrum. He blew out the candles, leaving the room in darkness. Dulcia was far more at ease without the light. Only a slight glimmer of moonlight remained to illuminate his path back to the bed. Quickly stripping away his clothes, he lay down beside her and gently worked the night rail up over her hips.

Dulcia kept her eyes closed tightly, a small part of her dying with each whisper-soft caress of his strong fingers on the most intimate parts of her body. With a silent prayer to the Virgin, she willed herself to be still, relaxing her limbs to let him have his way. It was her duty as his wife. Hadn't Sister Faith told her so?

Feeling her acquiesce, Lee took her limp resignation for acceptance of his lovemaking. He positioned himself over her and spread her legs, then slowly worked his aching, hardened staff into her soft, unresisting flesh. Dulcia was not wet and gyrating like the *putas* back in San Antonio or the more sophisticated women of the evening he'd known in Mexico City, but she was his love, his bride, pure, innocent, still virginally tender. He held back, stroking her flesh with his own, trying to override her convent-bred inhibitions. Finally he felt himself cresting.

Dulcia's arms, loosely held around his neck, tightened as she knew he neared the end. When he shuddered in release and collapsed on her with labored breath, he whispered hoarsely, "I love you, Dulcia, my wife."

She made no response but continued to hold his sweat-soaked body to her, stroking his back as her eyes opened at last to stare past him at the moonlight reflecting on the ceiling.

"Uncle Alfonso, I am so afraid. Texas is a wild, terrible place with no refinements. There are probably no dressmakers, no theaters, no balls or symphonies. Only savage red Indians and crude Yankees!" Dulcia paced in the study the following morning, hoping to enlist her guardian in dissuading Lee from his plan to go home.

Taking her by the shoulders, the old man sat her down in a chair by the big window. "Child, my princess, I understand how you feel, and I know it seems an alien and frightening world, but consider this." His blue eyes twinkled as he tapped his temple. "Lee has been living here in the midst of all the amenities you mentioned, moving in the best intellectual circles, speaking Spanish. But he's had this dream—a legacy if you will, from my wild young brother: Texas. He will not relinquish it until he's had the opportunity to return. Only then will he find where his true home is. Texas will be but an American land full of people he will no longer have anything in common with. Still, he must go and be convinced of this himself. If we could persuade him to stay here, we would gain an empty victory. He would be forever dreaming of Texas."

"But if I go with him to Texas and he sees for himself how it is now, he will not want to stay?" Dulcia's eyes lit with dawning comprehension.

"Bring him home, Dulcia. Home to me, home to Mexico."

Chapter 2

Galveston Harbor, January 1846

"The bay was named after a Spanish viceroy, Don Bernardo de Gálvez, over sixty years ago," Lee explained to Dulcia as they stood on the deck of *The Red Lion*, a British steamship they had taken from Veracruz the previous week. The weather had been raw and turbulent, and Dulcia suffered from terrible *mal de mer*. Fortunately, as they docked, the day had cleared and warmed. Lee hoped to cheer his despondent bride and distract her with a brief history lesson as he showed her the leading port city in Texas.

"I hardly recognize the place, it's grown so much. Look at all the ships along the wharves, Dulcia."

Dulcia implored, "Please, Leandro, don't even mention ships." The forest of bobbing masts ringing the harbor made her weakened stomach rebel once more. "I will be so glad to set foot on solid ground."

Lee put his arm protectively around her shoulders. "You'll be fine, but I'm afraid the solid ground is just loose sand. I'll carry you up the beach so you don't get sand in your slippers," he said gallantly, eliciting her first smile of the morning as he gazed into her blue eyes.

Suddenly he recalled vivid gold-coin eyes, a pouting child with sand in her slippers—Rafe Fleming's daughter, whom he had met so disastrously in Galveston four years ago. *I would never have carried that spitting hellion, that's for sure*, he thought ruefully to himself.

As if reading his thoughts, Dulcia broke in on his reverie. "You've been here before, haven't you, Leandro?"

With a guilty flush he replied, "Just twice—when I left Texas for Mexico over three years ago, and once earlier when Jim Slade sent me to Galveston for some brood mares. It's a booming port town, but we'll only be spending one night here. I'll book steamer passage upriver to Houston tomorrow."

"Is all of Texas so flat and open?" she asked timidly, shading her eyes against the surprising brilliance of sunlight reflected up from the water. This land looked primitive and menacing to her, but she held her peace, recalling Uncle Alfonso's admonitions.

Lee laughed. "First time I saw the gulf plains, I couldn't believe anyplace was this flat. The nearer we get to home, the more the landscape will change. San Antonio's nothing like this, believe me."

"Is it very far? I've journeyed more in the past two weeks than I ever did in my whole life," she said wearily.

"When we get to Houston, you can rest a few days while I make arrangements for our trip overland. I'm afraid it's almost two hundred miles, but the weather inland is drier during the winter. Once you're off the ocean, you'll be fine, my little sweet." He kissed the tip of her nose.

Why do I fear for her fragility and feel guilty for bringing her here? Mexican women colonized Texas over a hundred years ago. They thrive in San Antonio.

"You are right about the ocean. I will never be a sailor, but I will try to become a good *Tejana*, darling," Dulcia said with a tremulous smile that only increased his uneasiness.

Once disembarked, Lee arranged for their baggage and then began to escort his wife from the pier. He recalled the hotel where he and Melanie Fleming had stayed. It was near the waterfront, but clean, with a very good dining room. The city had grown a great deal and offered many more accommodations now, but he opted for the familiar and convenient.

As they walked across the creaking wooden planks, Dulcia began to wrinkle her nose. Placing a frothy lace kerchief to it, she coughed delicately. "Whatever is that stench?"

Lee, too, caught wind of the familiar smell. "Pouldoodies," he replied with a grimace and a laugh. "Oysters. A favorite

Texian delicacy and a sizable refuse problem. The smell is much worse in warmer weather!''

A few men had gathered near the end of the long pier just as Lee and Dulcia passed by a small sailing craft moored up close to shore. "I pernounce 'm daid. Neck broke clean when he wuz knocked off'n th' wharf in th' leetle set-to last ev'nin'," a loud voice proclaimed to the group of men standing on the deck of the boat.

"We gonna be here all day, Curley?" someone else chimed in. "We dunno who done fer Watkins 'n' me, 'n' Allen here's th' onliest ones whut come forward ta testify."

The tall fellow with black curly hair and a long beard of matching texture replied, "Yep. Hank Watkins's daid by th' hand—er fist more likely—o' party or parties unbeknownst. Hearin' dismissed! Abel, yew git a couple o' them niggers ta help ya bury 'em." With that, he reached down and casually flipped a filthy piece of gray canvas over the corpse lying in the bottom of the boat.

There was no way for Lee to escort Dulcia from the pier without passing the grisly drama taking place on the deck of the large flat-bottomed boat. As much as he could, he shielded her horrified eyes from the grotesque body and rushed her past the gaping onlookers at the "coroner's inquest."

"Is this how justice is done in Texas? Is there no law, no court?" Dulcia looked about ready to faint.

"I'm afraid the judicial system is rather primitive in many ways, especially when it comes to waterfront brawls between sailors. From what I've read, I suspect this kind of thing goes on in seaports from Liverpool to Veracruz," he answered gently. Eager to take her mind off her unsavory introduction to Texas, Lee scooped Dulcia up in his arms when they reached the beach, just as he had promised he would, and she responded with a delighted laugh.

That evening Dulcia ate little of the excellent dinner they ordered in the hotel dining room, sliding the rice and freshly caught whitefish around on her plate. Texas was every bit as ghastly as she had feared, filled with unbathed Anglos who were vulgar and loud and chewed tobacco incessantly. The streets were awash with the evil brown stains of their disgusting habit. Why, she had even seen a man engaged in a conversation with a woman (she would not design to call her a lady), and he was picking his teeth with a penknife as he talked!

"Are you still ill, little sweet?" Lee noted her lack of appetite and pallor with alarm.

"Oh, no. Not the seasickness, thank the Blessed Virgin," she replied. "I am just excited and overtired. I only need a good night's sleep in a real bed on solid land." *Pray the Virgin I will be allowed to sleep without any wifely duties tonight*, she implored silently. She had high hopes that she was with child, which would explain part of her violent *mal de mer*. It would also free her of all marital duties shortly. Smiling bravely at Lee, she clutched his hand and felt reassured by its strength. *I do love you, Leandro, and I will try. But now I'm so weary, so weary....*

Bluebonnet Ranch

"They should be there any day now, Charlee. I can hardly wait to meet Lee's bride," Jim Slade said as he strode across the kitchen from the washstand to the table where he embraced his wife. Tall and lean, golden-haired and hard-looking, he towered over the petite woman.

Charlee Slade snorted, "Bride! A seventeen-year-old child from a convent. Honestly, Jim, I couldn't believe he'd go and do something so crazy, but, of course, he's only twenty-two himself." She gave the large glob of bread dough she had been kneading a final swat and rocked back with her hands on her hips.

When she arched her back wearily, Jim reached over and began to rub it. "You having backaches again, Cat Eyes?" he asked. "You shouldn't be doing this. Lena can bake the bread for you until this little rascal is born." He reached over and gave her well-rounded abdomen a soft caress.

Charlee shook her head, and her long tan hair shimmered in the late afternoon sunlight. "I have too much energy to be sitting around doing nothing."

Jim said indulgently, "Nothing but fretting about Lee. Ever since we received his letter saying he was coming home with his new wife, you've been as excited as Will was when I gave him his pony. Anyway, why is Lee too young to marry at twenty-two? You were only eighteen when you married me."

She turned in his arms and said argumentatively, "I was almost nineteen, and besides, women are more mature than men. You were twenty-six. If you had married at twenty-two, you'd have ended up with someone like your old ladylove Tomasina Carver!"

Jim made a grimace of mock horror. "Well, I waited for you, so be grateful, woman. Anyway, you're not upset he's married at twenty-two; you're just upset that you weren't there to play cupid."

"But she's from an old, proper Mexican family. Lee is a *Tejano*."

"Who should have a *Tejana* for a wife," he added with a smile. "Well, it was his choice, Charlee, not ours."

"I know," she sighed. "I only hope she's able to fit in here. I do so want him to stay and do what he's always dreamed of."

"Rebuild his parents' ranch?" Jim replied. "Yes, I guess he did always want that, but you must realize, Cat Eyes, he's just spent nearly four years at the university in Mexico City, living with his uncle. The eighteen-year-old Texas boy who left here may just be a tad different and more mature when he returns. Maybe a little more Hispanic."

With a worried look clouding her bright green eyes, Charlee nodded. "That's what I'm afraid of."

When a messenger arrived the following morning to advise them that Lee and Dulcia would be arriving in San Antonio that afternoon, Jim could not discourage Charlee from heading straight to town. "I've started dinner and Lena is here to oversee it, so Weevils can't do too much damage," she insisted.

"You could give that young lady"—Jim pointed at her belly—"and your own backside a rest and let me escort them to the ranch."

"Who says this is a girl? Anyway, I have to set Dulcia a good example and show her the stuff we Texas women are made of."

"That's what I was afraid of," Jim replied.

As he stepped off the coach, Lee looked around the Main Plaza with the sweeping glance of a plainsman, taking in much quickly. Then he carefully helped his dusty, exhausted wife from the crude wooden conveyance. The sun shone brilliantly and the air was dry and crisp, a typical late January day, the perfect welcome for them. Thank heaven no blue northers had struck yet. He must get Dulcia safely to Bluebonnet before anything else befell!

Looking from San Fernando Cathedral to the old *cabildo* clock, hearing the rustling of the tall cypress trees and the twangy oaths of a Yankee teamster as he lashed his mules, Lee knew he was home. He watched Dulcia survey the wide expanse of the city's center with its unique mixture of Spanish adobe and Anglo frame buildings. Around the plaza, the larger limestone buildings dating from Spanish times still predominated. "Isn't it beautiful? Smell the air, Dulcia. No rotten oysters or wharf stench here."

A brisk, light breeze caught Dulcia's bonnet as she gazed around her in a daze. "It is very picturesque, Leandro. Larger and more like Mexico City than so many of the towns we've traveled through," she replied carefully.

"Look! Here come Jim and Charlee, and that must be little Will!" He pointed excitedly across the square to where a tall blond man was leaping lithely from a wagon with cougarlike grace.

Dulcia watched the rough frontiersman and realized that, except for the startling difference in their coloring and clothing, he and her husband were much alike. Lee looked elegant in his wool suit and gleaming dress boots, but he wore two of those terrible sidearms. Jim, dressed in a homespun shirt and buckskin breeches, was armed with a frightening arsenal of pistols. When they left Houston City, Lee had insisted he must carry weapons as they traveled into the interior. With each days' journey, he seemed less the gallant, handsome young scholar she had married, and more the *Tejano*, watchful and quiet, almost dangerous. The man striding toward them was older and harder but cast from the same mold, right down to the blinding-white smile and faultless Spanish with which he greeted her.

"Mrs. Velásquez, Dulcia, I am charmed to meet Lee's bride after all the letters he's written praising your beauty." He kissed her hand gallantly, then turned to introduce his wife and son.

The boy was a squirming, wide-eyed version of the father, but the woman! Well, at last Dulcia would meet the companion of Lee's youth. Charlee was as slight as she, fine-boned and slim with wide-set green eyes and a great mass of unruly multitoned tan hair. Her face was not classically beautiful, but instead was vivacious and strong with a zest for life that rather overpowered Dulcia, especially when the young woman reached out her arms and embraced her as if they were sisters. When she did the same to Lee, Dulcia was truly scandalized, for Charlee Slade was very visibly pregnant! Apparently she was as shockingly unconcerned with her condition as Lee, who practically threw her up in the air, laughingly commenting on how she had gotten fat in his absence!

"When's the blessed event, *chica*?" he had asked as he put her down.

"In about four months, maybe a little less. There's plenty of time for me to be in Austin for the ceremonies," Charlee replied.

Jim shrugged helplessly, a smile lighting the harsh angles of his face. "You see what Will and I have to contend with?"

Lee shifted his attention to the boy who sat in his father's arms, observing all the laughter and confusion of the reunion. "So you're William August Slade, eh?" When he switched to English, Dulcia could not understand all the words, but his manner and the way the boy responded to him made the meaning obvious. The child's serious, puzzled face split into a grin, revealing a goodly number of neatly spaced baby teeth as he reached out to leap into Lee's arms.

"I'm your Uncle Lee, and this"—he turned to his wife—

"is your Aunt Dulcia." Once more he switched to Spanish and said, "Let's hope we soon have some cousins to play with you and your soon-to-be brother or sister." He winked at Charlee, who laughed delightedly and looked over at Dulcia, who crimsoned.

Sensing the young girl's embarrassment, Jim interjected, "We have too much catching up to do to stand here in the street. Charlee, why don't you escort Dulcia to the wagon while Lee and I see to the baggage?"

Charlee nodded and reached out for the sturdy little boy. Will went unquestioningly from Lee to his mother, who hefted him easily despite her delicate condition.

Speaking to Dulcia in Spanish, Charlee suggested, "Let's pull the wagon up closer to where the driver let off your trunks. Oh, my, I bet you've brought gowns that would turn Deborah's purple eyes as green as mine with envy," Charlee giggled, seeming for a moment to be as frivolously girlish as Dulcia's school friends.

"Deborah?" Dulcia said uncertainly. Lee had spoken of so many people in Texas that her head spun with the names.

"Deborah is my dearest friend and a real Boston lady who loves beautiful things. She used to own my boardinghouse. Now she lives with her husband and children on a big ranch several hundred miles north of here in a rather isolated area."

As far as Dulcia could see, all of Texas was isolated, but she was too taken aback by the rest of Charlee's matter-of-fact statement to think of that. "You own a business—a boardinghouse?" Ladies did not work! At least not in Mexico. Did they in Texas?

Charlee smiled, measuring the confused and tired young girl before her. "I bought it from Deborah when she and Rafe left San Antonio over three years ago. But then Jim and I got married. It was too much bother to try running it myself from the ranch, so I hired a manager. I'm in town often enough to oversee it. I kinda like to keep my hand in, I guess. I suppose Yankee women seem different to a lady from Mexico, Dulcia, but this is Texas—one of the few places in the world where a woman at least has property rights outside her marriage."

Dulcia's blue eyes widened. "But—but if you love your husband, why would you need laws or courts to give you property?" she asked in puzzlement.

"Because I earned my property. So did Deborah. Oh, don't mistake me. We don't need protection from our husbands," she added with a wicked grin lighting up her small face, "but some women do. If a man has the right to protection under the law, so does a woman."

"I suppose there are cases . . ." Dulcia's voice faded into uncertainty again as they reached the big wagon, drawn by a team of enormous chestnut horses. Effortlessly, Charlee tossed young Will up on the spring seat and then climbed up, heedless of her ungainly belly.

When she offered her arm to Dulcia to assist her up, the younger woman reddened in chagrin. "Please, I can manage. I wouldn't want you to strain yourself in your state." As the girl very carefully lifted her skirts and climbed slowly up the big spokes of the wheel onto the wagon seat, Charlee laughed.

"My state is very pregnant, and I'm just as healthy this time as last. Best thing a woman can do to assure an easy delivery is to keep active. Words of advice from several of my older and wiser friends."

Despite her mortification, Dulcia was eaten up with curiosity, since she suspected that she at last might be carrying a child, too. "You aren't worried about the bouncing of the wagon?"

Slapping the reins, Charlee laughed easily again. "Can't hurt! I still ride Patchwork, my horse, although Jim sees to it I keep her to a rather tame trot!"

"But how can you position yourself properly on a sidesaddle?" Dulcia asked, almost in awe by now.

"Easy. I ride astride with a safe, solid stock saddle." Realizing how much Lee's child bride had to learn about Texas, Charlee let that sink in, then went on to tell her, "February nineteenth is the big shindig in Austin. Jim and I are taking Will. It'll be a historic occasion and I wouldn't miss it for anything—the Texas Republic will officially become the twenty-eighth state in the United States!"

"You will travel all that way to appear at a public ceremony in your condition! I mean, oh, I would be frightened, I suppose. In Mexico such a thing would never be permitted," Dulcia finished weakly, hoping she had not offended Lee's friend.

Charlee put her small but strong hand over Dulcia's small, fragile one. "You're in Texas now, Dulcia, married to a *Tejano*," she said gently. "You'll have to learn new ways. Some of them will seem pretty unconventional to you."

Before Dulcia could reply, they pulled up where the men were sorting through an immense array of boxes and trunks.

"This one's too heavy by half to be women's frou-frous," Jim said as he hefted one leather-bound portmanteau on his shoulder.

"Books. Uncle Alfonso was afraid my mind would languish in the Texas wilderness," Lee replied laughingly.

"Sort of like water in the desert, eh?" Jim said ironically, knowing how thoroughly Lee had used the extensive library at Bluebonnet while he was growing up.

They switched the conversation effortlessly from English to Spanish, Charlee included, as they loaded the wagon, deferring to Dulcia, whose understanding of English was very limited. Wanting to befriend the frightened girl, Charlee said as they rode out of town, "Lee taught me Spanish when I first came here from Missouri. The least I can do to repay the favor is to teach his bride English."

Dulcia returned her smile gratefully but prayed in her heart of hearts that she and Leandro would not be in Texas long enough for her to master the language.

Austin, Texas, February 19, 1846
"I hope we're not late, Joe," Melanie Fleming said as she kicked her horse into a slightly swifter pace and scanned the outskirts of the capital city.

"If we hadn't stopped to help them settlers with their

broken wagon wheel, we'd have made it in plenty of time," her nine-year-old brother, Adam, said impatiently.

"*Those* settlers," Melanie corrected automatically.

"Folks in trouble got a right ta expect a hand. That's Texas's unwritten law, youngun. Yew know thet," Joe De Villiers sternly admonished his young charge, who had pulled his horse alongside the slim half-breed's. "I 'spect we'll git there afore all th' speechifyin' is done, worse luck."

"Just so we get to see the flag raising," Adam said excitedly. "I wish Mama and Papa could've come—'n' Lucia, too!"

Joe De Villiers grinned. "Yore folks got them more important bizness ta attend to'n seein' th' Republic join th' Union."

"I don't see why havin' an ole baby is more important. We already got us—er, have Caleb," Adam replied, petulance etched across his dark, finely chiseled features as he referred to his three-year-old brother.

Melanie smiled encouragingly. "Maybe this time you'll get a baby sister," she said devilishly.

"Huh? I already got a big one! Who needs two of you to gang up on me 'n' Caleb? 'Sides, Lucia 'n' Joe already got a girl. Too many females on our ranch."

"Thet's where you're wrong, *mon ami*," Joe replied. "Lucia 'n' me 'spect ta have a whole dozen daughters. Won't be long 'n' yew'll git happier 'bout there bein' so many females round. Jist wait."

Melanie giggled, pushing a straggling lock of ebony hair from her forehead as she watched her young half brother squirm. In the years since she had come to live with her father and stepmother, the sullen, frightened twelve-year-old daughter of Lily Duval and Rafael Flamenco had been transformed into Melanie Fleming, a laughing, carefree sixteen-year-old of singular beauty and self-confidence.

When he came to Texas to reclaim his runaway wife, Deborah, Rafael had become a Texian rancher and built a new life for himself. Here he was known as Rafe Fleming, co-owner with Cherokee Joe De Villiers of Renacimiento,

the largest ranch in northern Texas. He and Deborah had
lavished their love and understanding on his octoroon mistress's cast-off daughter after the child's grandmother had
been killed in an accident over three years ago. Secure in
her place in the Fleming family and her life in Texas,
Melanie's childhood scars were forgotten on this sunny day,
so full of promise for them all. Texas was to become the
twenty-eighth state in the Union and she was going to see
Anson Jones, the last president of the Republic, hand over
the reins of the government to the first governor of the state,
J. Pinckney Henderson. Her mother's old friends Charlee
and Jim Slade were going to be present, as well. She could
hardly wait!

At the time of its creation in 1839, the capital of Austin
had housed a scant ninety souls on an outpost of the
Comanche frontier. Now, after nearly seven years of rivalry
between Houston and Austin, the capital was to be permanently
situated on the banks of the Colorado River. The log huts
with their dog-trot porches, so common across the Texas
frontier, were giving way to neat saltbox cottages and
temple-fronted dwellings. The population, by now grown to
a permanent base of over six hundred, looked forward to
conducting the business of government, leaving crass com-
mercialism to its rival on Buffalo Bayou.

"Shore is different 'n San Antonio," Joe said as he and
his young charges surveyed the wide, orderly grid of streets
and the Yankee architecture.

"So many people are here for the ceremonies, I hope we
can find the Slades," Melanie said, observing the milling
crowds around the capitol grounds. Men in frock coats and
tall stovepipe hats strolled between grinning teamsters in
ragged breeches, while hard-looking, buckskin-clad mountain men leaned on their long rifles and watched the pro-
ceedings with shrewd eyes. Dogs and children ran everywhere as farmers sat around makeshift campsites, pitched
beside their wagons. Everyone was here to see the end of
one era and the beginning of another.

"Let's stop at Miz Evans's boardin'house 'n' see if th'

Slades been there yet,'' Joe suggested. It was a familiar rendezvous place for respectable ranchers and their families.

"Aw, I want ta watch the fiddlers. Look, Mellie,'' Adam said, pointing across the street to where a group of men with violins and banjos were tuning up for the celebrations. "I bet Ole Sam'll be coming down this very street!''

"*Mr.* Houston's new title is United States Senator now, Adam, never 'Ole Sam' to the likes of a nine-year-old boy,'' Melanie scolded. She hoped secretly to catch a glimpse herself of the war hero who had twice served as the Republic's president. Deborah and Charlee both had met him and had told her tales of his wit and gallantry. He and Jim Slade were friends of long standing since Slade's service under him during the Battle of San Jacinto.

"Yew wait here and rest yer backsides whilst I check fer th' Slades. Now mind, don't go wanderin' off like a couple o' jugheaded mustangs,'' Joe admonished. Melanie and Adam dismounted, waving Joe on while they watched the show. Living for most of the year in the wilds of north-central Texas, the two young Flemings were relishing this sampling of city life as an incredible break from the daily chores and lessons of the ranch.

"Hey! Mellie, there's Billie Bledsoe. I knew his folks'd be here, I just knew it!'' With that, Adam dashed into the street and vanished into the press of horses and pedestrians, with Melanie in hot pursuit.

"Adam! Come back here! You heard Joe,'' she shrieked, pulling up her skirts to run after the speeding imp who was already across the street, engaged in a giggling exchange with his young friend from a neighboring ranch.

Intent upon retrieving her errant charge, Melanie collided with the solid chest of a tall stranger before she could stop her headlong rush. Breath knocked from her, she stumbled backward, only to find herself steadied by a pair of strong hands. Mortified, Melanie raised her flushed face to apologize, but the words froze in her throat as her eyes widened in recognition. "You!''

Lee's black eyes narrowed to slits as he appraised the luscious little morsel who had just flattened herself against

him. She was tiny of stature but very well put together; her
sheer mustard silk shirt revealed a full bosom, heaving from
her headlong dash. His hands could span her fragile waist.
He took in the enticing curves of her hips under the
scandalous split leather riding skirt. Expensive clothes but
not what he'd allow his wife to wear. As her gasping single
word of recognition registered in his ears, his eyes traveled
up to her face. And an exquisite face it was. Delicately
arched brows rose over enormous golden eyes fringed with
thick black lashes. Those eyes were slanted, following the
arresting lines of her high cheekbones. A generous pink
mouth was pursed in shock over a pointy, stubborn chin.
Her complexion was flawless, an olive-gold hue that was
complemented by masses of gleaming ebony hair spilling
down her back and around her shoulders. She knew him,
but who was she?

"Leandro Velásquez, home from your foreign adventures
at last. Whatever brings you to our parochial little celebration!" she asked, proud of her regained composure and
erudite vocabulary.

"I'm afraid you have the advantage," Lee replied, a
frown of concentration marring his chiseled features.

Melanie looked up at the tall man, more muscular and
mature than the reed-slim eighteen-year-old boy who had
struggled to rescue a humiliated and terrified twelve-year-
old from the clutches of a lecherous sailor on the Galveston
waterfront. Lee was still wonderfully handsome to her
infatuated eyes. *And he doesn't even remember me!* Smiling
oversweetly, she said, "After that brute of a first mate
almost squashed you like an insect, I'd think you'd be
grateful to the girl with the scissors who saved your life that
day on the wharf."

"Fleming's daughter," he choked out. "But you were
only a little girl—" He could sense her smirk even before it
began to spread across the lovely face. "All right. I suppose
that was four years ago, Melanie. You did grow up. Forgive
me?" He doffed his wide-brimmed hat, revealing that splendid head of curling black hair. When he smiled, the blinding

white slash in his dark face made her heart do a sudden lurch.

"Well, since you do remember my name, not just my father's, I suppose I forgive you," she said, returning the smile.

"But I'd say your scissors did more damage to me than the first mate!" What a hellish week that had been.

"Is that why you left as soon as my father arrived, not even saying good-bye?" she half teased, half challenged. How well she could still remember her devastation when she awoke that morning and her papa told her Lee was gone.

Lee, too, recalled his judicious retreat but was unaware it had caused a young girl's heartbreak. "Let's just say discretion was the better part of valor," he replied lightly.

Melanie was saved from an angry retort by her brother's sudden arrival. Remembering his hero from early childhood in San Antonio, Adam catapulted into Lee's arms. "Lee! Aunt Charlee told us you were living in Mexico. I'm so glad you're home. Wait till you see where we live now! Our papa has the biggest ranch in Texas. You gotta come visit us."

Smiling, Lee set the boy down and knelt by his side. "Afraid I can't do that just now. Dulcia's waiting for me back in San Antonio, *niño*. We're going to build a pretty fair ranch of our own."

"Dulcia?" Melanie asked, already dreading the answer.

"My wife. Didn't Charlee write Deborah? I was married last summer in Mexico City."

"Well, I hope you and your bride will be very happy in Texas, Lee. Adam and I promised to wait for Joe across the street. Maybe we'll see you after the ceremonies. I think they're about to begin." She turned quickly away and shaded her eyes, scanning the crowd around the grandstands.

With a nod, Lee gave Adam a final hug and rose. "I'd better find Charlee and Jim pronto. When you locate your friend, we'll be over by the right-hand side of the platform." With that, he disappeared down the crowded street as she stared blankly after him.

Chapter 3

El Sueño Grande, May 1846

Lee wiped the sweat from his brow and stopped to admire his handiwork in the clear noonday heat. The corral, with its sturdy high cross rails of oak, should hold at least fifty prime horses, culled from the wild mustangs he and his men had captured the past several months. Now they would begin breaking the best of them for sale.

With any luck, only one more trip out onto the open plains and he would have enough stock. He looked from the new corral to the rebuilt hacienda. The low-ceilinged, six-room stone-and-adobe structure he had built on the ruins of his parents' place was scarcely the grand mansion that would one day house his family, but it was a comfortable beginning nonetheless. Although Dulcia had made no protest when he brought her from Bluebonnet last week, he was sure it seemed primitive to her. At least here she was mistress of her own modest domain, with three house servants to see to her comfort. Still, he felt uneasy about her fragility in the face of frontier hardships. As he pictured his wife's soft features, another face floated in his memory, one with glowing, tanned skin and snapping gold eyes that mocked him.

What the hell am I doing remembering that little hellion? he thought incredulously. Feeling an unreasoning surge of anger at the way his subconscious had conjured her up, he was further upset with the immediate comparison between her and Dulcia that some perverse self-punishing instinct caused him to make. Neither fragile nor modest, Melanie Fleming fit in splendidly in Texas. Admittedly Lee had been shocked at how she had changed since their first encounter when she had been a twelve-year-old child. Even then he had thought the daughter of Fleming's octoroon mistress would grow into a striking woman. But her exotic beauty combined with earthy sensuousness had surprised him. Frequently over the past months, as he had slaved and sweated rebuilding his parents' dream, Lee had found Melanie haunting his imagination, causing him to wonder how she would respond to his touch. Scarcely the way a proper *criolla* would, he was absolutely certain of that!

Angrily he pulled his disloyal thoughts back to Dulcia, his gentle and patient bride who adored him. If she did not return his ardor in making love, that was to be expected from a woman with her upbringing. A lady did not behave with abandon. He felt a renewed surge of guilt for his wayward thoughts, especially now that she was pregnant.

Smiling ruefully, he recalled the evening when she had told him he was to be a father. It was the month after he had gone to Austin for the statehood hoopla. She had been so shy, yet proud about becoming the mother of his child. Of course, he had taken her agonizingly embarrassed plea to be relieved of conjugal duties with as much good grace as was humanly possible.

When in Mexico City he had been disillusioned with the morality of upper-class men who kept mistresses, thinking such a practice decadent and insulting to the women who bore their names and their children. He had even recalled Rafe Fleming and his illegitimate daughter, feeling sorry for Deborah's plight when she was forced to accept such a stepchild into her home. Now, faced with eight months of enforced celibacy, he was less inclined to be so puritanical.

"That's the only reason I've even given Melanie Fleming a thought, dammit," he muttered beneath his breath. Just then, hoofbeats coming from the direction of the ranch house interrupted his ruminations.

"Charlee tells me that congratulations are in order. That you and Dulcia are going to have a *niño* at year's end," Jim Slade's voice called out as he swung effortlessly from his big buckskin horse.

"I figured once the women started talking, all Bexar County would know," Lee replied smiling. "I only hope we have a boy like Will."

Jim's eyes lit at the mention of his son's name, but he grinned and said, "This time I'm hoping for a little Texas hell cat like Charlee."

Lee's face sobered. "Charlee takes so well to frontier life; I worry about Dulcia sometimes."

"She'll adapt. Look at Deborah Fleming. All the way from Boston, and Rafe couldn't ask for a better rancher's wife," Jim reassured his love-struck young friend.

Recalling his earlier uncomfortable thoughts about Deborah's stepdaughter, Lee murmured, "I suppose Dulcia will learn. I'm only glad we have the house furnished and a cook and maid to help her during her confinement."

Charlee had told her husband in no uncertain terms what she thought of Dulcia's ideas about "women's confinement" during pregnancy. Jim wanted to get off *that* subject quickly! "Some great corral," he improvised, striding over to run his hand along the sturdy oak railing.

"It'll be full of prime horse flesh in a few more days." Lee could not restrain the note of pride in his voice.

"You still working that blue roan stallion?" Jim asked.

"Sangre Azul," Lee said, eyes alight. "Yes, he's almost finished his formal education. I expect he'll be as much a one-man horse as Polvo." He indicated Jim's impressive buckskin.

"Blueblood," Jim translated the name his friend had given his new stallion. "You sure that time in Mexico City didn't turn you into a *criollo* snob, *mano*?" He was only half teasing.

Lee's face became serious. "Hardly that. God knows the political corruption in Mexico is causing chaos, and the fine aristocrats who head the government and the army are the cause of it. You heard any news from San Antonio lately?"

Jim's brow creased with concern. "We're really going to have us a war, Lee. That ass Taylor's moved from Corpus Christi down to the Bravo, claiming it's American territory."

"Which, of course, was never settled between Texas and Mexico," Lee said in disgust.

"Well, as Sam wrote me from Washington, President Polk wants California, and that means all the land above the Bravo or Rio Grande, whatever they call it—everything between here and the west coast is up for grabs."

"I guess our senator knows his president's game," Lee replied bitterly.

Jim grinned grimly, "Sam Houston knows *everybody's* game. Never be deceived. I only hope someone takes charge in Mexico City and is willing to negotiate before this thing gets really nasty. *Tejanos* and *Californios* are going to get caught in the crossfire. Already Governor Henderson has responded to Taylor's request for rangers to act as scouts for his inept dragoons. Jack Hays has formed up a company and headed out to join Taylor on the Bravo, where he's set up a fort across from Matamoros."

"'Remember the Alamo' all over again. Only this time the Texians can really get even, with the U.S. Army backing them," Lee said. His face was set in tight lines.

"You sound like you're ready to join the Mexican Army," Jim retorted angrily. "Jack Hays is an honorable man and a damn good Comanche fighter, I might add."

Lee waved dismissively. "Hell, I don't mistrust Hays, but there are plenty of Anglo rabble in San Antonio and all along the border who'd use any excuse to kill Mexican civilians, even those born on Texas soil. It's been so tense in the city the past months I haven't even taken Dulcia to visit her friends because of the drunken brawls and mob mentality of the 'noble militia.' If you ask me, we could use Hays right here in San Antonio to control the Texas volunteers for this damn undeclared war before they loot and burn an American city!"

Jim knew what Lee said was justified. Incidents between the companies of Texians forming up to fight with Taylor and the Texas-born Mexican populace, the *Tejanos*, had grown alarmingly common.

Jim said, "I fought with Houston at San Jacinto to free Texas from an invading army. I am sure as hell not going to march into Mexico and become the foreign invader. But Mexico's government, such as it is, has declared war on the

United States, and now Texas is a state. If they come here, I'll fight again.''

"But if they don't, you won't follow Taylor below the Rio Bravo," Lee finished for his troubled friend.

"'Rio Grande' in Texas," Jim corrected Lee. "No, I won't follow Taylor anywhere. He's no General Houston."

Lee snorted in agreement. "History sure has played some dirty tricks on us, *mano*."

"I don't know why you persist in disliking the girl so, Charlee," Jim said with irritation. "I know she's immature, but she's only seventeen."

Charlee swung up on her little paint filly's back with surprising grace for one who was eight months' pregnant. "Immature," she snorted. "Spoiled rotten is more like it. Lee treats her as if she were made of porcelain."

Jim walked Polvo alongside his feisty wife's horse in a leisurely after-supper ride. Charlee insisted it helped her digestion. "You sure you're not just jealous of how he dotes on her, Cat Eyes? If you like, I could get you a covered buggy like hers, and you could use a screen so the eyes of the vulgar couldn't gaze on that delectable little belly," he teased.

"Speaking of vulgarity, *Don Diego*, you're pushing the outer limits," Charlee replied with as much dignity as her expanded midsection allowed. "I might just get the vapors from being in such a delicate condition and tell you to go sleep in the guest bedroom tonight."

Jim laughed. "And deprive yourself? That'd be cutting off your pretty little nose to spite your face. As I recall, the day before Will was born you attacked me—"

Charlee reached over to swat playfully at her tall husband, who continued undaunted, "We were on a picnic, right out in front of God and everybody."

"We were not!" she shot back in mock anger. "We were in a very secluded copse of willows down by the creek and nobody saw us . . . well, maybe the cat and the horses," she amended as her husband laughed fondly.

"I'm afraid it's just Lee's Hispanic gallantry, all polished up while he was under the civilizing influence of his uncle, away from Texas riffraff like us. He's only twenty-two, Charlee, and being a new husband and prospective father is a lot of responsibility to take on.''

"Yeah, and considering her ideas about marriage, it sure isn't going to get any easier," Charlee replied darkly.

"Not wanting to appear in public while she's pregnant isn't an unforgivable sin, Cat Eyes," Jim remonstrated.

Charlee sighed. "That's silly, but if she wants to molder for nine months, that's her problem. It's the *other* that's unfair to Lee."

"You're not making sense," Jim countered.

Charlee sighed. "I don't guess I'm violating the sanctity of the confessional if I tell you about our conversation when she told me she was expecting—really, I told *her*, after she asked a bunch of very euphemistic questions. Then she was overjoyed.''

"Well, that seems natural enough. She does love Lee in her own shy way."

"She loves him all right, as long as she doesn't have to make love with him. Her first question to me after she was sure she was pregnant was how soon could she tell Lee it wasn't safe for her to 'submit' to him."

Jim burst out laughing, then sobered. "Come to think of it, that isn't really very funny, is it? I can just imagine what you told her," he added with a glint of devilment in his cougar eyes.

"I was the soul of tact and patience," Charlee replied primly, "but I don't think I convinced her. She's so young and full of claptrap and aristocratic pretensions, I'm afraid she's never going to make Lee the kind of wife he deserves."

"Well, if sheer devotion and youthful romance have any value, I wouldn't sell their chances short," Jim consoled her, hoping that it was only Charlee's inherent dislike of the snobbery she'd encountered from some of San Antonio's best Hispanic families that had shaped her judgment of Dulcia.

"Oh, Gertrudis, I am so lonely for Leandro," Dulcia practically wailed to her friend, the eldest daughter of the

Sandoval family, at whose lavish *estancia* she stayed while Lee was gone hunting a last elusive bunch of wild mustangs.

Knowing that San Antonio was a recruiting point for western militiamen who were forming very irregular companies of volunteers to "whip the greasers," Lee had feared leaving his wife alone with a handful of elderly servants at El Sueño Grande. Since she had disdained to stay with Charlee and had made friends with Jim's cousins, the Sandovals, Lee had left her in *Don* José and *Doña* Esperanza's safekeeping. But after two weeks of embroidery and gossip, Dulcia was restless. Her morning sickness had finally abated and she showed only the slightest evidence of being pregnant. Suddenly, after months of melancholy and crying spells, she wanted to see her husband. Lee's gentle charm and humor could lighten her flagging spirits.

Gertrudis, a pretty, flighty young woman of eighteen, engaged to a neighboring rancher's son, was instantly sympathetic. "I know how difficult it must be, dear Dulcia, but in order to build his ranch, Leandro must chase the mustangs. My father did it and so did Cousin Jim's father."

Dulcia still found it difficult to accept the fact that Jim Slade's mother had been a Sandoval, part of this proper and elegant family. "I know gentlemen work here in Texas, but must it be at such wild and dangerous things? Oh, Gertrudis, I wish to be there when he returns. Don't you see, if I am here, he will wait and work those dreadful wild beasts before he comes for me. He said two weeks. It is that and past already. I know if he isn't at the ranch, he will be by the time I return home. I could have the servants prepare his favorite foods and have the house readied for him if I left today. Ask your mother to see if your father would give me an escort home. It isn't that far. Please?"

Caught up in the romantic spirit, Gertrudis made one of her characteristic snap decisions. "Oh, posh, Mama and Papa will never agree to let you leave without Leandro's permission, but I could get Rosario and Lorenzo to escort us. They are very capable and very devoted to me. We'll have you at Great Dream Ranch for Leandro's homecoming by tonight!''

True to her word, Gertrudis got her father's *vaqueros* to hitch up Dulcia's rig, and the two women sneaked out immediately after the midday meal while the family was taking siesta. With their armed escort, they set out for El Sueño Grande.

"When yew git done with her, I want me a piece," the burly man called Griggs sang out to his companion, who was methodically cutting the clothing from a cowering Angelina, the Velásquez cook.

"She be a mite old fer ya, Griggs, but since I had ta kill th' younger one, I reckon I'll share."

As the cowering old woman pressed her body against the cool masonry of the *sala* wall, Jake Sears continued to undress her with his bowie knife, oblivious to the carnage around him.

En route to San Antonio from the open range to the northwest, Griggs and Sears planned to join one of the Texas volunteer companies they'd heard were forming to fight the hated Mexicans. When blind chance brought them to El Sueño Grande, they had seen what looked to be a prosperous little ranch owned by *Tejanos*. Few *vaqueros* were around, but two women worked in the yard around an open oven, baking bread beneath the canopy of a towering cottonwood.

The old man at the corral had been an easy target, and even the two armed *vaqueros* they had encountered had fallen quickly to the Patterson Colts of the two seasoned rangers. By the time they had entered the house, they found Angelina and Serafina hiding in the armoire in the master bedroom. The younger housemaid had found one of Lee's old rifles and had fired it ineffectually, grazing Sears and infuriating him. He retaliated by shooting her at point-blank range with his Colt.

They dragged Angelina, the graying old cook, out from the armoire and headed with their prize to search for food and liquor. Breaking into Lee's walnut bookcase, Sears searched for whiskey while Griggs raided the kitchen, bringing back a freshly baked loaf of bread and a haunch of cold beef. Finally, after destroying half the house, the marauders were satisfied they had found all the loot these greasers owned—a paltry few pieces of gold jewelry and plate, an antique pocket watch, and several bottles of old Spanish Madeira.

They ate, forcing Angelina to serve them, and then proceeded to get raucously drunk on the wine, as they turned their attention to the quaking old woman.

"Please, *señor*. I am sixty years old," she pleaded in heavily accented English. I am *Tejana*, not *Mejicana*."

Sears smiled evilly, showing a wide space where several teeth were rotted away. "I liked th' youngun's gumption better. Called me *rinche* and spit in my face. Course, it shore wuz a shame ta blow sech a piece of female flesh ta smithereens, even if she wuz a greaser."

"Hey, Jake, look see whut we got us comin' up. Quieten her real quick."

Hearing the sound of horses' hooves and the creak of a buggy, Sears complied with one well-placed blow from his meaty fist to Angelina's jaw. Scratching his greasy buckskins, he grinned at Griggs as he grabbed his Colt and ambled toward the window.

"Good thing them other three's layin' down near th' corral where our callers cain't see 'em," Griggs whispered hoarsely.

A *vaquero* was helping two young and very pretty Mexican women from the buggy while another horseman sat watching unconcernedly on his mount.

The minute he crested the rise and looked down on the ranch, Lee knew something was wrong. Neither old Juan nor the two younger *vaqueros* were visible around the area of the corral. The house was deathly quiet as he cantered his big blue roan toward it. A sick, still feeling began to tighten his gut, transmitting itself to the newly broken stallion. "Easy, Sangre," he whispered to the dancing horse, tightening his hand on the reins as they rounded the bend of the creek and crossed to the front of the house.

As soon as he saw Dulcia's rig standing unattended, he reached for the Patterson Colt in his sash, cursing the time he had spent helping his men put the newest mustangs in the far breaking corral. Then he saw Rosario Mendez, the Sandovals' head stable man, lying on the ground with a bullet through his head.

Silently he dismounted. *Dulcia, Dulcia,* his mind hammered out, but his throat was silent, closed off with fear and anguish as he moved toward the front door.

Not a sound could be heard but the beating of his own heart as it pounded in his chest. He knew with a dreadful certainty what he would find in the house. Another of the Sandovals' *vaqueros* lay just inside the door, alongside Gertrudis Sandoval. Both were dead. Obviously the poor girl had been savaged by her tormentor before he shot her. The *sala* was a wreckage of broken crockery and splintered bookcases, with Uncle Alfonso's precious volumes scattered across the floor. Chairs were smashed and overturned. Empty Madeira bottles and meat bones littered the large table across from the *sala* in the dining room.

Clenching the Colt in his hand, Lee stilled his trembling. Dulcia wasn't here. Apparently neither were the marauders who had killed Gertrudis and the Sandoval men and pillaged his home. But why was Dulcia's rig outside? He forced himself to turn toward the bedrooms. Angelina wasn't in the kitchen. A cursory glance through the door told him that. He found the young maid, Serafina, in the women's bedroom, crumpled on the floor. Only one place remained where he had not looked—the master bedroom at the end of the hall.

His feet dragged as if he were moving through quicksand. Even the most monstrous nightmares from his scarred childhood did not prepare him for what he found. Dulcia was alone in the big room, lying across their bed, the clothing torn from her body. Lee collapsed by the side of the bed and cradled her broken body in his arms, his gun thrown heedlessly on the floor. No one was alive in this house.

When the rapist had finished his bestial act, he had cut her throat. The pillows and bedding were stained a dark reddish brown.

Cradling his wife's head with its matted chestnut curls, Lee squeezed his eyes shut as acid tears forced their way past the lids, burning paths down his cheeks. "Oh, Dulcia, my sweet, innocent one, why did I bring you here—to die just like my mother? Like Josefina." He ran his hand over her soft, bruised body, resting it on the slightly swelling mound of her abdomen. With a ripping twist deep in his guts he imagined what being exposed like this must have done to one so modest and shy that she begged her own husband to douse the candles before he undressed her.

With a gripping feeling of suffocation, he reached down and pulled a blanket over her nakedness.

Why, Dulcia, why did I ever ask you to leave Mexico City? Your civilization for this wilderness—my wilderness?

He had been crumpled by the bedside with his wife in his arms for untold minutes when a voice rasped out in Spanish, "*Don* Leandro, oh, I am so sorry. Poor little one."

His stiffened muscles crying out in protest, Lee stood to face Angelina. "Who did this? Where did he go?"

The old woman's bruise-blackened jaw made it difficult for her to speak. "Two men, *rinches*," she spat out the border slang used as an epithet for rangers. "I heard them talk as they forced me to serve them food and wine, *Don* Leandro, before the ladies came. . . ." Her voice trailed away.

"How long ago?"

"Yesterday afternoon, late. When the carriage pulled up, one of them hit me and knocked me to the floor. I awakened to the sounds of screams. I could do nothing, *Don* Leandro, nothing. They had killed our men and the men *Doña* Gertrudis brought with her." Her eyes pleaded for understanding. "I hid out behind the well until they rode away this morning."

Lee stood up now, his face a frozen mask of hatred, oblivious of the terrified old woman's sobs. "Where were they headed?" His voice was ice cold.

"To San Antonio. They spoke of joining a company of rangers to fight against Mexico."

The tall, gangly Sears bent over to light a fat cigar, his back against the bar. Inhaling a deep puff, he let the acrid smoke drift out across the half-empty cantina. "We been waitin' round fer thet damn Captain Waller ta git his shittin' men mustered up all day. Lemmee see. . . ." He consulted the ornate gold watch. "Seven hours," he said and snapped the cover back across the face of the timepiece.

"Put that damn thing away, leastways till we git clear o' Santone," his heavyset companion said in a harsh whisper that carried across the deserted room.

One man, a big Tennesseean with an arsenal of weapons strapped to his person, slept at the corner table, coonskin cap over his face, snoring. A couple of men who worked as clerks at the mercantile played cards at another table. The bartender, a small man named Lyle Bricker, observed all that went on in his place but said nothing. The wild frontiersmen who frequented his establishment killed Mexicans, Comanche, even one another at the slightest provocation. They were loners, undisciplined and dangerous, none more so than Griggs and Sears, whom he knew had not come honestly by the antique watch with a Spanish inscription on its back.

Outside, a small boy was speaking rapidly in Spanish to a tall *Tejano*. "They are in there, mister, two Texian devils, just as you described them. One is skinny with long black hair and the other is big and fat with his front teeth missing. They rode in from the north this morning. I stabled their horses and heard them say they were to join Captain Waller's ranger volunteers."

Lee looked like a dark angel of death, his features graven in stone. He had searched every cheap hotel and cantina, questioning people and describing the two men as Angelina had to him. Finally he had hit pay dirt. He flipped the boy a gold piece and said, "*Gracias, niño.*"

As the boy scampered off, the *Tejano* checked his pistols one last time, then walked through the wide door into the dim, smoky room. His black eyes slitted as he scanned the bar for his prey.

"We don't serve Mex in here, sonny," Bricker said levelly.

As Lee sauntered toward the bar, something in his expression caused the proprietor to reconsider, that and the way the grim-faced young *Tejano*'s hands rested lightly on a pair of .36-caliber Patterson Colts.

"I didn't come to drink. I came to talk with these two." He motioned carelessly to Sears and Griggs.

Griggs put down his whiskey and looked over at the slim young man in dusty trail gear. Several days' growth of black beard gave his already icy-cold expression even greater menace. He was young, a *ranchero* by the looks of him. Suddenly the burly man knew who he must be. Reaching for his gun, he yelled, "Jake, it's her husband! Watch out!"

Caught sitting down, both men were at a disadvantage, made even worse by an afternoon of whiskey consumption. Lee's pistol barked twice, hitting the wide bulk of Griggs abdomen low before he could raise his gun halfway. Jake Sears got off a shot that grazed Lee's thigh as he spun and aimed his Colt. Before Sears' addled brain could focus clearly, Lee's next shot hit with sickening impact and knocked him backward, overturning his chair. He crashed to the straw-covered floor.

Griggs was unconscious, slumped back over his chair with his gun hanging in nerveless fingers. Sears was moaning and rolling on the floor as Lee knelt beside him, knife drawn. "Which one of you did it, you or your fat friend?" he rasped.

Sears' eyes bulged as he watched the light dancing off Lee's knife blade. He knew what the *Tejano* meant. "Griggs— he done it. I only. . ." His voice faded to a gurgling gasp as the blade descended in a swift and bloody arc, cleanly slicing his jugular.

Hearing the sound of a weapon being cocked, Lee whirled and drew his other Patterson, leveling it at the Tennesseean whose rifle had not yet sighted in. "These men killed three young women. One of them was my wife."

"How do I know yer tellin' th' truth?" Shrewd brown eyes took in the haggard but flinty face of the youth.

"The thin one's carrying a gold watch inscribed with the name Alfredo Santiago Velásquez." Lee motioned to Sears' body.

"I seen th' watch on 'em right 'nough." Satisfied, the backwoodsman slouched down in his chair, laid down his rifle, and pushed his coonskin back over his face.

Lee turned to scan the rest of the cantina. The clerks sat rigid in fright, and Bricker cowered behind the bar. He turned back to Sears and searched the corpse. He found the watch and placed it carefully in his pocket. Then he turned to Griggs. Once more the knife flashed.

"If I could've taken them alive, it wouldn't have been their throats I'd have cut," Lee said softly in the silent room. No one moved as he walked out the door.

He rode northwest for several days, avoiding Comanche raiders and bands of Mexican and Texian guerrillas. He was eager to shake the dust and dreams of Texas from his body and soul forever; that is, if he still had a soul. He doubted it. Lee headed toward Santa Fe, intent on losing himself in the vast wilds of the Apachería of New Mexico.

Chapter 4

Boston, 1851

The fire crackling in the grate cast a soft, warm glow on the faces of the three people standing in the library of the imposing brick mansion. Still straight and tall despite his seventy years, Adam Manchester interrupted his pacing to turn his intense gaze on the serene, lovely face of his daughter, Deborah. The gray-haired banker spoke quietly.

"Lord knows she's a brilliant student and a loving girl, Deborah. But I'm afraid you must prepare yourself. She is very different from the girl you were at her age."

Deborah's lavender eyes and patrician features softened as she smiled. "When I consider what a highly unconventional daughter I was, Father, I realize that you may be trying to soften a blow for us."

Deborah's tall, dark-haired husband interrupted. "Adam, exactly what kind of devilment has Melanie been up to?" Rafe Fleming's face at age thirty-nine had changed little since he had moved to Texas fifteen years earlier. Sundarkened and scarred, it was both fierce and arrestingly handsome at the same time. He scowled at his father-in-law, awaiting a reply.

Adam Manchester had not become a power in the New England business community by hedging. His level bluegray eyes locked with Rafe's glowing black ones. "She's joined forces with William Lloyd Garrison and his mobinciting revolutionaries, I'm afraid."

Deborah's eyes widened. "Garrison. Isn't he the abolitionist who publishes *The Liberator*?"

Rafe scowled. "One and the same, my dear. It's been foaming at the mouth about how the slavocracy of Texas trash should never have been allowed into the United States!"

"Since the passage of the Fugitive Slave Law last year, there have been several riots and disturbances. Even our city officials are helping slave catchers return runaways," Adam replied angrily. "I can't say I agree with Garrison's inflammatory rhetoric, but I do despise what's going on in Boston."

"And, of course, so does my daughter," Rafe said dryly.

"The right or wrong of slavery isn't the issue, however," Adam continued carefully. "It's the way the cause has affected Melanie that alarms me. When you sent her to me four years ago for formal education, she was a spirited young girl who loved to dance, read poetry, and even take an occasional carriage ride with an admiring young swain."

Deborah's face puckered in a mock grimace. "Quite

unlike her disgustingly bluestockinged mother, I warrant. I tried hard over the six years she lived with us to teach her to use her mind but still to enjoy life with more self-confidence than I had at her age. She was happy, Father, if a bit overeager to obtain a higher education than Texas could afford her.''

"She still *thinks* she's happy," Adam shot back.

"But you obviously don't think she is," Rafe interjected. "Her letters have been full of the starry-eyed idealism any bright young college student would prattle on about—male or female," he added with a nod to his wife.

"Yes," Deborah said. "She wrote about going to the women's suffrage convention in Worcester last year and even that she'd joined the Temperance Union. I'm scarcely surprised that she's added abolition to her list of causes. After all, Father, she has African blood and has every right to feel proud of it."

Adam threw up his hands and cast an exasperated look at Rafe. "You see, they're united against me, daughter and granddaughter, free-thinking females, God help us mere men!"

Rafe grinned ruefully. "After the way you spoiled them both, don't blame me for not curbing their willfulness! Seriously, though," Rafe said, his expression sobering, "I don't like seeing her involved with radical journalists like Garrison. She could be endangered. I think you were right to have us come collect her. We're Texians now and Texas is her home. She's had all the education she'll ever need— from books. It's time she got on with her life."

"You mean at the advanced age of twenty-one she's a virtual spinster," Deborah teased.

"Well, you thought you were when I married you at the 'advanced' age of twenty!"

Adam stifled a chuckle at his son-in-law's sally and tried to present his calm banker's facade for Deborah once more. "Much as I love my granddaughter, Deborah, I fear I agree with Rafe. She talks of nothing but dedicating her life to the abolition of slavery and the rights of womankind. Maybe if you take her away from all this agitation, she'll consider changing a few things. . . ."

"Such as?" Rafe questioned.

At that moment the subject of their discourse came dashing into the front hall of the Manchester house. Drenched from the autumn rain, Melanie's inky hair hung in tangles, clotted with mud and debris that the downpour had only partially washed away. Her cloak, however, was a total loss, stained with ground-in filth. She had been pelted with rotten eggs and garbage and pushed into a mud puddle by one of the slave catchers after she had scuffled with him.

Ramsey, the unflappable Manchester butler, took Melanie's cloak, carefully holding it at full arm's length from his immaculate black uniform. "I'll see that this is cleaned, miss," he said calmly, as if this were an everyday occurrence.

"Well, I managed to salvage the broadsides for Mr. Garrison!" Melanie announced with satisfaction as she took the bundle she had been shielding beneath her cape and placed it reverently on the polished marble table in front of a large beveled-glass mirror. She unwrapped the stack of printed broadsides that proclaimed in boldface type

CAUTION!!!
Colored People of Boston
Kidnappers and Slave Catchers are at large!

Glancing up into the mirror, she let out a small gasp of dismay. "Oh, drat! I'd better get upstairs and change before Grandfather sees me." Both her hands and her face were smeared with the same muck as her cloak. Although the cloak had protected her dress, her shoes were muddy and left tracks across the light rose-colored carpet and gleaming hardwood floor of the entry hall.

Just as she was in the process of removing one offending shoe, the study door opened and Adam, Rafe, and Deborah emerged.

"Ramsey, I thought I heard the front door," Adam said and stopped, frozen. Melanie, too, was frozen, stocking-clad foot planted daintily on the rug, thick-soled muddy shoe clutched tightly in one small hand. Speechlessly she glanced from her grandfather to her parents.

Deborah gasped in distress at her filth-encrusted stepchild; then her face brightened in a smile of welcome. The girl looked so guilty that Deborah couldn't be angry, especially when she saw Rafe's scowl as he looked at his daughter's ratty hair and disheveled appearance.

"Melanie, I'm so glad to see you," Deborah said, closing the distance to hug the girl. She bent her silverblond head to Melanie's dark one as they embraced.

Rafe crossed the room, and took the ugly shoe from Melanie's grubby fingers. "This is the kind of a stunt I'd expect from your brothers, not from a young lady of twenty-one." With grudging good humor he tossed the shoe aside, hugged her, and planted a kiss on her forehead. "Ugh, what is this stuff all over you?" He sniffed. "Egg— rotten eggs!" he said incredulously, holding her at arm's length now, freeing her from Deborah's protective embrace to inspect her. "You look like an escapee from some slum riot."

Melanie finally recovered her voice and her wits. "Oh, bother my clothes or a few silly eggs! What are you doing here? You never wrote you were coming for a visit. Did you bring Adam and Caleb and Lenore along?" Melanie's gold eyes were sparkling now, her initial shock fleeing as joy at seeing her parents replaced it.

Looking over her shoulder, Rafe saw the broadsides, picked one up, and scanned it. "This is not just a visit, young lady. We've come to take you home."

"I'm afraid your grandfather's letters have been a bit more explicit about your exploits than yours have, Melanie," Deborah remonstrated gently.

"Home? You mean back to Texas? To the ranch?" Her crestfallen expression was quickly masked as she replied with steel in her voice, "I have important work here, Papa, Mama. I just can't leave now."

"Is that *important* work posting these leaflets? And does it include being pelted with garbage?" Rafe asked in a voice heavy with sarcasm.

"And being involved in a riot or two, not to mention having her life threatened by one Cyrus Juline, a slave catcher from Georgia," Adam said with obvious distaste for the bounty hunter.

"Riot?" Deborah looked back at Melanie with concern.

"It was only a small riot on the Commons last month. I was out of range of the guns—"

"Guns?" Rafe thundered.

Melanie made a gesture of dismissal, as if shooting and mob violence were as commonplace for a Boston lady as attending the symphony. "Only a few men had guns, but the constabulary disarmed them before anyone was killed."

"One man was shot in the shoulder and three people were badly injured by rocks thrown during the melee," Adam added grimly.

"But the rock only grazed my temple. I hardly had a scratch! Considering all the Comanche raiders and renegades in Texas, I scarcely think you can consider it safer there," she countered.

"But, Melanie, look at you," Deborah chided. Ignoring the mud and garbage, she ran her hands over her daughter's hideous gray dress and looked down at the heavy high-laced shoe on Melanie's left foot. "You're dressed like an old lady, not the lovely young woman we visited here two years ago."

Melanie sighed. "I should think my clothes would please you. Honestly, Mama, you of all people should realize it's not how a woman *looks* but how she *thinks* that's important."

"Well I *think* you will take a bath, dress in some appropriate clothes, which your mother will select for you, and we shall continue this discussion at dinner," her father pronounced with finality.

"The letter must have followed us on the very next steamer," Rafe said dejectedly. He sat at Adam's desk, rubbing his fingers in small, tight circles on his temples.

Adam was surprised to detect a few faint flecks of gray in his son-in-law's curly black hair. "You must tell Melanie.

Lily was her natural mother. What will you do about Claude's estate?''

Rafe unfolded his long body from the chair and stood to face Adam. "I'll have to go to New Orleans and deal with *Maman*. The lawyers doubtless have her in tears by now. Damn that stubborn old fool, to die leaving me the whole estate just as if I'd stayed there and done as he wanted!" Rafe pounded the table in agitation.

The law firm of Beaurivage and LeBlanc's neat letterhead lay on the study table, as did another letter from the same packet, written in the bold, clear script of Rafe's brother-in-law, Caleb Armstrong. A late summer yellow fever epidemic had claimed both Claude Flamenco and Lily Duval Genet.

"I'll have to talk to Caleb about the estate. Hell, Adam, I don't want it! I told my father when I left New Orleans that he still had a daughter. He should have left his wealth to my sister and her husband as well as to *Maman*. I wanted no part of it or the hold it would have on me."

"You can never undo family ties, son. Maybe you and your mother can reconcile your differences now," Adam said.

Rafe gave a snort of disgust. "She and the rest of my illustrious Beaurivage and Flamenco cousins still refuse to admit Lenore and Caleb are alive, much less part of the family. When my sister eloped with an American, they disowned her forever."

"Yet your father willed you and your children everything, although you married an American."

"It's an old Creole tradition. Men can be forgiven any excess; women, none," he replied in disgust.

Adam half smiled. "Sounds like some of Deborah's ideas have been rubbing off on you over the years." He walked over to the desk and placed a hand on Rafe's shoulder. "You'll have to go to New Orleans and deal with the attorneys, son. Your sister doesn't need the Flamenco fortune, but your mother must be provided for."

Rafe's shoulders slumped. "If only I didn't have to drag Melanie into this."

"You have to tell her, son," Adam said gently.

* * *

"Why should I care if she's dead?" Melanie stood in the center of her bedroom with her hands on her hips. "She never loved me. She let *Grandmère* and Aunt Thérèse raise me—then you and Deborah. Deborah's my real mother, the one who loves me. Lily Duval never did!" Melanie's golden eyes were filled with pain. Her tiny body vibrated with fiercely restrained anguish.

Rafe understood her hurt. Lily had never accepted her firstborn child after the second one, a boy, died in an epidemic. Melanie reminded him of Lily in physical appearance, the high cheekbones and smooth olive skin with just a hint of copper in the complexion, the big eyes and long silky wealth of ebony hair. Yet anyone admiring the beautiful young woman would see the obvious resemblance to his own French-Spanish Creole ancestry and never suspect her Cherokee or African bloodlines.

"Lily's husband, François Genet, died last year in a duel, Melanie. The attorneys say she left everything to you now. There may be some mementos, something you might want to keep. I'll understand if you decide not to visit the house on Rampart Street, but we do have to visit your Aunt Lenore and Uncle Caleb and settle your Grandfather Flamenco's estate."

"Then home to Texas?" She smiled bravely though tears ran in rivulets down her cheeks as she slid into her father's waiting arms. "I'll think about what to do with her things," she murmured hesitantly.

"Talk it over with your mother," Rafe replied gently.

Everything is exactly as I remembered, Deborah thought to herself as she numbly unpacked in their old quarters, the private apartment across the courtyard connecting to the Flamencos' New Orleans house. Despite the high ceilings, the late fall humidity was oppressive. *Oh, for the dry air of north Texas*, she sighed.

"You hate it here, too, don't you?" Melanie, looking

small and forlorn, stood in the doorway to her parents' large bedroom. She had just left her own room at the end of the hall.

"I have little good to remember that isn't overshadowed by pain, that's true," Deborah said, a haunted note in her voice.

"At least *Grandmère* Céline is willing to admit you by the front door. If she had her way, I'd be sleeping downstairs with her slaves," Melanie said bitterly.

Deborah walked over and drew her daughter by the hand to the large four-poster bed. As they sat down, Deborah reassured her. "She won't have her way, because your father owns this house now and what he decrees stands. You are his child, just as Adam and Caleb and Norrie are, and equally loved."

"Oh, Mama, you are such a special person!" Melanie threw her arms around Deborah's neck.

"Remember the first time you called me Mama?" Deborah asked softly. "You were twelve years old, such a proud, fiercely independent, and lovely little girl. I used every wile I knew to win you over, and it was worth it. Don't let the old hatreds here touch you, dear heart."

"I won't," Melanie replied with a catch in her voice. "But when I think of how my *Grandmère* Marie loved me and how this one hates me . . ."

"As soon as we get legal matters straightened out, we'll go home," Deborah soothed.

"Do—do you think Aunt Lenore and Uncle Caleb will like me? I mean, they've lived here all their lives."

Deborah smiled confidently. "Lenore is much more like your father than like your grandmother. She and I were best friends when I lived here. That's why your baby sister is named for her. In fact, I helped Lenore and Caleb elope and scandalized the whole family."

"Including your papa," Rafe added from the door, remembering the bitter fight he and Deborah had had the night she disguised herself in Lenore's costume while his sister and her American slipped away from the masked ball and were secretly married.

Pain and guilt for the way he had treated Deborah were etched on his face as he came into the room. "Perhaps we should have stayed at Lenore and Caleb's house, and to hell with *Maman*'s hysterics," he said darkly.

Deborah rose and went over to embrace him, her body transmitting a warmth and love that erased all the old hurts. "No, we can stay for the few days it will take to settle matters. We'll see the Armstrongs and their brood tonight." Turning to Melanie, she said, "And I warn you, if you think two little brothers have been a trial, wait until you see all your cousins—Thad, Michael, Rafael, Burton, oh, yes, and one poor little girl as an afterthought—Alice!"

"And they all have red hair," Rafe added with a grin.

"Does Uncle Caleb have red hair?" Melanie asked innocently.

"If he didn't, your aunt would be in pretty big trouble by now," Rafe answered, and they all three laughed, breaking the tension and holding the past at bay.

They spent a delightful but exhausting evening with the Armstrong clan. Rafe's sister and brother-in-law and their children welcomed Melanie warmly, accepting the child of Rafe's mistress as openly as they accepted Deborah's natural children.

When they returned to the Flamenco house, Melanie was glad to sink into the soft bed in the room down the hall from her parents. Her five-year-old sister, Norrie, was already asleep next to her, and their brothers, Adam and Caleb, were doubtless drifting off next door, but Melanie lay awake ruminating.

Ever since she had come to live with her father and Deborah in Texas, she had been loved unconditionally, just as her *Grandmère* Marie and Aunt Thérèse had loved her back in St. Louis before their deaths. For the past four years her Grandfather Adam had loved her in Boston. But after meeting *Grandmère* Céline and sensing the animosity radiating from the old woman, Melanie felt like an outcast.

Melanie had been born in this city, only a few miles

distant, in a small white house on Rampart Street, a house she now legally owned. *That's really it. It isn't the color bar in New Orleans or the dislike of a grandmother I never knew. Even my being illegitimate isn't the real hurt. It's* Mère. Melanie lay very still as the thoughts washed over her in a tidal wave of fresh pain, like a newly opened wound, long suppurating and now freshly lanced. Willing herself not to cry and awaken her little sister, Melanie vowed to visit Lily Duval's house on the morrow.

"Are you certain you want to do this?" Deborah asked as the carriage pulled up in front of the small white house.

"Are you certain you do?" Melanie countered, remembering the painful confrontation between Deborah and Lily that she had witnessed sixteen years ago.

"Let's go," was all Deborah replied as she gave Melanie's hand a squeeze.

The house was much as her little girl's eyes had remembered it, expensively decorated and cluttered with too many pieces of doll-like furniture. Porcelain figurines and a silver tea service sat on delicately lacquered French provincial tabletops. Heavy brocade draperies were drawn against the sun. Despite the shade from several tall willows outside, the place was stifling with the musky aromas of perfume and death.

Both women were lost in the past as they walked inside, recalling old hurts. Here Deborah had confronted her husband's mistress and had discovered that he already had two children by Lily when she had just become pregnant for the first time. Despite the passage of years and the constancy of her husband's love, Deborah still felt the pain when she remembered Melanie as a small child rushing innocently into the midst of the bitter fight between wife and mistress. That child had been hurt most of all. Looking over at Melanie, Deborah said softly, "Let's go through her things and you select what you want to take home. Then the lawyers can sell the rest. You need never come here again, dear heart."

Melanie looked around and made a small moue of disgust. "She loved expensive trinkets—china, porcelain, sil-

ver, jewelry. Although I expect we're the same size, I don't
want her clothes. I know that,'' Melanie said with finality.

Although Melanie's overly plain and sensible wardrobe
was a continual frustration to Deborah, she knew the ''bird
of paradise'' clothes of a kept woman would be completely
unsuitable for her gently reared girl.

They spent several hours going through the small house
room by room. Lily's husband had been a fencing master,
killed in an affair of honor with another Free Man of Color
over a year ago. From the first time he had seen Lily's
daughter, Genet had hated her; she was a distasteful remind-
er that his wife had been a white man's property. He had
made her life a misery when she came back to New Orleans
from St. Louis after the deaths of her grandmother and aunt.
''We'll give all his things to the sisters to dispense to the
poor,'' Melanie said, and slammed his armoire door.

The expensive china and sterling they packed up carefully. Deborah offered a delicate suggestion to Melanie. ''Someday
when you're married and have a home of your own, you
might want these dishes—they're truly beautiful.''

''Only the rose crystal punch bowl and cups. They
belonged to *Grandmère* Marie,'' Melanie replied tersely.

When they finally came to Lily's jewel cases, both
women were amazed at the beauty and variety of the
pieces—emeralds, pearls, sapphires, and rubies, even the
icy glitter of diamonds, all set in delicate silver filigree or
massive gold mountings. Melanie ignored most of it, selecting
only a few old pieces of lesser worth that had belonged to
her *Grandmère*. When she opened one small black velvet
box and took out a heavy scrimshaw necklace, Melanie
heard Deborah's breath catch. Quickly she looked up and
saw an expression of anguish etched on her mother's face.
''Papa bought this for her in Boston, didn't he?'' Melanie
knew the ivory carving was a New England whaler's art. He
must have selected it for Lily during the same business trip
on which he'd married Deborah.

''Melanie, that was a long time ago. Rafael and I were
both different people then. I have a new life with my
husband now. She can't hurt us anymore. But she still can

hurt you, can't she?'' Holding her breath, Deborah reached over and gently took the necklace from Melanie's nerveless fingers and replaced it in the box.

"Why couldn't she love me? Why? Everyone else did—you, Papa, *Grandmère* Marie, Aunt Thérèse—but the woman who gave me life didn't even want me in the same house with her! I used to overhear her and Papa. They'd fight about me when I was little. She'd want to send me back to *Grandmère* in St. Louis, and Papa would want me to stay here.

"Once, when he came over, she had left me alone in the kitchen—her servant had gone to market and no one was here to watch me. She was still asleep and I tried to reach some fruit on the table. I knocked the bowl over and it broke. I cut myself on the glass. That's how Papa found me—cut and crying. I guess I was lucky I didn't eat any glass slivers with the grapes! After that, he let her send me to *Grandmère* a lot more often. . . .''

Once the monologue stopped, the tears began, slowly at first, then increasing to a torrent. For Deborah, who knew how long that agony had been locked deep inside the girl, it was almost as healing a relief as it was for Melanie. They held each other and wept.

By the time they arrived back at the Flamenco house late that evening, it was well past the dinner hour. Deborah had sent word by their driver not to wait supper on them. Eating in the same room with Céline was not conducive to good digestion for either Deborah or Melanie. The two went to the kitchen where the cook, Wilma, prepared them a delightful cold meal of thinly sliced roast veal, melon, and cool white wine.

While they ate and relaxed after an emotionally charged day, Rafe spent a bitterly unhappy evening with his mother and his cousins.

"Are the children asleep?'' Céline asked Rafe when he returned to meet them in the study. He nodded, adding conversationally, "Deborah and Melanie are taking supper now.'' He enjoyed reminding the intolerant Flamencos that his mixed-blood daughter was treated like the rest of the family.

"I've talked with the lawyers and they see no problem with my plans. All property will be given to you, Mother, but Caleb Armstrong will be executor." He looked meaningfully over at his cousins, Jean and Philippe.

Céline let out a gasp of horror and considered fainting. One glance at the stony countenance of her son convinced her of the folly of such a ploy. Once he would have rushed to comfort her, but no more. Now he'd let her drop to the floor in a heap! "You've become as savage and unfeeling as those wild red Indians in that accursed Texas! Your father wanted you to take care of me, Rafael. You are my only son. That's why he left you in charge of everything, to—"

"To bring me back to New Orleans, to my old life, *to heel*," he interrupted her tightly. "Well, he gambled and he lost, Mother." Then a sardonic grin split his face. "But I am grateful to keep the estate from being squandered by the Beaurivages, I will say that, even if I don't want or need the money."

"Now see here, Rafael. I've called many a man out for less." Philippe rose, red color infusing his cheeks.

"Really, cousin?" Rafe said, turning to stare Philippe down. "Would you like to challenge me? It would be my choice of weapons. I fight with a bowie knife now." He grinned like a shark, and Philippe quickly subsided.

"Please, children—Rafael, Philippe—you grew up together. We're all family. We must act together," Céline remonstrated.

"Caleb is family, too—my only sister's husband and a damned honest and sensible banker. He'll handle the estate for you, Mother, but you'll have to face your daughter and your grandchildren—something you resolutely refused to do while my father was alive. This is your chance. I won't stay here tied to the Flamenco wealth. I've made my own life in Texas, and that's where my family and I choose to live."

"You and your Yankee wife and your daughter kissed by the tar brush," Jean said mockingly. "Texas must be a very liberal place, indeed."

"The place we live is. Renacimiento is larger than some of the eastern states," Rafe replied levelly, his black eyes piercing his old drinking companion's facade, daring him to pursue the dangerous topic further.

"Nothing will change your mind, will it? You're going to give huge sums of money to your father's second family and let that odious American dole it out to me as well." Céline's voice was amazingly calm. Yesterday she had cried and pleaded, but Rafael had calmly moved Melanie into his apartments with Deborah's children. Deborah treated the girl as if she were her own. It was obvious that every social and cultural imperative under which Céline's world operated had been abandoned by her son. "Like a snake, you have shed your skin in the hot Texas sun. You are no longer Rafael Flamenco, but some American, Rafe Fleming, who I do not know." With that, she turned and swept imperiously from the room, leaving Rafe facing his two Beaurivage cousins.

Having lived a lifetime with Céline's theatrics, Rafe knew nothing would ever change between mother and son. Sighing, he turned to Jean and Philippe. "Gentlemen, the well has run dry. You can inform the rest of the family that my father's money will go where his son-in-law wills. I somehow doubt that Caleb Armstrong will be well disposed to subsidize your carousing."

"And what of you, cousin?" Jean asked of his boyhood companion, now grown a stranger.

Rafe grinned in relief, glad to be quit of the whole troublesome scene. "My family and I are GTT," he replied in English, then switched back to French. "We're gone to Texas, from where I plan never again to return!"

Chapter 5

Santa Fe, 1851

Dust hung suspended in the pale golden light filtering through the grilled window of the cantina. The air was still, dry, and very hot. It was late afternoon and a motley assortment of men were trickling into El Escondedero after their siesta. Despite its name, the barroom was not at all hidden, but a rather popular, if sleazy, gathering place off the main square of the bustling trade capital of New Mexico Territory. Two big Americans, burly and bearded, swaggered over to the bar and demanded beer. A handful of New Mexican *vaqueros* and the cantina owner played a highly vocal game of *Chuza* in one corner. Rosa and another plump, pretty young girl served drinks as they swished their brightly colored skirts and flashed their silver bangles at the customers, especially several off-duty American soldiers.

Lee Velásquez slouched in a chair in the rear of the room, his long buckskin-clad legs stretched indolently beneath the table in front of him. He'd taken his siesta in his seat, watching the play of light and shadow across the iron grillwork. He had nowhere to go, at least not until Fouqué arrived.

"Hot today, no?" Rosa, the barmaid, inquired as she leaned forward to place a glass of whiskey in front of him, hoping the gunman would take notice of the bountiful charms spilling out of her loose white blouse.

His black eyes narrowed in concentration on a shaft of light as he replied offhandedly, "Weather's the same as always." Without seeming to see it, he reached a slim dark hand toward the drink and tossed it off. Rosa swished away in irritation.

How much longer, Fouqué? As if in answer to his unspoken question, a small, wiry man in greasy buckskins strolled in the front door, spotted Lee, and motioned to Rosa to bring his usual drink to the table.

"Ah, *mon ami*, you are the smart one, here in the cool while like our mad English employer I ride in the heat." He spoke English, their common language, with a heavy Gascon accent. Gold teeth gleamed as he smiled.

"He's not my employer anymore, Fouqué," Lee said wearily. "I just want the money he owes me before he runs off with it like Armijo did."

Raoul Fouqué shrugged philosophically as he sat down. "That was the government; this is private business. Businessmen pay better than military governors, Mexican or Yankee."

Lee's face grew hard. "It's the same line of work."

"*Merde*, you rode with McGordy's bunch only a few months before the Mexican government fled and the Americans came. It was no surprise when the governor general took off without paying us. Bristol will not."

"Bristol better not," was the soft reply.

Fouqué looked at the younger man, studying his hard, dangerous face. Most women found his classically handsome features irresistible, so unlike Raoul's own irregular ones. But there was more to Leandro than a pretty Castilian face. He had the scars to prove it—one narrow white one vanished into his hairline, and another left a small line across his left cheekbone. They were indications of the kind of life he led, but not nearly so much as were his eyes, black and fathomless, like onyx polished to a pitiless sheen— eyes that no twenty-seven-year-old man should possess.

The Frenchman watched Lee surveying the room with seeming indolence, missing nothing, especially the two large and loud Americans at the bar. As a rule Lee didn't like Americans, although he'd ridden with a few under McGordy. Wanting to distract his companion's attention from the obnoxious pair, Fouqué said, "Where do you go if you leave Bristol?"

Lee shrugged. "Maybe California, maybe Oregon."

"Not Chihuahua, I know, since the governor still has a price on your head, but you could go to Mexico City, where you once lived." Fouqué's face was intense with curiosity.

"My uncle died three years ago, Raoul." Lee smiled grimly. "Besides, I'm not likely to fit in with the cultured academic environment I left there. I don't want to."

Fouqué chuckled. "Men like you and me, we make our own rules. You want a wild, open place, why not go back to Texas? There must be as many Anglos here as there by now."

Lee sighed. "That's true enough, but I'm afraid I've got a little problem with the Yankee law there. Besides, like Mexico City, it holds memories. . . ." His voice faded away as he gazed down into the empty whiskey glass.

Fouqué knew Lee's wife had been killed in Texas and that he had fled into Mexican territory five years earlier. The rest he only surmised, but it explained why Lee could not return to the land of his birth. "Speaking of Texas, I ran into a man yesterday with a Texian wife. *Quelle femme!* Big as a cottonwood rising by a wide river, with a voice to match. The two were returning to Texas, at the woman's insistence."

Lee smiled. "I knew a woman like that years ago. She owned a business back in San Antonio—don't get that look on your face. It was a very respectable boardinghouse."

"Speak of the devil, there is the Amazon's husband. No small fellow himself," Fouqué added, watching the man's immense girth fill the door frame. His long bushy red beard and hair to match almost obscured his face, but his blue eyes were merry and piercing. An arsenal of skinning knives and a Hawken rifle proclaimed him a trapper from the north.

"He looks familiar," Lee said pensively, realizing that for a man on the run, the blur of years and miles made many men seem familiar.

Just as the big stranger headed for the bar, a small Englishman clad in black broadcloth entered the cantina. He looked hot and harried.

"Over here, *mon ami*," Raoul motioned to Kenyon Bristol, owner of the largest silver mine in the territory. He was here to trade with the large American caravans from

Missouri, buying supplies for his mines. Bristol was a very shrewd bargainer.

He took the chair Fouqué offered and waved away the barmaid. "Damned rotgut swill," he muttered beneath his breath. "I'd sell a carload of bullion for one decent bottle of gin."

His precise English enunciation carried across the room to the nearby bar, where the two big Americans had been steadily drinking that very rotgut whiskey with beer chasers for the better part of an hour.

"We got us good American corn whiskey, all the way from Kaintuck. It ain't good 'nough fer his lordship here," one of the men announced to the assembly in a poor imitation of Bristol's accent.

A wealthy and powerful man, Bristol detested being in wretched places such as El Escondedero, but he had promised Velásquez and Fouqué that he would bring their money here. Now he was glad he'd brought two of his bodyguards as well. Although he was small and rumpled, there was a biting edge to Kenyon Bristol's personality that had warded off many a prudent man, but not the two drunk Americans.

"I scarcely think my drinking preferences are open to critique by a pair of oafish colonial ruffians." With that, he turned back to the table and shoved two heavy leather sacks across to Lee and Raoul. "It's all there," he said, dismissing the mountain men from his attention.

"For all the mules and horses alone, you owe us more than this," Lee replied in a tight, low growl as he hefted the gold-filled pouch.

"This here Bristol's a welsher?" one mountain man asked, shambling toward their table with a menacing scowl.

"We will settle our differences without your help, *mon ami*," Fouqué said softly.

The man scanned the two sitting at the table contemptuously. "Too damn many ferriners round Santy Fay—English lordships, Frenchies, 'n' greasers." He looked at Lee as he said the last.

"My ancestors were in New Mexico long before yours ever saw the east coast of North America. I'd debate who's the foreigner with you." Lee spoke levelly and remained seated, but the tension in his body had changed subtly as he watched the two drunken men and a number of other Anglos in the cantina who were observing the confrontation with increasing interest.

"Funny." The mountain man spat a wad of tobacco onto the hard-packed clay floor and said almost conversationally, "Yew don't talk English like no greaser."

"You scarcely speak English at all," Lee replied with deceptive geniality. "It's hot and the hour is late. Go back to your drink at the bar."

"I would do as he suggests, *mon ami*," Fouqué said. Bristol made a small hand signal to two inconspicuous gunmen at the far side of the room. They inched closer very slowly.

"We don't take no shit from froggies er greasers—er any other ferriners. Do we, Joe?"

"Wal, how 'bout from another Green River man?" The big redheaded hunter had moved with catlike grace from where he stood at the far end of the bar. "Chambers, I niver liked yew when we locked horns at th' meets 'n' yew ain't improved one lick o' spit on a buffalo's tongue since't."

The man called Sam Chambers asked in outrage, "Yew sidin' with them ferriners, Wash?"

Lee's eyes had left the two Anglo drunks to fasten on the red-haired giant. *Wash.* Where had he heard that name before? Then he remembered words Fouqué had used: *quelle femme,* when referring to the American's big Texian wife. "Wash Oakley?"

Lee recognized the big stranger, but it was obvious that the other man did not recognize him. "Last time you saw me I was a skinny seventeen-year-old kid at your wedding back in San Antonio," Lee reminded him.

"Shit, yore Jimmy Slade's friend from Bluebonnet," Oakley rejoined.

"Now ain't thet touchin', Wash. Niver did figger a good Kaintuck boy like yew fer a greaser-lovin' son of a bitch," Sam Chambers said nastily.

Washington Oakley swung so fast Chambers never even got his arm up to block the blow that sent him catapulting across the floor. The whole room erupted in chaos as the long-simmering tension between the victorious Americans and the defeated New Mexicans once more came to a head. Violence, always a way of life on the frontier, was commonplace in this old trade center, held by Hispanic governments for over 150 years and wrested away almost bloodlessly by Kearney's American Army in 1846.

Wash Oakley dispatched two American soldiers with his big meaty fists while Fouqué's knife disabled Chambers's belligerent companion. The *vaqueros* gambling in the middle of the room fell upon another group of American teamsters, fresh off their wagons from Missouri.

As chairs splintered and glasses shattered, men swore and swung, grunted and grimaced while the two women shrieked in fright and dodged behind the bar, where they cowered in terror.

In the midst of the pandemonium, Kenyon Bristol's bodyguards materialized by his side just as he reached across the table to where the two sacks of gold lay. Lee, his back to the corner wall, grinned as he brought a large knife down between the Englishman's splayed fingers with an audible *thunk*. Then he drew a .44-caliber Dragoon Colt and leveled it at Bristol's midsection.

"Call off your guard dogs, Kenyon, old chap, or I'll blow a hole through you and have five shots left over for them."

White-faced, Bristol raised his hands, greatly relieved to see all the fingers on his right hand intact. Backing away from the table, he said, "I was merely attempting to keep your payment safe in the midst of this melee. If you want to contract with me again, you know where to find me, Velásquez." With that, he and his men dodged their way through the cantina and slipped out a side door.

Lee was ready to take the gold and follow suit when an American soldier, reeling from a punch, lurched into him. Quickly sinking his knife into the straps of the leather pouches, Lee secured them to the table and turned to the soldier, delivering a knockout blow with one hand.

"Yew don't handle yerself half bad fer a runt," Wash guffawed as he took two good-sized men, lifted them off the ground, and bashed their heads together.

Dodging a punch from a drunken rancher, Lee yelled over his shoulder, "Where's Obedience? Fouqué said he saw her yesterday."

"I 'spect she'll be along shortly," Wash replied as he let his two unconscious victims drop to the floor.

Lee hit a rancher a solid right to the midsection and then picked up a chair to block the knife of an enraged yellow-haired man in the denim pants and homespun of a Yankee teamster. Just then a shotgun blast exploded deafeningly in the low-ceilinged room.

A woman stood poised in the doorway, filling it almost as completely as her husband had. Obedience Oakley stood six feet tall, solid as a stream-fed cottonwood.

"Now," she announced as her sharp brown eyes skewered in turn each embattled male in the place, "I got me another round in this scattergun. I don't figger ta piss it away on th' ceilin' a second time. Any o' yew gents care ta take th' next swing 'n' see whut I'll do with my cannon? I figgered yew didn't. Git!"

The men, Anglos and New Mexicans, soldiers and civilians melted away like snow in the Sangre de Cristo Mountains on a hot summer day. Finally only Wash, Fouqué, and Lee remained.

"Quit pointin' thet thing, darlin', afore it goes off," Wash said.

Obedience lowered the shotgun and uncocked it carefully. Then, peering across the debris-strewn room at the dark, slim man standing between the wizened Frenchman and the giant trapper, she bellowed, "Lee Velásquez, Jeehosaphat, if'n my ole eyes ain't failed me! Whut in tarnation er yew doin' here?"

The three of them sat in the bare room around a rickety table on crude pine chairs with high, straight backs. The remnants of a hearty meal of spicy mutton stew, corn bread, and a rich custard dessert had been shoved to the center of the table along with the coffeecups.

Sitting back, Lee smiled at the big woman across from

him and said, "That's the best meal I've had since I left Texas five years ago."

Returning the smile, Obedience noticed how the harsh, angular planes of his face softened when he was relaxed. She had scarcely recognized him as the boy with the sunny disposition who had grown up tagging at Jim Slade's heels or visiting her boardinghouse in San Antonio. This hard-looking *pistolero* bore scant resemblance to that Lee, until he smiled. But his smile was sad and haunted, and those fathomless dark eyes held pain as deep as a well. Obedience Morton Freeman Ryan Jones Oakley—for that was her full name after surviving her first three husbands and marrying Wash—had an intuition as big as all Texas when it came to sizing up people.

All through their jovial reunion supper, Lee had made pleasant small talk and urged her and Wash to describe their adventures in the Rocky Mountains. Always a spinner of tall tales, Wash had obliged. Lee had volunteered little about himself. But she knew that the Frenchman to whom Lee had returned one poke sack full of gold pieces was a cutthroat of the most dangerous kind. Everyone from Missouri to Mexico knew who Kenyon Bristol was and the kind of men he hired.

"I figger it's time fer somethin' stronger'n coffee. Wash, yew wanna do th' honors?" Obedience cleared the table of dishes and cups while the red-haired giant poured three generous slugs of clear liquid into clean tin cups.

Grinning, he gave one cup to Lee and held the second one in a hand so big it completely hid the drink from view as he tossed off a swallow. "Whoowhee! Still th' best we ever bought, darlin'."

Wiping her hands on her apron, Obedience took the last cup from where Wash had set it on the table. "It oughta be, considerin' yew traded a passel o' prime pelts fer a half dozen jugs o' this. Course, it shore is smooth," she assessed, wiping her mouth with the back of her sleeve after taking a sip.

Lee eyed the innocent-looking moonshine in his cup. Odorless and colorless, it seemed safe. Being used to wicked pulque and mescal, not to mention the rotgut corn liquor sold in more "civilized" barrooms, he braced himself for a deep throat-scorching burn as he swallowed. Nothing. He cocked one sculpted black brow at Obedience, who looked innocently over to Wash.

"Youngun seems ta be able ta hold his likker. Whut do yew think?"

"I think he needs a refill," Wash said heartily, and the evening was launched.

"You two going back to San Antonio? Why, after all these years of wandering and having such a good time?" Lee asked.

Still askin' questions 'bout us, not willin' ta open up 'bout hisself, Obedience thought as she said, "Done finished with my wanderin'. Been ever'where from Tennessee ta th' Oregon Territory, crossed th' Rocky Mountains so many times I done named nigh onta ever one o' em. An' I purely long ta see a real city agin. I got me roots in Texas."

"Like San Antonio?" Lee asked wistfully.

"Yew miss it, too," she answered.

Lee's face lost some of its shuttered coldness as he gazed across the room and out the window at the brilliant starlit landscape. Taking another sip of the potent alcohol, he said, "While I was a student in Mexico City, I couldn't stop thinking about Texas. Even now, after five years on the run, I still can't. Guess it kind of gets in your blood."

"Why not go home with us, then?" Wash asked. "Niver thought I'd agree ta settle down, but it's lookin' better 'n' better."

"I can't," Lee replied tightly, the mask once more slipped into place.

"Word gits out, Lee," Obedience said gently. "Deborah learned me readin' 'n' writin'. We keep in touch 'n' she lets me know 'bout whut goes on in Santone. I'm sorry 'bout yore wife, but Jim Slade knows a few folks in real high places. I 'spect he could get yore problem with th' law smoothed over like beeswax on polished oak—if'n yew wuz ta write 'n' ask him."

Lee shrugged too carefully, then drained his cup. Wash

unobtrusively refilled it as the younger man spoke. "Part of me wants to go back. Part of me can't face the memories."

"Memories of whut happened there—or whut you done here?" Obedience asked.

"Some of each, I guess. I came here to escape the Americans. I never wanted to hear English spoken again." He laughed bitterly. "I ran smack into the middle of the war. Less than three months after I arrived here, Kearney and Doniphan took the city without firing a shot! Everything from Texas to California was United States territory in a matter of months! I joined up with a man named McGordy, a Scots mercenary who worked for the Mexican Governor, General Manuel Armijo. It seemed the governor's regular troops couldn't handle the Apache and Comanche raiders who butchered civilians and burned trade caravans as far south as Chihuahua City."

"I heerd standard bounty's a hunert dollars fer a buck, fifty fer a squaw, 'n' twenty-five fer a kid," Wash said matter-of-factly, "paid by Mexicans er American." He had seen some of what the Apache had done up by Taos, and passed no judgment on Lee.

"I figured you knew who Fouqué was, even recognized Bristol," Lee said softly. "After a couple of years working with McGordy, the group split up. Gold fever in 'forty-nine. He went to California with a couple of Kanakas and Fouqué's brother. I headed south to Mexico City. I guess I knew sooner or later I'd have to face my uncle and tell him what happened to the little girl he cherished—how she died." He stopped and put the heels of his hands in his eyes, then shook his head and continued. "He was always so gentle, so loving. He never blamed me for taking her to Texas, but I knew he could sense the change in me, in what I'd become.

"I—I couldn't stay there, so I drifted north, back to Chihuahua City and hired out to a rich Mexican merchant whose caravans traveled all the way to St. Louis and back. By then I had a reputation like McGordy's. Men flocked to join me. We got scalp bounties and kept all the livestock we recovered from the Indians. We must have freed a couple of hundred white captives from the Apache and Comanche, mostly Mexican, some Anglos.''

"But it warn't enough ta make up fer th' killin'," Obedience said, her voice reflecting the sorrow of her young friend's tale.

"No, I guess it wasn't." He sighed and took another drink. By now the smooth alcohol was having an effect on Lee, as the Oakleys had expected it would.

"Yew need ta spit it all out, son, 'n' then git on with yer life. Put th' past behind yew," Obedience said, reaching her big work-reddened hand out to cover Lee's fine-boned, elegant one.

"I've killed so many times it's become part of me. I don't know if I can ever put it behind me," he said, withdrawing his hand from hers.

"Last March, after we brought back seventy-five captive Mexicans, mostly women and children, along with nearly a thousand stolen horses and mules—and over two hundred scalps," he added grimly, "I delivered the news to the governor. The mine owners and merchants had set up a private subscription to pay us for the scalps and buy the livestock we'd recovered from Apache raids. Well, the bill came to over forty thousand dollars. But it seemed the governor had appropriated the funds for his personal uses—buying new dress uniforms for his army. An army that couldn't protect their own civilian population!" he added scornfully. "The upshot of it was he refused to pay us. Fouqué and a few of his Shawnee friends stampeded the livestock out of town, drove it over the border, and sold what survived for over ten thousand. The governor tried to arrest me for the 'theft,' as he called it. I escaped and took the rest of my men to see the largest trader in town—the fellow who originally raised the subscription money. I, er, convinced him to pay us what was owed and send Governor Trias the bill to recover his loss."

Wash let out a snort of laughter. "Let me guess. Thet rich galoot couldn't git his money from th' Mexican government, so he 'n' thet Trias feller put a price on yore scalp!"

"I got out of Chihuahua with my scalp intact and the

money. Met Fouqué in Santa Fe and we divided what we had with our men. Then we took a job clearing out Comanche raiders around Bristol's mines.''

''So it 'pears ta me yew got yew a pretty considerable o' a nest egg ta go back ta honest ranchin' with—thet is, if'n ya *want* ta quit this here life,'' Obedience said. Seeing the desolation in Lee's eyes, she knew he did.

''What I want and what I'm able to do might not be the same thing.'' He rubbed his temples as if trying to squeeze back the memories—dark, tormented nightmares with blood running in rivers and grisly scalp poles carried like banners before the victorious army on its homecomings to Chihuahua City. He could still see those women in the desert south of Santa Fe—Mexican slaves they'd freed in a Mescalero camp they had overrun, women so dehumanized, burned, beaten, the soul's light snuffed from their eyes. *Do my eyes look like that?*

''Let me think about it, Obedience.'' He stood up slowly and gave her a lopsided grin. ''Hell, you got me so drunk I can scarcely walk, much less make a decision affecting the rest of my life—what there may be of it.''

He walked unsteadily toward the door. Wash caught up with him just as his knees began to buckle. Scooping him up and throwing him over his shoulder, the giant smiled at his wife. ''Now yew get thet extra bed made up. I 'spect this youngun's gonna need it, 'n' he ain't gettin' no lighter whilst I stand here holdin' him.''

Chapter 6

Renacimiento, 1852
Even after six months back home, Melanie Fleming was

finding her adjustment more difficult than she'd ever imagined. The coming of spring, with its eruptions of wildflowers
rioting across the hillsides in rust, orange, and yellow, could
only lift her spirits for a few hours' riding time. Then she
would return to the big stone ranch house, so full of the love
and laughter of her parents, brothers and sister, as well as
the Flemings' partner, Joe De Villiers, and his family.
Melanie loved Cherokee Joe, as much for his quiet, tolerant
attitude when she talked to him as for the Indian blood she
and the half-breed shared.

Joe had been the first one to sense her restlessness when
she had returned after four years in Boston. When they took
long rides he had listened to her talk about her feelings of
uselessness and frustration in the wilds of north central
Texas. As a young person growing up on an immense ranch,
she had loved the freedom to ride for hours, watch the men
as they captured and broke mustangs and branded longhorn
cattle. Small but plucky, she had even joined in with her
brothers, learning how to handle a hot iron, growing familiar with the pungent smell of singed fur and hide, the
swearing and clatter that were all part of ranch life. She had
helped Deborah and Joe's wife, Lucia, with their huge
vegetable gardens and fruit orchards, learning to cook and
preserve foods, tend sick and injured men and animals, to
be a contributor in the vast and varied work of the immense
kingdom of Renacimiento.

But when she returned last fall, it seemed everyone had
gone on without her. They welcomed her, but the ranch ran
just as smoothly and the men and women handled their tasks
just as efficiently with no help from her.

Her father's young foreman, Micah Torrance, was especially glad she had returned. When she'd left at age eighteen, he was just a line rider who looked in awe at the
boss's beautiful daughter. But after four years, Micah had
worked himself into the foreman's cabin and was looking
for a wife. Who better than Melanie? She was pretty,
hardworking and should be able to give him a passel of fine,
strapping sons.

That was the real burr under her blanket, as Joe sagely

pointed out to her. It wasn't that Renacimiento or its people didn't want her to be a part of the ranch. It was she who thought remaining here was burying herself far from the exhilarating support of noble causes that had given direction to her life back in Boston.

Deborah was in complete agreement with her about women's suffrage and abolition, if not overly enthusiastic about the absolute temperance vow Melanie had taken; but Deborah was a busy, happy wife and mother with a big household to run.

Melanie was certain she did not want that kind of life, at least not yet, not before she'd seen her causes win out over the benighted forces of male supremacy, African slavery, and drunken debauchery. And, as Joe had intuited, she did not favor young Micah as a suitor, even at some future time when she was ready to consider settling down.

On a bright, cool morning in April, Melanie arose from a restless night, squinted at the sun already high on the horizon, and dragged her body from the bed. "Once I would've been the first one up, down in the kitchen even before Papa, eager for the day to begin. Now look at me," she muttered as she inspected the dark smudges beneath her eyes.

Sighing, she padded over to the basin of cool water sitting on a massive dark-stained pine bureau. Like most of the furniture at Renacimiento, it was hewn from cleanly cut and crafted white pine and was stained a rich chocolate hue—very Hispanic and sturdy. She had always preferred it to the polished precision of the New England hard maple pieces her father had brought to Renacimiento for Deborah. But now, after four years in Boston, the maple furniture seemed a link with civilization.

As Melanie washed, dressed, and braided her waist-length black hair, she little imagined that she was the subject of an argument going on downstairs in the kitchen.

"We have to do something!" Rafe declared in frustration. "As her parents we can't just stand by and let her throw away her life."

"Just because she doesn't fancy Micah doesn't mean

she'll 'throw away her life,' darling," Deborah replied, striving to keep her voice even as she arranged a stack of biscuits on a platter.

"She doesn't fancy any man, as far as I've been able to gather. Look at how she dresses! If she wasn't so strikingly beautiful, even Micah wouldn't have noticed her. She looks like a crow, for God's sake!" Rafe took a gulp of his scalding coffee and grimaced in pain.

Deborah sighed. "I admit her wardrobe is sadly deficient, but if we arrange a shopping trip to San Antonio this summer, maybe between us, Charlee and I can remedy that."

"You don't seem to want to face the point, Deborah. Melanie *wants* to be as unattractive as possible. She left here with a whole closet of pretty clothes and came back from Boston with a collection of gray and brown gunnysacks and 'sensible shoes'!"

"Don't blame my father for the way she's changed, Rafe. Lord knows he tried to get her into society and offered her every advantage," Deborah retorted.

Rafe shifted defensively in his chair. "I'm not blaming Adam, but I do blame Boston and William Lloyd Garrison! All that crusade rubbish has made a beautiful girl into a professional spinster!"

"Ah, so now we have it." Deborah's violet eyes glowed as she poured a cup of coffee for herself and sat down facing her husband. "'A professional spinster'—rather like her frightful bluestocking mother, Boston-bred and all. Listen to yourself, Rafael. You're defining your daughter's whole life in terms of marriage. If she chooses to fight for such strange things as a woman's right to vote or control her own property, or for the end of slavery, she might scare away the timid souls who could rescue her from a fate worse than death—being an old maid! Would you rather she marry someone like Oliver Haversham?"

Rafe flinched. "That was a low blow, madam. Micah Torrance is scarcely like that rotten Haversham!" Oliver Haversham had been a fortune-hunting cad who had almost deceived Deborah into marriage before she had met Rafe.

"Micah is a fine young man, but Melanie isn't in love with him. Unlikely as some girls' choices are, their parents have to allow them leeway," she said firmly.

He looked over at her measuringly, his black eyes taking on an unholy glow. "Is that your subtle way of reminding me of how unlikely a choice your father thought I was for you?"

"Well, how many New Orleans Creoles marry Boston abolitionists?"

"You are sidestepping the issue, my clever bluestocking. My very real fear is that Melanie will never give herself a chance to love anyone because of her crusading zeal."

Deborah put down her cup and studied the grounds in its bottom. Choosing her words very carefully, she said, "Rafael, Melanie's childhood was not the easiest one, but she's learned over the years that despite Lily's neglect, many others found her lovable and cherished her—her grandmother and aunt, you and I, her grandpa in Boston, even her little brothers. But she's also learned to be proud of her heritage. The blood of Africa and the Cherokee Nation flow in her veins along with yours. It's natural for her to want to end slavery. Considering what the institution of 'second families' did to the women in her family, it's also understandable that she champions women's rights. If many men can't accept that, maybe it's better that she keep on crusading rather than forsake her ideals in order to marry and have children."

Rafe sat very still for a moment; then he asked quietly, "And do you feel as if you've given up your ideals? Would you rather be back in Boston standing up for women's rights than buried here at Renacimiento with me?"

Deborah fairly flew from her chair, half knelt, and threw her arms around his waist, burying her head against his chest. "Oh, beloved, no, no, never. I can't imagine my life without you, without our children and our home. My life is here with you, bearing our children and raising them, not crusading in Boston, no matter how worthy the cause. I love you, Rafael, more than anyone or anything on earth!" She raised her tear-filled eyes to his.

Rafe pulled her up onto his lap and held her tightly, his fingers tangled in the long silver hair that spilled down her back. "Oh, Moon Flower, sometimes when I think of all you've been through, all you had to give up—and now, being pregnant again—are you certain—"

She silenced him with a swift, fierce kiss. "Nothing could make me happier than this new baby. After all, Norrie's six. It's about time we had another one. I love my life and it *is* fulfilling—after all, I'm raising all our children to believe in the same ideals I do."

He smiled crookedly. "Whether or not their hapless father does."

"You can't deceive me, for all your airs of Creole male dominance. You only want your children to be happy. All I suggested to you was that Melanie has to find her own way. We can't make her into a conventional woman who'll choose marriage over her ideals. But who knows, maybe someday she'll meet a man like her father, who will be capable of learning to accept her radical ideas." She took his face between her hands and kissed him lightly.

"Well, at least *some* of those radical ideals," he echoed dubiously, returning the playful kiss.

Several loud childish squeals punctuated by a shouted command from an adult female interrupted them. Charlee Slade's voice carried from the front *sala* to the kitchen. "Sarah, hold on to Lee before he grabs that vase. Will, mind your manners and wipe your feet."

Deborah flew through the dining room and across the hall into the front *sala* where the young woman was fussing with her six-year-old daughter's dress with one hand while slicking down a recalcitrant cowlick on her nine-year-old son's head with the other. The girl, a reedy little blonde, caught her wiggling three-year-old brother just as he reached up to topple a vase of wildflowers from a low bookshelf.

Charlee broke into a broad smile and turned to rush into her much taller friend's welcoming hug, children forgotten.

"Deborah, it's been too long! Jim's so busy with spring roundup that he couldn't get away, and he figured Rafe couldn't, either. He couldn't abide my harping to go see you for one more day, so I offered him the alternative that several of his best hands escort us here for a visit." Charlee's cat-green eyes sparkled with devilment.

"Still leading poor Jim a devil's life, are you? Where's that moldy hunk of orange fur with the evil disposition?" Rafe took his turn hugging Charlee.

As the children took turns greeting Deborah and Rafe, Charlee replied, "Hellfire took off the minute the wagon stopped out front. An engagement with a mole—or are any of your female cats in heat about now?" she asked saucily.

In the midst of the excitement, Adam, Caleb, and Lenore burst into the melee from the courtyard, where they had been having a picnic breakfast. As soon as the adults induced Adam, at sixteen the eldest, to take the younger ones down to the corral to look at the new foals, Deborah, Rafe, and Charlee headed toward the kitchen.

"Have I got news for you! But first let me look at you," Charlee said when they entered the sunny, spacious kitchen. She held Deborah at arm's length for an inspection. "Yep, you're definitely pregnant. Your last letter said the end of July, right?"

Laughing at her friend's rather indelicate tally of her due date, Deborah replied, "Yes, I think the end of July or the first of August. And as I wrote you, I'm feeling wonderful."

"Reason I wanted to know," Charlee began matter-of-factly, as she bit into a fluffy biscuit, "is that there's someone in San Antonio who's dying to see you. It's been, let's see, nearly eleven years, and in her words, 'Jeehosaphat! Scarce a letter a year gits through them damn-blasted mountains!'"

"Obedience is back!" Deborah's eyes widened with joy, then clouded over. "Oh, Charlee, Washington didn't—he isn't—"

Charlee laughed. "No, he wasn't so inconsiderate as to die like her first three husbands. He's with her. But you know Obedience. She took it into her head that eleven years was long enough being a fur trapper's wife in the Rockies, and she 'plumb pined away fer a real city 'n' a soft bunk.' So—"

"Her defenseless husband didn't have a chance," Rafe said with a resigned expression. Both women burst into new peals of laughter.

"You never met her husband, obviously," Charlee replied. "Wash Oakley would fill that door and could pull those cottonwoods out back from the ground like garden carrots! They've taken over the boardinghouse for me, and I have to say I'm relieved."

"I thought Mrs. Raufing was doing a splendid job with it," Deborah responded.

Charlee let out a disgusted snort. "She was until old Cy Witherspoon up and married her and had the temerity to forbid his wife to work!"

"Imagine that," Rafe said innocently.

Deborah fixed him with a mock glare. "Just so you remember, darling, the only reason I sold the boardinghouse to Charlee in the first place was that we live too far away for me to oversee it."

Charlee added, "Bluebonnet was close enough for me to keep an eye on it when Gerta Raufing was managing it, but when she left I needed someone else. Who better than Obedience? After all, it was her place before you took it over, Deborah."

"I can't wait to see her. Oh, Charlee, has she changed much? Oh, how silly of me—you never met her before she left San Antonio."

"She and Wash are just settling in and have a lot of work to do fixing up the place. He'd adding a whole new wing on to the east side—four more rooms. The city's grown so much since your last visit, Deborah, you'd scarcely recognize it. You can imagine how amazed Obedience and Wash are with its size. We have a new soap factory on Laredo Street and a Dr. Heusinger has opened an apothecary shop on Main. The new courthouse and jail are finished. Oh, and a fascinating old man named Clarence Pemberton has begun a new newspaper, the *San Antonio Star*. Tell me you'll go back with us for a visit with Obedience. She's so eager to see you!"

"Oh, I'm dying to see her, too," Deborah said, looking over to Rafe.

Coming up behind her, he placed his arms around her slim shoulders. "Not until after the baby's born, Deborah. You're less than four months away from delivery. It's not safe to travel so far."

"I went to Austin for the statehood ceremonies when I was six months pregnant with Sarah," Charlee reminded him.

"Austin is only seventy miles from San Antonio and Jim was with you. We're nearly two hundred miles away. Quite a difference," Rafe countered. "And Jim was right to assume I can't go with Deborah now because of spring roundup here. It's just too dangerous in her condition," he said with finality.

Melanie had heard the squeals of the children and Deborah and Charlee's noisy reunion but was oddly hesitant about coming down. At times Charlee was shockingly outspoken, even what Grandpa's Boston friends would call vulgar, but Melanie liked that about her. However, Charlee had always been Leandro Velásquez's special friend. Melanie remembered that day in Austin at the statehood ceremony when she had watched Lee and Charlee together, almost like sister and brother. Charlee and Jim had named their youngest child after the outlaw.

"And that's what he's become," she sniffed, "an outlaw wanted for two grisly murders in a barroom brawl." Still, in the quiet of the night Melanie had often tossed and turned in her solitary bed, recalling a handsome dark face with piercing jet eyes and a slashing white smile: her first girlhood crush. Though five years had passed she could still remember the devastation she had felt in Austin when she found out he was married.

Banishing all the uneasy feelings about Lee Velásquez from her mind, Melanie headed downstairs to greet Charlee and her children. Just as she neared the kitchen door, Melanie overheard her father's pronouncement regarding Deborah's traveling while pregnant. Looking at her mother's swollen body, she thought angrily, *No man will ever have that kind of hold on me—to make me a prisoner of my own body.*

Charlee caught sight of Melanie in the doorway and turned to give her a hug. "At least one full-grown member of this family is only as big as I am," she said, hugging Melanie.

Just as she had done with Deborah, Charlee inspected Melanie and puckered her freckled nose. "Ugh, your mama wrote me you'd gotten some weird notions in Boston, but I never thought it meant you'd dress to hide all those terrific curves. Hell, six months pregnant I never had breasts that size!"

Deborah's face crimsoned even as she laughed. "Charlee, you'll never change!"

Melanie blushed nervously, all too aware of how men looked at her lushly feminine body. She had never liked it. *Except when Lee admired it*, a voice from nowhere cut into her thoughts. Squelching it, she said, "How are things in San Antonio?"

Charlee launched into a lengthy discussion about the city and all the exciting events of the past months. When she mentioned that a newspaper was being printed in San Antonio again and the publisher was from Massachusetts, Melanie's eyes lit up.

"What kind of paper? I mean, do they print stories from back east? About abolition?"

"Not much about that," Charlee replied dismissively, "but the editor is looking for someone to write a column about social events. San Antonio has fancy dances, teas, political dinners—all sorts of things. He needs a reporter. Say, didn't your mother say you wrote some things for newspapers back in Boston?" Charlee looked from Melanie to Deborah, then over to Rafe, who scowled silently.

"I wrote for *The Liberator*," Melanie replied with pride in her voice.

"A scurrilous rag that excoriated President Tyler and Congress for admitting Texas to the Union. Called it a victory for the 'slavocracy,'" Rafe said with rising ire.

"Oh, we had a real argument over *that* one," Melanie

said. "But Mr. Garrison's really a lamb. Only his rhetoric is fierce. I set him straight about all the Texians who don't believe in slavery."

"I can imagine you made an impression on him," Charlee replied gravely.

Rafe snorted and Deborah smiled quietly.

Melanie's gold eyes were glowing now. "I'm a trained reporter. I could work for that paper. I've even helped with presses. Do you think the editor might hire me?"

"Wait a minute," Rafe said, but Deborah placed a restraining hand on his arm.

"Rafael, if she *could* be employed as a ladies'-page reporter..." Deborah said slowly, her mind working swiftly.

Charlee immediately picked up on the idea. "Yes, of course she could get the job. I'm sure of it. She's a fellow New Englander—even if by adoption. And Obedience's boardinghouse would be a perfectly suitable place for her to live. Jim and I are close by. Why not?"

Two small smiling faces turned eagerly toward Rafe Fleming.

"Why go off to San Antonio? You just came home from four years in Boston. Your life is here, Melanie, with us," Rafe said softly.

Melanie turned to her beloved father, then looked intuitively to her mother for support. "Papa, I've loved growing up on Renacimiento, but since I came home from school, I haven't fit in. I *need* to work—to do something with my life. I don't want to go back to Boston, even though I do love Grandpa and liked working for Mr. Garrison. But there are lots of things in need of attention right here in Texas—that is, if I was in a city, working for a newspaper where I could raise an audience!"

Deborah nodded. "Maybe this is the very thing we've been in need of, Rafael—a way for Melanie to strike out on her own and make new friends. After all, San Antonio is a large city, full of many interesting, educated... people." *And eligible men.*

Rafe looked at his wife, then to Melanie and Charlee. Shrugging in defeat, he said, "If it'll make you happy, princess, I guess your mother and I—not to mention your sister and brothers—will just have to get along without you!" He grinned as Melanie rushed into his arms with a squeal of glee.

Chapter 7

San Antonio, 1852

"It's been so long since we were in San Antonio for a visit, I'd scarcely recognize your place, Charlee," Melanie said as the two women rode up to the boardinghouse.

"Well, it's not my place anymore. I'll be making the final arrangements to sell it to Obedience and Wash this week. All these years I kept it and had other people run it for me as . . . as sort of a symbol of self-reliance, I guess." Charlee paused thoughtfully.

Melanie looked over at the spunky twenty-eight-year-old woman who had become her fast friend on the journey to Bluebonnet. "I think I understand."

"Of course you do—Deborah raised you, didn't she?" Charlee shot back. "In a way, she raised me too, although we're much closer in age. I came to her boardinghouse a scared kid who'd just ended a disastrous relationship with a certain arrogant Texian rancher."

"Jim?" Melanie asked, although she was certain it must be Charlee's husband.

"Yes, I was a scrawny, clumsy, Missouri hill girl hopelessly in love with this elegant *ranchero* who was engaged to a fancy *Tejana*. Deborah made me over into someone who can pass for a lady—when I want to." She winked at Melanie, who emitted a burble of laughter. "Deborah also got me to thinking about what it meant to be a woman and stand on my own two feet, to be beholden to no man.''

"I know how you feel. Mama and I've had lots of long talks over the years since I came to live with her and Papa. You know she gives Obedience lots of credit for helping her learn to stand on her 'own two feet' when she arrived in Texas back in 'thirty-six. I've heard so many stories about Obedience that I can't wait to meet her.''

Charlee laughed. "Just wait, my formidable Boston abolitionist. You'll be overwhelmed. Even Hellfire keeps a respectful eye on Obedience Oakley since the time she caught him stealing a pork chop from a platter by the stove while she was making supper.''

Knowing the scrofulous old orange tom to be a fiercely independent beast, Melanie cocked her head inquiringly. "What did Obedience do to him?'' In Melanie's memory no one had ever crossed the huge battle-scarred cat and come off the better for it.

Charlee's green eyes danced. "I hate to tell and spoil his reputation. She grabbed him with both hands—one around his tail, the other in a choke hold—and pulled his head and neck back until he spit the pork chop out. His eyes practically popped from their sockets before he'd let go of his prize. Then she plunked him into a vat of pickling vinegar 'ta cool down th' consarn thievin' varmint'!''

At the picture of a soddenly pickled orange cat shaking mustard seeds and dill weed from his fur, Melanie burst out laughing. "I can't wait to meet her!''

"Jeehosaphat! 'Bout time yew got back, Charlee. Where's Deborah?'' A deep, braying voice boomed across the front porch of the large white frame boardinghouse, followed by the groaning of the wooden steps as Obedience came barreling down them. "Yew must be Deborah's daughter Melanie. She wrote yew took after yer daddy 'n' wuz a real beauty. Shore 'nough true, child.'' The rawboned giantess practically lifted Melanie off the ground in a bear hug of welcome. As she struggled to regain her breath, Melanie said, "I'm so happy to meet you, Obedience. Mama's told me ever so much about you.''

"Where's your ma 'n' pa? I been hankerin' ta meet thet feller fer a pretty considerable o' years now," Obedience replied.

It was difficult for Melanie to tell if Obedience's question about her father was merely curious or slightly hostile. "They're still back at Renacimiento, I'm afraid. You see, Mama's expecting again the end of July, and Papa wouldn't let her travel this far before the baby's born."

"I tried to tell the overprotective fool it wouldn't hurt her, but you know men," Charlee said with a patronizing air. "Jim is still convinced I shouldn't ride to town alone."

"Jeehosaphat! I *know* yew set him straight, but I can't figger my Deborah puttin' up with sech tomfoolery—unless she's doin' poorly." Her brown eyes squinted in concern as she looked at Melanie for confirmation.

"Oh, no. Quite the opposite. She's been feeling wonderful, but with roundup going on, Papa couldn't get away and they agreed that she'd wait until fall, when they can all come as a family. No one—not even Papa—makes my mother do anything she doesn't agree to," Melanie said staunchly.

Charlee laughed and started up the steps. "Let's go in and we'll tell you about Melanie's plans here in San Antonio. . . ."

"Yew think yew kin git thet prissy-ass Pemberton ta give yew a job writin' fer his newspaper?" Obedience asked. Then, observing the determined set of Melanie's jaw, she answered her own question. "Yep, mebee yew will, at thet."

"I'm a fellow New Englander, at least by adoption, and I've worked on newspapers in Boston," Melanie replied.

"We persuaded Rafe that you and Wash will be ideal chaperons for his eldest daughter," Charlee added puckishly.

"An' why not? I got me three granddaughters now, back in Tennessee. I reckon I kin take on a fourth one right here in Santone!

"I know I'm leaving you in capable hands, Melanie. Not that you need any help, mind," Charlee added quickly. "If

I'm to get home before one foul-tempered, yellow-haired Texian stomps in, demanding dinner, I've got to head back to Bluebonnet.''

Melanie couldn't resist a laugh. Having met the fearsome Jim Slade on numerous occasions, she was not deceived. Neither was Obedience. "Yew git on 'n' I'll bring them papers out from thet lawyer feller soon's he's got 'em writ up. Feels real good bein' a woman o' property agin after trapisin' clear ta th' Canady border 'n' back a half-dozen times in 'leven years." She paused to consider as they walked toward the front door of the big house. "Reckon ever' woman does a fool thang er two fer a man—onliest thang is ta be shore it's fer the *right* man!"

The older women laughed, but Melanie said with the certainty of untried youth, "You speak for yourselves. I don't ever plan to do anything foolish for *any* man."

"I reckon I'll wait on thet one," Obedience said with a slow wink at Charlee.

The newspaper office was a small cluttered place of roughly hewn whitewashed wood, squeezed between two large store buildings of Spanish style in the older part of town. The large glass window on the front door was neatly lettered *San Antonio Star.*

Melanie peered inside the grimy window and could see the familiar outline of a Washington Hand Press through the dusty gloom. It was early, scarcely eight A.M., but what good newspaperman wouldn't be busy at work by now? Straightening her unadorned straw bonnet and smoothing her businesslike gray suit jacket and skirt, Melanie knocked firmly on the door.

From behind the metal labyrinth of the press, an old man moved to open the door. He bobbed his head in a polite greeting. "Mornin', ma'am. Mr. Pemberton's not here yet. I'm Amos Johnston, his assistant."

Melanie smiled and offered her hand to the startled black man, who quickly wiped the ink from his fingers onto a rag he pulled from his pocket and then gingerly returned her salutation. She loved the familiar smells of linseed oil and carbon black. "I'm Melanie Fleming and I'm here to see Mr. Pemberton about a job."

Amos Johnston's wizened face took on a puzzled expression. "A job, ma'am?"

"Yes. As a reporter. My friends, the Slades from Bluebonnet, told me he was looking for someone to cover local stories."

"Oh, er, well, I don't rightly know. If you'd care to come back this afternoon, I expect he'll be back by then. He went out to try and get an interview with a fellow born and raised here who ran off and became a scalper down in Chihuahua. Just came back last week, or so Mr. Pemberton heard. He lives outside town, but if I know the boss, he'll track him down and get his story."

"So he's doing his own reporting as well as editorials and advertising. Are you his only employee?" Melanie asked as she drew a copy of last night's *Star* from beneath her arm.

"Yes, ma'am—er Miss Fleming. I came west with Mr. Pemberton all the way from Massachusetts. He's a good man with high standards. Guess that's why he hasn't hired a reporter yet," Amos said uneasily. *And he'll* never *hire a woman!*

"I can see that he's good—strong editorials, good bold headlines, clear type style. You're a fine printer, Mr. Johnston, but I still can plainly see the two of you need help. Mr. Pemberton's using the pieces submitted by the city council and the ladies' guild without editing or checking them, isn't he?" At a nod from his grizzled head, Melanie added, "I know. I'm sure he hasn't time to rewrite, but the style is clumsy, and the news can be repetitious and slanted when he just takes whatever is offered and runs it. I could cover council meetings, the court, even the ladies' circles and social events," she added with a hint of martyrdom in her voice.

"You say you did this kind of work before?" Amos could tell the determined young woman obviously knew something about newspapers.

"Yes, in Boston for nearly four years," she replied. "Tell your Mr. Pemberton I'll be back at two P.M. sharp!"

Clarence Vivian Pemberton was a tall, stoop-shouldered man with a slightly thickening middle and thinning head of white hair. Born in northern Maine, the second son of a prosperous farmer, he had moved to Philadelphia at the rebellious age of twenty-one. Facile of mind and capable of writing with acerbic wit, he quickly found his way into the printing trade. After an apprenticeship with a Philadelphia press, he had worked as a journalist for newspapers from Vermont to Virginia, and finally started his own small daily in Concord, Massachusetts.

As Pemberton dismounted at the livery that afternoon, he castigated himself for the thousandth time for his stupidity in coming to this godforsaken wilderness. "San Antonio, where the chapeau vies with the sombrero, the Paris of the Southwest," he muttered to himself as he rubbed his aching posterior.

"Somethin' wrong, Mr. Pemberton?" Whalen Simpson, the livery owner, inquired solicitously.

"Only that I rue the day man ever considered taming the equine species, my dear fellow. If only this accursed place had *roads* so one could use a rig."

"Depends on where ya wanna go," Whalen replied reasonably. *Damn fool Yankee. Lucky he warn't scalped!*

"I needed to go a good distance outside town to a burned-out ranch house. Unfortunately, my quarry eluded me," Pemberton said peevishly.

"Didn't know ya wuz a hunter," Simpson said, looking in vain for signs of a firearm on the slumping body of the newspaperman.

Rolling his eyes heavenward, the older man stomped off, cursing the wasted morning.

When Pemberton opened the door to the *Star* and found a young woman in wrinkled, oversized clothes primly perched on a chair chatting with Amos, his mood did not improve.

Cocking one shaggy white brow, he skewered her with piercing pale blue eyes. His New England accent had

evolved through fifty years into an intimidating twang.
"And precisely who might you be, young woman?" he
inquired.

She jumped up from the seat as if scorched by a hot stone
and faced his considerable height. "I'm Melanie Fleming,
Mr. Pemberton, and I've come to apply for a job as a
reporter. The Slades told me you were looking for someone."

"I am looking for a man to handle news gathering and
writing for me, yes. You scarcely qualify," he replied,
looking down at her dainty face and figure.

"I've worked on newspapers before—gotten the stories,
written them, even helped set type and deliver papers," she
replied gamely.

"She knows a case box upper from lower, I can tell you,
Mr. Pemberton. And she's worked with a Washington like
ours," Amos put in before Clarence quelled him with a
fierce scowl.

"Your 'bank president' look doesn't scare me," Melanie
said boldly, taking a gamble.

"Bank president look?" Pemberton echoed, a faint hint
of puzzlement in his voice.

"My grandfather is Adam Manchester, president of the
Union National Bank of Boston. He stands and glares at
people just like you do. Mostly they cave in."

"But you, I assume, do not," he observed waspishly.

"No. I do not. Nor do I ask for favors. I'm qualified to
work for you. Here are my references," she said, pulling a
sheaf of papers from her reticule and handing them to
Pemberton. "Since you're from Concord, you might be
interested to know I was there several times on Mr. Garrison's business when you were publishing the *Register*. I
covered the passage of freed slaves on the Underground
Railroad. One of the stopping houses was just outside
Concord."

"You wrote for Garrison's *Liberator*?" Pemberton's voice
betrayed just a smidgen of his surprise.

"Indeed I did—and for the *Sentinel* and the *Challenger*,"
she answered proudly.

"Still, that was New England. All well and good when

you're surrounded with intellectuals and bluestockings. This is the Texas wilderness, a horse of quite a different color." He grimaced at his own bad joke.

"Mr. Pemberton, I was raised in Texas, up north on a big ranch that my father carved out of the wilderness. I'm no tenderfoot and I've scarcely led a safe and comfortable life while living the past four years with my grandfather in Boston. I was in the thick of the Fugitive Slave Act riots on the Common in the fall of 1850. When the mob almost burned Mr. Garrison's office, I was with him. I've hidden with runaways in rat-infested basements and been attacked by drunken mobs, even shot at. Nothing here in San Antonio can scare me," she finished with bravado.

"And just what made you desert all that glamour in Boston for this wide place on the Camino Real?" he asked, with heavy irony lacing his voice.

"My family—my parents, that is, wanted me to return to Texas. It's my home," she replied evasively.

"Let me guess. You found ranch life too tame—merely escaping scalping by Comanche and fighting off Mexican banditti proved not enough of a challenge, so you rode into the sunset toward San Antonio to seek your fortune."

"The only reason you won't consider my references is because I'm a woman, not because of any lack of qualifications," she said with as much equanimity as she could manage.

"A woman in San Antonio is still subject to the mercies, or lack thereof, to be found amidst a populous of singular barbarity. Women can't fend for themselves on the frontier," he pronounced.

"Poor defenseless things like Obedience Oakley?" she shot back.

Pemberton cocked his head and raised an eyebrow. "Perhaps the formidable Mrs. Oakley is an exception, but she is not the one applying for a job."

"She and my mother went through the Texas Revolution together, and I'm living at her boardinghouse now. She thinks I can handle any assignment you give me. So do

Charlee and Jim Slade,'' Melanie said, growing more frustrated with each obdurate exchange.

At the mention of Jim Slade's name, Pemberton's ears pricked up. ''You know the Slades, do you?''

''Yes. I already told you that. In fact, I've even met Senator Houston at their house. Bet I could get you some great stories on Washington politics,'' she ventured, with hope once more rising.

Pemberton appeared to reconsider, glancing again at her references. That she had worked for several radical women's rights journals was hardly a surprise, nor the temperance crusade paper, but the recommendation from Garrison was highly unusual. Putting the papers down on his cluttered desk, he said, ''I went out this morning to interview a remarkable fellow. If he'd agreed to talk with me, I could have gotten quite a story. He's an outlaw of sorts, although he has been cleared of the crimes that led him to flee Texas. His criminal escapades in New Mexico and Chihuahua are out of Texian jurisdiction.

''You mean that scalp hunter? Amos told me that's where you went this morning.'' She hoped her voice hadn't squeaked.

''One and the same,'' Pemberton replied dryly. ''His life has been fascinating, and he's linked to our illustrious Senator Houston and Jim Slade, who incidentally secured his exoneration by state authorities. It seems the young cutthroat was only acting in retaliation for the deaths of his wife and several of the employees at his ranch when he killed the two rangers.''

Melanie's heart suddenly froze in her chest and her face went chalky as Pemberton continued.

''Yes, he's had quite a career—born here in Texas, university educated in Mexico City, a man with a price on his head for over six years in Texas—friend of Sam Houston, the infamous Indian lover, while at the same time a butcher who amassed a fortune in the Apachería by collecting bounty on savages' scalps. Yes, Leandro Angel Velásquez has quite a tale to tell—if he could be persuaded by feminine wiles to tell it.'' He paused and looked at her dowdy clothes and frozen face. ''Of course, you scarcely look the part of a femme fatale who could get him to divulge his innermost secrets," he said scornfully.

"If I get him to talk to me and write the story, do I have a job?" Melanie forced her breathing under control and waited until Pemberton turned to face her with frank surprise written on his face.

He was holding her, feeling her fragile, broken body fall lifelessly against his shoulder, her life's blood soak his shirt. He laid her back on the bed, staring down into her eyes, once so softly adoring, now dulled with horror and death. Then her face began to change, its chalky pallor darkening to a sun-burnished bronze, the delicate features coarsening. She was a Mexican peasant woman, some farmer's wife with her nose burned away from repeated torture, her eyes hopeless yet oddly pleading for understanding as she lay on the sere earth in front of Red Coyote's lodge. Flames leaped everywhere around her and an Apache lance pierced her side. Unprotesting, she lay dying, staring up at her tardy deliverer. He could smell the stench of burning flesh and greasy hair, hear the screams of the Mescalero warriors as they roused to battle and the equally fearsome yells of his own companions as they rode through the encampment, shooting, stabbing, clubbing. Once more the vision shifted, blood to more blood, this time congealed on scalp poles creaking and rustling softly with their gory burdens as the men rode toward Chihuahua City.

Suddenly the noise and stench of death evaporated into still silvery moonlight. Crying out on the warm night air, Lee sat up sweat-soaked, in his bedroll. He sank down and rolled over on his stomach, fighting the churning waves of nausea that threatened to overtake him. The nightmares, those damned nightmares from the pit of hell, were back.

Struggling to stand on shaky legs, he drew several deep breaths of clean, fresh air into his lungs and started to walk in no particular direction, just away from the jacal and his bedroll, away from the nightmares that pursued him like demons. "Damn nosy newspaper reporter digging through my past," he muttered to himself. "He dredged this up again." Lee swore, then smiled grimly as he recalled leveling the sights of a Sharps breech loader at the stoop-shouldered old dragon's midsection and watching him bounce away on the back of that swaybacked old nag he'd rented from Whalen Simpson's livery. Lee rubbed his eyes and let his thoughts wander back to the man he used to be, before the dreams, before the events that caused them. *Uncle Alfonso, no wonder you recoiled from me in Mexico City three years ago.* Lee could still see the shock and sorrow etched on the gentle old man's face. *You only imagined what I'd become. Thank God you never learned the whole truth!*

Forcing the past from his mind, Lee considered the future. Should he stay here? Begin again? His eyes were drawn toward the harsh outline of blackened ruins. His burned-out ranch house stood silhouetted against the starry night sky, the stone chimney of the big fireplace and the charred heavy timbers of the *sala* the only remains of his cherished dream. He had rebuilt the house burned by Comanche over twenty years ago and six years ago it had been destroyed again, this time by Anglos. Was it worth the pain to try again, when he had been twice vanquished?

What do I want from life? he ruminated. Certainly an end to the bloody carnage. But to rebuild his life, become a rancher, perhaps even reclaim his family's dream and marry again entailed a lot of risks and made him vulnerable to even more pain.

He walked down to where Sangre Azul stood, patiently watching as his master approached. The big blue stallion had become almost an extension of his own body, his companion on the headlong flight from Texas, his salvation on the tracking expeditions through New Mexico and Chihuahua, where a man's life often depended on the speed and endurance of his horse. Sangre had never failed him. Now the stallion knew his master wanted to ride. Swinging up bareback, the man kneed the big horse into an easy canter.

Feeling the coolness of the breeze hit his face, Lee rode, letting the soothing rhythm of Sangre's stride calm his confusion. He knew every part of this range, had since he was a very small boy riding with his father. Without knowing why, he headed south toward an open, shallow canyon, a favorite hideaway for him and his elder brother Tomás. The valley floor was divided by a meandering stream, part of the San Antonio river system that ran underground for hundreds of miles around the city, surfacing in enchanting creeks and pools such as this one. Lee dismounted and looked at the June grasses and flowering shrubs surrounding him. A stand of willows beckoned him from the end of the canyon where the creek vanished belowground once more. Jagged spikes of Spanish dagger stood scattered across the more arid sections of the sloping hillside like sentinels for sleeping conquistadores.

The scene was silvery and surrealistic, bathed in brilliant moonlight. He walked to the stream's edge and knelt on the sandy bank to dip his hand in the cold rushing water and drink. Just then, a flash of color caught his eye, a bright, buttery glow in the light from the night sky. He stood up and began to walk slowly, silently, almost as if stalking a wild creature. Wild it was and incredibly lovely, an evening primrose. Its soft petals stretched outward to embrace the moon, a flower of the night, never destined to exist in the scorching sunlight that brings all the rest of the desert to riotous life each day.

"Night flower," he breathed aloud, whisper soft as he reached out his hand, but stopped inches short of touching its beckoning beauty. "I wonder whether you'll be here next year to greet the summer moonlight? Will I?"

He contemplated the flower. Delicate as a woman, yet it had tough roots set deep in the harsh Texas soil. His roots were here, as well, watered by the blood of his family. "I'm alive, even if my parents and Dulcia are gone." He considered whether finding the flower was an omen. Each year, with the scant encouragement of a few nights of glory, it renewed itself. With so much more to gain, perhaps he could too.

Feeling hopeful, Lee mounted Sangre and rode back to his jacal to sleep the rest of the night, deep and dreamlessly.

Chapter 8

After spending a restless night dreaming of a chiseled aristocratic face with a blinding white smile, Melanie arose at dawn feeling uneasy. How could she reconcile that image, graven on her heart since girlhood, with the man Clarence Pemberton had described to her? Lee Velásquez was a renegade scalper, a bloodthirsty *pistolero* who was home because of the political influence of his old friend and mentor, Jim Slade.

"Perhaps I should begin my research with Jim," she mused aloud as she performed her morning toilette. "He could tell me about Lee." Odd that on the whole trip from Renacimiento to Bluebonnet, Charlee never mentioned her old friend; or, if half the bloody reports about him were true, perhaps not so odd. Sighing, Melanie looked at her reflection in the mirror. "No, I'm being cowardly. If I want to get this job, I have to face Lee Velásquez and ask him for myself."

With a firm scolding, she reminded herself of all the past hardships and dangers she'd endured—angry mobs and slave catchers. *But none of them were Lee Velásquez. Oh, damn!*

After riding a few miles on the livery nag she had rented, she was inclined to agree with Mr. Pemberton's dislike of Whalen's horses. She must write home and wheedle Liberator, her magnificent black stallion, from her father, although if he knew she was riding miles away from San Antonio, unescorted, in search of a dangerous gunman to interview, he'd drag her back to Renacimiento and bury her there!

She'd just have to think of a convincing reason to have her own horse, even though she was living in the largest city in Texas.

When she neared the burned-out ruins of the Velásquez ranch house, Melanie's uneasiness grew. There was no sign of Lee. She dismounted and began to investigate the site, recalling all she'd gleaned from several of the boarding-house's most gossipy old women. Miss Clemson remembered Lee quite well and even told her about his family, who were killed by Comanche back in 1830. *On this very ground*. She shivered as she recalled the rest of the story about the orphan raised by old Will Slade. Lee had gone off to Mexico City when he was eighteen and come home with a Mexican wife. Old Racine Schwartz said she was the prettiest young bride he'd ever seen. Melanie had felt a twinge of jealousy as the old roomer described Dulcia Velásquez's gleaming chestnut hair and wide blue eyes.

All anyone knew was that the girl and her friend, one of the Sandovals' daughters, were murdered, and after Lee killed two rangers in retaliation, he had fled into New Mexico Territory back in 1846. It must have been only a few months after she had left for Boston, after they had met so briefly at the statehood ceremony in Austin. How oddly their lives had been interwoven since she first met him in Galveston ten years ago. *Both of us left Texas and then returned. Almost against our wills*.

Her ruminations were suddenly interrupted by an angry male voice. "What are you doing here?" Melanie gasped and jerked around in fright. "You!" Lee's voice registered amazement as he recognized her arrestingly lovely, heart-shaped face and wide gold eyes. But her raven hair was drawn unbecomingly into a tight knot and her voluptuous curves, so tantalizingly revealed six years ago in a silk shirt and split riding skirt, were now swathed in a shapeless hot-looking brown linen suit. "I repeat, Miss Fleming, what are you doing trespassing on my land?"

Melanie's throat had collapsed around her vocal cords. As she struggled to speak, she stared at the man Lee had become. Still tall and gracefully slim, he had a rangy, corded leanness to his body now, like a panther poised to pounce. His face was frightening! Gone were the flashing smile and sunny innocence. This man's black eyes were hard as obsidian, narrowed in insolent appraisal of her person. Melanie returned his inspection while she recovered her voice. She could see a thin scar just below his hairline, though it was partially obscured by curling black hair that tumbled to meet his arched brows. His nose had been broken and another small scar nicked his left cheekbone. He needed a shave and a haircut, but despite the harsh new lines and scars on his face, it was still arrestingly handsome in a barbaric sort of way.

She searched his eyes. "I scarcely recognized you, Lee. You've changed." Well, at least her voice was back and even presentably clear.

"You still haven't answered my question, Melanie," he said harshly. "What are you doing here?"

She took a deep, steadying breath. "Looking for you. I want to find out if the Lee Velásquez I knew is the same man who fled into the Apachería six years ago with a price on his head. A renegade."

His face darkened and he scowled. "The only price on my head now is in Chihuahua, and I don't plan on going back there."

"I know in Texas you're free and clear, thanks to Jim Slade and his friend Sam Houston. If you were innocent, why did you run, Lee?"

His sculpted lips hardened into a slash. "You are a naive child. I killed two Anglos—rangers signed up to go kill Mexicans. Do you honestly think a *Tejano* would get a fair hearing in Texas on the eve of the war?"

"No, but—"

"You're still evading the issue. Why are you here, two hundred miles from your papa's ranch, alone, trespassing on my land?"

His piercing eyes made her feel like an insect wriggling on a pin. "It's a long story."

"Try me."

Damn! She was supposed to be interviewing *him*. "Well,

I came to San Antonio with Charlee Slade to live with
Obedience and Wash Oakley. I—I had nothing to do at
Renacimiento after I came home from Boston. In Boston I
worked for the abolitionists and women's suffrage movements.''

His harsh face relaxed a fraction, and a smile twitched on
his lips. "Still tilting at windmills, Melanie?"

Recalling his condescending allusion to Don Quixote ten
years earlier, she replied tartly, "I'm no longer an ignorant
twelve-year-old schoolgirl who never read Cervantes, Lee."

"But you still feel compelled to raise your standard for
the downtrodden. Better to fight for abolition in Boston than
Texas, little girl."

She felt her cheeks heat with anger as she shot back,
"There are enough downtrodden in Texas to make it an
admirable place for me to 'raise my standard.' ''

"What brings you to my ranch to launch your crusade?"
He had moved from defensive anger to condescension, then
to frank curiosity.

Recalling Clarence Pemberton's description of how Lee
had run him off at gunpoint, Melanie knew she had to go
carefully. "There may not be many slaves to free in west
Texas, but there are other issues—like the way *Tejanos* are
treated. You said yourself, a *Tejano* who kills a ranger or
any Anglo isn't likely to get a fair trial."

"I never thought of placing myself in the ranks of the
defenseless downtrodden," he said sardonically.

Looking at the tall, heavily armed man in front of her, she
was inclined to agree. "Don't you care if Texas citizens of
Mexican ancestry are denied their rights?"

His brows arched quizzically. "And just what could you
do about it?"

She took a deep breath and plunged in. "I could write a
story about you for the *San Antonio Star*, explaining what
happened to you and what you plan to do with your life
now."

It took a minute to register. Then his face hardened once
more. "That Yankee prig sent *you* to interview me after I
ran him off! Of all the spineless, harebrained, idiotic ideas
I've ever heard!"

She stood facing him, hands on hips, furious anger lighting her eyes to golden flames. "And why is that—just because I'm a woman? I'll have you know I'm a trained journalist, and there's no good reason I shouldn't be able to talk with you just as well as a male reporter."

"I don't talk to reporters, male or female," he replied harshly. "So get your pretty little ass back on that horse and ride out of here before I paddle it—that is, if I can find it beneath all those wrinkled layers of skirts!"

"You arrogant, crude brigand!" she shrieked at him, furious beyond reason. "Mr. Pemberton was right—you did murder whole villages of Indians for their scalps, didn't you? And now you're back here with your blood money, skulking in these ruins like some wild animal licking his wounds! Mr. Pemberton's not the coward—you are!"

As Lee listened to her diatribe, his face paled beneath his swarthy tan. He stood very still, staring down at the tiny, furious woman in front of him, willing himself to remain calm and ignore his craven itch to put his callused hands around that slim golden neck and squeeze.

Sensing the direction of his thoughts, Melanie quieted but stood her ground doggedly. "If you don't talk to reporters, everyone will assume the worst about you."

"They do anyway," he said tightly.

"You're impossible, Lee Velásquez, but I'm going to get your story no matter what. Do your damnedest to stop me!" With that, she whirled and stalked toward her horse without a backward glance.

By the time she had ridden halfway back to town, Melanie's heart slowed its trip-hammer beat. *He might have killed me. He's a cold-blooded monster*, she thought to herself. Still, somewhere beneath the renegade's menace must remain a semblance of the smiling young man who had haunted her dreams and fantasies since she was a child. Surely the real Leandro Velásquez was still there.

Obedience was up to her elbows in flour, kneading an enormous quantity of bread dough in the boardinghouse's big kitchen. "Give me more flour, Sadie," she called to the elderly black woman who had worked for the establishment the past twenty years.

Sadie scuttled over to the sack of flour and scooped some into a pot. "This be 'nough, Miz Obedience?"

"Jist dump it on me," Obedience replied, her rawboned, muscular arms working the huge blob of dough rhythmically. Both women were interrupted in their task when Melanie came dashing into the kitchen. "Yew look whiter'n this here flour. Whut's wrong, girl?" Obedience asked as her shrewd brown eyes took in Melanie's pallor and agitation.

Melanie fidgeted, feeling guilty for not telling Obedience about her challenge from Mr. Pemberton to interview the infamous Lee Velásquez. She was loath to confess her failure after having sneaked from the house at daybreak to attempt the thankless task. She sat primly on the edge of a chair and arranged her clumpy wrinkled skirts carefully, avoiding two pairs of curious and probing eyes.

"Dat chile done been up ta somethin', Miz Obedience," Sadie said emphatically.

Obedience just waited, knowing full well her charge would explain in her own good time. Turning back to the dough, she resumed kneading.

Realizing the boss and her ward had some sorting out to do, Sadie nodded to Obedience and excused herself to go and change bed linens upstairs.

"Well, you know I wanted to work for Mr. Pemberton at the *Star*," Melanie began hesitantly.

"Yep, 'n' last night yew tole me he wuz gonna give yew a sorta trial job cause o' yew bein' female 'n' all." The pounding and squeezing on the dough never missed a beat.

"What I didn't tell you was the kind of test—er, assignment— Mr. Pemberton gave me . . . more of a dare really. He couldn't get Leandro Velásquez to talk to him, so he sent me out to his place to try and get a story," she blurted out all in one breath. "Do—do you know who Velásquez is?"

Obedience let out a whoop of laughter and pounded the dough so hard a white floury cloud rose up and surrounded her. "Jeehosaphat! Do I know Lee? Girl, your mama 'n' me come here in 'thirty-six 'n' thet little tadpole wuz underfoot ever since't, taggin' on Jim Slade's heels ever'where he went. Wash 'n' me run in ta him in Santy Fe last year 'n' convinced him ta write Jim 'n' git shut o' his trouble so's he cud come home.'' She stopped and laughed again, wiping her arms on her apron after she plopped the dough into an immense stone crock to rise. ''I kin jist see thet prissy New England prune Pemberton runnin' like a stampeded jackrabbit when Lee fixed them black eyes o' his'n on th' old fart!'' She guffawed and then observed the girl's shaken demeanor. ''Say, I figgered a pompous ole windbag like Pemberton ta run, but yew? Thought yew cud stand up ta any man!''

Melanie flushed in shame, angry and confused over her feelings about Lee Velásquez. ''I stood my ground with that—that scalper! He's a crude, mean, low-life, muleheaded...'' Her voice trailed off as she ran out of expletives and Obedience's laughter drowned her out.

''Always figgered yew two'd tangle when ya met.''

''We always have,'' Melanie replied. Then, at Obedience's look of curious prompting, she continued, ''We met twice before.'' Quickly she gave the older woman an edited version of her earlier encounters with Lee. ''I don't understand how someone could change so much, Obedience. He was always full of himself, puffed up with insufferable Hispanic vanity, but he was teasing and smiling. Now he even looks different, hard and dangerous. When Mr. Pemberton told me he'd been a scalper in New Mexico, I didn't believe it, but now I think it's true. What kind of a man hires himself out to go and kill whole villages of people?''

''Mebbe,'' Obedience replied slowly, ''th' same kinda man who comes home as a twenty-two-year-old kid ta find his wife 'n' unborn baby murdered—her 'n' her friend 'n' three o' his ranch hands all dead. Them two drunk rangers whut done it raped her and abused her somethin' awful, then cut her throat. I spect when a man lives through thet, somethin' inside o' him snaps. He found 'em in town 'n' kilt em—two ta his one. But they wuz volunteers fer th' army ta fight Mexico 'n' his folks wuz from th' enemy country. It made no never mind he wuz borned here.''

"So he had to run," Melanie interjected as her mind envisioned the horror of the blood-soaked scene he had found on the very spot where she encountered him that morning. "But that doesn't erase his becoming a bounty hunter, killing whole villages of Indians for their scalps."

Obedience looked levelly at Melanie. "I ain't sayin' whut he done wuz right, er thet mine owners 'n' traders got th' right ta pay fer scalps, but they's two sides ta ever' fight, child."

"You mean because the Comanche killed his parents, that gives him the right to kill any other Indians? Well, I don't see it that way." Her retort sounded self-righteous even to her own ears.

Obedience ignored it and said gently, "I seen things whilst travelin' with Wash through th' Rockies 'n' down in New Mexico Territory. Things yew niver dreamed o'—whole towns 'n' wagon trains o' settlers kilt—women, children, babies. Both sides's done wrong. Lee didn't start th' war— he wuz borned dab smack in th' middle o' it. Santy Fe's a rough place. Not much fer a kid with a price on his head 'n' no money in his pockets ta do. Lee's seen whut Apache 'n' Comanche done, not jist when he wuz a boy, neither." She paused. "He tell yew 'bout any o' it?" At Melanie's negative nod, she said knowingly, "Didn't think so. Took a quart o' whiskey ta git him ta tell it ta me 'n' Wash. He freed hunnerts o' slaves when they raided in Apachería— mostly Mexican women 'n' younguns."

Obedience proceeded to describe Lee's sojourn in New Mexico and Chihuahua, the men he dealt with, and the situation facing traders and settlers. She told Melanie about the hellish way captives were treated and how the blood lust of his companions as well as that of the Indians had driven Lee to quit and return to Santa Fe. "If'n yew want th' truth o' why he got a pardon from th' gov'ner, yew go 'n' talk ta Jim Slade. He'll set yew straight 'bout whut kinda man Lee Velásquez is!"

Nodding slowly, Melanie agreed to do so. She had a great many things to consider and to learn. And she was going to

get that job with Clarence Pemberton! She rode out to
Bluebonnet for a talk with the Slades that very afternoon.

The following afternoon Lee rode into town, bathed and
shaved. He had decided it was time for a haircut and a new
wardrobe, and also a talk with Gerhart Grosman, a big
mercantile owner who doubled as the town's leading banker.
Since Texas law prohibited incorporated banks, the large
freighters and merchants provided banking services across
the state. Lee had deposited a sizable sum with the German
merchant and decided it was time to draw some out and get
to work.

He had spent almost a week alone since returning to
Texas, camping on his land, brooding over the past and
wondering if he should rebuild. After all the trouble Jim had
gone through holding the title for him the past six years,
Lee had felt duty bound to at least confront all the bitter-
sweet, lost dreams at the ranch. Discovering the night flower
had awakened a new resolution inside him. He would begin
once more. When he was done, the Velásquez name would
be one to be reckoned with in Texas.

After spending the morning outfitting himself with clothes
and visiting the barber, he felt more like a rancher and less
like a renegade. Wearing a soft white shirt, tan wool suit,
and gleaming new boots, he headed across the Main Plaza,
intent on visiting several of the largest and most popular
cantinas, the best places to spread the word that he wanted
to hire *vaqueros* for Night Flower. "Night Flower." He
rolled the new name he had chosen for his ranch on his
tongue.

As he walked, preoccupied, across the busy square, two
pairs of female eyes watched him with great interest. Larena
Sandoval and her cousin Teresa Ramirez were out for a late
afternoon stroll on their way to confession at San Fernando
Cathedral.

"That is *him*, Larena," Teresa whispered from behind
her parasol. "Leandro Velásquez."

Her friend, a slim dark-haired girl of striking beauty,
stared at the tall, lean stranger who walked with such catlike
grace. "He looks different than he did six years ago, that is

certain," she said hesitantly, noting his wicked-looking knife and pistol and the harsh, angular planes of his handsome face.

"But still gorgeous! I think the scar on his cheek makes him dashing!" Teresa sighed.

Larena remembered the young man and his pretty bride who had been fast friends of her older sister Gertrudis. Now both Gertrudis and Dulcia were long dead, and so were their murderers—at the hand of this dangerous-looking stranger. She could not deny there was a certain frightening fascination to him.

"I've read the terrible story about him and what he did in New Mexico," Larena said, recalling the story in that morning's *Star*. Teresa babbled on about the tragedy of his lost youth and unfair treatment at the hands of the Anglo government.

"But my cousin James has had him pardoned," Larena replied to Teresa's diatribe. "I wonder what he's going to do now. Perhaps rebuild his ranch?"

"Let's ask him," Teresa said, giving her friend's arm a yank and propelling her on a collision course with the long-legged man.

Lee was preoccupied with his plans and did not see the two young women until he had almost trampled them. Catching himself an instant before he lost an eye to the sharply pointed edge of Teresa's parasol, he pulled back sharply as the pretty young woman flipped it back with a feigned gasp of dismay, as if the last thing in the world she had thought to do was to run into him.

Doffing his wide-brimmed hat, he sketched a bow and smiled at the conspiratorial pair. The cute little brunette who had nearly blinded him was simpering coyly, but her delicately beautiful friend with the lustrous ebony hair was obviously embarrassed at their ploy. "A thousand pardons, ladies. I was not watching where I was going. Are you hurt?"

"Better to ask that of you, Leandro. Teresa wields a wicked parasol," Larena said, with color staining her cheeks.

Lee chuckled and then looked closely at her, realizing she

was familiar. "You have the advantage of knowing my name. Might I presume to ask yours?"

"I am Larena Sandoval—Gertrudis's sister," she added quietly.

His expression betrayed a hint of pain, but it vanished in an instant, replaced by amazement. "But the last time I saw you, you were a schoolgirl with braided hair, in short skirts!"

"It was six years ago. Schoolgirls do grow up," she said with a dimpling smile. "Oh, and this rather dangerous young woman is my cousin Teresa Ramirez."

Lee smiled at Teresa and she was lost. Lord, how handsome he was! "As an old friend of our family, you must come calling some day soon. You've been back in San Antonio for weeks, and after the story in the newspaper, I'm certain Uncle José and Aunt Esperanza are very concerned for your well-being," she said primly.

"Story in the newspaper?" Lee looked from Teresa to Larena as a sickening feeling settled in the pit of his stomach. *She wouldn't have dared.*

"The *Star* carried a long story about your life, Leandro," Larena replied. Seeing the anger that darkened his face, she quickly went on, "Oh, it was not an unfavorable story. It told of the injustice done you by the government and how you were deserving of the pardon. In fact, it was very flattering to the *Tejano* community."

"I'll bet," he said tightly. "If you ladies will excuse me, I have to go read a newspaper." He tipped his hat and stalked off determinedly.

Lee stormed in the front door of the boardinghouse and nearly collided with Violet Clemson, who gasped and leaped out of his way with surprising alacrity for someone of seventy-plus years. Ignoring her fright, he strode toward the kitchen and the sound of Obedience's voice.

Without a greeting, he slammed the *Star* on the table and glared at her. "Why the hell did you tell her all this? It *was* you, wasn't it? And don't deny that Melanie wrote this story, even though no name is on it."

Thoroughly unintimidated, Obedience continued slicing the haunch of venison that was to be served for the boarder's midday meal. "Yep, I tole her part o' it. She talked to Jim 'n' Charlee, too. Anythin' in it not true?" She looked at him patiently.

Wanting to lash out at someone, he shifted his weight from one foot to the other, furious with Obedience and the Slades. "Why did you help her? I didn't want the past dredged up, and I don't want people's sympathy because I was a *Tejano* who was done wrong by the Anglos."

She shrugged philosophically. "If'n yer gonna make a life here, Lee, yew gotta figger folks is gonna dredge up th' past whether er not yew like it. Question 'pears ta me ta be, is someone gonna set 'em straight? Till now, them ugly rumors 'n' lies, 'bout yew wuz the onliest things they had ta go on. Yew have th' truth tole now, without yer havin' ta go over 'n' over it with ever'body. Folks is willin' ta fergit yer mistakes in Santy Fe now thet they know why yew went 'n' how yew come back." She looked at him, gauging that his anger was cooling slightly. With a twinkle in her eyes, Obedience added, "She done a helluva a job, didn't she?"

Chapter 9

Father Gustav Schreckenberg wiped the sweat from his brow and ran his fingers through the thick swatch of straight yellow hair falling on his forehead. Unconsciously he pushed it back and placed his hat over it once more. *And I thought it was hot in Munich!* The July heat was nearly unbearable. How far away the cool, dark green mountains of Bavaria seemed from the gold and azure of Texas with its brilliant skies and parched adobes.

Here at least the air moves, he consoled himself, remembering his landing in Galveston on a becalmed day when the humidity and sun had combined to drive even stray dogs and hardy burros to seek shade. He patted the small, sinewy beast he rode at a slow, gentle pace. "A long way we have come from Galveston to San Antonio," he said aloud, practicing his English on the burro.

The priest observed the city as he neared the eastern boundaries. Mercifully there were some tall cottonwood trees welcoming him with their shade. The river, too, was lovely as he followed its twists and turns, watching small dark-haired children with glistening brown bodies splash and cavort in the shallows while their mothers scrubbed laundry on the rocks at the water's edge.

So far everyone he had met appeared Hispanic. Where were all the Anglo and German settlers? The young priest's fair complexion was sunburned to a fierce cherry glow, adding to the cherubic appearance of his round, pleasant face with its bright blue eyes and generous lips. Seeing the young padre's cassock and collar, many of the young men and children called greetings to him in Spanish. Smiling, he blessed them, making the sign of the cross and nodding but venturing no further communication.

As he neared the center of town and began to see more northern European faces, he relaxed. Perhaps someone here spoke English, even German. Then the tall dome of San Fernando came into sight. Recognizing it at once from the description he'd been given in Galveston by Bishop Odin, he urged the little burro in that direction, cutting through the thronging melee of the crowded market conducted daily in the Main Plaza. He was suddenly diverted from his goal by the *baah* of a nanny goat that was quickly drowned out by the shrill cries of a small child and the rumbling bass curses of a fat merchant.

Turning to stare in the direction from which the noise was coming, Father Schreckenberg saw a small Indian boy pulling frantically on a rope fastened around the neck of a protesting nanny. Boy and goat were fleeing the wrath of a cantina owner whose ample girth greatly impeded his speed.

Brandishing a broom, the fat man swatted at the boy and missed, overturning several crocks of milk, which elicited furious shrieks from the woman who was selling it. He ignored her and swore as the boy overturned a stall of oranges in his path. The youngster raced through a clutch of chickens, tripping over the squawking, fluttering fowl and losing his hold on the goat's tow rope. The latter quickly turned her attention to several spilled crocks of corn and an overturned jug of milk.

By this time a gaping crowd circled the peace disturbers. The fat man, whose loose, soiled cotton pants and shirt marked him as a member of the lower class of *Tejanos*, grabbed the child and hauled him up roughly. The boy was small and painfully thin, dressed only in ragged pants, bare chested and shoeless. His straight black hair and high cheekbones marked him as being of Indian ancestry.

The cantina owner took a broad swipe at the boy with one hand while holding the squirming, bony little body with the other hand. A nonstop torrent of Spanish accompanied the blow and several more, which the child endured in silence as he struggled to free himself from the man's grip.

Father Schreckenberg observed the uneven contest for several seconds, then quickly dismounted and made his way through the crowd. The young priest was short but stocky and muscular. When he put his hand on the bigger man's arm, his fingers restrained a blow aimed at the dazed boy's head.

Whirling like an enraged bull, Enrique Santos snarled, then seeing the cassock and crucifix which the interloper wore, he quickly subsided. In Spanish he asked, "What do you want with this Indian trash, Father? He's stolen my goat from the back of my tavern. They all steal, you know."

"That is a lie! I took her only to milk her," the boy shot back, also in Spanish. "I worked all day sweeping and scrubbing his place for that milk, and he refused to let me have it when I was done."

As the two argued in rapid-fire Spanish, one standing on each side of him and the crowd milling and staring, Father Schreckenberg felt his face redden in consternation—as if the merciless heat of the Texas sun weren't bad enough! *The bishop warned me about interference. Why do I always get in these situations?* Aloud he blurted to the irate cantina owner, "Please, it is wrong to raise your hand in anger, my son." Rattled, he spoke German without realizing it.

Santos, who knew little English and nothing of German, had never seen a priest who couldn't speak Spanish. "What kind of father are you?" he asked in his language.

Before the priest could respond, the boy seized his chance and darted away. Quickly grabbing the child's arm, Father Schreckenberg said, "Not so fast. You wait, too. Stealing also is a sin."

The boy's large black eyes silently mirrored the suspicion that Santos had verbalized. What strange guttural language did the foreign one speak? He squirmed while the cantina owner yelled.

"You aren't a priest, are you? Why do you wear the holy robes? I'll take you to Father Calvo!" He took a menacing step forward, his big hamlike hands grasping the priest's cassock, tearing his clerical collar.

Just then the crowd split to admit the slight figure of a dark-haired girl. "Perhaps I can help, Father, although my German is really rusty," Melanie said haltingly to Father Schreckenberg. Then turning to Santos she said rapidly in Spanish, "He is a priest, only from a faraway land, like the farmers to the north in New Braunfels."

Not loosening his hold on Schreckenberg, Santos said, "I never saw a priest in San Antonio who couldn't speak Spanish, or at least English."

"English! Ja, English. I speak English! I practice on my burro," the priest said, proud to regain his bearings.

"Ha! What burro, *tonto*?" Santos asked sarcastically. The boy, who had squirmed from Father Schreckenberg's grasp when the big *Tejano* attacked him, had shinnied up on the burro and kicked him into a startlingly fast gallop through the crowd.

"I told you, *indios son ladrones*!" The barkeep made a self-satisfied pronouncement, then scowled once more at Melanie and Father Schreckenberg. Looking at the girl, he said, "You always meddle where you are not wanted. This man let a thief get away from me, and now he must walk for his sins. It's God's punishment on him for pretending to be a priest," he said furiously, raising his hand once more in a fit of temper.

The priest quickly interposed himself between the small woman and the larger man, but before the confrontation could get uglier, a cool voice interrupted. "Let the priest go, Santos." Lee stepped from the crowd, hand resting lightly on the Colt at his hip, the threat palpable in the air.

Santos squinted his black eyes and stared at Lee in amazement. "He let off a thieving Indian, one of those half-breed brats who follow the Yankee soldiers. You, of all people, should want him punished." He spat on the ground in disgust.

"He's still a priest and a foreigner. He doesn't know about Indians. Go home, Santos." It was not a request.

Muttering to himself, the big man shambled off, pulling the goat with him.

Looking at the spilled crocks and overturned produce bins, the young priest said in his thickly accented English, "Always trouble seems to follow me. Why, I ask? But never does the good Lord find time to answer me." He chuckled. "Perhaps because I keep him too busy sending angels of mercy to rescue me, ja? I thank you both."

Lee smiled darkly, looking at Melanie, daring her to dispute his claim to being an angel of mercy. "I'm Lee Velásquez, Father, a rancher. This adventuresome young woman with more gumption than sense is Melanie Fleming—"

"Who works for the *San Antonio Star*," she interrupted, casting a quick glance at Lee, daring him to dispute the veracity of the article she had written about him.

"I am Father Gustav Schreckenberg—Father Gus, please. It is easier to say, ja?"

"You must've just arrived in San Antonio, Father Gus, or else you'd know not to tangle with Santos. Or get your burro stolen by one of those half-breed kids," Lee added darkly.

Melanie bristled. "The boy only took the burro to escape Santos. I'm sure I can get him to return it."

"If his kin haven't eaten it first," Lee replied.

"The boy did look hungry," Father Gus said hesitantly, appalled that his boon traveling companion might suffer such a fate.

"All those children are hungry," Melanie answered. "The boy said he'd worked all day for Santos in return for some of that goat's milk. Just like that cur to try and cheat a child!"

"These children—they are Indians, ja? What tribe?" Father Gus asked.

Lee shrugged carelessly. "Actually they're a nuisance more than anything else—scarcely dangerous. They're a mixture of tame Indians—Tonkawas, Caddos, Kickapoos, even a few Lipans. They hang around the soldiers stationed here and move with them. Some of the men, mostly Lipans, act as scouts and meat hunters. The women are camp followers."

"Living off the scraps so generously thrown from U.S. Army mess tents," Melanie interjected acidly.

"But—but small children like that—do the soldiers not care for their own offspring?" Looking from Lee to Melanie, he sighed. "Always it is the same with armies the world over. But these are conquered people who signed treaties. I have read your government is supposed to provide for them."

Lee snorted in disgust. "Try and provide for the wind. They come and go! The men drink up their earnings and the women whore for the soldiers. The children . . ." He gestured in helpless disgust.

"The government back in Washington is corrupt and so are the state authorities," Melanie countered angrily. "Everyone from the Indian Office to those lousy whiskey-selling traders takes a cut, and nothing's left for those children."

Tiring of the argument, Lee tipped his hat to the priest, motioning to the large church across the plaza. "I have to get back to my ranch, Padre. I think you'll be putting up over there tonight with Father Calvo."

"Father Calvo, *ja*, he is in charge of San Fernando. Bishop Odin told me in Galveston I must report to him. The bishop wants more schools. Already the good Ursulines educate young girls here in San Antonio. Now he wants the boys also to learn."

"But none of the church's schools have ever taught Indians—any more than the government feeds them," Melanie said indignantly, sensing a potential ally in the young priest.

Lee didn't deign to reply but simply said good day to the priest and sauntered back to his big blue stallion without a backward glance at the furious girl.

Calling out his thanks once more to Lee, Father Gus turned his attention back to Melanie. "Now, tell me, *Fräulein*, about the situation with these poor Indian children. . . ."

As Lee rode, he fumed. Damn that girl! Why did she get under his skin so much more than any other female in memory? Here he was, on his way to luncheon with the Sandovals, to meet that pretty Larena again and all he could think of was Melanie Fleming. Her ridiculous uniform of drab baggy clothes amply disguised her body, and that glorious mane of midnight hair was pulled back in its ugly knot at the back of her head. But when he tried to envision Larena's soft dark eyes and delicately boned face with its sweet smile, all he could see were the flashing golden eyes and scowling countenance of that hoyden. "She's as much a mongrel as those Indian camp followers outside town. Only difference is she's been educated and spoiled rotten by her father and that Boston grandpa!" he muttered aloud in disgust.

As he neared the Sandoval house on a quiet, tree-lined street off the plaza, Lee was unaware he was being scrutinized from the *sala* window. "Look at those weapons—a gun and a knife! I tell you, I do not like it." *Doña* Esperanza Sandoval looked at the tall man dismounting in front of their house.

Her husband, José, watched as Lee carefully placed both pistol and knife in his saddlebags and then handed the horse to their stable boy. "He's ridden from his ranch, dear heart.

It is a long and dangerous journey. See, he does not come to
the door armed. He is a good friend of my nephew James,
and the Velásquez name is an old and honorable one. We
have no reason not to receive him.''

Esperanza sighed, "I suppose so, but he does have a
frightful past to live down, even if he was forced into that
desperate life because of a tragedy that touched us all. If
only Larena—'' *Doña* Esperanza stopped short as she heard
her daughter's very unladylike haste as she came down the
hall to greet their caller.

Don José's dark eyes were soft. "If only Larena wére not
so smitten with him? But, Esperanza, she is nearly nineteen.
Far past the age of betrothal. You cannot keep her at home
forever.''

"But if she married him and went to live at that terrible
place where our baby : . .'' Esperanza's voice broke and she
stopped, hearing the murmur of Larena's soft soprano
blend with the deep resonance of Lee's baritone.

"It is a new time, and I think a man such as Leandro
Velásquez would be well able to protect her,'' he whispered,
ushering her toward the *sala* door.

Larena could hear her parents' footsteps nearing and felt a
twinge of annoyance at her perpetual chaperonage. Ever
since she'd run into this handsome man in the plaza last
month, she had wanted a chance for them to talk privately.
But every time they met, someone was with her.

Lee looked at her delicately pretty face, flushed and
smiling. For all her shy, ladylike ways, she was not manipu-
lative as Dulcia had been. Her clear brown eyes met his
straightforwardly and she never giggled or pouted as his
wife had. *Am I really considering marriage again?* If so,
Larena would make a splendid wife, a true *Tejana* who
wanted to make a home in the land of his birth, as he did.
He smiled and greeted her parents as they approached.

Larena watched Lee as they made small talk during
dinner. There was something dark and compelling in those
obsidian eyes. They held terrible secrets and a well full of
pain. *I am the one to heal your hurts*, her eyes said silently.
Did he intuit their message?

* * *

"It was an outstanding article and you know it, Clarence Vivian Pemberton!" Melanie enunciated every syllable of his name with precision, eliciting a smothered chuckle from the printer, Amos, who quickly returned to setting type in the crowded rear of the *Star* office.

"Don't get testy with me, young lady, just because you read my private correspondence and found out from my infernally nattering sister about that absurd middle name with which our mother insisted on punishing me!" Pemberton responded.

"You're evading the issue, you old curmudgeon you," Melanie replied doggedly, watching Amos's brown eyes dance with mirth. Few people knew how to get past the intimidating acerbity of the editor, but Melanie seemed to have a special talent. "I deserved to have my name on that story about Lee Velásquez and you know it. Everyone's been talking about it for the past month!"

"It got you a job as a reporter. That's all I promised," he replied.

"It sold your newspapers—hundreds of them! And you ran it without giving me credit. Everyone I talk to assumes you wrote it. It isn't fair."

Pemberton sighed in aggravated martyrdom. "Life, my pet, is not fair. Men write news stories and report on danger, politics, the criminal elements. Women write about balls and charity drives and fashions." He paused and looked disdainfully at her rumpled navy suit and dingy gray print blouse. "A subject about which you are obviously abysmally ignorant!"

"Oh, bother fashions and teas!" she shot back. "All right, if you can't sign Melanie Fleming to my stories, how about a nom de plume? You have heard of George Sand, haven't you?"

Raising one shaggy white brow, he replied with heavy condescension, "And just what nom de plume did you have in mind, Baroness Dudevant?"

Melanie snorted. "I scarcely have a titled family name to protect as George Sand did, only one timid newspaper editor. How about Moses French?"

"Has a certain ring to it," he conceded pettishly. "The surname I ascribe to your Creole ancestry, but Moses?" He flipped the reading glasses from the top of his head down to the lower half of his nose and looked through them at the young woman before him. "Do you propose to be the new law giver for San Antonio?"

She shrugged dismissively, not quite ready to tell him about her black or Indian antecedents. Being female was hardship enough for openers! "Let's just say I plan to lead the readers of this fair city out of the desert of ignorance and into the promised land of truth."

"The land of milk and honey, hallelujah!" Amos interjected in his best Baptist-revival voice, his hands never slowing their lightning deftness as he set type.

Ignoring the insubordination, Pemberton handed Melanie a sheet of paper with brusque dismissiveness. "Well, Moses French will have to wait while Melanie Fleming writes a column about the social scene in the city. I want to know who's engaged or married, who has recently been blessed with new offspring, with what galas the ladies of our fair city plan to break the pall of midsummer doldrums. You get the general idea."

Sighing, she took the list. "Do you want obituaries, too, or is that too newsworthy for a female to handle?"

Smiling at her benevolently, he answered, "Only if the poor unfortunates die of natural causes. Come back for further instructions if you hear about a murder."

After a whole morning listening to Althea Dallman talk her ear off about the big ball to fete U.S. Senator Sam Houston, Melanie had a roaring headache. Dejectedly she headed back to the *Star* office to make some sense of the piles of scribbled notes she had stuffed in the oversized canvas sack she used as a reticule. In addition to copious information on guest lists, menus, and decor for the ball, she had a pile of pages covering births, deaths, marriages, and engagements. Only one event was of any significance to her, however. Why did it bother her so much that the Sandovals had just held an elaborate fiesta to celebrate the engagement of their daughter Larena to Leandro Angel Velásquez? "Another prim and prissy Mexican sweetheart," Melanie sniffed, determinedly telling herself they deserved one another.

His ranch, which he had renamed Night Flower, was prospering. Lee had overcome his scandalous, bloody past and was taking his place in the elite ranks of San Antonio's wealthy Hispanic community. Small wonder such a pillar of society would choose to wed a Sandoval. Still, for perverse reasons she refused to admit, Melanie felt wounded afresh, but not nearly so painfully as she had been in Austin six years ago when she learned about Dulcia.

Rounding the corner on Commerce Street while deep in thought, Melanie suddenly collided with a very solid object. She reeled backward against the hard limestone wall of a building, her "newswoman's possible sack" flying from her grasp.

"*Fräulein* Melanie, so sorry I am! Here, let me," Father Gus said as he reached to help her stand clear of the rough wall, then knelt to retrieve the scattered scraps of paper. Melanie crouched down and helped him as she struggled to regain her breath.

"I'm the one who should apologize, Father. I was wool-gathering, I'm afraid," Melanie said distractedly.

"And what is this gathering of—wool? Like a shepherdess?" His blue eyes were merry as he rose and handed her the last of her notes. "It looks here as if you gather news, not sheep."

"It's just an expression, Father Gus. It means I wasn't paying attention to where I was going."

"How goes your career as a reporter?" he inquired.

Melanie sighed in disgust. "*That's* what I was woolgathering about . . . sort of." She paused and looked into his cherubic, earnest face. "All Mr. Pemberton wants me to do is write gossip columns about parties and dances and that kind of silly stuff. I want to write about important things.

Speaking of which, how goes *your* career of trying to start a school for those poor Indians?''

Now it was Father Gus's turn to sigh. "Father Calvo is very solicitous but says the bishop is first concerned with the children of white settlers. The government is to take care of the Indians.''

Melanie snorted in derision. "He's just like all the rest of these good Texians—Anglo or Mexican. They all fear Indians, even the ones like the Lipans and Cherokees who work for the army.''

"Even among themselves the San Antonians quarrel,'' the priest said, half in sorrow, half in irony. "The Spaniard, Father Calvo, dislikes Germans. The Germans dislike the Anglos and the Anglos dislike the Mexicans.''

"And everyone hates the Indians,'' Melanie added to his litany. They both laughed. Then she said, "You have been gathering a fair number of German Catholics for your masses, though, haven't you?''

"*Ja*, a few come, but so many are more concerned with making money. On the Lord's day they still work in their shops and stores.''

"It's an old Texas custom, I'm afraid,'' Melanie replied. "Religion always has taken a back seat to business.''

"All the more reason to minister to those in greater need—the hungry children of those Indian scouts, *ja*, and the women who follow the soldiers,'' Father Gus said with a hint of iron in his voice.

Melanie's mind was racing as she looked past the young priest, down a wide street lined with frame houses and sycamore trees. "If your white parishioners can spare you— and if Father Calvo will allow—I just might know someone who could help. If she'd lived two thousand years ago, she'd have helped feed the five thousand,'' Melanie said impishly.

"I think you and Father Gus will have a good deal in common,'' Melanie said as she introduced the priest and proprietress of San Antonio's best boardinghouse.

"I got me no quarrel with this here black robe er any

other, long's they don't try 'n' git a old hard-shell Baptist like me ta switch!'' Obedience reached out a red, meaty palm and pumped Father Gus's hand in an enveloping grip.

Father Gus stood his ground and returned the vigorous handshake. "*Ja*, I think we will be friends, *Frau* Oakley."

"Now, whut's this here scheme you two have cooked up? Feedin' them Injun kids 'n' all."

Melanie explained that she and Father Gus had just located a deserted old adobe on the edge of town where a makeshift school could be held for the half-breed children and a number of impoverished *Tejano* children as well. "The problem is getting them to come. They're starving and ragged. And no one, not the church or any of the citizens who own stores or market stalls, will contribute food or clothes. So, we thought—"

"Jeehosaphat! Caint' larn readin' when yer belly's growlin'. I cotton ta thet." Looking from one to the other of the conspirators, Obedience sighed. "I'll git Sadie 'n' Lena ta work on fixin' a feast ta tempt a saint, much less a passel o' hungry little pagans."

Chapter 10

"This isn't social news, but it is a story about people—a real story, Clarence Viv—"

"Don't say it or I'll rip that paper up and feed it to you one strip at a time," the old man intoned gravely.

Bubbling over with excitement, Melanie ignored his threat. "Oh, I promise, Mr. Pemberton, never again to tease you about your heinous middle name but—" she stopped abruptly.

His brows rose diffidently. "Pray continue."

"But you must read this story about Father Gus's school

for underprivileged children! San Antonians do have hearts. Obedience got all the big ranchers to donate one steer each to the children's fund. Well, not all of them—that nasty old land speculator Laban Greer refused, and so did Noah Parker; but even Lee Velásquez agreed, after Obedience threatened to thrash him.'' Melanie chuckled at her mentor's description of *that* interview! ''And that's not all. Charlee Slade got a whole bunch of women in town to gather up all their children's older or outgrown clothes and fix them up—even donate blankets. And the three of us went to all the storekeepers and got them to give Father Gus a set of readers and ciphering books for the school! Here. Read about 'The City with a Saint's Heart'!''

Clarence Pemberton scanned the pages with his lightning-quick eyes, taking in every detail . The girl was good. Clear style, tight organization, yet with just the right touch of sentiment and emotional appeal. He hated to, but he said, ''We'll run it under your name.''

With a squeal of delight she leaped up and kissed him on his jowly cheek. He restrained her with a frosty raising of his eyebrows.

''I'm scarcely surprised Laban Greer and Noah Parker refuse to help your impoverished Indians,'' he said, returning to the story he was writing.

Melanie's eyes strayed to the copy, and she seized it before he could stop her. '' 'Militiamen plan a bold raid on marauding Comanche at dawn this day. . . .' '' she read aloud, then scanned the rest of the rough draft and notes in haste. ''Quite a story. How did you find out? I haven't heard a thing about it.''

Clarence looked smug. ''I have my sources, child. Men will confide to other men in a, er, libational setting, shall we say.''

''Oh, you got them drunk, huh?''

''Another thing a male reporter can do which a female cannot, I daresay,'' he patronized.

''But I can ride and shoot, something Texians can do that Massachusetts Yankees can't—*I* daresay,'' she sassed as she shoved her story about Father Gus's school into Amos's hands. "This should sell a few papers this week, Amos. I'm off!" With that, she whirled with her heavy-soled shoes clumping across the oily wood floor past Clarence Pemberton.

"And precisely where are you going, young woman?" he called after her retreating figure.

"To get a story," she yelled over her shoulder before vanishing through the front door.

Pemberton sighed and Amos chuckled.

Twilight was deepening when Melanie stole down the back steps of the boardinghouse, through the kitchen, and out the side door. The last pink streaks of sunset were leaving the sky and the kitchen was deserted now. Good. Melanie didn't want to be detected, especially in the clothes she was wearing. The old black cook might mistake her for a prowler and take her broom to the youth in baggy patched buckskins and shabby boots.

Melanie had checked her appearance in the mirror repeatedly as she dressed in the carefully assembled costume, mostly "borrowed" from old Racine Schwartz, the boarder who used to be a mountain man in his youth. He was small and wiry and possessed the most disgusting-looking clothing she could readily lay her hands on. That afternoon she had dug the worn, greasy buckskins and boots from the bottom of a chest in his room and smuggled them into her wardrobe. Before she put on the worn clothes, she had flattened her breasts with a tight wrapping of linen toweling to disguise the ample evidence of her sex. Her hair was pulled into a tight knot and hidden beneath the brim of a battered felt hat. After sneaking out the back door, she had liberally smeared herself and the buckskins with dirt so that even her fingernails were encrusted with filth. That last detail made her sure she could pass as a rather runty young man.

Melanie walked quietly toward the icehouse behind the garden, where she had tethered a rented horse of no distinguishing quality to await her predawn rendezvous. Her Hawken rifle was loaded and set in the scabbard. On her person she carried an Allen and Thurber pepperbox, a gun small enough for her to handle. She had also filched an old skinning knife from Racine. Armed, tough, and dirty looking, she hoped to blend in with the band of volunteers under the leadership of a local ranger captain, Seth Walkman. It was, according to Clarence's notes, to be a hunting expedition in search of a band of Comanche raiders who had burned out several ranches and stolen cattle southeast of Fort Inge. The undermanned and woefully ill-equipped soldiers couldn't stop the Comanche, so the citizen militia of Texians would do the job.

Jim Slade had made several exceedingly unfavorable comments about Seth Walkman and his rangers, lamenting the departure several years earlier of his old friend Captain Jack Hays, who had headed for the California gold fields. Walkman lacked Hays's leadership skills and essential decency. The men who rode under him tended to be drawn from the dregs of west Texas society—gunmen, drifters, and scalp hunters. Melanie wondered if Lee Velásquez would ride with this punitive expedition, but decided that no matter how great his hatred of Indians, he'd never deign to take orders from a Texas Ranger.

Still, when she pulled her horse up by the riverbank south of the city where the men were gathering, she was relieved to see that Lee was not with them. *He might recognize me,* she said to herself. But she was glad that he had truly left his bloody past behind. She did recognize a number of the men hunched around the campfire, drinking coffee. Walkman, rawboned and rangy, with stringy gray hair and eyes the lusterless color of pewter, conferred with Laban Greer, a rancher from the western part of the county who doubled as a land speculator in town. Greer was short and thickset as a bull, with a disposition to match. Turning her attention from the unappealing duo, she observed a number of rangers who regularly rode with Walkman and about a dozen assorted townsmen, small ranchers, and drifters who apparently had nothing better to do than chase Indians.

As she scrutinized the crowd, Melanie committed to memory as many faces as she could without being obvious about it. She was careful to stay clear of Laban Greer, who knew her from their hostile encounter when she had tried to get him to donate cattle for Father Gus's Indian school. *He'd rather shoot Indians than educate them.*

When the command came to mount up, no one paid particular attention to the "boy" hovering in the shadows of a willow tree near the riverbank. Several youths, drifters who worked cattle and doubtless did less honest jobs, were among the riders. A sense of grim determination seemed to infuse most of the men. Jocular comments were infrequent, but the men did talk among themselves. Melanie learned one of them, a settler named Ben Haycox, had lost his ranch house and most of his herd in the recent raid. Another, who now worked as a blacksmith in town, had suffered the same fate as Lee, having his family killed by Comanche when he was a small boy. An icy sense of foreboding washed over her as she eavesdropped on their conversations.

They rode for several hours as Walkman, who was a skillful tracker, watched for signs and shifted directions several times. The moon flitted in and out of cloud cover, slowing their progress when it vanished. Still, Walkman seemed to know where he was going—almost as if it were prearranged, Melanie thought uneasily. But if they were tracking a band of raiding braves, how could Walkman know where they'd head?

Her unease grew through the night. Then, just as the first warning haze of false dawn lighted the sky, Walkman signaled for the group to dismount and be quiet. He and two of his rangers left the others behind and rode slowly down a narrow ravine off to the west. About half an hour later they returned.

"We got 'em, boys. Clean ta rights." Walkman's whisper crackled across the still dawn air like a whiplash. "You, Jonas, get a dozen men 'n' follow Miller here. Tatum, take the rest 'n' go with Abe. Greer, you 'n' your boys come with me."

As the men fell into informal ranks as directed, Melanie slipped in with Marsh Tatum's group, where she would be less likely to be recognized. Few of the men had even noticed the taciturn youth or spoken six words to "him" on the grueling night's ride. Keeping her head down and her rifle ready, she followed the men as they stalked silently through the rough, hilly terrain toward a destination known only to Walkman and his two rangers.

Expecting to come on a campfire and a host of Comanche warriors sleeping out in the open, Melanie was amazed when they crested a low rise of land at the lip of the ravine. Below, strung along several hundred yards of a twisting stream, lay a small village. The loose brush arbor shelters built by Comanche women resembled the Mexican jacals constructed by peasants from San Antonio to Sonora. She could hear a sleepy child cry and a woman's voice raised in reprimand. Then several more women became visible; obviously the first to arise in the sleepy encampment, they headed toward the stream to fill their cookpots.

The village was awakening. Two dogs chased a naked boy who splashed and giggled in the water. Finally a male, clad only in a breechclout, appeared from beneath the crude shelter of a jacal, stretching and rubbing his eyes as he ambled out to greet the dawn. As was their custom when encamped in the wild canyon country of Comanchería, the Indians had posted no sentries and had pitched camp haphazardly along the water with no defensible perimeters.

When the white men opened fire, the small boy and his dog were the first ones Melanie saw hit. After that, chaos reigned and everything happened with horrifying rapidity. Men on horseback fired their six-shooters into the shrieking, milling Comanche. It was hard to miss at point-blank range. Their horses trampled the flimsy brush shelters and smashed anything in their paths. Most of the braves had still been asleep and came rushing at their attackers with whatever weapons they could grab upon leaping up when the shooting began. Few were able to reach guns or bows before they were cut down by bullets and rifle butts.

The carnage was completely indiscriminate. Melanie stood rooted to the ground as she watched men she had known in town, civilized white men, shoot women and children with the same unhesitating dispatch they employed on the fearsome warriors. One woman—really, she looked to Melanie's keen eye to be little more than an adolescent girl—sheltered a baby with her body as Seth Walkman sent a .44-caliber slug ripping through her back. When she slumped lifelessly to the ground, Melanie could see the bullet had passed through her body and killed the infant as well.

Hiding behind a sharp outcropping of rock and using her horse as a shield, Melanie crouched and watched the holocaust exploding around her, praying she would not have to add to the wanton slaughter to protect her own life. In truth, she had little to fear, for the sleeping Comanche had been so thoroughly surprised the uneven fight was over in a matter of minutes. No one came near Melanie's hiding place, not even to steal her horse and escape.

The rangers and their militia had been devastatingly effective. In five minutes, not a man, woman, or child was left alive. When Laban Greer raised his fat hand and fired into the still moving body of an old woman thrashing on the ground, Melanie almost cried out, but bit her lip until it bled to stifle her useless protest. In the frenzy of their blood lust, these men would doubtless see to it that she shared the fate of the Comanche women if her disguise were detected.

Wanting to keep busy and attempting to drown out the ugly laughter and brutal comments of the men, Melanie followed the half-dozen riders who were sent to round up the villagers' horses. Known far and wide as the best riders and horse breeders on the plains, the Comanche possessed valuable mounts that could be sold anywhere across Texas.

As they left the village, Melanie ate trail dust, riding drag on their booty while the smell of burning brush and the acrid stench of roasting human flesh assailed her nostrils. Walkman had ordered the village and all its inhabitants fired. As dry as the weather had been the past weeks, the savage scene was quickly reduced to smoldering ashes.

When they neared the Greer ranch, which had large corrals to hold their captured livestock, the majority of the men went with the owner to see to their cut. A small handful stayed with Walkman and his rangers, who were headed to San Antonio, and several other of the ranchers split off to ride for their homes. The mission was accomplished. Still terrified of being discovered, Melanie stayed with the dusty, milling herd of Indian ponies until they neared the corrals. Then, when no one was watching, she quickly cut her horse into a small brushy swale off the trail and waited until everyone was gone. She rode for town by a circuitous route, as if pursued by demons, when in fact the real demons were ahead of her on the road to San Antonio.

Clarence Pemberton's usual facial expressions ranged from boredom to sardonic ill humor, then back to boredom. But as he read the copy Melanie had just handed him, his world-weary countenance changed, his complexion going chalky white, eyes rounded in shock, and mouth pursed in concentration. After carefully perusing the lengthy article in its entirety, he took his glasses from their precarious perch on the tip of his nose and laid them very carefully on the desk. His light blue eyes pierced her gold ones and held them while he cleared his throat. "Every word of this is accurate," he said. It was not so much a question as a statement of horrified incredulity.

"Right down to Laban Greer's shooting an old woman as she lay on the ground," she replied quietly. "Even babies and their puppies were cut down. The river was pink from all the blood—"

"I get the picture. Your prose style is startlingly graphic," he interrupted. The look of repugnance on his face was not directed at her, but at the events her words chronicled.

"Will you print it?" She held her breath.

"I'm a newspaperman, and ghastly as this is, it's news. Of course, we must protect your anonymity. We'll run it under the Moses French name."

"Of course," she replied gravely as relief surged through her. The people of Texas would learn of this perfidy.

But the people of Texas had lived for generations with Comanche depredations. They were not disposed to shed sympathetic tears for the fate of one lone Comanche village.

The destruction rained on their own towns from Victoria to Linnville in the previous decade had hardened them to the fate of Comanches, even if the victims were women and children. Many citizens were inclined to be philosophical about the deaths, recalling the Council House killing of Comanche chiefs on the very streets of San Antonio, provoked by their refusal to relinquish a dozen white captives held by one southern Comanche band. The fault lay with both sides, but this was war.

Other readers were simply disbelieving. Civilized men, townsmen and ranchers they greeted on the streets daily, could never do what that eastern meddler Pemberton and his mysterious reporter Moses French said they did. Others like Lee Velásquez, themselves victims of Comanche attacks, were disgusted and furious with the graphic description of a battle reenacted on the Texas plains dozens of times each year. What use to describe the horrors both sides perpetuated? It would only end when every last Comanche was dead.

If the majority of the citizenry was disposed to scorn or ignore the *Star*'s blazing condemnation, a vocal handful were of a more violent bent. Seth Walkman and Laban Greer, along with Zeb Brocker, Pike Miller, Marsh Tatum, and Jeff Jonas, had been mentioned by name in the article. Greer was at his ranch, above mingling with the saloon riffraff who were incited to riot by Brocker and Miller. Seth Walkman, as the head of the local rangers, stayed discreetly in the background while his lieutenants went from cantina to cantina gathering a mob the evening after the *Star*'s hairraising story broke. By dusk they had a sizable group assembled and were vocally calling for more "brave Injun fighters" to join them on the plaza.

Lee was on his way to have dinner with the Sandovals when he heard the ugly commotion. He assumed it was nothing but a drunken fight the local constabulary would handle. When he was greeted by Larena Sandoval at the door, *Don* José was with her, clutching a copy of the *Star* in his hand.

"I wish those foolish easteners would go home and leave Texas to deal with her own problems," he said tightly.

"That's what all the shouting down on the plaza's about?" Lee asked in disgust. "I read Mr. French's inflammatory rhetoric."

"Inflammatory is an understatement, " *Don* José replied. "The fool is obviously as ignorant of the volatile nature of our so-called 'militia' as is his editor. They'll burn that newspaper office to the ground. I only hope the fire doesn't spread to other businesses adjacent to it." *Don* José's normally genial face was harsh as granite.

"Father, what about the people who work there? Besides Mr. Pemberton, there's that frail old printer and Miss Fleming. Her parents are good friends of the Slades," Larena said with genuine concern.

Lee stiffened. "It's late. Surely she's back at Obedience's boardinghouse by now. Devil take old man Pemberton and his printer, especially his 'star reporter,' Moses French!"

"I don't know, Leandro. Charlee told me the other day that Melanie often works late, finishing up her columns and then helping Amos Johnston set type. She said Mrs. Oakley was complaining that the girl had every towel in the place ink stained."

Snorting, he said in disgust, "Yeah, that sounds like Melanie Fleming, all right. I suppose I'd better see if she's safely tucked under Obedience's wing." Taking his fiancée's fingertips in his hand, he saluted them lightly. "Please forgive me for delaying dinner, but I do feel an obligation to Jim and Charlee to see that the pesky girl's all right." With that, he turned and quickly retraced his steps toward the Sandovals' stable and Sangre.

A rock came sailing through the window, spraying the floor of the *Star*'s office with glass shards. Amos Johnston bent his gray head as he kicked at the sharp-edged piece of stone, sending it rolling across the floor. "I think they're getting nasty, Miss Melanie. You head out that back door real quick while I—"

"Oh, no, you don't, Amos. If you and Mr. Pemberton

stay, *I* stay. After all, it was my story that caused that trash to come here in the first place.'' Melanie stood her ground in front of Amos while Clarence Pemberton peered through the glass window of the front door.

"Exercise judicious behavior for once in your disaster-prone lives, both of you,'' the old editor said. "Amos, while I go out to calm them, you and Melanie slip out the back before those Neanderthals recall there is an alleyway along Commerce Street."

"We wanna talk ta thet Frenchie feller,'' one nasal voice hiccuped.

Another more strident one yelled out, "Give us Moses French er we'll do ta yer newspaper whut them Comanch done to Noah Parker's ranch house."

Melanie braced her feet and shook off Amos's hand. "See, they want Moses French. When you can't produce 'him,' what do you think they'll do to you?''

"Better an old man than a young woman," Clarence said with surprising calm.

"Make that *two* ole men. Now you all git!'' Amos said, attempting to mimic a southern black's accent.

"Not on your lives! Do either of you have something so un–New Englandish as a gun in this place?''

"Balderdash! Of course not. What would you have me do, place my sights on the ringleader and shoot him between his beady little eyes?''

"Something like that—only, given your aim, I'd better be the one handling the shooting. If only I'd brought my rifle with me,'' Melanie fumed, "or even my pepperbox.''

Another rock came sailing through the window, punctuated with several stray bullets. The flickering glow of the mob's torches cast eerie shadows across the wreckage of the *Star*'s glass-strewn office.

"I'm going out and face them down,'' Pemberton said.

"With what—withering sarcasm? Somehow I don't think it'll work.'' Melanie quickly grabbed the old man's arm. Looking past him, she yelled through the broken glass, "Brave Texians all—throwing rocks and shooting at two old men and a woman! You should be ashamed of yourselves.''

"Thet French feller's th' one whut's got him first claim on bein' ashamed," the whiskey-hoarse voice of Jeff Jonas croaked out.

"I hear you, Jonas, and I see you Zeb Brocker—you and Pike Miller. The Texas Rangers ought to be real proud of your day's work—yesterday and today!" Melanie was abruptly grabbed from behind by steel fingers and whirled around to confront Lee Velásquez's furious face.

"Will you shut that loud mouth of yours before they storm this place, you little hellion?" he ground out, shoving her into Pemberton's arms. "All three of you stay back!"

"You can't. They'll—" Melanie's protest stilled as Lee vanished through the front door, slamming it behind him.

"This the way you rangers keep law and order, Miller, Brocker? Where's your boss, Walkman? If he's too big to bother with a couple of old men and a girl, how about someone who knows how to fight back—Texas style?" Lee's voice dripped with scorn but carried across the crowd with chilling impact, every syllable cutting like a lash.

"Yew an Injun lover like them Yankees, Mex?" one drunkenly weaving drifter slurred.

"I don't talk much about loving—or killing," Lee said quietly as his right hand rested lightly on the gun at his hip. His left hand caressed the hilt of his bowie knife as he stood poised and waiting.

The implication was clear to most of the men in the crowd who had heard the stories about how he had slit two rangers' throats and collected scalps in the Apachería of New Mexico.

Watching the confrontation, Melanie shivered at the implacable stance of the man confronting the mob. "He'll kill that drunk if the fool doesn't let up," she whispered to Amos. The tension grew to crackling proportions as Zeb Brocker shoved the drunk out of his way and planted one boot on the edge of a watering trough near the front of the *Star* office. His narrow-set eyes blazed at Velásquez as he dared the slim *Tejano*, "You got a real mean reputation, for a greaser. But I been shootin' greasers an' Injuns for years, Velásquez." His hand rested on his six-shooter.

"And I've shot rattlesnakes since I was a boy," Lee replied matter-of-factly.

"You dirty Mex—"the ranger's hand *flashed, but he never pulled the revolver from its holster. Lee vaulted across the water trough and kicked him squarely in the solar plexus. Brocker was knocked backward to the dust and Lee landed on top of him, knife drawn and strategically placed at the big man's jugular. "Any more slurs on my ancestry, *rinche*?" he asked in a harsh whisper.

Brocker only wheezed, struggling to regain his breath.

Just then a loud blast ripped the air, sending the already chastened mob into frenzied retreat. Wash Oakley's enormous girth loomed over the edge of the crowd as he stood at the corner of Commerce Street with a shotgun aimed at the center of the mob. Obedience, only slightly less formidable, appeared at the opposite end of the street from behind the newspaper office.

"We got us a Mexican standoff, gents," Wash said genially.

"An' I'll plug th' first feller, Mex er gringo, whut moves anyways but away from thet buildin'," Obedience added. "Jeehosaphat, skedaddle!"

By now the mob had erupted into blind panic and was scattering up and down the street, evaporating between buildings. Soon the area was deserted except for the Oakleys, Lee, and the semiconscious Zeb Brocker.

Melanie, Amos, and Clarence slowly emerged from the building. Before Wash and Obedience could reach the *Star* office, Lee whirled on Melanie and grabbed her roughly away from the two men. "You belong at the boardinghouse, little miss, not here inciting a riot!"

"You're the one who nearly got yourself killed! Why blame me? I was only doing my job in my own place of work," she responded furiously, jerking her arm free of his bruising grasp.

"Your place of work—your *place* seems to be anywhere there's trouble," he retorted.

"And I suppose I should be sitting in the parlor knitting, huh? I happen to be a reporter and I write about trouble. I don't make it.'' She looked into his narrowed black eyes, daring him to bring up the subject of her story about him.

He didn't. Instead, he turned to Pemberton and said, "You're all three lucky to be alive—and that bastard French who started the whole thing isn't even around. You ought to fire this girl and hire a gun hand if you want him to keep writing about downtrodden Indians.''

Melanie let out a furious hiss of breath, too angry to speak.

Observing the heated exchange between the young pair, Obedience warned Wash to silence when he started to speak up. She turned to Lee and said, "Why don't yew take this here gal back home whilst me 'n' Wash see ta gettin' th' trash off th' street.''

Eyeing Brocker, Wash reached down and hauled his six-foot-two frame up as if lifting a rag doll. Tossing the coughing man over his shoulder, Oakley whistled cheerfully down the street, calling out, "Fetch me th' horses, woman, 'n' I'll dump this garbage clear o' town.''

Shrugging at the Oakleys, Lee once more grabbed Melanie's arm and began to drag her away from the amazed pair of old men standing in the *Star*'s doorway.

"I'm not going anywhere with you, Leandro Velásquez!'' Unsuccessfully, she attempted to yank her arm free. Looking to Clarence and Amos for help, she was amazed when they both vanished precipitately back into their ink-stained lair.

Melanie gritted her teeth as he hustled her along the sidewalk. "Why don't you shower all this chivalrous attention on Larena Sandoval? I'm certain your fiancée would be more appreciative.'' The instant the words escaped her lips she hated herself. The smirk that twitched at his sculpted lips was positively infuriating.

"Why, Miss Fleming, don't tell me you're jealous? Larena told me what a perfectly lovely article you wrote about our betrothal fiesta.''

"And I'll be even happier to write about your wedding ceremony—if only you take your demure little bride off to Night Flower Ranch and—pollinate!'' she finished in an infuriated huff.

He threw back his head and laughed. "Why, Melanie, what a perfectly indelicate thing for a lady to say. But then, I keep forgetting you're a reporter, not a lady." He looked down distastefully at her ink-stained nose and rumpled clothes. "Don't you own anything that fits?"

"How do you know whether or not my clothes fit— unless you've been peeking through keyholes while I dress!" she shot back defiantly.

He recalled how delectable she had looked in a silk shirt and riding skirt that day in Austin over six years ago. Angry at the unwanted stirring evoked by the memory of her curvaceous little body, he stopped short and pulled her suddenly into his arms. "Have you ever been well and truly pollinated, Miss Fleming? It begins something like this." He bent down suddenly and kissed her startled, opened lips, holding her head prisoner in one hand while his other arm pressed her body tightly to his.

They were alone on the deserted street and it was full dark now. Melanie was so startled by his mercurial mood changes from anger to humor to this unexpected passion that she did not protest when his mouth closed over hers. His tongue ravaged inside, sending strange darts of warm, liquid pleasure through her body. She could feel the way his hard chest flattened her breasts as he pressed her closer to him, molding their bodies together in a shockingly intimate fashion.

Having been kissed by a variety of beaus, from the young cowboy Micah Torrance to the intellectual swains in Boston, Melanie had thought herself rather sophisticated about men. None of them had dared take the liberties Lee Velásquez was taking. But then, why shouldn't he do with her as he wished? He considered her no lady, merely a mongrel with despised Indian blood in her veins! She tore her mouth free of his bruising kiss and pushed with surprising strength against his chest. Lee freed her so quickly she almost lost her balance.

Humiliation washed over her for the way he had made her feel. Even now she could sense the male triumph radiating from him as he looked with amusement at her heaving breasts and flushed face. She stumbled backward, braced herself, and delivered a stinging slap that wiped the arrogant grin from his face. "I'm not your plaything, Leandro Velásquez! Go inflict your attentions on your fiancée."

He was rubbing his jaw when he caught up with her as she stomped up the street. "For such a little bit, you sure pack a wallop. Just a lesson—be careful who you talk to about risqué subjects, Melanie."

"I certainly won't talk to you about anything, ever again," she retorted as his long-legged strides easily overtook her far shorter ones.

"This is the best corn bread I've ever eaten, Obedience," Charlee Slade said, wiping the golden-brown crumbs from her mouth as she savored the last morsel of one of Obedience's famous corn dodgers.

The two women sat in the big boardinghouse kitchen late one afternoon, catching up on the past week's gossip. "Yew never miss runnin' this here place, Charlee?" Obedience asked.

"Oh, sometimes, when Will and Sarah are fighting or little Lee's just broken half the dishes in the china cupboard, but mostly, no. I have more than enough to do at Bluebonnet. Speaking of past proprietresses of this establishment, you and Deborah ought to be getting together shortly. That baby's due any day now, and I know she's dying to come for a visit. Wait till you see how Adam has grown."

"The Flemings got them quite a brood now, ain't they?" Obedience said fondly. "I wuz worried somethin' fierce when Deborah's first letter come from thet ranch, sayin' she 'n' her Frenchman wuz back together."

Charlee laughed. "So was I, but obviously it's worked out rather well for her and Rafe. You'll like him, Obedience. He reminds me of Lee in some ways—all that fierce Latin arrogance on the surface, but beneath it, they're both good men with a lot of love to give the woman strong enough to stand up to them."

"Jeehosaphat, Deborah fills thet bill, fer shore!" Obedience said with a chuckle.

"Larena Sandoval doesn't," Charlee replied darkly. "She's too much like Dulcia. Oh, Obedience, Lee's trying to recapture the past. That's no way to build a future."

Obedience's shrewd countenance reflected her agreement. "Purty gal 'n' right nice, but no grit. She'll be bowin' 'n' scraping' ta him th' rest o' their lives."

"When she isn't in a 'delicate condition' and unable to *submit* to him," Charlee said cryptically. Then, seeing her friend's confusion, she told her the tale of Dulcia's distaste for her marital duties.

"Why 'n hell would a feller as bright as Lee want ta get hitched up ta sech a unnatural female a second time?" Obedience looked baffled.

Charlee signed. "He's full of Hispanic pride and still cherishes his boyhood notions about a fairy tale romance that never really existed. He's a man now and ought to have more sense, but last week he was lecturing Jim about exercising more *control* over me while I was in town to help Father Gus with the new school!"

Obedience guffawed. "Fer as long's thet boy's knowed yew, he shore ain't figgered much out! I reckon it takes a good tussle with words now 'n' again afore a man 'n' woman get a good tussle in bed."

Charlee laughed out loud. "Jim used to say unless a man's mad enough to strangle a woman, he's not really in love with her." She paused and then added darkly, "Of course, when I consider how near Jim came to marrying Tomasina Carver, I'm really concerned about Lee. Men are such jackasses."

Obedience said cheerfully, "All men's purely worthless—"

" 'Cept fer *one* thing," Charlee finished for her. "Deborah passed your sage words on to me years ago."

Both women shared a chuckle as they thought about the past. "Yew 'n' Deborah 'n' me, we done real good pickin' menfolk—not countin' my second and third husbands, o' course. Shore wish we could do somethin' 'bout thet youngun o' Deborah's, though."

"Melanie?" Charlee asked in surprise.

"I been watchin' her 'n' Lee. 'Pears ta me they fight like cornered bobcats ever' time they meet up." Obedience proceeded to tell Charlee about Melanie's first encounter with Lee in Galveston, the interview for the *Star*, and the dangerous episode of the near riot a few weeks earlier.

Charlee listened in rapt attention, turning over in her mind the idea of the two of them together. She definitely liked it! "Lee's mentioned her to me, as well," she said when Obedience had finished. "After he came back from Galveston—hell, it must've been ten years ago. Even as a little girl she got under his skin. I remember it now. And you should've seen how they reacted to one another in Austin. Of course, she looked like a woman then, not a crusader." Charlee sighed, recalling her own painful metamorphosis from tomboy to belle.

"I was just as ignorant as Melanie. My mother wanted me to dress and act properly, and I looked as bad as Melanie does now. Deborah's had a fit over the wardrobe Melanie came home with from Boston."

Obedience scratched her chin in consideration. "Didn't Deborah teach yew how ta dress 'n' act 'n' sech so's yew cud ketch Jim Slade?"

Charlee chuckled. "I'm way ahead of you. Now I owe her one for her daughter."

Chapter 11

"Absolutely not! I refuse to break my neck in high-heeled shoes or mince around in dresses so tight-waisted that I swoon for lack of oxygen." Melanie glared across the big desk at Charlee when she broached the subject of more fashionable clothing. They confronted each other in the boardinghouse office, where Charlee had taken Melanie after dinner for a private talk.

"If you could have heard me ten years ago, that's exactly how I felt about looking like a female." Charlee chuckled, then turned serious. "Melanie, look at yourself. At least I had a reason for the breeches and shirts and bare feet. I was comfortable that way in the Texas heat." She let the vision of an adolescent Charlee McAllister dressed scandalously like a boy register with Melanie, then continued, "But you're *over*dressed. That jacket and skirt must weigh twenty pounds, not to mention the soles on those mud clompers you call 'sensible shoes.' I'd guess we're about the same size, but those shoes are so big I could get both feet in one of them!"

Melanie looked a little sheepish. "Well, they are too big—"

"Too big! Hell, Obedience could wear them with room to spare!"

"They don't come in small sizes. They're made back east for women with bunions," Melanie retorted, as if that explained everything.

"Well, heavens be praised, you'll never have to worry about bunions, just blisters!" Charlee exclaimed in disgust.

Melanie's lips curved in an unwilling smile. "You sound like Grandpa when you say 'heavens be praised.' He was always yelling that at me—at Mama, too, when she was a girl."

Charlee had her opening now. "Whatever else she did to stir him up, I know Deborah Manchester always looked lovely, and she taught you how to dress as well. These hot, ugly clothes you've adopted are a disguise, young lady."

Melanie's breath caught in surprise. Charlee had hit far too close to a painful truth she did not want to discuss. "So I don't want to look pretty and catch a man. That's not my goal in life," she said stiffly.

Charlee searched the arrestingly beautiful face of the twenty-two-year-old who stared defiantly at her. Very slowly and carefully she chose her words. "I admit I wanted to learn to be a lady so I could take Jim away from his fiancée, Tomasina Carver. She was aristocratic and perfect, from the best family, just like the Slades and Sandovals. Did you know Jim's mother was a Sandoval?" At Melanie's surprised expression, she continued, "Well, he's descended from real fancy bloodlines on both sides of his family. I was only a Missouri hill girl. My father, Lord rest his soul, was a drunk and my brother was killed in a blackmail scheme. But your mama convinced me I was somebody, that I was worthy in my own right, the hell with who my family was." Charlee paused a beat.

"She told me it was harder to find a man if you were a bluestocking than if you had African or Cherokee blood," Melanie said, smiling with such sadness it tugged at Charlee's heartstrings.

"So that's it! You're Rafael Flamenco's child by an octoroon woman and you're afraid no man in Texas will want you if they know about your background."

"My mother, like generations of Duval women before her, grew up to be an ornament! Be beautiful, Melanie. Dress carefully, Melanie. Watch how you walk, what you say—learn to flirt! All so you can get a rich young man from the very best family to *place* you. The Duval women are very particular, you know. We only sell ourselves to the highest bidders!" She was sobbing now and turned her face toward the bay window to stare blankly out at the street.

Charlee quickly crossed the distance separating them and took Melanie in her arms, turning the girl to face her. Melanie buried her head against Charlee's shoulder and struggled to regain her composure.

"You're not going to have that kind of life! Rafe and Deborah raised you to be the eldest Fleming daughter! You're not some backstairs relation they've hidden in the closet, Melanie. You have every right to expect a fine marriage with a man you choose," Charlee said emphatically. Then more gently she continued, "Oh, Melanie, you're bright and good—and, yes, beautiful. There's nothing wrong with being attractive to men. Don't hide from yourself. Give yourself a chance to find the right man.''

"And tell him I'm a bastard with African and Cherokee blood in my veins?'' She looked at Charlee measuringly.

"If he's the right man, he'll want you for being you. The rest won't matter. I ought to know. So should Deborah.'' Charlee's green eyes met Melanie's gold ones straightforwardly.

Melanie walked back to the desk and began to fiddle nervously with the untidy stack of papers on it. ''Maybe even if I could have a proper marriage and all that—what if I don't want to be tied down? To be fat and pregnant and have to do what some overbearing man says all the time?''

Charlee burst out laughing. ''Yup, Deborah raised you, all right! Melanie, have you ever considered how seldom women like Deborah or me or Obedience do what we're told by our husbands? How often we do as we damn well please?''

"Still, women can't vote or control their own lives any more than slaves. I want to work to change those things,'' Melanie said obdurately.

Charlee sighed and tried another approach. ''Clarence Pemberton assigns you to attend social events and write about them for the *Star*, doesn't he? Well, don't you think if you looked comfortable and presentable at dances and teas, you might get folks to talk to you more naturally? Tell you all sorts of gossip they wouldn't confide to someone standing out like a crow in a flock of swans?''

Remembering Clarence's sardonic comments about male reporters being able to ply information from men in bars, Melanie considered the fact that she might very well make her sex work for her, too. A man might just tell a pretty woman all sorts of things he'd never tell a stuffy Massachusetts reporter. She said neutrally, ''Maybe I could fit in better.''

Pressing her advantage and testing the waters at the same time, Charlee said, ''You bet you could. Why, just the other day Larena Sandoval told me she felt sorry for you standing all alone at the Mendozas' barbecue like a poor waif.''

"Poor waif! She felt sorry for me, did she, the mealy mouthed twit! Let's go shopping, Charlee!"

In the following weeks, an amazing metamorphosis took place in Melanie Fleming. Despite an occasional ink smudge on her nose and the inevitable pencil and writing pad in her reticule, she became a strikingly attractive woman. The old women clucked in amazement at Obedience's boarding-house while the younger San Antonio belles cast envious glances. The men just stared. And they talked. Anything she wanted to know, Melanie found she could pry from an eager admirer.

The women, too, wanted to be included in her news articles. Her society column was filled with all the latest tidbits of gossip, news about fashions, engagements, weddings, and births. Even secret recipes were confided to her.

Feeling particularly superior and charitable one afternoon at a luncheon for the ladies who helped Father Gus's Indian school, Melanie deigned to initiate a conversation with Larena Sandoval and her mother Esperanza. Both women, she was dismayed to discover, were intelligent and gracious, and Larena was far too pretty. Larena mentioned Lee several times, speaking in such glowing terms about her fiancé that Melanie doubted they knew the same Leandro Velásquez.

Eager to get away from Larena, Melanie caught Father Gus's eye across the room and excused herself, saying she had to discuss a matter of importance with him. Such proved to be the case.

"And you're sure renegade Comanche chiefs are trading stolen livestock to *licensed* traders in return for whiskey and guns?"

"*Ja*. Lots of investigating I've been doing these past months." The young priest's face split in a cherubic grin. "Letters I write, dozens of them to the Indian Office in Washington, even to our illustrious Senator Houston. And he so kindly replies."

"He lived among my grandmother's people for many

years. Some say he's the only real friend the Indians have in Washington," Melanie said quietly.

"And in Texas, I think. That is not spoken as praise but condemnation. Many things my schoolchildren hear about those evil men who steal from the Indians. Licensed traders—licensed by Satan himself! *Ja*, and so few Texians care," Father Gus added, his anger evaporating into sadness. The priest had learned a great deal during the past months since he had begun his campaign to sustain the impoverished children who existed on the periphery of San Antonio.

"Many people will help orphans of Mexican parentage, especially the wealthy Hispanic families prominent in local politics. But the Anglos and the *Tejanos* want nothing to do with Kickapoos, Shawnees, Tonkawas or Caddos," Melanie said. "Even the Lipans, whose own fathers served faithfully with the rangers as scouts against the Mexicans and Comanches—even they are turned out to forage."

"Enlisting you and Obedience has done great things, you know." Father Gus's eyes twinkled.

"Oh, it's only because we're friends with Jim and Charlee, and Jim's related to the Sandovals. Once Charlee got *Señora* Sandoval on our side, well, a handful of charitable women can wring contributions from the worst tightwads in the country," Melanie replied.

"But such benevolence on your ladies' parts should not be necessary if the government keeps its promises."

The idealistic young priest and his unorthodox female protégée were learning a lesson a day, and some were brutal to digest, but both of them were sure that they had a mission in Texas. Father Gus felt God had sent him halfway around the world from cool, green Bavaria to hot, dusty Texas. As for Melanie, Texas was already her home, and she would fight for it, for all its people, but not necessarily with the saintly patience of the gentle young priest.

"The men sent by the Indian Office from Washington, many are good men, *ja*—like Robert Neighbors. But these men have no real authority. And the state officials, never will they protect red men—not if it means keeping white settlers from moving farther west. Mr. Neighbors wants the rangers to stop traders from bringing whiskey to the Comanche.''

Melanie grew increasingly incensed. ''Those Comanche raids last June that led to that massacre I wrote about could've been avoided if those fools in Austin had listened to men like Robert Neighbors!''

Father Gus shrugged. ''Perhaps. Always the Comanche do not keep their word, either. But this much I do know—as long as the whites push west and plow the land, kill the game, the reds will fight back.''

''Until they're all dead,'' Melanie said bleakly.

Father Gus sighed. ''That I fear is the state government's plan. For many ranchers and traders here, I *know* it is their wish.''

''Father, what do you know about these licensed traders who're selling whiskey to the Comanche?'' Melanie's mind was turning over a dozen ideas as she waited for the priest to reply in his slow, careful English.

''Several of my students' mothers are, er—'' He struggled for a way to put it delicately to a lady.

''They are common-law wives to white soldiers,'' she supplied helpfully.

''*Ja*, sort of like that. These boys hear many things. They tell me about how traders like Lucas Blaine deal with renegades, selling them rifles in return for stolen horses.''

''Right here in Bexar County?''

He made an expansive gesture. ''*Ja*, even here.''

''I think I'll just keep an eye on our Mr. Blaine,'' Melanie said, her gold eyes narrowing.

Already Father Gus didn't like the dangerous turn of the conversation. A nice young lady like Miss Fleming should not get involved with Indian traders or their ilk. Still, one look into those blazing eyes told him how useless it was to argue. He laughed good-naturedly. ''Why is it, *Fräulein*, that I feel if I don't help you, you will use the skills of a reporter and get your story anyway?''

* * *

Word arrived the next day from Renacimiento that Rafe and Deborah were the proud parents of another son, Joseph Paul, weighing nearly eight pounds, a fine healthy child. The posts being so uncertain and the elements so trying, there was no way to determine for sure exactly *when* little Joey had been born. The letter's ink had been smeared when it was exposed to a sudden dunking in some swollen stream between Renacimiento and San Antonio, erasing the date at the top of the first page. Melanie was glad her mother and new baby brother were doing well. Obedience couldn't wait to see the whole brood, as Deborah indicated they would be arriving for a visit in a month or so, as soon as she was feeling up to making the trip.

While they discussed this exciting news over breakfast at the crowded boardinghouse table, Melanie received an unexpected summons. A small, dark face with enormous black eyes and a wealth of shaggy straight hair peeped through the kitchen door, with Sadie's voice ringing out from the kitchen.

"Now, git back here! I done tole yo Miz Melanie's eatin'." With an arthritic black hand she snatched at the boy's shoulder to drag him back into the kitchen.

Practically overturning her chair in her haste, Melanie called out, "Wait, Sadie. That's Lame Deer. He's a special friend of mine from Father Gus's school."

Melanie ushered the child out onto the back porch, away from the curious boarders inside, then asked eagerly, "What do you have to tell me, Lame Deer?"

"I see the Fat Firehair go into the saloon, and I sneak up to watch who he talks to and what they say," the boy told her.

Fat Firehair was the unflattering designation for Lucas Blaine, the paunchy trader with carrot-red hair and beard.

"The *rinche*—ranger—he told Fat Firehair a big herd of cows will be held near the Cedar Fork cutoff of Clear Creek. There will be few *vaqueros* guarding them. He told Firehair that Buffalo Gall should steal the cows. Firehair gives the renegade guns in return for the cows. The two men, they are as evil as Buffalo Gall," Lame Deer whispered fearfully.

"This ranger—describe him," Melanie prodded.

"Big, tall. Gray hair with eyes the color of bullets," the boy said. "He is a chief among them, I think."

"If'n thet ain't Seth Walkman, I'd miss hittin' thet there post with my scattergun," Obedience said grimly.

Melanie turned to confront the intruder. "Obedience, this is a private conversation between a reporter and an informant."

"Jeehosaphat! This is plumb foolishness, thet's whut it is! Walkman's meaner'n a poked rattler, 'n' no gal reporter oughta git near him."

"I've already been near him, and he doesn't scare me! Thank you, Lame Deer, for watching Blaine for me. When I get this story it'll be better than—well, never mind, it just will!" She gave the boy a hug and sent him scurrying back to Father Gus's place for the start of school.

Melanie had changed into a dark brown riding skirt and was buttoning a peach silk blouse when Obedience knocked and peremptorily entered the room. "Who is—well, come in!" Melanie said.

"Fool thing ta say seein's how I already am in." The big woman stood with meaty red hands on her ample hips and a no-nonsense glare in her eyes. "Yew fixin' on follerin' Walkman 'n' his bunch o' cutthroats, ain'tcha?"

Melanie considered denying it, then realized how useless it would be. "Look, Obedience. I've had a whole bunch of the boys from Father Gus's school watching and listening for information about what's happening between Blaine and the renegades. Now I know Walkman's involved, too."

"'N' when yew find them thievin' varmints, yew'll write a great story tellin' all Santone 'bout it, just like yew did thet raid on th' Comanche camp." She waited for a reaction.

Melanie's eyes widened, feigning surprise. "Obedience, you don't mean to say you think I'm—"

"Moses French," she finished the sentence emphatically. "Yep, 'specially after I got plumb tired o' hearin' old Racine Schwartz caterwaulin' 'bout how his favorite buckskins 'n' knife wuz stole from his room. Then they come home all by theyselves a week er so after thet story wuz printed. Right remarkable." She shook her head in reproof. "Gal, what yore doin'll be the death o' yew."

"This won't be nearly as bad as that massacre, believe me. All I'm going to do is sneak up where Lame Deer told me Blaine is meeting the renegades. I'm not fool enough to try and shoot it out with a bunch of gunmen and Comanche!"

"They ketch sight o' yew 'n' yore as dead meat as them cows," Obedience yelled after the small woman, who had quickly slipped past her and dashed down the back steps. Fuming and cussing, the big woman shambled after the girl, realizing the futility of trying to catch her. Small, agile Melanie would be traveling too quickly for a man of Wash's considerable bulk to outride her. Frantically Obedience cast her eyes up and down the street as she stood on the front porch of the boardinghouse.

"Whut's frettin' yew, sweet pea?" Wash said, coming up behind his wife and placing his enormous bear-paw hand on her shoulder.

"Jeehosaphat! We gotta find someone ta stop thet fool child afore she ends up buzzard bait er worse!" Quickly she told him that Melanie was Moses French and described the dangerous situation about to take place if someone didn't stop the girl.

"I seen Lee Velásquez up th' street 'bout two minutes ago. I'll git him. Yew fetch thet Injun kid back here so's he kin tell us where she's gone." After issuing those commands, Wash moved with surprising speed toward his big bay gelding while Obedience yelled for their hired man, Chester, to bring Bessie, her mule, from the stable.

"She *what*?" Lee's eyes blackened with fury and incredulity.

"She's Moses French, ya see, 'n' she got them fool Injun kids spyin' on thet thievin' rascal Blaine," Wash explained further, as if dealing with a simpleton. "Someone's gotta ketch her, 'n' yew know this country and kin track. I'd go, but ole Gentry here'll never outrun thet little gal."

With a curse, Lee vaulted onto Sangre's back in front of the Sandoval house, where Wash had intercepted him. "I'll head to Father Gus's school and find that boy," he called out as he vanished in a cloud of dust kicked up by the big stallion's hooves.

After an hour on the trail at a punishing pace, Lee was as
hot and sweaty as the big blue roan, who was enjoying the
exercise. His rider was not. He cursed Melanie Fleming in
English, then Spanish, then switched back to English; it
had more uniquely graphic words with which to express his
feelings. All sorts of horrible images of her small body
lying bullet-riddled and bloodied on the hot Texas earth
flashed through his mind. Then he pictured her as she had
looked at the Slades' fiesta last week, all frothy in a cream
lace dress, dancing with one of those mooning cowhands of
Jim's. The vision of her earthy, sensuous beauty haunted
him as he rode. She had a good half hour's head start on
him. If only he were in time.

As he rounded a curve in the road, he could see he was
near the Cedar Fork area of Clear Creek. When he heard the
distant bawl of cattle, he knew the stolen herd was not far
ahead. He reined in Sangre and considered, *Where would I
go to spy on them if I were Moses French?* Then he saw a
brushy thicket that stretched along a rise of ground on the
far side of the creek. A natural observation point—if the
Comanche and Blaine's men hadn't concluded the same
thing and posted a sentry who'd already killed her! Slowly
he backtracked and headed toward the thicket from the
opposite direction.

All his years in the Apachería had honed Lee's instincts
for survival. He knew how to smell out an enemy and had
never been taken by surprise. When he sighted several
renegade Comanche and Lucas Blaine standing over the
inert bodies of two cowhands, the raiders were unaware of
his presence. Obviously the savages had surprised the luck-
less wranglers at their campfire and killed both men. Now
they were haggling with Blaine over the guns while the
trader's men drove off the cattle. *Where the hell is Melanie?*

Lee tied Sangre in a low-lying willow copse across the
creek. The horse was trained to silence and would never
give him away. Then he moved toward the rise on foot,
crawling up the steep, rocky pathway noiselessly. He could
hear the sounds of the Comanche riding off. Then when he

crested the hill he saw her, kneeling behind a jutting rock, watching the scene below intently.

Silent as an Apache, he stalked her, crouching down as he neared the edge of the precipice.

Melanie watched as the last of the renegades prepared to ride away, sporting several new rifles each. One Comanche stayed behind, however, searching the campsite of the unfortunate cowboys, apparently looking for anything of value to pilfer.

If I can capture him red-handed, Wash and Jim can wring the truth out of him about Blaine. Melanie's mind was fixed on the renegade across the creek. Just as she started to get up, a set of steel fingers tightened over her mouth and a powerful arm squeezed the breath from her rib cage.

Lee Velásquez's voice was unmistakable, even through clenched teeth as he whispered in her ear, "Don't do anything else stupid like scream and bring those savages down on us. Now I'm going to release you—promise to be quiet?" At her affirmative nod, he let her go.

Melanie jerked away from him and hugged herself around the middle where his iron-hard grip had bruised her. "Ooh," she whispered, laboring to regain her breath, "I think you've broken my ribs. What are you doing here?"

He arched his brows in a fierce scowl and shot back, "What is a lone female doing riding after cutthroats and Comanches, might be a better question!"

"Look, they're gone—all but that one fellow," Melanie said, turning to watch again.

"Good. We can get the hell out of here before he sees us." Grabbing her arm, Lee began to pull her back from the overhang.

Melanie jerked free furiously, hissing, "I'm not going anywhere with you! I'm here for a story to expose Lucas Blaine and his thieves. Go back to your San Antonio belle and rescue her when she has the vapors. I'm going to catch a murderer before he gets away."

When she tried to storm past him, he grabbed her roughly with both hands and shook her until her teeth rattled. "Get this straight. I didn't ride Sangre into the ground to save your pretty little ass for my own amusement or out of some misguided sense of chivalry. I came because the Oakleys asked me. Moses French has written her last story!''

Her eyes flashed fiery gold like a cornered she-cat. "I don't want your help—I don't care if the Blessed Virgin and the Archangel Michael sent you!" She tried in vain to wriggle free.

As they engaged in a silent struggle punctuated by heavy breathing, Lee looked over her head at the clearing across the stream. The last Comanche had mounted up and was leaving the scene of their crime. "Your quarry's getting away, Moses. Give it up," he said, now half amused at her fierce resistance.

She turned and emitted a furious oath when she saw the rider escaping. Lee began to release her when she stilled her thrashing. Then she reached in the pocket of her skirt, pulled out a six-shot pepperbox, and aimed it directly at his chest.

"Now back off or, so help me God, I'll shoot you! I'm going to stop him!" She heard the hiss of air escape from between his clenched teeth as he looked down at the lethal Allen and Thurber. His face lost all expression and he stepped back a pace, still standing directly in her path. "Move!" she ordered.

"He's gone, Melanie. What're you going to do—ride him down? A Comanche? Never aim a gun at a man unless you're prepared for the consequences." He didn't budge.

Suddenly she sensed he was dangerously angry, in a different way than he had been moments earlier. She could feel the trembling in her knees spread upward to her hand holding the small gun, which now seemed to weigh fifty pounds. "How dare you presume to rescue me when I obviously don't need help?" she demanded, trying to keep the edge of her own anger sparked to stop her shaking.

Lee's face betrayed none of the savage fury coursing through him. "Do you recall what I did to Zeb Brocker when he tried to pull a gun on me?" he asked levelly. "I could snap that pretty little neck of yours." His eyes commanded her to get rid of the gun, even though he continued to stand deceptively still, poised cat-taut, waiting for her to obey.

Melanie's fright grew, but so did her rage. "Order your sweet little girlfriend around, but don't play lord and master with me, you—you scalper!"

As she vented her spleen, Melanie gesticulated, moving the gun the tiniest bit off center. It was the split second's opening Lee needed. With one lightning sweep he knocked the gun flying, numbing her hand with the force of the blow. His other hand reached for her, grabbing at her shoulder, but she twisted away. Lee caught the thin silk of her shirt, ripping it all the way to her waist and revealing the swell of her breasts over their tight confinement in a lacy camisole. She backed up a step, clutching at the torn fabric to cover herself. He moved forward a step, but made no further attempt to touch her.

His black eyes locked with her golden ones. Then his hypnotic gaze slowly lowered to her parted lips to watch as she moistened them with her tongue, breathless with fright and some other emotion he knew she had never felt before. His scorching eyes traveled to her voluptuously rounded breasts, then down to her tiny waist and flared hips, perfectly encased in the tailored riding skirt. "Your taste in clothes has certainly improved."

"If admiring my clothes inspires you to rip them off me, I'll go back to my old wardrobe, thank you," she said stiffly.

He watched the rise and fall of her breasts as she stood with her arms crossed protectively over them. "I've had you under my skin ever since we collided in Austin six years ago," he said, more angry at himself than at her because his reaction to her had always made him feel disloyal to Dulcia.

Melanie could feel the leashed fury and sexual tension uncoiling in him. Cornered and desperate, she made a swift lunge to get past him.

Lee was too quick for her. His hands once more imprisoned her shoulders. When she raised her fists to swing at him, he quickly grabbed her fragile wrists. In their struggle her torn blouse once more fell open. As Melanie thrashed against his imprisoning grip, one camisole strap snapped. She could feel the tight lace garment riding down until her right breast was exposed. In humiliation and shame she kicked out at him in a frenzy to escape. Her pointed boots stabbed his shin and he let out a snarled oath of pain, which swiftly changed to a hiss of agony when she raised her knee to his groin. The action was inadvertent on Melanie's part as she flailed and kicked wildly.

"You little bitch," he ground out, yanking her against his chest so hard they both lost their balance and tumbled backward to the ground. Lee's body cushioned the fall for her, but the breath was knocked from both of them. Gasping for air, Melanie tried to pull free, but he rolled them over and imprisoned her beneath him.

"Now, let's see you try that sweet trick again," he panted as he threw one leg across her thighs, immobilizing her lower body. Her fingernails raked across his face before he secured her wrists. He stared down at her small, beautiful face.

"Please," was all she could get out in a hoarse, terrified whisper. Her eyes glowed like liquid gold, shimmering with unshed tears of fury and fright. Her hair had come free from its pins and tangled around her shoulders. Holding both her hands in one of his, he took the other and seized the cluster of gleaming ebony curls. Her hair smelled of wild roses, delicate and sensuous, like the night blossom he'd found at his ranch.

He could feel her shivering terror. Slowly the red haze of lust abated, leaving a bemused gentleness. He stared into her golden eyes, then lowered his mouth to kiss first one, then the other. "Don't cry, little Night Flower, don't cry," he whispered raggedly as silvery droplets squeezed through her brushy black lashes. He continued his softened assault, trailing his lips down to her mouth and brushing it feather lightly until he cold sense her opening to gasp in surprise. He centered his mouth over hers then and kissed her deeply, his tongue entering the virgin recesses to tease and tantalize.

Melanie sensed the change in him from brutal predator to gentle seducer. Every nerve in her body seemed stretched tight, no longer in terror but now in some new unnamed and unknown emotion. She heard his whispered endearment, but the words didn't register because the warm, probing magic of his lips and tongue had taken her reason away. She could feel the bone-crushing hold he had on her wrists loosen then relent as he moved his hand downward, between their bodies to trace a scorching pattern around her bared breast. The nipple contracted in a frisson of pleasure, and she found herself arching up for yet another caress.

Her fingers ran through his shaggy black hair, then clutched convulsively at his shoulder when he deserted her lips and moved his head lower to her breasts. Slowly, like a man unwrapping a treasure, he eased the camisole all the way down, baring both rounded globes with their hard rosy points. He circled one tip with his tongue while his hand continued to caress the other.

Melanie heard a whimper of pleasure and dimly realized it was her own voice. Now her writhing was not in protest but in ecstasy. Never had she felt anything like the sensations flowing through her body, which seemed to have a will of its own, instinctively reacting to his practiced hands and mouth. She clung to him, letting him bare her breasts and suckle them, run a lean, callused hand down her thigh and reach beneath her skirts. Then he stroked back up her sleek little leg toward the warm, liquid core of her body. She arched and pleaded incoherently.

Lee sensed her acquiescence. Unpracticed but eager, she was instinctively sensuous and passionate. He lost himself in her soft rose-sweet flesh, so intent on discovering the delights of her body that he did not hear the approaching horsemen until they were practically upon him.

"Lee, what the hell are you doing?" Jim Slade's unmistakable gravel drawl interrupted the lovers.

"Velásquez, I'll kill you for this." Rafe Fleming's silky voice held a deadly menace for all its quietness.

Chapter 12

Rafe Fleming slid from his big sorrel stallion with the effortless grace of a Comanche, his movements sinuous and swift. Before he could reach Lee, Jim Slade intercepted him with a restraining hand on his shoulder.

"Don't do anything you'll regret, Rafe," he said in a low, intense voice.

Lee quickly rose from the dusty ground and pulled Melanie up behind him, shielding her from the prying eyes of the half-dozen riders still mounted behind Slade and Fleming. *Damn, as if they haven't all seen enough!*

Fleming's black eyes glowed like embers as he looked from his daughter's torn clothing to Lee's scratched face. "The son of a bitch attacked her, Jim." Rafe saw only what he wished to see, his cold voice and tightly coiled manner belying the white-hot rage hammering inside him.

Jim, who had seen the girl ardently returning Lee's attentions, was decidedly the calmer of the two, afraid only that Rafe would try to kill his childhood companion before the situation was clarified. "Let's just discuss this before we decide anything," he replied easily.

Melanie could feel her father's eyes assessing her disheveled state as he walked past Lee and took her in his arms. She frantically tried to pull the shredded blouse up with one hand while smoothing down her wayward skirts with the other. Silently he slipped his buckskin vest off and offered it to her. Although far too large, it did at least hold her silk shirt together at the shoulder. Cringing in shame and shock, she listened to the men's strident voices as if she were overhearing them from a great distance.

Lee turned from the father and daughter to face Jim Slade. "I followed her to keep her from getting killed. She was ready to ride after one of the men who shot those wranglers." He gestured across the creek to the campsite.

Seeing the slain men left by the rustlers, Jim barked terse orders, "Wash, Asa, check and see what's gone on over there and wait for us across the creek."

As the mounted men wheeled their horses and departed in mute embarrassment, Jim looked quickly between Lee and Rafe, knowing he had to stay calm and keep control of the situation. "All right. I know Wash sent you after her and I know what she was up to, but that doesn't explain how we found you." He cast Rafe a quelling look, praying the arrogant Creole would not act precipitately.

Lee took a long, steadying breath, trying to gather his badly scattered wits. How to explain the unexplainable, the irrational? "I won't make excuses, Jim. She pointed a gun at me and when I took it away from her we struggled. Then, oh, shit, I lost my head, and—"

"And tore the clothes from her body because she defended herself?" Rafe interrupted with deadly softness.

"It wasn't quite that simple, Fleming," Lee replied angrily. "She was out here on a fool's errand and tried to shoot me for the trouble of saving her hide—and, I might add, it's not the first time since she came to San Antonio that I've had to keep someone from killing her." ·

"That doesn't give you the right to manhandle her, *mano*," Jim replied levelly, knowing there was much more to the encounter than Lee was revealing.

"I regret my actions and I apologize," he said woodenly, looking at Melanie's small dazed face, now smudged with dust. Her eyes were downcast and her lips were bruised from his fierce kisses. He felt a renewed surge of that bizarre combination of desire and fury rise in him once more.

"So," Rafe said, releasing Melanie and stepping up to confront Velásquez, "you apologize, do you? After half a dozen cowboys from Bluebonnet saw her pinned to the ground under you and you with your filthy hands all over her body. I'd say it's a little late for regret." His voice finally rose a notch.

Two sets of fiery jet eyes clashed. Looking at the men, Melanie was shocked at how alike her father and Lee were, tall, dark, and hard-looking—dangerous. She knew Lee was a killer, and she had heard rumors about Rafael Flamenco's early days in Texas. Then Lee's words jarred her from her ruminations.

"I can't undo what's done and I won't crawl for it, Fleming. Anyway, you and all the others could see the lady wasn't exactly fighting me when you happened on us. She gave me the distinct impression she was enjoying what we were doing."

Melanie let out a gasp of indignation, coloring at the shameful accuracy of his words. "You border ruffian! You—"

Rafe lunged toward Lee, but Jim interposed himself between the two. "Now cool down, both of you. Look, Rafe, I hate to say it, but, well"—his amber eyes flashed at Melanie's crimson face for a moment—"she did seem to be, er, responding to him, not fighting him."

"He dishonored my daughter, Jim. I'm sorry he's your friend, but he can't just tip his hat and walk away," Rafe said through gritted teeth.

"I never intended that he should," Jim said, a wicked white grin slashing his tanned face as he looked from one set of hard, dark features to the other. He had done some quick calculating while Lee talked, watching Melanie's reactions and replaying the scene between the two lovers over in his mind. There was no doubt that they had been loving, not fighting. "The only honorable thing for Lee to do is marry Melanie."

Everyone grew silent for a second, then spoke at once, but Melanie's shriek of indignation cut across all the rumbling baritone voices. "Wait a minute! Everyone here—every *man* here has had his say. I'm a twenty-two-year-old adult, and I have some small stake in this, too! I wouldn't marry him if he'd ravished me in front of a whole company of Texas Rangers!"

"I think by the time we get back to San Antonio every ranger and *civilian* between here and California will have heard about it," Rafe said, eyeing his furious daughter speculatively. She *had* allowed Velásquez's liberties, unless his eyes were going bad, which he doubted.

"I can't marry her, Jim. I'm already engaged to Larena, *your* cousin Larena, in case you've conveniently forgotten," Lee said.

Remembering Lee's relationship with his first dutiful Hispanic wife, Jim said tersely, "Break your engagement, *mano*."

"I second the motion, Velásquez," Rafe said with the beginning of an evil smile tugging at his lips.

"Papa! You can't mean to go along with this insane scheme!" Melanie turned beet red, then chalky as she looked from man to man.

Jim's amber eyes and Rafe's obsidian ones both locked on Lee's set face, united now in their purpose. All three ignored the woman.

"You think this'll solve anything?" Lee questioned incredulously, looking from Rafe to Jim.

"The way I see it, you owe a debt of honor, Velásquez. You do have a fine old family name in these parts and a respectable ranch—and you are free to marry my daughter. That's one way to settle it. The other way—"

"There won't be any other way, dammit," Jim cut in, the famous Slade temper finally getting the better of him. "How the hell will it help Melanie's reputation if you kill each other? Don't either of you mistake it—you'd both lose. I know you too well."

"I'm not standing here and listening to another minute of this rubbish. You can all three shoot it out—and them, too," Melanie yelled, gesturing broadly to the men across the river, as she whirled and stomped off toward the base of the bluff where her horse was tethered.

"Oh, Rafael, I don't know. This is so sudden, so crazy." Deborah laid their infant son, Joey, in his crib and turned to face her husband. She looked pale and shaken. They had just arrived at the boardinghouse when Obedience rushed out with some insane story about Melanie pursuing a band of outlaws to get a newspaper story.

"You're exhausted, darling," Rafe said as he took her in his arms. "It's been only six weeks since Joey's birth. I knew we should have waited longer before you traveled so far."

"I'm fine, only worried about Melanie. If we hadn't come, what would have happened to her? What *will* happen, Rafael? She can't marry a man she's only met a handful of times in her life." Deborah's violet eyes were wide with apprehension.

Rafe turned and paced, running his fingers through his shaggy black hair. "Hell, Deborah, you knew me only a few weeks before we married," he replied ruefully.

"And it took us only seven years to work things out," she countered acerbically. "I've known Lee since he was a boy and I've always liked him. But since the tragedy of his first wife's death, he's grown into a hard, dangerous stranger."

Rafe quirked one elegant brow at her. "I seem to recall you thought the same thing about me when I found you at this boardinghouse!"

"But that was us, Rafael. This situation is different. They're not committed to each other. There are no children to consider."

"If we hadn't come along when we did, there might have been," Rafe said darkly.

Remembering Melanie's torn clothing and disheveled state when she returned to town that afternoon, Deborah nodded. "Yes, yes, I know it must have looked awful. I always suspected she inherited your passionate nature and simply directed it in channels acceptable for a female."

"Well, it certainly emerged today! Anyway, there's nothing wrong with her showing some natural womanly feelings. She's twenty-two years old. And Lee Velásquez is a solid figure in the community, good family name, educated, owns a prosperous ranch. He's settled down from his renegade days and he's a strong enough man to handle Melanie."

"Our daughter is a handful, I'll grant you," Deborah said

with approval in her voice. "But she is also a grown woman, as you just pointed out, and we can't force her to marry him. This is 1852, not the Middle Ages!"

"It's best for her," he replied arrogantly. "Her reputation is in shreds here in San Antonio. If she refuses, the only alternative is to send her back to your father in Boston."

Deborah heard Joey fret in his sleep and knelt by his crib to give him a reassuring pat. Shaking her head, she sighed. "If she let him take such liberties, she must love him whether or not she realizes it. But does he love *her*?"

Rafe snorted in derision. "He was giving one hell of a good imitation of it when we caught the bastard!" Seeing his wife's distress, he pulled her up gently and whispered, "Don't worry. I've talked to Wash and Obedience. They know Lee and Melanie both. They think it'll work. We really have no choice, Moon Flower. If Melanie's too stubborn to acknowledge her own feelings after today, someone's got to force her to confront them."

Ever since they were eighteen-year-olds, Lee Velásquez and Charlee McAllister Slade had been as close as siblings. Of course, as he thought of it now, Charlee had been a lot more grown up at eighteen than he. But that was ten years ago and he wasn't the carefree boy who lived at Bluebonnet Ranch anymore. Still, here he was riding out to see Charlee and seek her advice once more.

God, what a mess! Melanie Fleming under her parents' protective wings, Obedience threatening to take her rolling pin to certain portions of his anatomy, and Wash ready to throttle him with one hand. Of all the times for the Fleming family to come for a visit! Of course Jim and Wash would've found him and Melanie anyway. He sighed. If there was any way out of the tangle, Charlee, the master schemer, would think of it!

Charlee's opinion about his looming nuptials dumbfounded him. Arms akimbo and cat-green eyes aglow, Charlee Slade planted her small, slim body squarely in the center of her kitchen and asked, "When's the wedding—tomorrow or sooner?"

"I came here for your help, not to be greeted like an Inquisition victim," he replied sourly.

"I happen to know *exactly* how Jim and Rafe found the two of you, Leandro *Angel* Velásquez," she said saucily, the emphasis on those two words speaking volumes.

He winced. "Look, I know I acted like a jackass—all right, a real bastard—but marrying the girl just because of what *almost* happened is ridiculous. I'm already engaged to Larena. She and I were talking about a fall wedding only last week."

"Melanie Fleming will make you a much better wife than Larena," Charlee said flatly.

Lee's eyes almost popped from their sockets. "You can't be serious! That wild hoyden! She's no lady!"

"Sounds just like the way Jim used to describe me," Charlee said, eyes dancing.

"That was different," he said dismissively. "He wanted to marry Tomasina Carver and we all know what she was like."

"Yeah. A real lady. Fancy manners, soft words, knew her place around men, all right," Charlee said sarcastically.

"If you mean to imply she was anything like Larena, that's ridiculous, Charlee, and you know it," Lee replied angrily.

"I wasn't comparing Tomasina and Larena, but Larena and Dulcia," Charlee said softly.

Lee's head jerked up and a look of bleak, shocked pain flashed into his eyes. "Don't, Charlee, don't."

"Sit down," she commanded with no nonsense in her voice. When he folded his tall frame onto a chair, she pulled out a chair for herself. Before sitting down, she selected two glasses from a cabinet and took a bottle of whiskey from a shelf. "I got this from Wash. He brought it all the way from the Rockies."

Lee groaned. "The last time I drank that stuff was in Santa Fe. I swore off."

"Never knew you to be temperance," she replied cheerfully, handing him a glass. "Lunch is served," she said, swallowing a sip carefully.

He took a gulp. It was fiery and smooth at the same time.

Charlee let him stew in silence for a moment, then plunged in. "Lee, I know Dulcia was your first love, a sweet, dutiful, lovely girl—and I hate to dredge up the pain of the past, but your whole future is at stake."

"And you think I chose Larena because she reminds me of Dulcia?"

"Well, let's just say you're hung up on Hispanic pedigrees. Larena is ladylike, from a family with *pureza de sangre*. I know you set great store by that, but I also know that if you and Dulcia had stayed married, you'd have ended up keeping a woman on the side."

Lee looked at her in incredulity. "How the hell can you say that?"

"I know what she thought of 'submitting to her husband,'" Charlee said baldly. "She was raised that way, Lee—to be timid and proper, to be afraid of honest passions— passions Melanie felt with you." She paused a beat, then continued, "Jim was very graphic in his description of just how he found the two of you."

"I'll bet!" He stood up, unable to decide whether to be furiously angry or terribly embarrassed. "It seems all my faults, past and present, are laid bare," he said coldly.

Charlee stretched out a small, tanned hand and grasped his fist, pulling him back into his chair. "They're not *your* faults. Dulcia didn't fail to respond because of anything you did wrong, Lee. But Melanie sure responded because of what you did right! She responded because she feels something very strong for you—and you do for her, too. Tell me honestly, did you ever kiss Larena that way?"

"That's different," he said evasively.

"Why? Because she's a lady? Lee, you can't have a real marriage with a mirage, an idealized dream. You need a real flesh-and-blood woman."

"And you think Melanie is that woman?" He shook his head in amazement and disbelief.

"Melanie will be the woman," Jim said determinedly from the back door. He had overheard the last bit of their conversation as he walked quietly across the back porch. "Either you do the decent thing and marry her or you're finished here in San Antonio, Lee. As for the Sandovals, Uncle José will never let you marry Larena now with all this scandal. You made your bed on that hillside with Melanie Fleming, Lee. Now you'll just have to sleep in it,'' he concluded with a lopsided grin.

Lee had never felt so powerless over the course of his life as he did that afternoon. After his surprising conversation with the Slades, he visited Father Gus for counsel. Jim Slade and Rafe Fleming together had had a long talk with the priest the previous evening. By the time he left the sympathetic but regretful cleric, Lee realized he was only postponing the inevitable. He must break his engagement with Larena and marry Melanie Fleming. He had felt more self-possessed riding alone into Mescalero camps in the wilds of the Apachería than he did approaching the Sandoval house.

Larena refused to see him, so he was forced to make his apologies and explanations to her father. *Don* José was impeccably polite but decidedly cold. It *was* easier to describe what had occurred between him and Melanie to another man than it would have been if he had spoken to a gently reared girl. Still, it hurt him when she would not see him, and he felt bitterly guilty for causing her such undeserved humiliation and sorrow.

Melanie wandered aimlessly through the orchards in back of the boardinghouse, nibbling without appetite on a peach plucked carelessly from a low-hanging bough. The sun was warm and the breeze light, a clean beautiful Texas afternoon. ''How can the day be so lovely when I'm so miserable?'' she asked aloud of no one and everyone.

Dinner last evening had been a horror, with her whole family present, all her younger siblings silently puzzled, itching to know what had happened. Their papa had brought her back to the boardinghouse with her hair tangled, face dirt-smeared, and clothes ripped. No one openly discussed it, but Obedience and Wash, as well as Rafe and Deborah, engaged in private conversations before the meal. Several of the lady boarders stared at her as if she had sprouted horns and a tail, but old Racine Schwartz seemed secretly delighted about the situation.

She had fallen into a restless, exhausted sleep filled with feverish dreams in which she and Lee replayed the furious, hurtful scene on the hillside over and over. She awoke sweaty and trembling near dawn and could not go back to sleep. Visions of her father's stern features and closed expression haunted her. He and Jim Slade had arranged her life, forcing a man who despised her—whom *she* despised— to marry her! Damn men and their infernal rules of honor!

She finally worked up her courage and went to plead her case with Deborah, only to find her father was waiting with her mother. They were in agreement. She must marry Lee Velásquez. Everyone, it seemed, agreed but the bride and groom! The Slades, the Oakleys, even Father Gus. She had not had the courage to approach Clarence, wincing to imagine his scathing sarcasm at her most typically female fall from grace while on a news assignment!

She felt betrayed by her friends and family, alone and frightened. *What kind of life can I have as a rancher's wife? No, be honest, as Lee's wife?*

As if in answer to her question, she caught sight of a tall figure striding purposefully across the orchard toward her. *Lee.* She stopped and took a quick calming breath, willing her heart to stop its trip-hammer beat. Oh, why had she thrown on this girlish muslin dress? She felt at a disadvantage with her hair in a simple braid and low-heeled slippers on her feet, confronting his hard, menacing presence. He towered over her, dressed in his usual uniform of buckskin breeches and white shirt open at the throat, revealing an indecent amount of that springy black chest hair. She forced herself to meet his eyes.

Lee watched her brace herself, like a spitting, cornered wildcat, ready to claw at him. Her physical allure still amazed him, reaching out, scorching him with desire. He remembered the feel of that soft, voluptuous body beneath his hands, the arching breasts so full and ripe, the undulating hips and small, delicately formed calves. Her simple yellow dress clung to every wickedly enticing curve in whisper-soft folds. The breeze blew the sheer fabric, molding it to her, reminding him of what lay beneath. Absurdly,

he wanted to grab the fat, shiny plait of hair and pull her
into his embrace once more. *What is it about her that makes
me act like a rutting schoolboy?* If he wanted to succeed
with the plan he had formulated this morning, he must get
all such thoughts out his mind immediately.

He scowled and removed his hat, letting the wind ruffle
his hair with blessedly cool air. ''I've discussed the marriage with Father Gus. He's making arrangements for San
Fernando Church. Tomorrow. I know it's not much time to
select a wedding trousseau, but considering everything, I
imagine it's best if we return to the ranch and skip the
honeymoon.'' He paused and looked at her widening gold
eyes.

''So you've made all the arrangements. How efficient,''
she said contemptuously.

''*I* merely followed up on what Jim and your father have
already arranged. It seems neither of us has a choice in the
matter.'' He watched the seething emotions boiling just
below the surface, ready to erupt. ''Look, Melanie, we're
going to have to go through with this charade. The whole
damn town is united against us.''

''This isn't a charade—a game! It's the rest of our lives
you're talking so calmly about! It's marriage!'' she cried
desperately, hating the panic in her voice.

He assessed her emotions and decided to plunge ahead.
''It wouldn't have to be a real marriage. If it weren't
consummated, we could wait a year or so, until things cool
down here, and then apply to the bishop in Galveston for an
annulment.''

She stared at him blankly. *Not consummated.* Her golden
skin flushed crimson as his meaning sank in. ''You'd deceive Father Gus and lie in church? Promise to—to . . . and
then. . . .'' She turned her head and groped with one hand
for a tree limb on which to steady herself.

''Don't get religion so late, Melanie. It doesn't become
you. You've flirted with disaster ever since I met you on the
Galveston waterfront ten years ago. This time I can't just
rescue you and turn you loose like before. Your irresponsible behavior created this mess. A temporary marriage is the

only way out. Surely a woman as free and unconventional as you won't worry about the scandal of shedding a husband.''

"You bastard," she whispered. "*My* irresponsible behavior! You took it on yourself to be my rescuer. I didn't ask you to follow me! And I for sure didn't ask you to grab me and—and do those awful things to me!'' Her voice rose steadily as she spoke until it ended on a shrill cry, echoing across the empty orchard.

"You seemed real receptive to those awful things by the time your father and Jim came on the scene! If you hadn't had your arms and legs wrapped around me, they'd have killed me on the spot and solved both our problems at once! Think, dammit!''

Melanie squeezed her eyes shut in humiliation. He was right. Why had she acted that way, let him—no, *encouraged* him—to touch her so intimately? She stiffened her spine with pride, now her only defense. Forcing herself to gaze on his hard, handsome face, she replied flatly, "I'm a very unfeminine crusader, as you've reminded me more than once. You're the experienced man of the world. You took advantage of me, and now you're only marrying me to save face and keep my father from killing you! How do you expect me to react to such a cold-blooded proposition? With joy for my shredded reputation? 'Well, at least he married the chit!' I can hear Violet Clemson's spiteful tongue already!''

"Can you think of an alternative? That is, if you consider me brave enough to defy your formidable father?'' he asked sarcastically. She made no reply. "You just moved to San Antonio. You have family and friends in other places. After an annulment you could move to Nacogdoches or Houston— even back to Boston. But I was born here and this is the only home I've ever known. As it is, I've lost the woman I planned to marry because of what's happened. Larena won't even see me,'' he said bitterly.

"So now we get down to it, really,'' she responded, forcing the words from her aching throat. "Your fiancée from her pure-blooded family! You wanted a dynastic alliance with the Sandovals—a woman to breed heirs for your *estancia.* Mindless and dutiful—oh, yes, and exceedingly ladylike!''

''Nothing like you, that's for damn sure,'' he shot back.

Tears of furious rage suffocated her, closing her throat and making her voice raspy. ''Yes, me—a bastard born of a misalliance with the blood of Indians and African slaves flowing in my veins! You couldn't dream of giving the precious Velásquez name to any mongrel children of mine, could you?''

Lee stood riveted to the earth, unable to deny the truth of her painful accusations. Here she was, having made chaos of his life, now making him feel guilty! He forced himself to calm, lest he say even more hurtful things to her, then shrugged carelessly. ''It really doesn't signify whether or not I'd consider you a fit mother for my children, since we don't intend to have a real marriage. You don't love me and I don't love you. We just have to make the best of this disaster for the next year or so.''

Melanie turned over in her mind what he had said. *Forget the pain—you've always lived with it. It'll never change. You are who you are, and you don't need any man.* ''All right,'' she began in a low, rational voice, ''we'll get married in name only. After things settle down'' *and my parents go back to Renacimiento*, she thought with a stab of desperation, ''I'll go to Galveston and get the annulment. Maybe Clarence knows an editor there who'd hire a good reporter.''

''What's wrong with Boston? You've got a grandfather there and all sorts of crusades to join,'' he said, guilty once more over the image of a tiny woman alone in a rough port city.

''Texas is my home too, Lee. My parents and brothers and sister are all here,'' she replied, angry again.

''Be grateful they're alive, Melanie,'' he said softly, looking out across the fields with a shuttered expression on his face.

She felt an unexpected surge of pain for his losses. *That will always be between us, won't it, Lee?* Forcing her thoughts to more practical considerations, she said, ''Let's bury the past and think of the future. We'd better settle how this so-called marriage is going to work. I'm not your household ornament and bed warmer. I'll want other more useful things to do."

"Such as?" He quirked one brow, knowing what she was leading up to.

"I intend to keep my job at the *Star*. It's not that far from Night Flower Ranch to San Antonio."

"Haven't you gotten in enough trouble—nearly got me, you, Pemberton and that poor old printer all killed with your escapades? Moses French is dead, Melanie," he finished on a note of flat finality.

"Moses French may be, but I will still do my society news and gossip columns," she shot back angrily. "And I'll continue to help out at Father Gus's school, too." Her gold eyes flashed, daring him to refuse.

He shrugged with seeming indifference, realizing how impossible a hoyden she'd always be. "Do your good deeds and write about teas and dances. But as long as I'm responsible for you, I'd better never catch you risking that pretty little ass again!" His black eyes glittered, daring her to refuse.

After a long, hard look at her proudly set jawline and rigid stance, he turned sharply on his heel and stalked back toward the boardinghouse, saying only, "I'll see you in church."

Melanie stood watching him until he had vanished from sight. Then she finally released the tears held in check for so long. *Anger, pure venomous anger, that's all it is,* she told herself as the silvery droplets deluged her cheeks. She clung to the tree trunk and slid down its scratchy surface to huddle forlornly against its base, sobbing brokenly, damning Lee Velásquez with every ragged breath.

In the years since his ordination, Father Gus had performed numerous marriages, but he would never forget this one. The bride was wooden and subdued, ushered into church by

her parents and younger siblings. Adam, a tall replica of his
darkly dangerous-looking father, was as impassive as his
parents, seeming to understand that all was not well with his
sister's hastily arranged private marriage. Caleb and Lenore
were boisterous, happy children behaving with their best
"church manners" while the baby Joey slept peacefully in
his mother's arms. The priest made a mental note to speak
to her in a few days about the child's baptism. For now he
would not press the issue, for Mrs. Fleming looked sad as
she attempted to soothe her unhappy stepdaughter.

Rafe Fleming seemed protective of his daughter but
sternly forbidding, as if he and she had exchanged sharp
words earlier, doubtless about the necessity of the marriage.
Father Gus smiled. Melanie was a willful daughter. Small
wonder Rafe looked so grim.

But Fleming's mien was mild compared to Lee's fierce
scowl yesterday when he'd come to make his confession and
seek guidance. What guidance could the priest give? The
wronged girl's father and Jim Slade had discussed the
matter with him the preceding night—rather forcefully.
After his careful interrogation of Lee the following morning,
he concluded that their insistence on the marriage was
justified. Lee had acted abominably toward the girl and
exposed her in a shameful scene in front of a large group of
men.

Watching Melanie's nervous glances toward the back of
the church, he said in his most reassuring voice, "Never
fear, daughter, soon he will be here."

"That's what I am afraid of," she replied tartly before
receiving a quelling look from her father.

Melanie reached down and smoothed her silk gown in
agitation. *What a lovely picture she makes*, Father Gus
thought to himself, so different from that drably dressed girl
he had met his first day in San Antonio. Now she was a
vision in pale green silk. The gown was plainly cut with a
high neckline and long sleeves, but its very severity emphasized her delicate features and dramatic coloring. Had Lee
Velásquez been responsible for this transformation?

Just then Lee's footfalls echoed down the aisle of the

quiet church. He was accompanied by the Slades and their noisy brood, much more at ease in the familiar church they attended every Sunday than were the Fleming children. Perhaps Jim and Charlee looked more positively on the forced marriage than the Flemings did, he mused.

The towering hulk of Wash Oakley and his Amazonian wife completed the small company here to witness the private marriage ceremony. Being of fundamentalist religious background, they were obviously uncomfortable with the ornate grandeur of the vaulted-roofed San Fernando. Still, when Lee walked over to stand beside Melanie, the priest was sure he saw Wash and Obedience exchange a wink and a grin. If only the bride and groom were as pleased as their friends!

Lee reached out his hand, palm up, offering to take Melanie's hand. She responded woodenly, visually prodded by her father to do so. Lee's slim dark hand enveloped her tiny pale one, and they knelt before the altar.

Father Gus carefully went through the preliminary explanations about the permanence and sanctity of the sacrament of marriage.

Then in a strong voice, struggling to overcome his thick German accent, the priest read, "If anyone can show just cause why this man and woman may not be joined together, I exhort him to make known such objections or forever hold his peace."

Silence. Breathing a sigh of relief in spite of himself, he began the ceremony. When the time came for Lee to place the ring on her hand, Jim Slade stepped forward and handed it to the bridegroom. Lee hesitated for a moment, his eyes flashing in amazement back to his friend's. He recognized the antique gold band set with rubies and had not expected it to be the ring he would place on Melanie's hand.

The priest cleared his throat, waiting patiently for Lee to continue. Finally, reluctantly, he slid the ring on her finger and repeated the words. Father Gus could see Melanie's wide golden eyes staring up at her groom, confused and angered by his last-minute hesitation.

As he pronounced the final benediction after the mass,

Father Gus couldn't help but sigh with relief, thanking the Heavenly Father that the church was still standing. Already he anticipated a great many hours on his knees, praying for the success of this most unlikely union.

"I should have told him first," Jim said to Charlee as they stood on the church steps watching Lee lift his tiny bride into the carriage for their ride to Night Flower Ranch.

"If you had told him, he would have refused to give it to her and you know it," Charlee said emphatically. "It was his mother's ring, and it should belong to Melanie now."

"When you found it in that attic trunk of Pa's, I should have given it to him for Dulcia," Jim replied uneasily.

"I was saving it for someone special," Charlee said with a gamin grin. "Don't worry, no matter how much he fumes now, he'll come around."

Jim grunted. "Melanie didn't look any happier than Lee. I only hope she comes around, too."

Chapter 13

They rode in strained silence for several minutes, as they left the whispering cypress trees and stout adobe buildings of San Antonio behind on their journey to Night Flower. Thinking of the months to come living in his house, Melanie nervously twisted the ornate old ring back and forth on her finger. Finally she worked up her courage to speak. "Why did you hesitate—about the ring, I mean?"

At first she didn't think he'd reply. His profile remained impassive as he stared straight ahead. Then he sighed and said quietly, "It was my mother's ring. I hadn't seen it since Will Slade pulled me off her body that day. . . . I was seven years old then, but I still remember the ring. It's been in our family for generations. I guess old Will kept it hidden somewhere, and Jim and Charlee only recently found it.''

Melanie nodded mutely. *You would have given it to Larena but not to me.* She fought back the hated tears.

Lee could sense her mute misery. Guilt and anger tore at him as he gazed surreptitiously at her bowed head. *Damn, if only you weren't so beautiful, so desirable.* He forced his thoughts away from that dangerous consideration.

''Can you cook?'' he asked abruptly, wanting to change the subject.

''No,'' she answered frostily.

''I didn't think so,'' he replied glumly. ''Well, you'll just have to get used to Kai, then.''

''Kai?'' she questioned, looking up at him.

''Molokai—shortened to Kai by the hands. He's Kanaka— from the Sandwich Islands in the Pacific.''

''I know where they are located. I studied geography,'' she interjected with asperity.

He slapped the reins lightly and groused, ''Never learned to cook but you studied geography. It figures.''

''How did a Kanaka,'' she stumbled over the foreign word, ''get halfway around the world to Texas?''

''He escaped from Molokai as a kid. It was a leper's colony then.'' At her look of horror, he said quickly, ''He's not contaminated—that was over thirty years ago. He signed on a whaler and ended up in Mazatlán. That's a city—''

''On the northwestern coast of Mexico,'' she finished impatiently.

Smiling in spite of himself, he continued, ''Well, anyway, I met him through Raoul Fouqué, a, er, business associate in Santa Fe. We three rode together for a few years. He's six foot seven and very good with knives,'' he warned her.

''Can *he* cook?'' she asked, undaunted.

''Yep. That's why I hired him. He hated life in the Apachería. Funny, he's really a gentle giant once you get past his intimidating face and size. He showed up at the ranch a few months ago, not long after I'd begun to rebuild.''

"What's it like, the new house? All I saw that day were the burned-out ruins of the old place." She was curious about her new home, even if it was to be only a temporary one.

For the first time she felt him warm to a subject. "It's more beautiful than either of the first two houses. I had money to buy the best materials this time. I built it on the pattern of a traditional Mexican *estancia* with a central courtyard and a fountain. It's set alongside an underground stream that bubbles to the surface for several hundred yards and twists its way through a lush shallow canyon. The interior isn't quite finished yet. I expect it could use a woman's touch. You can select any furnishings you want—that is, if you want to bother." He looked over at her, his expression once more guarded.

"I—I'd like that very much, Lee," she answered, surprising herself with the answer. Then, remembering how lovingly her father had built Renacimiento for her mother, filling it with all Deborah's belongings, her heart ached. *He built Night Flower for Larena, you fool, not you!* They lapsed into silence for the rest of the ride.

Suddenly Lee pulled the horses up and pointed to the valley floor below. There, nestled between a twisting creek and a copse of cypress trees, sat a lovely house of whitewashed adobe, sparkling pristinely in the afternoon sunlight. The low, thick walls shaded by trees would keep it cool on the hottest days.

"What a beautiful setting," Melanie said, taking in the gently sloping trail to the canyon floor, carefully graded to allow wagon and carriage traffic.

"I didn't want to build on the old ruins a second time," Lee explained as he urged the horses on. "Too many memories, I guess. Anyway, I've loved this place ever since I was a boy. When I first came home, I camped where you found me by the ruins. One evening I couldn't sleep." He paused, recalling his nightmares. When she looked questioningly at him, he continued, "I rode here. It was as if I were drawn irresistibly. I was trying to decide whether or not to stay and start over. That's when I found them."

"Them?" she asked softly, oddly pleased for him to explain this much to her.

"The evening primroses. They grow along the edge of the stream by the canyon wall."

"Night Flower? You named the ranch for them," she said in sudden understanding.

"I thought of it as sort of an omen, I guess. Fouqué would say I spent too much time with Indians," he added, scoffing, abruptly breaking the mood of closeness between them.

When they arrived at the house, an enormous man, even bigger than Wash Oakley, stood outside the front entrance, apparently awaiting them. His dark mahogany skin was scarred and his expression forbidding.

"That's Kai?" Melanie asked, suppressing a tremor of uneasiness.

Lee gave a low chuckle. "I told you, he's really a lamb." The young rancher called out a greeting in an unfamiliar melodic tongue.

The big man replied in the same language and then reached up to help Melanie from the carriage, a smile now creasing his face. Several front teeth were missing, but despite that and his fearsome scars, Melanie sensed his instinctive kindness. "Hello, Mr. Molokai," she said politely.

"Welcome to your new home, *Señora* Velásquez," he replied in English that was oddly accented with Spanish. "Please call me Kai. Everyone does."

"Only if you call me Melanie." She smiled at the giant and he was won over. "I understand from—my husband," she almost stumbled on the words, "that you are a very good cook. Perhaps you can teach me?"

"It would be an honor, Melanie." He went around to the rear of the carriage and began to lift her trunks as if they weighed nothing.

Lee stood beside her, watching her charm Kai, feeling surprised at her easy camaraderie with the Kanaka. Larena had been terrified of him. "Let's go inside and I'll show you the house," he said, taking her arm with surprising possessiveness.

The interior of the house was as lovely as the outside promised, with spacious, airy rooms and an enchanting central courtyard. Lee ushered her across the wide front *sala* and out onto the patio. "It's beautiful," she exclaimed, looking from the sparkling water tumbling down into the shallow limestone pool to the scattered pots filled with miniature orange trees, fig trees, and other flowering shrubs, many so exotic she'd never seen their like.

"I had the patio plants brought up from Mexico City. My Uncle Alfonso was an amateur botanist of sorts," he said. "I'll show you the rest of the house if you like."

The rooms were indeed sparsely furnished, with only a few massive oak pieces in most. The white walls and dark stained furniture made a dramatic contrast, crying out for brightly colored rugs and wall hangings to accompany them. "I saw a bright orange and yellow rug at Frascatti's Emporium last week that would be perfect for the *sala*," Melanie said impulsively after they had briefly inspected the dining room, library, and smaller sitting room off the *sala*. "That is, if you would like those colors," she amended quickly, remembering that this was meant to be Larena's house.

"As I said, it's not finished and needs a woman's touch. One of the hands can take you to town tomorrow and you can buy whatever you want." His expression was shuttered and Melanie felt her enthusiasm wane.

Tomorrow I must go to the Star office and explain to Clarence, she thought with a shudder of dread, imagining his scathing reaction. She said nothing aloud to Lee.

"If you want to freshen up before dinner, I'll show you your room," Lee said stiffly, not bringing up their agreement, yet reminding her of it subtly.

When they turned down the other wing of the house, where the bedrooms were located, Kai was in the process of setting the last of her trunks in a large bedroom at the head of the hallway, obviously the master suite where Lee slept. The bed was large, made up with a bright blue spread. The masculine room was furnished with a tall oaken armoire and a wide library table spread with papers and books. A gun belt was slung carelessly over one chair and the makings for cigarillos lay spilled on the table. Several butts had been crushed out in a heavy brass ashtray. *As if he spent a sleepless night here last night*, Melanie thought immediately. Before she could frame anything to say, Lee interrupted with a command.

"The *señora* will not be using this room, Kai. Put her things in the room at the end of the hall, next to Genia's."

The Kanaka's face was impassive, but Melanie knew he was wondering about the sleeping arrangements. Obviously he had been under the mistaken impression this was a real marriage, she thought in humiliation. "Are you sure you'll be safe with only three rooms between us?" she muttered when Kai had taken the first trunk down the big hallway.

"Are you sure *you'll* be?" he countered darkly.

"Who is Genia?" she asked quickly, changing the subject.

"The housekeeper. She came from Mexico City. She worked for my Uncle Alfonso until he died. When I finished this house, I sent for her. She's probably out in the garden, selecting some herbs to sweeten our bridal bed," he added sarcastically.

"How shortsighted of you not to have explained the nature of our arrangement," she replied stiffly, affronted at his temerity.

"I did, but Kai and Genia believe what they want to believe."

Genia was a plump, smiling woman of indeterminate years with a heavy Spanish accent. Lee was right about both his house servants' attitudes. He had married Melanie in church; therefore, the match was sealed, and she was mistress of the ranch.

As they chatted in Spanish while Genia unpacked her clothes, the housekeeper said bluntly, "I do not like your being so far from *Don* Leandro's room. At least you should be in the adjoining one."

Melanie colored in mortification. "Genia, Lee must have told you we were forced into this marriage. It isn't—that is, we aren't going to . . . sleep together."

"And the sun will not rise in the east," the older woman scoffed in disbelief. "You are both young and fine-looking.

Put a match to kindling and watch sparks fly! You both have
passion. I can tell,'' she said, chuckling at Melanie's horrified expression. ''Sooner or later it will happen. Not even
three walls between you can stop what is meant to be.''

You both have passion. The old housekeeper's words
haunted Melanie as she lay staring at the ceiling in her big
lonely bed that night. How true that was! If not for his fierce
lust and her inexplicable response to his kisses, they would
not be trapped in this travesty of a marriage. Painfully she
reviewed her relationship with Lee Velásquez. Ever since
her first encounter with him as an impressionable and
frightened twelve-year-old girl, she realized, there had always been an attraction. The chance encounter in Austin
just after his first marriage had devastated her. There, she
had finally admitted it to herself, aware it was after that
meeting that she had first begun to rebel against being
female. Boston only gave her a rhetorical vocabulary with
which to rationalize her feelings.

Tears again. They slipped from her eyes and ran down her
temples, soaking into her thick ebony hair. ''Damn him for
making me cry,'' she gritted aloud in the silence of the
night. *Damn him for making you want him*, the night
whispered back.

Lee could not sleep either. Visions of his wife's soft,
golden body and gleaming ebony hair haunted him. He
could still feel her breasts and hips, so generous for a
woman with such a tiny frame. He remembered the smell of
her, like wild roses. Her wide eyes were the color of the
night flowers blooming outside his bedroom window. Rolling over in anguished frustration, he scoffed at himself,
''You named your home after her, you fool, and you didn't
even know it!''

Passionate little bitch, he thought angrily, *no doubt just
like her octoroon mother*. All the fancy schools in Boston
and the airs Rafe Fleming led her to put on couldn't disguise
the fact she was a *placée*'s daughter. She exuded an innate
sensuality that drove men to act irrationally. *And you, you*

dumb bastard, want her—just like Fleming wanted her
mother—as a mistress, not as a wife!

But Lee knew he could not take her now, not while they
were married. That would shackle them together for the rest
of their lives. He desired her, but he knew her accusations
that day in the orchard were true. He did not want children
of mixed blood carrying the Velásquez name. He wanted a
woman with a fine old Hispanic name, someone traditional,
dutiful, decidedly not like Melanie. Even if she hadn't been
an octoroon's bastard with hated Indian blood in her veins,
she was still headstrong and spoiled, filled with all sorts of
crazy ideas about women being equal to men! Of course,
raised by Deborah and hanging around Charlee and Obedience, that was scarcely a surprise. He stared at the ceiling
and forced himself to think of Larena. Somehow he would
win her back.

Melanie awakened in the strange bed, hearing familiar
noises outside her window. The cowhands were down at the
corral saddling up. She could hear muffled curses and
shouted greetings echoing across the valley floor. Dim gray
light filtered in the window. Sweeping the covers from her
body, she sat up and looked around the room. Like all the
others, it had roughly plastered whitewashed walls and was
innocent of furnishings except for the bed in which she slept
and one heavy, low chest. Genia had unpacked her combs
and brushes and had set up her dressing mirror. A white
porcelain pitcher and bowl sat alongside her things on top of
the chest. At least she could wash her face and perform a
simple toilette. The stone floor was chilly to her bare feet as
she stood up and stretched. It was rainy and gray outside,
weather that reflected her feelings on the first morning of
her married life.

Although she dreaded it, Melanie knew she must go to
town and face Clarence. Of course, with all the gossip, the
shrewd old editor would know all the humiliating details
about her face-saving marriage. "If only I can convince him
to keep me on," she murmured under her breath. Then,
remembering the story about the rustlers who killed Jameston's
men and stole his cattle, Melanie knew what she would do.

Rummaging frantically through her book trunk, she came up with pencils and note pad. Sitting cross-legged on the bed, she began to write.

Feeling refreshed and self-assured, Melanie walked down the long hall toward the heavenly smells emanating from the kitchen. Dinner last night, for all the strained tension between her and Lee, had been superb. "At least I won't starve to death on his accursed ranch," she muttered as she inhaled the fragrance of coffee and fresh-baked bread.

She hesitated on the threshold of the kitchen, half afraid Lee might be there, scowling at his late-rising wife. *Wife.* She was married to a hostile stranger who wanted no part of her. His feelings had been abundantly clear last night at the supper table when all Genia and Kai's efforts to make the bridal meal festive and special had met with irritation and impatience on his part. He had eaten perfunctorily and quickly, then had excused himself to go outside and smoke a cigar.

Little hoping his mood had improved with a night's sleep, Melanie had dallied until she was certain he had left the house. She did not relish a fight over her ride to town this morning. It would be just like him to renege on the bargain struck that day in the orchard and forbid her to work at the *Star* in any capacity. *Of course*, a voice niggled at her conscience, *you're reneging on the bargain*. She would not only file Moses French's story about the rustling and murders, but continue to pursue leads to uncover who was working with Lucas Blaine.

Taking a deep breath to bolster her courage, Melanie opened the door to the *Star* office and stepped inside with a jauntiness she did not feel.

Clarence scarcely looked up from behind the cluttered barricade of his desk to acknowledge her. Without skipping a pen stroke, he continued writing and spoke at the same time. "Are we to assume the honeymoon is over so soon?"

"As I'm sure you've deduced from the circumstances of

our marriage, there *was* no honeymoon,'' she shot back, heading for the small table in the corner that doubled as her desk. ''I have the story about a herd of cattle being stolen and the murder of two hands—renegade Comanche did it.''

''Old news,'' he replied. The pen continued its scratching.

''I have a new angle—Lucas Blaine.'' She waited. The pen stopped scratching.

Clarence's white brows arched sardonically and his eyelids drooped. ''Pray continue.''

''One of my Indian children followed Blaine and overheard him discuss the theft with Seth Walkman. The Indian trader and our illustrious ranger captain are thieves and murderers,'' she stated baldly.

''I assume you can prove this sweeping assertion—that is, other than by the testimony of red urchins from Father Schreckenberg's school? I scarcely think the citizenry would find an Indian a credible witness against such illustrious pillars of the community as Blaine and Walkman,'' he said in a voice laced with irony.

''Well, not yet, but—''

''I thought not.''

''I *will* find proof. In the meanwhile, here's the story about the raid. There are no accusations against Blaine in it, but Moses French was an eyewitness to the theft. I'll get you the rest of the story!''

''And what will your husband say when you go chasing about the countryside, following charming characters like Walkman?'' Clarence leaned back in his chair and regarded Melanie's agitation with a distressingly fatherly air.

''Lee and I have an agreement. I'll continue to work for the *Star*,'' she replied with bravado, trying to convince herself as much as the cynical old man sitting in front of her.

''Well, all things considered, I'm glad 'true love' hasn't left you soft and dewey-eyed,'' he said, reverting to character and once more lowering his head to the pages he was editing.

Melanie swished briskly by him with her copy and

headed to the case boxes. "Where's Amos?" she asked as she began the laborious task of setting her story.

"Said something about going out to purchase you a wedding present," he answered with feigned absentness, ignoring the wad of paper she threw squarely between his shoulder blades.

Amos returned a scant fifteen minutes later, laden with a wooden crate from Cincinnati filled with bottles of ink. Seeing Melanie at work at his compositor's table, his eyes almost popped from their sockets. "Miss Melanie—I mean Mrs. Velásquez, what're you doing here?"

She looked up at his incredulous face and nonchalantly brushed a curly wisp of hair from her eyes with ink-stained fingertips that left a dark smudge across her cheek. "I happen to work here, Amos, and don't start calling me Mrs. Velásquez. I'm still Melanie."

The old man shrugged and placed the crate on the floor. Having heard the same gossip as Clarence, he was aware of the rather unusual and hurried circumstances of Lee and Melanie's marriage. Quickly he went to work alongside her, as if nothing was at all amiss in a woman spending the day after her wedding working in a newspaper office.

After a couple of hours, the front door opened and a tall young man entered. Flashing a wide, disarming grin, Adam Fleming introduced himself to Clarence and Amos. "I figured you'd be here, sis, and I wanted to talk to you, away from Papa's eagle eyes."

As he turned to Clarence, Melanie was once again struck by his uncanny resemblance to their father. She wondered what he was up to and feared she knew the answer. When Clarence briskly told Adam to get her out of Amos's hair so he could finish setting type for her story, the youth immediately offered to buy her lunch.

As they strolled down the street, garnering more than a few curious stares, Melanie said uneasily, "Everyone is wondering what I'm doing in town so soon after my marriage. Taking up with a strange man, at that," she added, trying for a teasing note.

"Anyone looking at us could scarcely miss the family

resemblance, Mellie, but they do have good reason to wonder about why you're here instead of being with your husband." Adam's black eyes had the same eerie, penetrating power as their father's.

Melanie suggested a nearby cafe run by a Mexican couple who served adequate meals for those with little money. It was dark and quiet inside, a good place to talk in privacy. In passable border Spanish, Adam ordered their lunch and then turned to his sister.

When they had first met ten years ago, he had been a jealous boy of six, she a frightened and spoiled girl of twelve. Distrust and rivalry had gradually changed over the years into a genuine companionship few siblings shared.

"We never had a chance to talk before you married him, sis. When I found you in the *Star* office, I knew my guess was right. You only went through with the wedding because he and Papa made you. Is—is he treating you all right, Mellie?"

Melanie stared into his dear face, so full of love and concern. Of course, it if weren't for all her family's love and concern, she could have refused this marriage, and Lee Velásquez be damned! "I can take care of myself, Adam, as you can plainly see," she replied waspishly. Then, realizing it wasn't his fault she was in this mess, she quickly amended, "Oh, Adam, I'm sorry. I know you only want to help, but there's nothing anyone can do. We've reached an agreement. He lives his life and I live mine. I'll keep working at the *Star* and he'll run his ranch." She tried for a bright smile, but it wobbled.

"You don't really have a marriage, do you, Mellie?" he asked earnestly. "Papa wanted you to marry him so you'd settle down and have children. Be happy like Mama and Charlee. I tried to tell him it wouldn't work with you." He sighed. "At least not this way, not with *him*."

Melanie felt her face flaming as she realized her brother had guessed at the sterile relationship she and Lee shared. With a start she remembered that their own father had been less than a year older than Adam when she was born! Why was it boys were given the facts of life and turned loose so

early while girls were sheltered and deceived? It just wasn't
fair, dammit!

Adam watched her mute misery for a moment, then
reached across the table and took her cold little hand.
"Mellie, I'm the one who should be sorry for butting in, but
I just wanted you to know, if you ever need help—if he ever
does anything to hurt you—"

"No, Adam." She shook her head, interrupting him.
"Thank you, dear, for your offer, but Lee and I will settle
this between ourselves." She had to smile at the way he
refused to mention Lee by name.

"How can you settle it if you go on like you're not
married? Say, you're not planning . . ." He hesitated, uncertain of how to broach such a delicate topic, even with his
beloved sister. "That is, he hasn't offered to get the marriage annulled?"

"I never could keep secrets from you, could I?" she
replied with a soft, sad little laugh. "Please don't tell
anyone, Adam. I know why Papa and Mama wanted this
marriage, and it would break their hearts to know what
we're going to do."

Adam watched her fidget with her cup and spoon, stirring
the thick cream into the coffee until the liquid was too cool
to taste good anymore. "I remember back in Austin, at the
statehood celebration, when you and Lee," he forced himself to use his brother-in-law's name, "when you two
collided and you acted kinda funny all day afterward.
Mellie, you aren't in love with the man after all, are you?"

The spoon clattered against the side of her cup. "Of
course not! Don't be absurd! He was an arrogant bully full
of Mexican machismo even then." She could not meet
Adam's eyes. Wanting to change the subject, she looked
outside the open door to the busy street. "Looks like we
have another ranger in town to add to Seth Walkman's
wonder brigade," she said disdainfully.

Adam followed her narrowed gaze to the big man filling
the door. He had shaggy tan hair, long sideburns, and a
narrow mustache, and he wore buckskins and a yellow
neckerchief, a uniform of sorts often affected by the irregularly

attired militiamen. But it was his carefully oiled .44 caliber Walker Colt that most clearly marked him as a ranger.

Adam's face split in a wide grin. "That's Jeremy. I met him at the boardinghouse yesterday." Quickly he hailed the stranger who sauntered over to their table. "Jeremy, this is my sister, er, my older sister, Melanie. Mellie, meet Jeremy Lawrence, a friend of Jim Slade."

Lawrence was a man in his mid-twenties with keen blue eyes and a dazzling smile that fairly lit up his angularly handsome face. "Pleased to meet you, Miss Fleming," he said politely with the faintest hint of a Virginia drawl.

"My name's Velásquez now," she replied stiffly, hating the way her voice betrayed her. "I was recently married."

"Yesterday morning," Adam put in unhelpfully.

"Congratulations, ma'am," he responded politely.

Giving her brother a quelling look, Melanie ignored the look of puzzled interest that flashed across the ranger's face and inquired, "You're a friend of Jim's? I've never seen you here or heard him or Charlee mention you. Are you from far away?"

"Fact is, ma'am, I just met Jim Slade the other day. We have mutual friends," he said vaguely, seeming to want to change the subject.

"Like Sam Houston," Adam stated baldly. Then at Jeremy's sharp look of curiosity, he added quickly, "I overheard you and the senator late last night out by the ice shed. I—er, that is"—he cast a nervous glance at his sister—"I know this girl who works for Obedience and I had just walked her home. I was returning by way of the back orchard when you two were discussing your new boss, Captain Walkman."

Lawrence's face took on a shuttered look and he muttered an oath under his breath, then quickly apologized to Melanie. Grabbing a chair, he sat down and leaned forward, speaking intently in a low voice. "Look, what Houston and I were discussing is dangerous for you to know. I want your word it'll go no further than this table. My life could depend on it—and yours, too."

Adam gulped in surprise, but Melanie's gold eyes took on

a catlike gleam and she whispered, "This little assignment that brought you from the capital to San Antonio wouldn't have anything to do with a polecat named Lucas Blaine, would it? He and that scum Walkman are thick as thieves. They *are* thieves, in fact." At the ranger's look of amazement, Melanie quickly told him about the story that would appear in that day's edition of the *Star*.

"You mean *you* rode out after a band of renegades and got involved in those killings?" He couldn't keep the incredulity from his voice. "You could've been shot or worse!"

"Those possibilities have been pointed out to me," she said darkly. Glancing over at her brother's wide-eyed stare and not wanting to chance his divulging any of her professional secrets to their parents, Melanie said sweetly, "Adam, didn't you say you and Papa were supposed to go look at some breeding stock out on Bluebonnet this afternoon?"

Adam Fleming knew the pugnacious set of his sister's little chin. Sighing, he stood up. "Yep, I did and I am late. You just be careful, both of you." Uneasily he nodded and signaled Serefin, the owner of the place. When the old man had taken his money for the meal, Adam headed back toward the boardinghouse with grave misgivings. Mellie never had answered his question about Lee Velásquez. At times like this, he almost felt sorry for the poor bastard!

Once free of Adam's youthful curiosity, Melanie quickly explained to the ranger about Moses French and her article for the *Star*, outlining her contacts with the Indian children. "So you see, I think we can work together, Mr. Lawrence. You want to nail a crooked ranger and stop the whiskey and gun traffic to the renegades, and I want the story. Of course, I won't print anything until you have all the facts and make the arrests," she added hastily, sensing he was about to refuse.

"I don't know, Mrs. Velásquez. This isn't a game. These men are very dangerous," he said measuringly.

"So were the men with Walkman that day they massacred a whole village of Comanche up on the fork of the Guadelupe," she said quietly.

"Moses French was there, too, I take it," he replied, whistling low in amazement. "You are one incredible woman, Melanie Velásquez. Just what does your husband think of all your adventures?"

"That they're over," came the terse reply from behind them. Melanie let out a gasp and whirled to face Lee's set features. "Come on, wife, we're going home," he commanded while his black eyes bored into Lawrence's blue ones.

Jeremy stood up across the table. Although not quite as tall as Lee, he was heavier with thickset bones and tightly knit muscles. "I take it you're Lee Velásquez," he said gravely, sensing the undercurrent of hostility between husband and wife. He did not offer a handshake to Lee, instinctively sensing the *Tejano* would refuse it.

"Clarence said you'd likely be here, Melanie, but you were supposedly with Adam." Lee hated the jealous tone in his voice.

Refusing to justify her perfectly innocent actions to the tyrant looming over her, Melanie replied oversweetly, "Adam had to go. Jeremy and I were discussing some *Star* business. Whatever are you doing in town? I thought you had a ranch to run."

"I do and I need to get back to work—that is, as soon as I see my wife safely home. Clarence assured me he and Amos can put the paper to bed without your help," he added sarcastically. His fingers bit cruelly into her arm as he virtually dragged her from her chair.

"I'd hate for you to get the wrong impression, Velásquez," Jeremy said very softly. "Mrs. Velásquez and I were only discussing my arrival in San Antonio so she could mention it in the social news."

"Sometimes my wife works too hard on the *social* scene in this city. Right now she's needed at Night Flower," Lee replied as his obsidian eyes dared the big ranger to cross him.

Suddenly Melanie realized she was standing between two armed men, both with quick tempers. Violence hung suspended in the air. *Very dangerous.* Jeremy's words about the renegades came back to her. All Texian men, on either side of the law, were dangerous. "Calm down, Lee. Mr. Lawrence is a peace officer, not a border ruffian." The minute the words escaped her lips she wanted to call them back. They were the very words she had used to describe Lee three days ago!

Lee flashed an evil, wolflike smile at the younger man. "Strange, I'd never thought of calling a *rinche* a peace officer—unless you consider there's peace when every *Tejano* in the country's dead and buried!"

Jeremy stiffened at the hated epithet *rinche*, used by *Tejanos* as the crudest insult to a ranger. "Because your lady's here, I'll let that pass, Velásquez. You're not the reason I'm in San Antonio, but I wouldn't get in the way of the law if I were you."

"I somehow suspect your law and mine don't exactly mesh, Lawrence. Go after your renegades, but leave my wife out of it." Lee's voice was low and steady as he measured the Texian, wondering if he'd try to start a fight. Feeling a primitive blood lust surge through his veins, he hoped the younger man would oblige him.

But Lawrence was under strict orders and knew he must obey them. Tipping his hat at Melanie, he said, "I don't involve women in violence, Velásquez. Take care of her." He walked slowly out the door.

Once he was gone, Melanie whirled on Lee like an enraged wildcat. "You wanted to kill him! You insulted him and goaded him like some cheap saloon brawler!" Seeing the gaze of several customers across the room traveling to the sound of her strident voice, Melanie subsided in humiliation.

Lee ignored the sprinkling of curious customers and replied heavily, "We agreed you could do your social and gossip news, Melanie, but don't play me for a fool. That ranger isn't social news. He's trouble. Remember, Moses French is dead." With that, he steered her toward the door, never relinquishing his iron grip on her arm.

They rode back to the ranch in silence. Melanie's mind whirled with all the possibilities working with Jeremy Lawrence could provide her. But she must keep Lee off guard and let him think he'd won. What if he locked her up at the ranch and kept such a close watch on her that Moses French couldn't operate? No, she must help Jeremy and he'd help her. Together they could see Walkman and Blaine in jail. What a story she would have then!

Chapter 14

You aren't in love with the man after all, are you? Adam's words echoed in her mind as she lay in her bed that night. Her initial excitement about working with Jeremy Lawrence had faded, and her desolation had grown as they neared the ranch. Lee had been angry and silent on the ride home, his limitless Hispanic vanity wounded because she was seen in a public place with a strange man the day after her wedding. Facing his brooding presence across the dinner table that night, she was reminded of the empty year ahead of her.

But if they were going to go their separate ways at year's end, she would be free to live out her life as she saw fit. Then why these bitter tears? Why the ache in her heart? *Have I grown to be such a fool as to hope, after all these years, that he'll love me? That I can have a real marriage?* Punching her pillow, she rolled over and tried to sleep, not liking the answer the night wind gave.

After the third sleepless night in a row, Lee knew he was dangerously close to losing his control. He had agreed to her insane scheme, allowing her to go to town and work at the *Star* after they were married. But when he had returned to the ranch for the midday meal the very day after their wedding, Kai had informed him she was in San Antonio!

She could not even wait a decent interval before returning to work.

Furiously angry, he had ridden Sangre hard to the *Star* office, only to be told by that supercilious old editor that she and her brother were lunching down the street. Prepared to lecture her on propriety, then ask her to accompany him to Frascatti's Emporium to select some furnishings for the house, he had found her engrossed in conversation with a strange man. A ranger! Not another woman alive would do such a reckless, unthinking thing. His wife with a ranger—a big, handsome Anglo with a southern accent. *Just the type to charm her fickle soul*, he thought angrily. He would be well rid of her at year's end.

Forcing himself to consider that, he went over his re-hearsed speech to Larena once again. He could not leave things as they were between them, with her thinking he had a true marriage with Melanie. If he could make her under-stand that he would be free at the end of the year, then perhaps she would forgive him and wait until he could offer marriage.

He refused to admit that seeing Melanie with Lawrence had triggered his decision to seek out Larena so soon. Originally he had planned to wait a month or two and allow things to cool down. But Melanie had dealt his pride a terrible blow, taking off without a by-your-leave when he had planned the afternoon as a sort of peace offering. The day before she'd seemed pleased with the idea of decorating the house and had even mentioned the dry-goods importer's warehouse. She could furnish the house or not; he didn't care anymore. He would doubtless want to have Larena redo it anyway—if she loved him enough to wait.

Realizing his tactical error in going to the Sandovals' house the first time, where her parents would prevent his seeing her, Lee decided on another strategy. He sent a note to her through her cousin Teresa, asking Larena to meet him in a secluded area behind San Fernando Church. She and her cousin went to confession every Wednesday afternoon at two o'clock. At two-thirty he dismounted from Sangre and tethered the big blue near a small park down the street from the church.

Numerous young ladies strolling in the park with their *dueñas* noticed the tall, handsome *caballero* who walked like a stalking panther. His chiseled face was arresting, enhanced rather than disfigured by the thin scars on his cheekbone and at his hairline. He ran his long, elegant fingers through curling black hair, pushing it off his high forehead. The tightly molded black suit with its fitted jacket and flared pant legs left little to the imagination. He was lean with rangy, hard muscles that projected an aura of grace and danger.

Noticing one very pretty, very young girl's brown eyes on him, he flashed her a wicked grin. She blushed but boldly returned his smile with an enticing wink before her *dueña* yanked her away toward San Fernando Church. The girl reminded him of Melanie when he had first met her. He swore under his breath. Would nothing get that damnable woman off his mind? His wife was no longer a high-spirited waif but a willful schemer who placed him in jeopardy every time he came near her. Come to think of it, she'd done that even when she was twelve years old!

Larena had spent a sleepless night after receiving Lee's message. Should she risk her reputation by answering the request in his note? Teresa had urged her to go to the tryst, but she was uncertain. He was a married man now, beyond her reach, and propriety forbade their having any further association. She knew his bride and admired Melanie Fleming, although the circumstances of the sudden marriage shocked her. Larena Sandoval was a sensible and cautious young woman. She gave the situation careful thought, then knew what she must do.

"He looks nervous," Teresa said to her cousin as they peered through the thick foliage of the garden behind the church.

"Well, he should be, seeking out his ex-fiancée within a week of his marriage," Larena said with a touch of impatience. Teresa saw everything through the rosy glow of hopeless romanticism.

"You seem a bit nervous yourself, cousin. Could it be you love him enough to break your own strict rules just for a kiss?" Teresa's eyes glowed.

"Wait here and see that no one catches us. All I need is for someone to find out what I've done and tell Mama." With that, she parted the leafy curtain and slipped quietly into the small bower.

Quiet as her tread was, Lee sensed her presence at once. He turned and doffed his flat-crowned black hat, smiling sadly at her but making no move to touch her. She looked every inch a lady, dressed in a cool pink silk gown with a matching rose silk parasol and slippers. Her black hair was neatly piled on top of her head beneath a rose bonnet tied with frilly ribbons. Larena was enchantment. "I'm most grateful you came, Larena. I feared you wouldn't."

"I wasn't going to, but I reconsidered," she said in a breathless voice.

"I owe you an explanation about what's happened, and my personal apology as well. Understandably, *Don* José didn't want me to talk with you." He paused, uncertain of how she was going to react to what he would say. "I guess you know my marriage was forced on me against my wishes. I went after Melanie to stop her from risking her life on one of her infernal crusading stories for Clarence Pemberton."

"She is a very remarkable woman, Leandro, to do a man's job so well. I admire her work for the *Star*," Larena said guilelessly, awaiting his reaction.

"She's a wild little fool who nearly got us both killed! She even pulled a gun on me. I guess that's when I saw red and lost my temper. I had to literally wrestle her to the ground and, well, I won't make excuses for myself or offend your sensibilities by describing the rest. It's enough to say that we were both guilty. When her father and Jim found us, they forced the marriage issue. She didn't want it any more than I did.

"Larena, nothing happened out there on that hillside and nothing's happened since. We have an agreement. It will be perfectly legal and moral for us to have the marriage annulled within a year. I want to marry you—that is, if you'll have the patience to wait for me and be willing to endure the scandal of marrying a man with such a reputation." His face was grave yet beguiling at the same time as he stretched out his hand and enveloped hers gently.

How could Melanie Fleming resist him? Blessed Virgin, I find it nearly impossible, and I'm not living under the same roof! Larena looked up into his face, framing her reply very carefully. "You said nothing happened out on that hillside, Leandro. Yet very obviously something did, else my cousin and your wife's father would not have felt so strongly about the matter."

"Larena, we exchanged a few kisses and—yes, I did have her blouse opened, but that's as far as things went," he said, hating the turn the discussion was taking. A gently reared lady like Larena would certainly be appalled by the animal passions that had flamed between him and Melanie.

She fixed her liquid brown eyes squarely on his face. "And if no one had interrupted you, would that have been 'as far as things went'?"

He dropped her hands and turned away to pace back and forth, making an anguished shrug. "I don't know. I honestly don't know. Larena, what goes on between a man and a woman like Melanie isn't anything a lady like you should know about."

She arched one delicate black brow. "Really? You make it sound as if she were one of the residents of those houses on Soledad Street. All this time I've heard she comes from a good family and was university educated in Boston."

Lee felt himself trapped. He couldn't give out the secret of Melanie's birth and upbringing prior to her coming to Texas. How to make Larena understand? "Yes, she's educated—too educated, filled with nonsense about women's suffrage. That's why she refused to quit working even after we were married."

"But I assumed she kept her job precisely because this wasn't a real marriage," Larena interjected, feigning bewilderment.

"She'd keep her job if she were eight months pregnant,"

he blurted out. Then, mortified at making such an indelicate statement in front of a maiden, he began to apologize.

Larena smiled shyly and waved off his attempts to speak, saying, "Your friend Charlee Slade, as I recall, used to ride astride to town when she was quite obviously with child. It seems to me that you and Cousin Jim have always admired her."

"Charlee's . . . Charlee," he replied weakly. "Jim should control her more. I've always told him that."

"Yet you do see how well-suited they are, don't you?" she asked earnestly.

"Yes," he admitted grudgingly. "Larena, what are you trying to tell me?" Now it was his turn to stare into her eyes, demanding a straight answer. "Don't you want to wait for me? Won't you marry me if I get an annulment?"

"I don't think an annulment would be a wise idea—or perhaps even possible in another year," she replied carefully, her heart still a bit tender, rebelling over what she was about to say.

He lifted one arched brow sardonically now. "Perhaps you'd care to explain that?"

"You're being obtuse, Leandro, and that's not like you," Larena said impatiently. "There's something between you and Melanie—some very strong attraction that neither of you can deny. The incident on the hillside certainly proves that! But it's more than just a physical attraction, I think. She's bold and bright, educated and outspoken. She's seen the world, Leandro—the whole world outside my small one here in San Antonio. So have you."

"Yes, I've seen it, but there's much I didn't like about it," he replied darkly.

"Still, for all you've endured, you've survived, Leandro, and so has your wife. She can match your fire and your intellect. I—I could do neither. You'd grow bored with me and I . . . I fear I'd grow frightened of your passions and ambitions." She faced him squarely, trying to hide her pain beneath a facade of reasonableness.

"Tell me you don't love me, Larena," he commanded softly.

"Tell me you feel no passion for your wife," she countered.

On the long ride home Lee mulled over Larena's words. The things Charlee had said to him returned to haunt him, as well. He reassured himself Larena and Dulcia were not alike. Certainly he did not relish a return to the childish pouting and frigid timidity Dulcia had exhibited during the brief course of their marriage. But they had both been so young then, he excused. Larena would never shrink from him—or bore him. And he *knew* he didn't want a wife who challenged his every male prerogative the way Melanie surely would. Let Jim Slade and Rafe Fleming put up with that insanity!

"No, I want a woman who knows her place—gracious, genteel, patient, and loving, someone to raise my children and make a home for us—not some hoyden in riding skirts out chasing renegades!" He shouted the words to Sangre, kicking the stallion into a gallop for the ranch.

Melanie had not seen Lee leave that morning and assumed he had gone to work stock with his men. She had ridden to the *Star* office, worked on her society column, stopped by to visit Father Gus's children and get a report from Lame Deer, then headed back to Night Flower early, wanting to bathe and change before Lee arrived home. She wanted to leave him in doubt as to whether or not she'd even left the ranch. Let him ask her for an itinerary, if he dared!

On the way home the skies opened up in a sudden fall shower. It was a mud-spattered, bedraggled *Señora* Velásquez who trudged into Kai's spotless kitchen late that afternoon, requesting a bath. He cheerfully put water on to warm and sent Manuel, their young houseboy, to haul it to her room when it was hot.

Stripping off her sodden clothes, Melanie hummed softly as she pinned the waist-length coil of night-black hair up on top of her head in a haphazard knot. With rain-curled tendrils falling free of the pins, she looked like a pixie, young and vulnerable. For several moments she stood poised in front of her mirror, surveying herself from the crown of her head down to her toes and back up. Gingerly she ran her hands over her cool skin, still damp from the long rainy ride. She seemed pale golden in the flickering candlelight, her satiny skin in contrast to the gleaming jet of the hair on her head and at the juncture of her thighs. Melanie inspected critically. She was short, a scant five feet, with fine bones, but her body was curvy and lush. She hefted her breasts, which were full, like ripe melons. Despite their heaviness they stood proudly upthrust. Her hips flared out from a minuscule waist and her legs were delicately tapered with slim ankles. *I am pleasing to look at*, she said to herself, trying to convince herself it was all right to possess feminine allure. She examined her face, which was younger looking in the mirror's dimly reflected light. She could see resemblances of her beloved papa in the aristocratically formed brows and nose, the firm chin. Yet the slanted cat-gold eyes that stared back at her and the high Cherokee cheekbones were pure Duval. *I won't ever be like her—never!*

A jagged streak of lightning hit the ground outside the house and the wind gusted furiously. Glad of the thick walls and the beckoning hot bath, she let herself sink into the steamy water for a brief respite of blissful relaxation. Before Genia went to set the table for dinner, she had placed fluffy towels and rose-scented bath oil beside the tub. Melanie poured a generous dollop of the oil on the water, laid her head back on the rim of the heavy brass tub, and dozed.

Lee bypassed the kitchen and headed straight for his room, intent on getting out of his ruined suit. As if the day hadn't been disquieting enough, he had to soak his best dress clothes. He peeled off his jacket and shirt, then sat down to struggle with his boots. After getting them and his hose off, he stood up and reached for the buttons at his fly, only to hear a crash of glass coming from the end of the hall.

The damn storm must have forced the latch on a bedroom window. He walked swiftly and silently to Melanie's room, cursing her for leaving the window unattended. "She probably forgot to lock it," he muttered, shoving open the door. He stood frozen at the sight that greeted him.

The gust of wind had torn open the casement window and

Melanie was startled awake. After gathering her scattered wits, she began to rise from her tub when she heard the door open. Lee stood in the doorway, bare-chested and barefoot, clad only in a soaked pair of black dress pants. His eyes glowed like onyx coals as they raked over her shivering body. She reached for a towel, then thought better of it and submerged herself beneath the sudsy water, all the while returning his stare like a small wild thing hypnotized by a savage predator. He said nothing, just continued to look, as her enormous gold eyes did the same.

Melanie watched in fascination as small droplets of water slipped from his head to fall glistening onto the corded muscles of his shoulders, then catch once more in the dense mat of black curly hair on his chest. His desire was obvious as his wet pants clung to his body. Passion was reflected with equally startling clarity in his face. Slowly he stepped inside the room and closed the door.

Attempting to keep her body submerged, Melanie reached out again to snatch up a towel, but before she could open it, his bronzed fingers circled her wrist, stopping her. He took the towel and unfolded it. Then, bemused, he held it up for her, as if performing the duties of a lady's maid. "You'll freeze if you stay in that water," he whispered, the hoarseness of his voice apparent even over the noise of the storm.

The towel was large and offered her more protection than the now cold water. Lowering her thick fringe of black lashes to hide the warring emotions in her eyes, Melanie grasped the edge of the tub and rose, allowing him to enfold her in the linen, then quickly broke free of his hold, clutching the towel securely around her shivering golden body.

He smiled like a wolf. "There's nothing I haven't already seen, Melanie," he said in that same disconcerting whisper.

Part of her felt a kindred flare of desire leap between them; she wanted to shed the fragile protection of the towel and fly into his arms, yet she held back. He desired her, but he did not want her as his wife, only as a beautiful, available vessel to assuage his lust.

"No, Lee. We had an agreement," she said, her voice

strangling as she fought the tremors of desire pulsing through her.

"A man can't be expected to resist such temptation, Melanie—naked, smelling like night flowers, looking at me with those golden eyes, waiting for me," he replied, advancing on her slowly.

"I wasn't waiting for you!" she cried.

"And I suppose you weren't looking at me, either!" He laughed silkily. "Your face gave you away, just as your body gave you away that day on the hillside." One lean brown hand took a tumbled ebony lock of hair and twisted it softly around his wrist, pulling her nearer.

"I'm not your whore, Lee! You can't just barge in here and expect me to melt in your arms like . . . like . . ." her voice trailed off in whispering humiliation.

"Like an octoroon *placée*?" he taunted.

As if struck by the lightning raging outside, Melanie stiffened and yanked the curl from his hand. "You *do* think of me that way—not as a wife but some expensive harlot! Only remember your bargain, *husband*," she hissed. "If you don't want children kissed by the tar brush—or worse yet, with *Indian* blood, then don't touch me or I'll give them the proud Velásquez name as surely as I'm Lily Duval's daughter!"

He dropped his hands and clenched his fists in frustration. "I've never forced a woman in my life," he gritted out. "I won't start now. Sleep in your cold bed." He turned and stalked toward the door, then turned with his hand on the knob. "I'd close that window, unless you want to catch pneumonia and save me the trouble of an annulment!" With that, he slammed the door behind him with a crash that matched the raging elements outside.

The sun shone with obscene brilliance the next morning, awakening Lee when it hit him full in the face. He was sprawled across his bed, covers kicked off, head throbbing wickedly from an excess of brandy. Very carefully he slid his legs over the side of the bed and then raised his upper torso, cradling his head like fragile crystal in his hands as he sat up.

After the disastrous scene with Melanie, he had stalked into the library, where he kept an oak cabinet stocked with fine liquor. He had no idea how he had negotiated the way between the library and the bedroom.

He sat in misery, contemplating the forthcoming year of living under the same roof with a gold-eyed temptress: smelling her perfume, watching her lithe little body as she moved through his house, imagining her as she had looked naked in her bath—or spitting at him in hate-filled defiance when he tried to touch her.

He rose and cursed his precipitous words and actions last night. He had said cruel, hurtful things to her—words he did not mean. No wonder she had refused him! She was his wife, and he was certain he had treated her worse than Rafe Fleming had ever treated her mother. But after the things Larena had said to him that afternoon and the months of celibacy since returning to Texas, damn, she had pushed him past the breaking point! To find his beautiful little Night Flower that way—it was more than any man should be asked to endure!

Lee considered his options. Hold to his plan for an annulment and send her away at year's end? Impossible. He dismissed the idea immediately. Try to seduce her and settle for the marriage Charlee and Larena seemed to think would be so good for him? But would it? Could Melanie ever become a dutiful, loving wife? Or would she always cling to her infuriating ideas about women and Indians?

Then, too, he had to examine his own prejudices. She flaunted her mixed blood, and as she said, it would be Velásquez blood if he lay with her. Did that matter to him? He didn't know; he honestly didn't know. The only thing he did know was that he wanted her as he had never wanted any other woman in his life.

Chapter 15

The following week passed in stony silence. Only the barest civilities were exchanged between the honeymooners. Each spoke with Kai and Genia, using the hapless household servants as intermediaries whenever possible. Everyone was on edge waiting for something to happen. Then on the following Wednesday, Melanie returned from town with some news she had to share with her husband.

Lee was in his study having his before-dinner whiskey, a ritual that he indulged in liberally since his marriage, fortifying himself for the ordeal of sitting across the dining room table from his coldly hostile wife. When Melanie knocked on the door, he called absently for her to enter, expecting one of the servants. She stood poised on the threshold, watching him down a generous slug of amber liquid. As he stood by the large window, his tall, lean body was silhouetted in the twilight. She waited for him to turn, and when he did she could see surprise and some other darker emotion flash across his features.

"To what do I owe this honor?" he asked with a sardonic lift of his brows. "You only enter my domain to borrow books when I'm away."

"You might try reading instead of drinking when you're in this room. You'd feel better in the mornings," she answered acerbically.

"I can think of something else that might make me feel better in the mornings," he replied with a slyly taunting lilt to his voice.

Melanie clenched her fists and stepped closer, daring him to persist with his innuendos. "I have to talk to you, Lee."

"So, talk," he replied, giving up the game and returning his attention to the sunset outside the window.

How to put what she had to say—to ask, really. She began carefully. "My family is leaving for Renacimiento the day after tomorrow. I've spent only a few hours with Mama and Papa and have hardly seen Norrie, Caleb, and Joey. Adam came to the *Star* and we've had lunch several times. . . ." She hesitated, remembering the first day she and Adam had had lunch, when he introduced her to Jeremy Lawrence with such disastrous results.

Lee's face betrayed nothing. "I presume this is leading up to something. A family gathering to say farewell?"

"Jim and Charlee are giving a dinner for Mama and Papa and the children. The Oakleys will be there, and we're invited, too." She waited for his reaction.

"A command performance," he said, setting his glass down on the cabinet rather forcefully. "Your father must see that I'm not abusing you before he can go home with a clear conscience."

"Call it what you will," she said dejectedly, too emotionally overwrought to argue further. "Will you go or shall I make your excuses to Charlee?"

He chuckled in spite of himself. "*No one* makes excuses to Charlee Slade when she gets her mind made up. I'll be there—and never fear, I'll play the doting husband so well Junius Brutus Booth would be fooled!"

The evening began with cautious politeness between Lee and his in-laws. Deborah acted uncertain but conciliatory. Rafe watched his son-in-law with a measuring eye as Lee laughed and talked with the Slades and Oakleys and roughhoused with the Slade children. Norrie and Caleb warmed quickly to him as well, taking to his teasing and charm easily. Adam even surprised his father by going out of his way to show Lee that he was welcome in the family. Indeed, the bridegroom showed decidedly more animation than did the bride.

Melanie was quiet and watchful before the meal, listening to the children's laughter ring through the house. Lee's natural ease with them made her think about how good he would be as a father. *But a father who wants his children to have* pureza de sangre.

The men spoke of the weather and probable road conditions on the Flemings' forthcoming trip home, and the women adjourned to the kitchen to assist Charlee's helper, Weevils, in putting the finishing touches to a magnificent feast of roast pork and sweet potatoes.

With appetites sharpened by horseplay, the children settled down to serious eating when called to supper, and the noise level around the table abated. Melanie was aware of Jim's attempts to draw Lee and Rafe into conversation about ranching.

Responding to his father-in-law's question about Night Flower's future, Lee said to Rafe, "I'm running about five thousand head now, but that's all I've had time to buy or gather on the land. After the ranch's being deserted for so long, it'll take awhile to gear up to the sort of operation you have. At least this time I have the capital to hire men and purchase all the materials I require."

Rafe smiled and looked over at Deborah. "When I came to Texas, I was in a situation similar to yours—only instead of lying unattended for six years, Renacimiento had not been worked for nearly fifty. It was lucky for me that I had some cash to start off with, but even with that it took years of backbreaking work to get the place going. If Joe hadn't been there, we'd never have made Renacimiento succeed."

"Your partner?" Lee questioned, vaguely recalling the name.

"*Cherokee* Joe De Villiers. He's half Indian, and he's been like an uncle to all of us. Hasn't he, Adam?" Melanie interjected, addressing her remark to her brother but watching Lee's reaction.

The interchange was not lost on Rafe, who was a survivor of many a strained dinner-table conversation at the Flamenco household in New Orleans. He flashed a quelling smile at his daughter. "Yes, Joe and his wife, Lucia, practically raised Melanie. They'll be so happy to hear that she's settled down and married now."

"Oh, I may be married, Papa, but I'm still working for Clarence—mostly covering social news, nothing dangerous," Melanie cooed.

Lee smiled tightly. The little bitch was baiting him, flaunting her damn Indian blood and hoyden activities right in front of the assembly to see if she could get a rise out of him. "*Only* a gossip column for the *Star*. After all, Mellie, you don't ever want to place yourself in danger again, do you?" His voice was soft, but the message came across loud and clear.

Melanie gritted her teeth at his added insult in using the pet name only family members called her. Deborah's violet eyes flashed warily between Lee and Melanie. Rafe sat back, waiting to see what his daughter would do next—and wondering what his son-in-law would do to counter. Jim coughed, hiding a grin behind his dinner napkin while Charlee kicked him under the table.

"Jeehosaphat," Obedience interjected suddenly, "I purely do hope yew two git saddled with a passel of younguns real quick 'n' take ta stayin' home. Keepin' up with either one o' yew's 'nough ta tire out a lantern-jawed jackass! Keepin' up with th' two o' yew's nigh onta killin' a old gray mare like me!"

"I agree," Charlee said with a chuckle, her cat-green eyes dancing as she looked at Lee. "What you need is a couple of hell-raisers like Will and Caleb to keep you close to home."

"What about me? I keep Mama and Aunt Lucia real busy," Norrie said with a mixture of childish pique and pride.

The adults and other children around the table joined in the laughter, but Lee looked at Melanie with a question in his night-dark eyes.

Melanie returned the searching look briefly, uncertain of what it meant. Did he really want her children, or did he simply lust for her body—the body of a beautiful kept woman?

* * *

"Why do you suppose ole Sam's come all th' way from th' U.S. Senate jist ta dance in Santone?" Obedience speculated as she gave a final swat to the big blob of bread dough she was working in the boardinghouse kitchen.

"Politics, I guess. Sam likes to talk to his constituents," Charlee replied, munching on a corn dodger as she visited with Obedience.

"Jeehosaphat, 'pears ta me he might cud be oilin' th' waters over this here Injun mess. Folks in west Texas is plumb unhappy with th' way the' gove'mint back in Washington's been handlin' things," Obedience said shrewdly.

"From what I can get my tight-lipped husband to divulge, I think you're right. Sam's always been on the Indians' side, trying to keep white settlers from crowding them out of Texas."

" 'N thet don't make voters hereabouts none too happy," her friend averred.

"Especially with the Comanche raids increasing around Bexar County this past year. Why only last week another family sold their land to Laban Greer and took off for California after being burned out."

Obedience nodded. "Th' Ryans. Good folks, even if ole man Ryan wuz a bit shiftless. Course if'n his woman an' younguns warn't in town draggin' him outa th' saloon, they'd all be kilt dead by them bloodthirsty Comanch."

"There have been so many settlers leaving. Lots of folks say it's the Congressmen in Washington who are to blame for not sending the army enough men and supplies to fight the Indians," Charlee said with a touch of doubt in her voice.

Obedience let out a snort of derision. "I kinda 'spect our senator won't take real kindly to thet talk. Whilst Houston's here medin' fences, yew don't suppose he 'n' Jim'll be lookin' into whut Blaine 'n' some o' his cronies er doin'?" Her shrewd brown eyes surveyed Charlee. Obedience knew Jim Slade had secretly worked for Houston when Sam was president of the Republic.

"You know, Mrs. Oakley, you'd make a hell of an agent. Maybe I can speak real sweetly to Sam at the dance tomorrow night and get you a job," Charlee said with a chuckle.

"Speakin' o' sweet talk, how er Lee 'n' Melanie gettin' on? Been nigh on ta three weeks since't her folks left. She's been galavantin' round town fer thet old Yankee Pemberton, but I scarce kin git her ta light 'n' talk ta me."

Charlee nodded sagely. "I think she's avoiding us. She knows we want her and Lee to work things out, and it's not going well."

"Yew don't think them two young folks is still sleepin' in separate beds, do yew?"

Sighing, Charlee shrugged. "She's so scarred by her past and he's so damnably proud, I don't know. After the combustion between them when they first met, I was positive it would be inevitable. It sure was for Jim and me, and we weren't even married!" She had the good grace to blush, but only slightly as Obedience slapped her thigh and let out a hearty guffaw.

"Since't her mama's not here 'n' yew know Lee bettern'n anyone hereabouts, mebbe yew better have a talk with thet gal 'n' set her straight. Ain't natural fer a female ta ignore a man like Lee Velásquez 'n' pay attention ta one like Clarence Pemberton."

Charlee's eyes lit up. "Clarence is scarcely Lee's rival, but there is one other possibility." Her agile mind quickly went into high gear as she began to plan her strategy for the dance the following evening.

Melanie was covering the big gala ball given in honor of Texas' illustrious senatorial visitor, the hero of the revolution and twice president of the Republic. Of course, Lee felt compelled to attend so his wife would have an escort. They had ridden to San Antonio in the afternoon and reserved a room at a local hotel. Since the boardinghouse was filled to capacity, Melanie insisted that she and Lee would make their own sleeping arrangements. She knew Obedience would put them in one small room, deliberately attempting to force them together. Instead, Melanie had rented a suite with a comfortable sitting room off the bedroom; it was equipped with a large sofa on which she planned to spend the night.

Standing before the mirror, Melanie held up the gown she had bought last week, inspecting it critically. It was a deep golden yellow satin that gleamed in the afternoon sunlight. The complement to her ebony hair and sun-kissed skin was apparent, but the way its luster exactly matched the color of her gold eyes was what had really drawn her to choose it.

"Now you need high-heeled slippers and your hair piled high on your head. Something with lots of coils and a few loose, springy curls—soft but adding height," Charlee said musingly from the doorway between the bedroom and outside sitting room. "I let myself in when you didn't reply to the knock. Lee said you were up here unpacking."

Melanie dropped the ball gown on the bed and turned away from the mirror. "Why all this sudden interest in what *I* wear? Shouldn't you be getting all dolled up to dance with the senator yourself? After all, he's your guest at Bluebonnet."

Charlee grinned. "Sam's already reserved a dance for me. He and Jim are out strolling around town—putting an ear to the ground 'to listen for signs'—that's Sam's expression for observing the political climate. I have lots of time to get ready. Brought my dress clothes from the ranch this morning. Sadie's pressing my gown right now. Speaking of gowns," Charlee said casually, picking up the gold satin cloud from the bed, "this is really beautiful. There's hope for you yet. Try it on and let's see how it fits."

Melanie knew Charlee was up to something, and it related to her persistent matchmaking. "It fits just fine—well, maybe a bit lower cut in the front than I'd prefer, but once she'd measured me, the seamstress insisted I wear it that way."

Charlee chuckled. "Your mother had to persuade me to wear a low-cut dress once. Of course, if I had all the assets you have to fill it out, I might have been more willing to give it a try. One thing we do have in common, though—our height, or lack thereof."

"So?" Melanie shrugged indifferently. "I've never found being short a disadvantage."

"To quote your mama again, 'It is if you want to catch a tall man,' " Charlee replied.

Melanie turned abruptly and picked up the dress, fingering the slick fabric. "Who says I want to catch *any* man, much less that tall *Tejano* you're thinking of?'' Her nervous gesture belied her insouciant tone of voice.

Charlee sighed. ''This is really getting tiresome, you know that? I've played this scene before—only I had your part. Luckily Deborah cared enough about me to shake some sense into me. She got me past my mulish Missouri pride and made me admit I wanted to catch Jim. Whether or not that damned Creole pride of yours will loosen up is another matter, but I know you want Lee, young lady, and I aim to see to it that you get him. Look at it this way: you've got one hell of an edge. You're already married to him, even if the marriage hasn't been consummated yet.''

Melanie dropped the gold dress as if she had been scorched by it. ''How did you—'' she blurted, then stopped short, her cheeks aflame in humiliation.

Charlee put her arm around Melanie's shoulders and gave her a sisterly squeeze. ''I've known Lee Velásquez for a long time. He's proud and stubborn, and he doesn't like being forced. He's also got some very dumb ideas about the kind of woman he thinks he wants for a wife. It's up to you to show him the light.''

''All this is predicated on the assumption that I want this marriage to work,'' Melanie said with her own share of stubbornness.

''Humor me. Wouldn't it be satisfying to watch him eat his heart out with jealousy while you're the belle of the ball? Just think of it as sweet revenge for all that smug male arrogance you've endured.'' Charlee cocked her head and waited for Melanie's reaction.

''Well, if you put it that way . . .'' A smile played around her lips.

As Charlee arranged her charge's hair in an upswept masterpiece, she said devilishly, ''That young ranger Jeremy Lawrence is a handsome devil. Wonder if he can dance? I hear he and Lee almost had a brawl a few weeks back.'' Feeling Melanie stiffen, she paused, then continued, ''If you think Lee doesn't care for you, why is he so all-fired jealous of Lawrence?''

''I'm his wife. I bear the proud Velásquez name, much as

he may resent that fact. If I'm caught in a public place with any man under the age of sixty, he thinks I need a chaperon!'' Melanie's eyes blazed with golden fire as Charlee put the finishing touches to the hairdo.

''Not just *any* man—he knows that ranger is young, single, and very attractive to women. You can make that work to your advantage, you know.''

''Charlee, you're still laboring under the misconception that I *want* Lee's attention,'' Melanie said in exasperation.

''Just think about it tonight while you're in his arms dancing. You might find you like it there,'' Charlee replied tenaciously.

Lee had avoided their hotel room all afternoon, leaving his wife to get ready for the big gala while he took care of some business at the bank and freight office. He dreaded the coming night. Not that he was worried about their sleeping arrangements. She'd seen to that. But he did have to escort her to Houston's ball, and for appearances' sake he supposed he'd have to dance with her. That meant touching her, taking her in his arms, smelling the rose-sweet fragrance of night flowers.

Ever since the night of the storm, when he'd seen her naked in her bath, he had been warring with himself. Even though he knew he deserved it, her rejection stung his pride. The past weeks had been a misery of enforced celibacy for him, but every time he had considered visiting a discreet brothel he discarded the idea almost immediately. Perversely, he wanted no other woman but Melanie. She was in his blood, and he hated himself because he could not break free of her spell.

He stood outside their room, debating whether or not to knock. *What the hell, I'm paying for the room.* Preemptively he slid the key in the lock and turned the knob. The vision that greeted him took the breath from his body. ''My God, you *almost* have a dress on!'' The words burst forth before he could stop himself.

Melanie preened in front of the mirror, giving him a little smirk as she eyed her overflowing cleavage with hidden misgivings. "It is cut a bit low for my, er, shape, but Charlee assured me it was in excellent taste," she answered primly.

"You're about to spill out the top!"

"You sound like a *dueña*," she said dismissively, watching with uneasiness as his jet eyes raked her from head to toe, inspecting the dress which clung to her tiny waist and flared with golden perfection over billowing hoops and crinolines. She couldn't resist one twirl in front of the mirror. The sleeves were puffed slightly at the shoulders and fitted at her slim wrists. From the daring plunge of the V neckline to the hem of the full skirt, it was utterly unadorned, relying for the dramatic effect on the way the satin clung to each curve of her body. She gleamed from her bouncing ebony curls and gold eyes to the tip of her high-heeled satin slippers peeping out beneath her skirt.

"Would you fasten this? I've been trying without luck." She held out a topaz pendant like a peace offering. Slowly he walked over to where she stood and took the necklace, careful not to touch her fingers as he did so. But when she turned to face the mirror and watched him reach around her neck to fasten the clasp, his hard warm fingers were trembling. She felt a small frisson of pleasure course through her. What if Charlee was right?

Melanie looked at their reflection in the glass. With her high heels and this hairdo, she fitted splendidly next to him. He was dressed in very traditional clothes, a severely cut black suit that hugged his lean body, emphasizing long limbs and hard muscles. *And he thinks my dress is too tight!* God, how splendid he looked with his white satin stock framing that swarthy, chiseled countenance. The black and white suit was relieved by the lavish silver trim that edged his jacket and ran up the sides of his pants legs. The only color in his ensemble was a sash of deep crimson. Just then their eyes met in the mirror. His were amused, smirking, for he had caught her staring at him with schoolgirl fascination.

"I'm not that twelve-year-old girl on the Galveston wharf anymore, Lee," she said quietly, turning away from his gaze.

"I can see that," he responded huskily, ushering her from the room.

"You will introduce me to Sam Houston so I can get my story?" Melanie needed to calm her nerves as they entered the big ballroom, festooned with red, white, and blue bunting. A big banner proclaimed, "Welcome Senator Sam," attesting to the affection of Texians everywhere for the hero of San Jacinto.

"It's been a few years since I met Houston—ten, to be exact," he replied, looking at her small, elegant head as she scanned the crowd. "It was on my way to Galveston to pick up some stock for Bluebonnet." At that her gaze flew to his face before she could stop herself.

"I hope the disaster of meeting me didn't ruin your visit with the president," she replied sourly.

He gave a mirthless chuckle. "Houston and Slade are thick as thieves, always were. It really wouldn't signify whether I liked Sam or not. But as it happens, I do admire him and he's done me a favor or two over the years."

"Just how much did he have to lean on the governor to get you that pardon?" she inquired sweetly.

He scowled. "Quite a bit."

Just then a big voice boomed out across the room. "Jim told me you'd be here with your fair bride. God, boy, I must be getting old. Last time I saw you you weren't dry behind the ears." The speaker was a giant of a man, towering over Lee's six-foot frame as they exchanged greetings. Houston was still an impressive figure dressed in an elegantly cut gray wool suit that hid his slightly thickened waist and emphasized his wide shoulders. His hair was white and thinning, but the high forehead and blunt, strong features were as arresting as ever, especially the piercing blue eyes that danced with merriment as he looked from Lee to his lady.

"Jim said you married a stunning woman, Lee, but all his praise could not do you justice, madam." He made a courtly bow and kissed Melanie's hand gallantly.

"You've not lost your legendary charm with the ladies, I see," Melanie replied, glowing under his admiring gaze.

"Did Jim or Charlee also happen to mention that I work for the *San Antonio Star*? You see, I would very much like to write a story about you for my newspaper, Senator."

Throwing back his leonine head in a hearty laugh, Houston replied, "Charlee told me you were as straightforward as a Boston bluestocking. I would be honored to give you an interview, Mrs. Velásquez, if you would favor me with the first dance."

"Done, Senator," she replied.

After a big fanfare, in which the mayor praised the senator to the assembled crowd, Houston said a few words and urged everyone to enjoy the festivities. With no more ado, he motioned for the musicians to strike up a lively tune and claimed Melanie for the promised first dance.

The gala was held at the Pearsons', one of the newest, and by far the largest, house in San Antonio. With the rugs rolled up for the occasion, the front parlor did double service as a ballroom. The planked floors were smooth and polished, perfect for dancing. Nearly a dozen musicians played fiddles, horns, and even a piano whose tinny sound bothered no one a whit.

Melanie and Houston danced and talked easily. For such a large man he was extraordinarily graceful. When she commented on his skill, his face fairly beamed. "I owe my appreciation of music and what poor abilities I possess as a dancer to my beloved Margaret. She has endeavored over the years to refine this crude frontiersman's taste and make him appreciate all things beautiful. She plays the piano for me every evening when I'm at home."

"You miss her and your children, don't you?" Melanie had heard lots of gossip over the years about the May-December marriage between the Texas giant of forty-seven and the Alabama belle of twenty. Despite all predictions of disaster, the marriage had worked out splendidly over the past dozen years, and Sam proved to be a model husband and father.

At the mention of his family, Houston's blue eyes glowed. "Yes, I miss them a great deal."

"Tell me, Senator, is it true Margaret actually convinced

you to take a temperance pledge?'' Melanie's eyes danced as she dared to ask the audacious question. Houston's drinking had been prodigious in years past, but he was known as a model of abstemiousness since his marriage.

He roared a great laugh but never missed a beat as they danced. ''Why is it, young woman, that I suspect your sojourn in Boston has something to do with your zeal for the temperance movement? Ah, you see, I, too, did my homework.''

''I'm sure the Slades were a gold mine of information about my background,'' Melanie said with a smile that hid her apprehension. She prayed they had not discussed the reasons for her precipitous marriage! ''Indeed, I did embrace the cause of temperance while living in Boston with my grandfather.''

''My wife's espousal of temperance had little to do with crusading idealism and much to do with her Baptist upbringing. She has endeavored to bring me to the light of true religion for some years,'' he said, eyes filled with deviltry.

''And did she succeed as well with your religious conversion as she did with your temperance?''

''I was finally prevailed upon to take the plunge, in literal terms, last year. I was baptized by immersion in Rocky Creek.'' He shivered in remembrance. ''The water of life liked to have sent me to my grave with pneumonia!''

''But did it wash your sins away? That is the burning question, Senator,'' Melanie parried gaily, thoroughly enjoying the conversation as well as getting a wonderful story with which to dazzle Clarence.

Houston appeared to consider her remark, then replied, fervently, ''If that creek was indeed the instrumentality that absolved all Sam Houston's mortal sins, then God help the fishes down below!''

Lee stood by Jim and Charlee, watching his wife's lively exchange with the guest of honor. When he heard her trill of delighted laughter echo across the crowded room, he scowled sourly. ''She must be getting one hell of a story for the *Star*.''

Jim smiled. ''Sam always could charm the ladies, *mano*.

You know, you might just cut in on him and dance with your bride. I'm sure Sam would understand, under the circumstances.''

Lee shrugged indifferently, casting an eye across the room to where Larena Sandoval stood, flanked by her parents. He had not seen her since their meeting in San Fernando's secluded garden. ''I expect my bride will keep barraging the senator with questions until he cries off without my help. I think your aunt and uncle want to talk with you, Jim. Since they obviously don't want to see me, I'll just wander over to wherever they're dispensing liquid refreshments.''

Charlee watched him walk off, her face creased in a thoughtful frown. ''Let's do say hello to the Sandovals, Jim.''

''Why is it, Cat Eyes, that I suspect you're plotting something?'' Jim's expression was faintly troubled, but he knew better than to try and stop Charlee when she got an idea into that mulish head of hers.

It didn't take long for Jim to discern her plans. She artfully cajoled Larena into accompanying her to the refreshment tables while Jim became engaged in a political discussion with his aunt and uncle. Shortly thereafter, she ''accidentally'' bumped into Lee and then orchestrated his asking Larena to dance. If there was any doubt about Charlee's motives, one look at Melanie's furiously wounded eyes convinced Jim that the girl was indeed jealous. What would she do about it, he wondered uneasily, damning Charlee and her machinations.

Just then, as if arriving on cue, Jeremy Lawrence walked up to the small assembly, which Houston was regaling with a humorous tale about the French Ambassador to the Texas Republic. Melanie had danced with several men after monopolizing the guest of honor for as long as she dared, but Lee had not approached her all evening. Not even one dance with his new bride! As if her pride were not stung enough, she then saw him in Larena Sandoval's arms. Two could play that game. Maybe Charlee's harebrained idea about making him jealous might work. It would certainly salve her bruised ego. She smiled a warm greeting at Jeremy.

Within a matter of minutes they were gliding across the floor and she had the young ranger completely in thrall. "You seem to know the senator, Jeremy. Where did you meet?" she asked as they danced.

"I'd rather not tell an inquiring lady reporter about that, Melanie. Remember our discussion about my boss Captain Walkman and Blaine?" At her watchful nod, he continued, "Well, let's just say it's no accident that I've been assigned to Bexar County. Leave it at that for now. All right?"

"You've been sent by Houston to investigate the whiskey-running to the Comanche?" she whispered. "I've always heard he was concerned about the Indians."

Lawrence frowned. "Yes, he is, but there are those who'd jump for joy to see every Indian in Texas dead."

Melanie followed his line of vision until she saw the squat, bull-necked frame of Laban Greer. She shuddered in the young ranger's arms.

"What is it, Melanie? You know Greer? Oh, that story. . . ." His voice trailed off.

"Yes, my story. I watched him kill an injured woman—a frail old woman lying helpless on the ground. He shot her in cold blood." She could feel Greer's cold eyes on her, almost as if he were penetrating her disguise as Moses French. Forcing herself to block from her mind the scene of carnage she had witnessed, Melanie returned Greer's piercing, rude stare boldly. "Just let him have the nerve to ask for a dance."

Jeremy laughed softly. "Somehow I don't think he's got the heart for it."

"Oh, yes he does. Here he comes," she said levelly. Feeling Jeremy stiffen protectively, she placed a hand on his arm placatingly. "It's all right. He doesn't frighten me, and I won't back down from him and hide behind your badge, Jeremy."

When Greer bowed quite politely to the young ranger, he unwillingly relinquished his partner. "Why do you do me this honor, Mr. Greer? Surely a big rancher like yourself isn't interested in a mere gossip columnist for the *Star*, especially since I'm an old married woman now," she added with a silent curse for her absent husband.

Greer's thick, blunt features did not conceal his keen intelligence. He smiled coldly. "I was merely wondering if you've ever met this Moses French fellow. After all, you do work for the paper, after a fashion."

The condescending male arrogance of his last statement infuriated Melanie but also indicated to her that he did not believe she was Moses French.

"Surely Pemberton is too old, and that nigger of his would scarce have the nerve. Who might that leave?" Greer continued, prompting her.

Gritting her teeth, she replied, "Yes, Mr. Pemberton is too old for such active undercover reporting, and, no, it certainly isn't *Mr.* Johnston, although there's nothing lacking in his nerve."

Greer laughed nastily. "I forget myself. You are a Boston abolitionist, aren't you? Just keep out of Indian affairs, lady. Texans don't like women meddling in things that don't concern them."

"Things like decency and justice, Mr. Greer?" she replied curtly. "If you'll pardon me, I see some old friends I need to greet." *Was he fishing to see if I'd get so rattled I'd tell him who our reporter is? Or does he suspect me?*

As she quit the floor and headed over to where Larena Sandoval and her mother stood, Melanie forced a smile for her rival. Even amenities with Lee's old flames were preferable to one more minute of that odious man's oily and intimidating presence.

She talked briefly with the Sandovals and then danced with several other men before Jeremy once again claimed her hand. "What did Greer have to say?" he asked worriedly. "He doesn't know you wrote that article?"

"No, of course not. I'm just a meddlesome, addlepated female to him. He did try to find out if I knew who Moses was, though. Fat chance!"

Jeremy laughed. "Just you be careful, Melanie. And for God's sake, don't mention my connection to the senator to a soul. When this investigation is over and we've cleaned up the corruption here and in Washington, you'll have a whale of a story, I promise you. But in the meanwhile, it could be very dangerous for you to get any further involved.''

"Now you sound like Lee," she rejoined hotly. "Stay out of harm's way, little girl.''

"Well, I wouldn't call such an elegant lady a 'little girl,' for certain,'' he replied with a gallant smile and admiring sweep of her hairdo and costume.

She blushed.

Sitting off on the sidelines, Lee observed his beautiful wife dancing and flirting with a succession of admirers as the evening wore on. All seemed enamored of her, but none infuriated him half so much as the handsome young ranger who was her most frequent partner, even escorting her over to the buffet tables and filling a plate for her.

While he watched, he drank and brooded, still confused about his ambivalent feelings toward his wife. After she had gone off to dance with Houston, Charlee had maneuvered him into dancing with Larena. Then he had stayed near the table where drinks were dispensed. A number of the men were lacing the watered-down punch with a significantly stronger libation. Each time Fernando Rojas passed the whiskey bottle, Lee poured a generous slug into his glass. *Temperance unions be damned! All Boston crusaders be damned!*

Melanie felt Lee's eyes burning into her as she danced with Jeremy, but he made no move to approach her himself. He danced with his ex-fiancée but not his own wife. As if their scandalous marriage weren't fueling enough gossip already, his behavior tonight was the final straw.

Jeremy watched Velásquez working up to a mean and dangerous drunk, wondering if he would have to fight the man because of his wife. As much as he admired Melanie's wit and beauty, he knew she was a married woman and there was a strong if antagonistic attraction between her and her husband. At his afternoon meeting with Slade and Houston, Lawrence had discussed the situation in San Antonio and the role he was to play in trapping Blaine and Walkman. He could ill afford to become involved in a confrontation with

Velásquez and jeopardize his assignment. But if Melanie remained this unhappy when the mission was completed, he vowed to do whatever was necessary to help her.

Around midnight the guest of honor departed for Bluebonnet Ranch with Jim and Charlee Slade, but he urged the younger revelers to continue dancing. His war wounds were acting up, he said, and he required a good night's rest. Although surrounded by swains eagerly asking her to dance, Melanie felt frazzled and tense, more than eager to depart, as Houston had, but her husband was nowhere in sight.

When Jeremy cut in on one particularly obnoxious young cowhand whose maladroit dancing was as annoying as his roaming hands, she was relieved. Suddenly she felt the sting of tears in her eyes and attempted to dash them back. "Would you see me to the hotel, Jeremy?" she whispered in a choked voice.

He put his fingertips lightly on her cheek. "Don't cry, Melanie. It's been a long night and I know you're tired, but think of the wonderful story you can write about the senator," he said softly as he escorted her from the floor. He returned a moment later with her wrap, a soft white wool shawl to ward off the cool night air. Very carefully, as if she were breakable, he placed it around her shoulders and then took her hand and tucked it beneath his arm proprietarily.

The tender gestures were not lost on Lee, who stood behind the glass doors to the side porch, watching his wife and her escort. Jeremy and Melanie said their farewells to the Pearsons. Lee left the house, walking with ground-devouring, purposeful strides toward the hotel and the suite he would share with his wife that night.

Chapter 16

Melanie and Jeremy walked slowly through the cool starry night. When she shivered and pulled her wrap closer, he offered her his suit coat.

"No, thank you, I'm not really cold. I just need to walk for a bit and clear my head." She smiled tremulously at him and then looked up at the sky. "Ever since I came to Texas as a twelve-year-old girl, I've been astonished at the night skies here. It's as if you could reach up and touch the stars, as if they were diamonds sprinkled on a crumpled black velvet cloth."

Lawrence smiled. "As an adopted son of Texas, I'd say there's no place on earth this special—big, open, free. There's so much waiting for people here." He stopped walking and almost reluctantly she paused, too. "Melanie, look, I know it's none of my business—that I have no right to come between a husband and wife, but Velásquez was drunk and mean tonight. No telling where he's gone or if he'll come back to the hotel. I could take you to the Oakleys or even back to your ranch if you want."

Melanie took a deep breath and swallowed the tears clogging her throat. *Why couldn't I have met someone like you ten years ago, Jeremy?* Aloud she replied, "It's all right. I do thank you for your concern, but I can take care of myself. I may not be native-born, either, but I'm a real Texian, too."

They resumed walking, heading toward the hotel, both full of silent misgivings they knew they dared not discuss.

When Jeremy walked her to the top of the stairs and down

the long corridor to her suite, he took the key from her hand and unlocked the door. Standing in the hall, he gave her one last, searching look. The pugnacious set of her little chin said it all. Firmly she took the key back from him and stepped inside the sitting room. "I'll be fine, Jeremy. Good luck with your mission. If Lame Deer or any of the children hear any more news, I'll be in touch. Thank you."

Feeling as if he could drown in her luminous gold eyes, the ranger nodded. "Just give a holler if you need anything," he reiterated, then turned and walked reluctantly down the hall.

As his footsteps faded, Melanie looked nervously around the room. There was no sign of Lee, she thought with relief. She walked over to the porcelain wash pitcher on the table and poured its contents into the matching basin. The maid had filled it and left it for her in the sitting room as she had instructed. Dispiritedly she stripped off slippers and stockings, then the beautiful golden gown and all its underpinnings, tossing them carelessly over a horsehair chair in the corner. *All that trouble with fabric selections and fittings—for what?* she thought, trying to work up some rejuvenating anger over the shambles of the evening.

She returned to the pitcher and washed her face. Then, feeling the dull throb of a headache coming on, she began to pull the pins from her hair as she rummaged across the table in search of her brush.

"Looking for this?" a voice whispered from the bedroom door. Lee leaned indolently against the door frame with her ivory-handled hairbrush dangling from one bronzed hand. His eyes roamed over her bare shoulders and penetrated the sheer lace camisole and pantalets, all the remaining clothing on her body.

Almost as if protecting herself, she combed her fingers through her waist-length hair and pulled it across her breasts to cover herself. The gasp of fright and surprise that had escaped her at his pantherlike entry revealed her vulnerability. Standing barefoot in the center of the room, she knew she had nowhere to run, nothing to do but brazen this situation out as she had the night of the storm.

But this time Lee had been drinking. His slouched pose
and heavily lidded eyes gave that away, although when he
glided into the room, his step was surprisingly steady. He,
too, was barefoot and mostly undressed, clad only in his
black suit pants, as if her untimely arrival had caused him to
stop in the act of disrobing for bed.

When he took several more steps near her, Melanie
forced herself to stand her ground. *If I retreat, he'll corner
me like a frightened deer*, she thought frantically as she
stared into his eyes. They were as black as a starless night
yet they glowed with a strange dark fire. Without a word he
reached out a hand and pulled on a lock of her hair, drawing
her nearer, then raised the brush and began to draw it
through the thick ebony masses. He stroked down the heavy
coils lying across her breasts, then turned her back to him
and worked the brush through the rest, pulling it all down to
the curve of her buttocks, massaging with the heavy brush
until the tangles and curls of her coiffure were smoothed out
and the whole length crackled in ebony splendor.

This gentle ministration was the last thing she had expected
when she saw him standing in the doorway, scrutinizing her
barely clad body. At a loss as to how to respond, she let him
work the sensual magic of the brushing without protest,
remaining bemused, almost relaxed. Then he took a fistful of
her hair and raised it to his face, inhaling the fragrance of it.

"Like the primroses, sweet as night flowers," he whispered
near her ear. When he stretched his arm around the front of
her waist and pulled her against his body, he could feel her
stiffen; yet she offered no resistance.

Lee held her immobilized for a moment, savoring the
sweetness of her lush body. He had heard her murmured
good night to Lawrence, listened to the rustle of her clothing
being discarded, heard the splashing of water as she performed
her toilette. Then he had opened the bedroom door and seen
her searching for the brush. Like a sleepwalker he had
picked it up from the bedside table by the door and made
her aware of his presence. Did her quiescence mean she
would accept what she had wanted that day on the hillside
and had refused the night of the storm?

All evening he had watched her, a glorious golden butterfly, flirting and dancing, laughing and talking with a succession of men, especially that bastard ranger. Lawrence seemed to single her out for his particular attentions, and she was more than receptive to them. "If this were Lawrence instead of me, his hands on you instead of mine, what then, princess?" he grated out in a low, tormented voice.

"You have no right to ask me that," she cried out, stung half by his unfairness, half by her own guilt, for she had wished fervently that she could react to Jeremy the way she reacted to Lee.

"I have every right—to anything I want," he growled, turning her to face him, his hands no longer gentle but firm and unrelenting. "I'm your husband and I think it's long past time we had our honeymoon night."

"You promised me—the annulment was your idea. You despise everything I believe in, everything I am!" she cried out in small, wounded gasps as he kissed her, crushing the breath from her body, trailing his lips from her ear to her neck, then down where his hand cupped the fullness of her breast. He pulled it free of its lacy confinement to suckle fiercely on it. All the remembered sensations from that insane, breathless day on the hillside came rushing back to jolt her with the force of a stampede. "No, Lee, please," she moaned.

"Yes, Lee, please," he echoed, lost in the golden promise of her body, that lush, voluptuous body he'd lain awake dreaming of for weeks. He could feel the points of her nipples as they hardened beneath the subtle persuasion of his hands, the pounding of her heart as he brushed his lips in the deep vale between her breasts. "You were made to be loved, Night Flower," he whispered, ignoring her gasped moans of dismay.

"No! You don't love me—you only want me," she cried out with more force, struggling to break the heated magic his body was working on hers. "It's the same as it was the first time—just lust!" She pushed herself free of him at last and stood flushed and trembling, pulling her unfastened camisole up to cover the bounty of bare rose-nippled breasts.

He straightened up, fury and frustration etched across

every plane and angle of his hawkish face. "You've be-
haved more than once as if you're well acquainted with lust
and not at all averse to it! You and Lawrence put on a
touching little show at the end of the dance tonight," he
rasped out bitterly.

"How would you know? You left me alone! You never
paid the slightest attention to me all night long. Between
attending to Larena Sandoval and the punch bowl, I'm
amazed you even noticed I was alive!" Her eyes blazed like
molten gold as anger raged through every nerve of her body.

"Well, I'm noticing now, and I have a right to sample
what you've probably already offered Lawrence. Is that it,
Melanie? Have you and that ranger bastard been lovers? Is
that why you don't want me to touch you—afraid I'll find
out the truth?" The moment he spat out the accusations he
knew they were untrue. Her face blanched and her eyes
dilated in shocked, horrified denial, but she uttered not a
sound, standing proudly before him as if daring him to do
his worst.

Rather than assuaging his racing desire, her obvious
innocence fueled it anew. He would be the first, and by God
he would have her! When he reached out both arms and
took her by the shoulders to pull her back into his embrace,
she stood woodenly, like a sleepwalker, in shock over his
monstrous accusations and raging jealousy.

With her hair down and high heels off, she was tiny as a
doll. He bent down and lifted her, pressing the length of her
soft curves against his chest and belly, groaning in exquisite
torture, "Oh, Melanie, Night Flower, I must have you, I
need you. I can't wait any longer."

Before she could answer, his mouth swooped down to
fasten on hers, hot and firm, as his tongue insinuated itself
between her lips. With a volition of its own her mouth
opened and allowed him access. He tasted faintly of tobacco
and more pungently of whiskey. Her senses swam as his
tongue entwined with her own and his lips continued their
almost savage onslaught. He was holding her very tightly,
lifting her feet from the carpet so she hung suspended in
midair, clinging to him. Melanie had been angered at the

presumption of his assault, but she became bemused, acquiescing to the anguished pleading of his last words.

He needs me, he desires me—he was jealous just like Charlee said he'd be! Confused thoughts dashed helter-skelter through her mind as she felt her senses reeling and that hypnotic heat once more stealing through her body. All reason fled as she gave herself up to this mysterious, inexorable need. *I need him, too* was her last coherent thought before he swept her up in his arms and silently carried her into the bedroom.

When he reached the bed, Lee slowly set her down alongside it, all the while nibbling soft, wet kisses from her mouth to her shoulders and around her throat. Then he slipped the camisole straps down her shoulders and shoved the frilly bit of fluff to her waist, tearing the buttons off in his impatience. Leaning back, he gazed breathlessly at her breasts, completely bared and standing proudly upthrust. He filled his hands with them, hefting and massaging them. "For a body so small to have these so large . . ." he whispered in awe, feeling her arch into his palms, thrusting the aching points of her nipples against his fingertips.

Melanie's small hands sought the rock-solid expanse of his chest, flattening her soft palms against it and running her fingers through the thick springy mat of black hair. Electricity, like summer lightning, flashed between them. When he reached down to suckle her breasts again, she eagerly accommodated him, her long nails digging into the muscles of his shoulders, pulling him against her this time. Scorching heat spiraled out from her breasts, dipping lower, uncoiling in her belly, then lower still.

Reacting instinctively, he pulled her lower body firmly against his, then guided her hips in a slow rotation against the burgeoning heat of his erection. Feeling the soft pressure of her pelvis, he groaned with the exquisite torture and grabbed the fastening of her pantalets, yanking the lacy drawers below her hips. Then he scooped her up and deposited her on the bed.

Melanie looked up at him, her wide gold eyes glazed with passion as he quickly slid the pantalets off her and tossed them on the floor. She was completely naked and vulnerable, yet a languid, hot paralysis held her in thrall. Watching the expressions play across his taut features, she knew he thought her body beautiful. His burning hands traveled from her breasts to her tiny waist, then lower over her hips, pausing at that small tangle of black curls between her thighs, then lower still to caress her sleekly curved little calves. One lean bronzed hand encircled a fragile ankle and then moved upward, retracing the course to her flushed face. "You are perfection," he ground out as he stood up and began to unbutton his pants.

In the dim recesses of her mind, Melanie knew that she should feel embarrassment at his savoring perusal and bold words of praise for the most intimate parts of her body, but all she could do was wait with her eyes riveted to his swarthy male beauty as he roughly yanked his tightly fitted suit pants free of his body. Having three younger brothers, Melanie was familiar with male anatomy, but it had never looked like this! Once freed of the constraint of his pants, Lee's pulsing shaft seemed enormous. Remembering his earlier accusations about Jeremy and knowing his opinion about the morals of a *placée*'s daughter, Melanie grew suddenly afraid. What if he hurt her? She struggled to remember Deborah's explanations about what went on between men and women, but everything was confused as her mind skipped back and forth, torn between fear and desire.

Lee looked down at her small expressive face and followed the path of her wide golden gaze. *She's afraid of me*, he realized in sudden amazement, remembering all too well the fiery, passionate little creature that day on the hillside. But now, naked together in bed, it must seem different to a virginal woman. She was so tiny and fragile, for all her lushly curved feminine allure. He took a deep, steadying breath and knelt on the bed once more, splaying his fingertips across her belly and running them delicately in ever-widening circles, caressing her breasts and thighs but avoiding the core of her that enticed him with its untried innocence.

As he stroked her, Melanie felt the fearfulness abate, replaced by another kind of tension, a tightly coiling ache.

She looked up at his dark beauty, hesitantly raising her own hand to trace the pattern that was formed by the black hair on his chest. It narrowed in an arrowlike descent on his belly. Her busy fingers stopped midway down.

With a low, wicked laugh, he caught her wrist and pulled her hand the rest of the way toward his erection, then slipped it around the hard, pulsing flesh and stroked up and down slowly. Struggling to keep from crying out, he released her hand and rolled onto his side to lay next to her.

"Kiss me, Night Flower," he commanded raggedly and was rewarded when she moved toward him and reached her arms up to grasp his shoulders. He pulled her beneath him as they joined their mouths in a sealing kiss. This time she parted her lips and entwined her tongue with his eagerly. As he deepened the kiss, he slid his knee between her thighs, then reached down with one hand to stroke the dark curly mound. He felt her tense and instinctively arch upward toward his hand as he parted the hot, wet core of her. She whimpered and writhed as he stroked the sensitive aching tissue. Her eager desperation was all the more beguiling because it was untutored.

Lee felt the throbbing in his groin growing almost unbearable as he raised himself up over her and guided his shaft home—home to enter the hot, velvety sleekness of her body. He forced himself to pause just inside the welcoming lips, probing carefully for the barrier of her maidenhead.

Melanie felt him begin a desperate plunge, then stop short, laboring to breathe and calm himself. But the heat and hardness that was positioned at the seat of her desire drove her to seek completion of the act. Heedless of her earlier fears, she arched up, clawing at his back and tightening her legs around his hips.

With a muffled oath he responded, unable to stop himself this time as he tore through the thin membrane in one fast, hard thrust. He heard her small gasp of surprised pain, but was beyond the point where it registered. He continued to thrust in and out, rhythmically, joyously, after waiting so long.

The initial penetration was hurtful, but not nearly so much as Melanie had first imagined when she had looked on

his swollen phallus. The pain quickly receded as he continued to labor over her, driving into her in steady, even
strokes. That heat and ache, her constant companion since
that day on the hillside, once more took over, driving her
wild with a need for something beyond her imagination, yet
something as elemental, as necessary as air. She struggled
for it, looking up into his passion-glazed eyes as she
watched him arching to meet each stroke, unaware her eyes
were as revealing as his.

Melanie didn't understand what was happening as she
pulled him closer, fixated on her own blinding need. It was
as if she wanted to absorb him into her body. He suddenly
stiffened and cried out her name—as if in protest. She could
feel him swell even larger inside her as he made several
fast, hard thrusts that gave her what she had been so
desperately seeking.

Lee bit his bottom lip in an attempt to prolong the
exquisite, torturous rapture throbbing through his whole
body. *Stroke slow, easy, don't stop, don't ever stop*—"Oh,
Mellie, no, no!" The cry was torn from him as she gasped
and clawed at him, arching her back and driving him over the
brink into a final burst of meteoric fury that spent him utterly.

As he stilled and collapsed on her, she tightened her
knees around his hips and lay still while the rippling
contractions radiated outward through her entire body.
Gradually, as she came to herself she realized she had been
panting and crying like a wounded animal!

*So this is how a man bends a woman to him, enslaving
her mind and her will, making her breed for him and obey
him.* She squeezed her eyes closed tightly and buried her
face in the curve of his shoulder, feeling his heart thud next
to hers as both gradually returned to a slower rhythm.

Lee sensed the unnatural stillness in his wife's small body
and felt the wetness of her tears against his shoulder.
Completely drained and exhausted, he wanted only satiated
sleep, but he could not ignore her. She had followed him
over the edge, he was certain of that. After all the times
Dulcia had lain stiff and still, filled with his seed, her body
totally unaffected by what they had done together, he knew

the difference well enough. For all her virgin's pain, Melanie had clawed at him, impaling herself and moving with him, as hot and desperate as any woman he had ever encountered. And in his travels from Mexico to the Apachería, Leandro Velásquez had encountered many women.

Demanding, passionate little vixen—you almost caused me to finish without you, he thought through a groggy haze of oddly mixed pleasure and guilt. As he rolled away from her, he pulled her small soft body up against his hard long one and fell blessedly asleep.

Melanie did not resist his hold on her. She lay staring out across the darkened room. The wick light had long since burned out. Lee's even breathing indicated to her that the combination of the alcohol and his sexual release had made him fall asleep. She was grateful, wanting the time to think and regain control of her emotions.

It was so intense, this man-woman thing. The feelings were so confusing and contradictory—pain and pleasure, fear and trust, lust and love. *Love?* No. He found her beautiful, he desired her, but had wanted her tonight out of a perverse sense of possessive anger and pride, not out of love. She was certain of that. He had watched her with Jeremy and misread everything. *But what did you expect, little fool? He thinks you have the morals of a whore—at least the inferior bloodlines of one.*

As the tears overflowed, she refused to consider why his bigotry could hurt her so much. She focused instead on what giving in to his physical demands would mean. *I'll be tied to him, enslaved as surely as my black ancestors were.* Even if she were of impeccable Hispanic lineage, she would still be a possession to a man like Lee Velásquez, a woman to preside over his household and bear his children. *I can't live that way, I can't.* . . . Frightened and confused by all the new needs and emotions awakened in her that night, Melanie finally fell into an exhausted sleep.

Lee awakened the following morning with a foul hangover throbbing at his temples and a long-unfamiliar sensation prickling at his consciousness. He was in bed with a woman. For all the plenitude of whores he'd used in the past six years, Lee had never slept with one after she dispensed her services. He had deliberately paid them and sent them on their way.

The soft warmth curled beside him was definitely feminine. The sweet fragrance of night flowers filled his nostrils. He turned his head and was almost glad for the hammering agony inside his skull. It was a penance for his stupidity. The preceding evening came back to him in shadowy edged visions—visions of the ebony-haired beauty lying so innocently asleep in his bed. She had driven him wild with jealousy, a golden butterfly flirting and dancing with all those besotted men, especially that damned ranger. He had watched and seethed and drunk. Drunk. Yes, that described it. A dangerous combination—fury and liquor.

He looked at her sleeping face, framed by the billowing clouds of black satin hair. She was so young and vulnerable with those wicked gold-coin eyes closed, their thick brushy lashes fanning her cheeks. The night had been cool and she snuggled near him for warmth, pressing her lush curves tightly to his body. What man, drunk or sober, could resist Melanie Fleming? *No*, he amended, *Melanie Velásquez. His wife.* He supposed it was inevitable that she become his wife in fact. But not the way it had happened—in a fit of drunken lust. Although he knew her passion matched his own, he despised his roughness in taking her, and even more, he despised the naked hunger, the need that he had revealed in his drunken weakness last night.

Suppressing that thought, he brushed a lock of silky hair off her cheek with his fingertips, grinning as he remembered her cries of passion and the startled expression on her face when she climaxed. *So unlike Dulcia*, the thought flashed traitorously into his mind. He scowled darkly, feeling a renewed surge of guilt when he remembered the comparison he'd made between her and Melanie last night.

Melanie was certainly unlike Dulcia, and had he a choice, he would never have married this fiery, passionate little she-cat sleeping beside him. But all that was behind him now. For better or worse, he had taken an irrevocable step last night and now he must make the best of it and try to build a life with his Night Flower. First he must apologize for his drunken temper, he thought with a sigh, wishing the pounding misery in his head would abate so he could think more lucidly. She stirred.

"Good morning, I think," Lee whispered, wanting to keep noise at a minimum in deference to his splitting skull.

Melanie sat up, then, realizing she was naked, yanked up the tangled mass of sheets from the foot of the bed and pulled them defensively around her body. She had been cuddled up to him like a damn lapdog and he had been watching her, no doubt with a self-satisfied male smirk! She heard a slight rumble of baritone laughter and scooted across the narrow bed, turning to confront her nemesis with as much dignity as she could muster.

"Why the qualification? Aren't you sure it's a good morning? Could your fondness for whiskey perchance have something to do with your doubt?" she inquired with acid sweetness, trying desperately not to look at that dark, hard body, so virile with black curly hair set in cunning patterns. She had caressed every inch of him last night! Now just the thought of looking into his jet eyes made her quake.

He swung his long legs over the other side of the bed and stood up gingerly, rubbing his head as if it were made of fragile crystal.

"A temperance lecture—just what every man needs in the morning," he groused. Seemingly unconcerned with his nakedness, he walked slowly over to where a pair of buckskin breeches lay, tossed carelessly across a chair. Lee slid the soft old leather up his lean, hard legs and over his narrow hips, standing in profile to her as he buttoned the fly. She blushed and looked away. Did he notice?

"Mellie, we have to talk about last night." He hesitated, looking at her, so small and lovely, huddled on the bed like a doll. She gasped in affront at his use of her family's pet name. He knew she disliked it on his lips, for some perverse reason. Shaking his head very carefully, he was rewarded with a slight clearing of his vision as he walked over to the bed. He sat down and looked at her. "Look, what's done is done. I'm sorry I drank so much. I didn't want—"

She bounced off the bed like a coiled spring. "You're sorry! Too bad it means the end of your plans with Larena Sandoval! Get drunk and rape me and then beg pardon!"

Lee's face first went blank in amazement, then hardened like granite as she finished her tirade. "Raped you! Why you vicious little slut! You cried my name and clawed my back, clung to me and met me thrust for thrust. You found your release as surely as any hot-blooded Creole belle kissed by the tar brush ever did!" He stood up and glared down at her, fists clenched at his sides.

Melanie was blinded by a knifelike pain squeezing the breath from her, blinding her to all reason. Unthinkingly she dropped the sheet and reached up to slap him with all the strength her tiny hand could muster. "Yes, I'm kissed by the tar brush—a *placée*'s daughter, a dirty Indian breed! All those filthy inferior things you despise, and yet you want me! You desire me and you hate yourself for it. You'd take a woman like me in any bordello and never think twice. But I'm your wife—I bear that vaunted Velásquez name, and now I might even be carrying your child! Something to be sorry for, indeed, *Don* Leandro!"

He almost struck her back; he was shaking so badly his teeth chattered. "Bitch—you beautiful little bitch!" he ground out as he struggled to keep his arms at his sides. "You know all the tricks to tease and torment a man, just as surely as your Creole mother ever did. But she was more honest—she just wanted a man to support her in return for her favors. You—you don't want me. You don't really want any man, just your goddamn causes. I hope you find temperance and suffrage comfort you in bed at night, madam. I can assure you, you will sleep alone. No other man will touch my wife, and I don't choose to!"

Melanie stood trembling and breathless through his diatribe, afraid he *would* strike her. Wasn't he a scalper, a man who had killed, maimed, lived outside the law for years? She had never seen such hell as those tormented night eyes revealed. But Lee spun on his heel and grabbed his boots and shirt, leaving the room in a few stiff, controlled strides.

When she heard the door to the outside hall slam, it

sounded painfully final, like closing the door to a crypt. She was young and alive, yet shackled for life to a man who despised her, a man who had just sworn to hold her in a cruel travesty of a marriage with no care for her feelings, her dreams, her *self*. She ached but refused to give in to another self-pitying bout of tears. With the same rigid control Lee had exhibited, she began to dress for the day.

Chapter 17

That same morning Jim Slade sat watching the sunrise at Bluebonnet. It was a magic time, especially on a cool, crisp fall morning as the golden rays touched the dew-drenched grasses and shrubbery surrounding the front veranda, setting everything ablaze like a million fragments of diamond. Slade reclined on a sturdy oak bench, sipping a cup of coffee, surveying his land from the veranda. This was a morning ritual of his from early spring when the wildflowers turned the hillsides to riotous blue violet, to late fall when the mustard weed made them blaze yellow and bronze. Born and raised on this piece of land, he could imagine no life elsewhere.

"This is one of the loveliest spots in the Almighty's creation, I do believe." Sam Houston's sonorous voice interrupted Slade's ruminations. Cup in hand, he walked out the front door and sat down beside his younger friend. The two men sipped their coffee, drinking in the morning as much as the scalding black liquid.

"Your friend should be here soon," Jim said, finally breaking the companionable silence. They had important matters to discuss, matters that related to the very beauty and tranquillity surrounding them.

Houston shrugged. "I don't really know a good deal

about Jeremy Lawrence personally. I met him in Washington last spring for the first time. When this matter first came to my attention, I, er, investigated his background and decided he was the right man for the job.''

Jim grinned and took another sip of coffee. "With your usual thoroughness, I'm certain you know what he eats for breakfast and who his maternal grandmother was.''

Houston threw back his leonine head and laughed. "As always, Jim-boy, you ascribe more virtue to me than I possess. Still, I did find Lawrence has lived off and on in Texas since leaving Virginia as a youth. He has several years' experience as a peace officer and rode with the rangers during the war. Jack Hays spoke highly of him, and the few men in the Indian Office I trust also think he's honest and capable.''

Slade nodded. "Sounds good to me. How long has he worked for the office?''

"He was an agent for the superintendent in St. Louis for one year. In fact, that's why he was in Washington—to speak before Congress when they passed the Indian Office Appropriations Act last winter, reorganizing and expanding the office. He worked closely with the special investigating commissioners Campbell and Temple, whose mission in Texas was all too brief.'' Houston swore and pounded his big, meaty fist on the smooth oak bench. "If only those fools in Congress had extended the financial support for that commission, we might not have the mess we have now.''

Well acquainted with his mentor's political frustration in the nation's capital, not to mention its state counterpart in Austin, Jim sighed. "Well, we do know we've got some traders selling whiskey and guns to Comanche renegades, and their raids are getting pretty close to San Antonio. Any idea if these scum are licensed traders or just illegals who've slipped in to meet with the Comanche?''

Houston laughed mirthlessly. "Despite the fact that the idea of licensing traders to deal with the Indians was my own, I must confess it a dismal failure in practice. All the licenses have done since our illustrious Whig administration took power is serve as a form of spoils. We might as well have the army *give* them their military issue to sell to the renegades! I'm afraid the licensed traders are hiding behind corrupt deals with highly placed people in Congress and in the Interior Department. I know for certain that Lucas Blaine is getting direct payments from the Indian Office for alleged debts run up by half the Comanche Nation—who all conveniently seem to purchase goods on credit from his post."

"Convenient—eliminate the middleman," Jim said disgustedly.

"One way or another, those white carrion get government money and deliver nothing but inferior goods and pestilence to their red brothers," Sam added sadly.

"You think Blaine is one of the whiskey traders?" Jim asked.

Houston scoffed. "As my old friend Chief Bowl used to say, 'Does a bear shit in the woods?' The trick is going to be catching him actually dealing with the renegades. He may be defrauding the government by taking Comanche allotment money for inferior or nonexistent pots and blankets, but the real danger is that he's also selling them guns and spirits. Obviously the Indian Office can't reimburse him for those items."

"And since he isn't in this for philanthropy, we can be sure the renegades are trading him something in return—horses and cattle stolen from ranchers around this area," Jim supplied.

"And if Blaine is operating this close to San Antonio, he has to have the cooperation of someone with the rangers," Houston said.

"No way would this go on if Jack Hays was still in charge," Jim agreed fervently.

"Let's just hope our undercover ranger will be able to nose out everyone involved before the whole of west Texas erupts into full-blown war," Houston added, then looked up. A horseman was approaching the house.

Jeremy Lawrence swung down from his mount with the careless ease of a man who has spent a lifetime on horseback. His tan hair blew free in the breeze and his mustache gave his face a hard-edged look, like a Texas ruffian, the perfect sort to fit in with Seth Walkman.

He ambled up to the porch and shoved the flat-crowned hat to the back of his head. Reaching out his hand to Houston, he said, "Mornin', Senator. Mr. Slade, a pleasure to see you again."

As the two men shook hands, Jim smiled and said, "Call me Jim, Jeremy. Sam here's been telling me all about you. You know this is going to be a hell of a dangerous job. But first, let's go in and get breakfast. Be grateful Charlee's cooking this morning, not Weevils."

Over stacks of hot buckwheat cakes and molasses, the men sat around the kitchen table and talked.

"What do you know about Seth Walkman?" Jeremy asked Jim, his level blue gaze measuring and steady.

Jim grimaced and took a swig of coffee to clear his throat. "I wouldn't trust my back to him. He's kill-crazy mean and hates Indians. You tangle with your 'boss' already?"

Lawrence grinned wolfishly. "Nope. I'm just a quiet boy from Virginia who used to shoot a few buffalo for a living. I'm not making any waves around my superior officers yet."

"You'll learn a great deal that way. Jim here can tell you that from experience," Houston interjected dryly.

"I have already learned a number of fascinating things," Lawrence said quietly. Both the men fixed their eyes on him expectantly. "Newspaper reporters are a great source—especially when they're beautiful women, to boot."

Jim dropped his fork with a clatter. "Melanie Velásquez?" he croaked. "Damn, I should've known she'd get involved after all her Indian crusading."

Houston's face lit with glee. "After you yourself married a strong-willed woman, Jim-boy, you should not be shocked by a female reporter unearthing these facts."

"I am when she's married to Lee Velásquez," Jim said with decided unease. "What did Melanie tell you?" he asked Lawrence.

Jeremy leaned forward. "She has some Indian kids—boys from that school the German priest runs—who can observe all sorts of things for her. They found my Indian-hating boss, Walkman, being rather chummy with a fellow named Lucas Blaine, who's licensed to trade with the

Comanche. Walkman not only keeps his rangers from crossing tracks with Blaine, he gives Blaine tips about good pickings—livestock for Blaine's renegade friends to raid.''

"Like that herd of cattle stolen from the Jameston place?" Jim interjected with dawning understanding. "That fool girl is really in over her head! If Walkman or Blaine ever finds out she can tie them together, they'll kill her or sell her as a slave to Buffalo Gall or one of his cronies!" He well remembered when his own headstrong Charlee had narrowly escaped such a fate a scant ten years earlier!

"I've told her she's to stay out of this from here on, but I don't know that she'll do it," Jeremy said with a sigh. "She *has* agreed to tell me everything she gleans from the children. At least we do have a link substantiated between a ranger captain and a whiskey trader. Now we have to bait a trap for Blaine and his renegades." He looked from Houston to Slade expectantly.

Houston said shrewdly, "Not Jim. He's too well known and tied to me. We need someone newer around here—a rancher who lives farther out, with smaller numbers of men working for him—someone they'd never suspect." He looked at Jim.

"You're thinking of Lee." He sighed. "The way he feels about both Indians and rangers, it'll be the devil's own time convincing him to help us."

"But if his own wife is endangered by these men, surely—" Jeremy replied vehemently.

"He'd probably sooner lock her in a closet than work with you," Jim bluntly interjected.

Lawrence shrugged. "I did detect, er, a bit of hostility from him the first time we met, but I attributed it to jealousy over his beautiful lady, not to my ranger uniform—if you can call these buckskins a uniform," he added ruefully.

"He'll work with you, the young rapscallion, or he'll answer to Sam Houston," the senator replied with finality.

"I just itch to know what a man with Walkman's crazy hatred of Indians is doing helping a trader who barters them guns," Jeremy said speculatively.

Houston and Slade exchanged grave looks. "What better

way to touch off a full-blown war of extermination?'' the senator asked.

Lame Deer tasted blood as Fredo Rojas's large beefy knuckles connected a second, then a third time with his split lips.

"Dirty Indian, renegade trash, hanging around our city trying to act white," Felipe taunted, struggling to hold on to the much smaller boy as his brother pummeled him mercilessly.

"You stay away from our library," gritted Fredo as he landed a telling blow to the Indian's stomach.

"Yes. Just come to our father's house and clean the privies. That's good work for a shit-eating savage," Felipe said with an ugly laugh.

Using his last surge of blinding, hate-filled strength, Lame Deer wrenched free of Felipe's hold and butted his head like a battering ram into Fredo's ample midsection, knocking the youth into the thick dust of the street. As they rolled and thrashed, Felipe grabbed the smaller boy, pulling Lame Deer off his brother. Viciously he twisted the Indian's straight black hair, forcing Lame Deer's bloody face into the dust, caking it with dark reddish mud. Fredo now rolled up and began to punch at the downed Indian's back and sides.

Lame Deer could feel the fierce blows raining all over him, but their impact was lessening as his vision began to blur and he slipped into semiconsciousness. Then the weight of Felipe's body was suddenly lifted off him and the shrill, angry cries of the Rojas brothers were silenced by a deep baritone voice speaking in rapid Spanish.

After Lee's fight with Melanie, he had stormed off to the livery stable. He was on his way back to the ranch when the sounds of boys scuffling had distracted him. Lee held twelve-year-old Fredo and fourteen-year-old Felipe, one in each hand, by the scruffs of their necks. "Why are the two of you beating up one small boy?" His piercing black eyes and fiercely scowling face turned from Fredo to Felipe, waiting for an answer.

"He's just an Indian who works for our housekeeper. Why do you care what happens to a dirty Apache?" Felipe asked, half in bewilderment, half in fear.

"I am a Lipan!" Lame Deer cried furiously, heedless of his split lip and aching jaw as he dragged himself to sit up, spitting mud and blood from between his teeth.

Lee released the two larger boys, saying, "That still doesn't explain why the two of you set on him behind your house."

"He was reading a book from our papa's library! No dirty Apache," Fredo said, looking defiantly at the smaller boy again, "has the right to read our books. He stole it!"

"Yes! We chased him out here," added Felipe.

Lee knelt by the Indian boy's side. Knowing the fiercely independent pride of Lipan Apaches, he made no attempt to comfort the beaten child, but simply asked, "Did you steal a book, Lame Deer?"

The child's eyes were already swollen almost closed and his face was so cut and mud-covered it was nearly unrecognizable, but he replied with surprising dignity, "I stole nothing. Mrs. Mendoza gave me permission to read in the library after I finished my chores in the back."

"Our housekeeper wouldn't let an Indian in Papa's library," Fredo shrilled, taking a menacing step toward Lame Deer again.

"Anyway, Indians shouldn't be able to read," Felipe added scathingly.

"Father Gus is teaching me. I can read better than Fredo. Despite the fancy tutors his papa hires, he is stupid," Lame Deer added defiantly, beaten but unbowed before the menacing brothers.

Deciding the ten-year-old had no broken bones and was able to walk, Lee stood up and motioned for Lame Deer to do the same. "Let's just go see Mrs. Mendoza and find out who's telling the truth here." He looked from the younger Indian child to the two tight-lipped Rojas boys.

All three preceded Lee back toward the house beyond the high adobe wall surrounding the garden.

Mrs. Mendoza was a kindly woman, well past fifty but

vigorous and efficient. She took pride in her work. When Lee introduced himself to her, he could see the obvious Indian heritage stamped on her strong impassive features— high cheekbones, flat broad forehead, and prominent nose. She stood in the kitchen of the Rojas house, looking with obvious distress from Fredo and Felipe to Lame Deer.

"When I told him he could read for a bit when he finished his chores, I never dreamed this would happen. He replaced the book yesterday evening—I saw him do it. It was one about Indians with drawings in it. Then he left after thanking me." She nervously wiped her hands on her apron, looking at the Rojas brothers. "I did not think they would attack Lame Deer for it."

Lee looked at Felipe and Fredo with a scowl. "So he stole a book, did he?"

"What does it matter? That crazy German priest has no right to teach Indians how to read!" Felipe pointed a finger at the small muddy boy.

"*He* shouldn't touch our papa's things, either," Fredo added spitefully.

Mrs. Mendoza gasped and crossed herself at his insult to Father Gus. "He is a man of God, and you will confess that sin tonight!"

Lee added, "And as for touching your father's books, you might do well to spend a little more time reading in his library yourself and a lot less bullying boys half your size in the streets. That was a coward's act."

Felipe looked ashamed and faintly fearful that his father might indeed exact punishment for brawling with a common Indian servant, but Fredo only gave Lee a sullen, silent pout and stared down at his shoes.

When Mrs. Mendoza wanted to cleanse Lame Deer's injuries, the boy stubbornly refused, saying only that he was late for his lessons at Father Gus's school. When he would have slipped away, Lee restrained him and, upon assuring Mrs. Mendoza that he'd see to the boy, departed with him.

As they walked out the back way, Lee noticed how the child stoically ignored his injuries and labored to keep up with his own long strides. He mounted Sangre and reached down to scoop the small battered child up into his arms. "You work for the Rojas family long?" He switched from Spanish to English now.

As he suspected, Lame Deer followed the language shift naturally. "No, only a month or so. I help the gardener and do some chores for the housekeeper lady."

"Your family need money?" Lee asked, knowing that was the situation with most of the tame Indians living on the periphery of the city.

The boy nodded. "My baby sister's sick and needs milk." Then he ducked his head suddenly.

Lee's eyes narrowed. "That has a familiar ring to it. Last spring in the Main Plaza market—you were the boy who tried to steal the goat! You *did* steal Father Gus's burro."

The boy looked his rescuer in the eye. "I returned the burro to the holy father. He forgave me."

"And taught you how to read, too, apparently," Lee said dryly. "Why try to read in the Rojas library? Of all places to pick, I'd guess it's the least hospitable."

"We have so few books at our school. Father Gus writes to his friends in St. Louis and in Germany, but they can spare little. There aren't enough books to go around," he said wistfully. "And the Rojas library is grand, with books full of drawings, even!"

Lee smiled in spite of himself, recalling a small boy sneaking into Will Slade's imposing library to read late at night. Of course, he had Will's full blessing to read all he wanted. Somehow, knowing Felipe and Fredo's father, he was certain no such invitation would ever be tendered to Lame Deer.

"Ach! Lame Deer, what has happened?" Father Gus's eyes widened to saucer size as he saw Lee dismount with his bloodied pupil. He rushed from the door of the small adobe on the outskirts of the city that served as his free school.

"I am all right, Father, honest," the boy remonstrated to the priest, who was kneeling in the dust examining cuts and swellings. "Only one tooth is gone and it was a baby tooth I was to lose anyway. It was loose or they'd never have knocked it out," he said with bravado.

"They? Who are these 'they' that beat small children?" Father Gus's blue eyes blazed.

"The Rojas brothers," Lee supplied. "I'll tell you all about it while we get this young man cleaned up."

"*Ja*, come," Father Gus picked up the unprotesting child and walked resolutely through the door as Lee quickly explained about the fight he'd interrupted.

"Jeehosaphat! Child, whut's happened ta yew?" Obedience Oakley stood in the middle of the courtyard behind the schoolroom. The adobe oven in the center was flanked by several crude trestle tables with a big cook fire over to one side. A large pot bubbled over the fire and Obedience was in the process of taking six pans of golden corn bread from the oven. She dropped the last pan carelessly on the table and scuttled over to the injured boy.

"I fought two boys. It is not really that bad, Mrs. Oakley, honest," Lame Deer said as she ushered him over to the fountain spilling down the far wall of the courtyard.

"Jist set a spell 'n' let me see whut need's doin'." She grabbed a large towel from the table and soaked it in the fountain, then began to clean the caked mud and dried blood from the boy's face as Lee explained.

Father Gus shook his head sadly. "We need books and there is no money to ship them. English or Spanish, just any books. So many bright young minds I have here, so willing to learn, if only the tools were available. But we do what we can, *ja*?" He turned to Obedience and she nodded, intent on the squirming child who was more disquieted about being bathed than having his injuries treated.

"This day I go to visit *Señora* Rojas. She must be told what kind of cruelty her children do," Father Gus said sadly.

"Won't do no good, Father. Them rich folks don't want th' likes o' us mixin' in with them 'n' their younguns. Them boys is purely spoiled rotten," Obedience averred.

"I'm afraid she's right," Lee agreed.

"Anyway, I go. They must know that Lame Deer did not steal. Who knows what lies are upon the souls of those boys even now?"

"Never seen a man with sech grit, I'll give yew that, Father," Obedience said, chuckling. "Even if'n yew do wear them funny dresses all th' time." She gestured to his cassock. "Ain't hidin' nothin', are ya?"

Looking down, the young priest's eyes danced and he lifted the hem of his cassock. "See? No hooves."

Lee looked baffled as Obedience and Father Gus exchanged a hearty laugh. "Hooves?"

"Ach, I forget. You were not here." He wiped tears of mirth from his eyes and explained, "Last week a wagon train comes—from Alabama, bound for California. Two small ones, no bigger than Lame Deer, follow me across the square from San Fernando's after mass. When I stop to talk with my abbess here at one of the market stalls, the younger of the little ones, a girl, she rushed up to me and . . . lifts my cassock in the back! Suddenly I feel a draft and I turn."

"He ain't got no tail, ner no hooves neither," Obedience interjected, mimicking a small girl's voice. "Them children wuz tole th' same thing I wuz tole back in Tennessee. Reason yew priest fellas wear long dresses 'n' hats like ladies is ta hide yer horns 'n' tails 'n' cloven hooves 'cause yer th' devil's own!"

Lee grinned. "What did your two emigrant children decide when they couldn't find any incriminating evidence?"

Father Gus shrugged good-naturedly. "An argument between the girl and her brother began. She said I had no—er, extra appendages. He was afraid to come closer but yelled that she was lying. As red as a beet my face was with all the stall keepers laughing. And this one"—he gestured at Obedience—"she grabs my cassock and pulls it free to rescue me. Then she asks them where is their mama."

"Jist then this here woman comes tearin' through th' crowd 'n' yanks th' girl by her ear 'n' gives her a swat. Th' boy follered her off like he wuz scalded, both o' them younguns lookin' over their shoulder at Father Gus." She paused to scratch her head. "Still wonder who won thet argument—th' girl er th' boy. . . ."

"Mother Obedience here, besides being my rescuer in time of distress is also our school cook. And a splendid one she is, indeed. One good meal each day the children receive while they learn,'' the priest said fondly.

Obedience looked up warily. "I'm jist a good Baptist lady doin' my Christian duty feedin' hungry younguns. Don't yew sweet talk me with thet 'Mother Obedience' stuff agin. Too many o' yew Catholics round hereabouts ta make me rest easy, even if'n yew ain't got no hooves er tails,'' she added with mock gruffness, looking from the grinning young priest to Lee.

As if sharing an old joke, Father Gus said, "Ach, good Mother Obedience, what a splendid abbess you will make! Daily I pray for it—and your conversion first, of course.''

"Jeehosaphat! Reverend Foster done like ta drowned me when he baptized me in th' Tennessee River back in twenty-seven. I ain't never doin' no more convertin' fer shore, ner lettin' a preacher near me with talk 'bout baptizin' me agin! No siree!''

"Wash Oakley might just have something to say about losing his wife, Father,'' Lee said cheerfully, winking at Lame Deer, who had begun to giggle despite his painful cuts and bruises.

"*Him* I would make a bishop!'' Father Gus said triumphantly. "He could fill the pulpit in Galveston Cathedral and thunder at the city elders: 'Send Father Gus more books!' '' he intoned in a rumbling bass voice.

Chapter 18

Melanie sat alone in the hotel room she and Lee had shared, staring bleakly at the door he had slammed with such finality a moment earlier. She felt numb with shock as the enormity of what they had done the preceding night washed over her. All their plans for a discreet annulment were impossible now. She was truly married for the rest of her life. Slowly, unwillingly, yet with a quivering stir of curiosity, she walked to the mirror, letting the sheet she had wrapped around herself trail carelessly to the floor.

Naked, she stood in front of the long oval floor mirror and inspected herself critically. *Do I look changed? Will everyone be able to tell what happened last night when they look at me?* Were her eyes haunted by a new knowledge? She ran her hands down from her shoulders, over her breasts, across her flat little belly, then around the flair of her hips. *I don't look different,* she reassured herself, but she felt different; she *was* different.

Melanie bathed and dressed, preparing to go to the *Star* as if it were merely another ordinary day. Despite her best revolve, every time she passed a store window or mirror on her long walk from the hotel to the office, she found herself staring at the sad-eyed woman reflected in it.

Taking a deep breath, Melanie opened the door to the newspaper and stepped into the dim interior from the bright sunlight of the street. The place smelled comfortingly of dust and linseed oil.

Amos grinned at her and continued setting type, his dexterous fingers moving across the case boxes with blurring rapidity. Clarence cleared his throat and gave her his usual cursory inspection, a gesture that normally elicited no more than a saucy swish of her skirts as she went to her desk. Today she actually felt herself beginning to blush, the heat stealing up over the primly starched collar of her white blouse. *He can't know—he just can't!* She stood rooted to the floor for a moment.

"I assume you danced with the senator and got all the latest Washington gossip?" he said at length, apparently ignoring her flustered appearance.

"Yes. I'll write it up immediately. I have a good story about Houston, and all the frills and furbelows the ladies wore at the ball," she said in an overeager rush to get past his scrutiny.

"Your Mrs. Wolcott was here this morning again, sancti-monious old crow," Clarence muttered waspishly.

"She's not *my* Mrs. Wolcott, but she is a fine woman—a truly visionary leader in the temperance cause," Melanie said defensively. "I plan to do a series of articles on temperance as well as gambling and prostitution. Your female readers will love it."

"I'm rather more worried that my male readers will hate it," he replied sourly.

As she worked, Melanie considered how right Stella Wolcott was in her condemnation of demon rum. *If Lee hadn't been drinking last night* . . . She stopped what she was writing and furiously balled up the paper, tossing it angrily on the floor. Her concentration was abysmal, but somehow she got through the day and finished a credible series of stories, one on Sam Houston, a gossip column about the dance, and even a brief article using the news items Stella Wolcott had delivered for her that morning.

Lee had already left for the ranch when she finally returned to the hotel. A terse note lay on the dresser beside her hairbrush, admonishing her to come home before dark and to use the buggy he'd left at the livery. One of the *vaqueros* was waiting in the hotel lobby to carry her valise and drive her to the ranch. The hotel bill had, of course, been paid. She felt like a kept woman.

On the long ride home Melanie dreaded confronting Lee. She could still see the blazing anger in his face, sense the leashed fury holding his body taut as he delivered his scathing rebuke to her that morning. *You don't want me. You don't really want any man—just your goddamn causes!* His words still rang in her ears. Was he right? Was she an unnatural woman, cold and unfeeling? Then why did she feel so bereft when he had told her he regretted touching her—and vowed he would never do so again? But would he keep his word? Did she want him to?

"You all right, Miz Velásquez?" Ray asked.

She had buried her head in her hands and huddled back in the corner of the buggy like a wounded child. "Yes, yes, of course, Ray. Just a little tired from a long day's work."

Finally the ranch house loomed ahead. She felt an odd mixture of dread and welcome. It was so enchantingly lovely, nestled beside the stream with the trees whispering above it. Their cool, leafy fingers caressed the roof like a lover. *Why did I think that?* she scolded herself as she climbed down, her resolute step belying her anxiety.

Genia greeted her warmly and already had bathwater heating. Delicious smells wafted from Kai's kitchen. As she sank into the tub in her room, she thought wistfully, *I could love this place like home if only . . . if only he could love me.* The thought seemed to complete itself. She bolted upright in the tub, splashing water over the sides with her sudden exertion.

Would it really be so bad to love him? To have him love her? To have a real marriage? Slowly she sank back in the tub to consider all her whirling thoughts. *You both have passion*, Genia had told her. How right the canny old woman had been. But passion alone was not basis enough for a marriage; it took love, trust, respect. Given her background and his bigotry, there seemed no solution for them.

She dressed for dinner that night as if preparing to do battle. *If I've acted like a passionate* placée, *I might as well look like one.* Rummaging through her closet, she selected a gown she'd never worn, a deep cranberry-red velvet trimmed with deep black lace. It clung to every curve of her body. She decided it was the sort of gown that Lily Duval would have liked. If Lee thought her yellow satin with its billowing skirts was outrageous, wait until he saw this. That priggish Hispanic *don* would probably have apoplexy! Of course, no one but he and the servants would ever see it.

Nervously she pulled on the lace at the rounded low-cut neckline, trying to fluff it up a bit to conceal her cleavage. Then, considering what Charlee would say about her endowment, she smiled archly and smoothed the lace back down. She left her hair loose, caught over to one side and adorned with a small cluster of the wild primroses that she had picked near the house. Very simple, casual, the artless way a *placée* would appear for her lover. Scorn her he might, but he *would* suffer for what he'd said.

Lee had arrived at the ranch early that afternoon and had busied himself with stock work for several hours, hoping the exhausting riding would take away some of the tension still simmering inside him. Last night had turned his world upside down. A long afternoon of backbreaking labor left him aching and tired but no nearer to a resolution of his confused feelings than he had been when he awakened with Melanie in his bed that morning.

When he came into the ranch kitchen, dusty and sweaty despite the cool fall air, Kai grinned broadly.

"Bathwater's heating for you. Figured you'd need it. Genia's taken care of your wife already."

Lee grunted as he hung his hat on a rack by the door. "I assume she just returned from town."

"She put in a full day at the newspaper. She wrote all about Senator Houston. Promised to read me the story tomorrow," the big Kanaka said with almost childlike enthusiasm.

The servants were certainly won to her. Genia's acceptance he'd expected, since she was a born romantic, but the fierce old scalper Kai was Melanie's devoted friend as well. Lee felt the subtle pressure both of them placed on him. Kai continually sang Melanie's praises, and Lee was sure Genia had told her mistress what a splendid husband he could be if only . . .

Lee sighed in perplexity as he stripped off his dusty clothes and threw them on the floor of his bedroom. By the time he had finished undressing, Kai was there filling the tub. Gratefully he sank into the water, trying to think of anything else other than Melanie and the fact that he would have to confront her across the dinner table. Idly he considered packing up an assortment of books from his library and sending them to Father Gus for use in his school. He felt an unreasoning surge of anger when he recalled the Rojas bullies beating up that small Lipan boy this morning, then laughed at the irony of Lee Velásquez rescuing an Indian, even if he was a child.

A child. If he and Melanie had children, they'd have Indian blood, a fact she had repeatedly thrown up to him whenever he had weakened and tried to touch her. Now she could be carrying his child. No, he dismissed the idea. It was very unlikely after only one night, and he had promised her he would never again force himself on her—a promise far more easily made in the heat of anger than kept in the long years stretching ahead of them. There would be no annulment, no other marriage. What if there were no children to carry on the Velásquez name, to inherit the ranch he had sweated and struggled so long to build?

As he brooded and turned those disquieting thoughts over in his mind, his bathwater grew cold. Finally he roused himself and quit the tub, drying off quickly. Kai had laid out a fancy ruffled shirt and one of his best wool suits. Ignoring this obvious hint from the Kanaka, he donned a simple open-collared muslin shirt and buckskin pants, then headed to the library to select some books for Father Gus's school.

When Melanie came into the dining room, Lee was nowhere in sight. Then she heard a noise from down the hall. Following the sounds of rustling pages and thudding books being tossed onto a pile, Melanie paused in the door to the library, puzzled. Lee was standing with his back to her, rummaging through the shelves against the window wall, pulling down volume after volume, flipping through each, replacing some, tossing others onto the growing heap threatening to spill from the desk.

She observed his casual attire, feeling angry at his cavalier attitude and embarrassed because she had overdressed. Nevertheless, even in a simple pair of buckskins and homespun shirt, he was elegantly handsome. While he was unaware of her perusal, Melanie watched the play of lean muscles beneath the thin fabric of his shirt, the way the soft leather pants hugged his long legs. One inky lock of hair spilled over his forehead, which was creased in concentration.

Suddenly he sensed her presence and looked up. If she'd poleaxed him between the eyes, he would not have been more stunned. Covering the surge of breathless pain her beauty evoked, he asked harshly, "Aren't you a bit overdressed for a simple dinner at home?'' With insulting thoroughness he surveyed her lush curves encased so revealingly in red velvet.

"Perhaps I felt I owed you something," she replied cryptically, fighting down the dizzying wash of humiliation his inspection brought. She walked over to the desk and picked up a Latin grammar, blowing the dust from its pages. "It seems an odd time to clean out your library," she commented, wanting desperately to change the subject.

Now it was Lee who felt an unreasoning surge of embarrassment. "I was just packing up a few old books for Father Gus," he said nonchalantly, turning back to his task.

Her eyes widened in surprise. "For his school—for the Indian children? Lee Velásquez helping Indians? How out of character!"

"No more so than a women's rights crusader wearing a dress like that," he shot back, tossing the last of the books from the case onto the desk.

Just then Kai appeared in the doorway to announce dinner. He could sense the crackling tension between the boss and his wife. Both of them seemed glad to quit the library and file silently into the dining room to eat the superbly prepared meal. It depressed Kai to realize that neither would taste a bit of what they consumed.

The next morning two of the *vaqueros* from Night Flower Ranch pulled up to the weathered adobe schoolhouse with a wagon filled with books. One of the men handed the overjoyed priest a terse note.

Dear Father Gus:
    Please don't try to make me a Cardinal for this, but I thought you could use these. I brought them from my Uncle Alfonso's library in Mexico City many years ago. Jim Slade saved them for me while I was in exile. Since it was his father who first gave me a love of books and a chance to read, I only repay a debt of long standing by passing them on to you.

                                              Lee Velásquez

Melanie left early that next morning for town. Lee was already down at the corral making work assignments to the men, trying to concentrate on the business of running his ranch. He wanted nothing more than to forget his wife, at least for the day. Seeing two horsemen approach, he recognized Jim Slade's big buckskin, Polvo, at once and a broad smile crossed his face. Then seeing the man with his friend, he immediately scowled. It was that damn ranger Jeremy Lawrence! *What the hell is he doing on my land?* His hand went automatically to the Colt on his hip.

Jim nodded tersely to Lee, noting the way he looked at Jeremy and touched his gun. "You won't be needing that, *mano*. I'll vouch for Lawrence here," he said levelly.

"I don't want rangers on Velásquez land, Jim. You know that," Lee replied tightly.

"Will you forget all the old hates just long enough to listen to what we have to say? It's important, Lee. I'm asking you as a friend." Slade's amber eyes pierced Lee's armor.

Shrugging, Lee let his hand drop away from his gun and swung up on Sangre. Several *vaqueros* lingered around the busy corral, curious about what was going on. They were aware of the hate their boss had for the *rinches*. Ignoring them, Lee said, "Let's ride out a ways where we can talk in private."

After a few minutes of riding in silence, Jim said, "What I have to ask you comes direct from Houston, Lee." As he expected, Lee's eyes narrowed in surprise, then shifted to Lawrence. "Jeremy works for the Indian Office. He was an agent for the superintendent in St. Louis for several years. Now he's been assigned to Texas."

"What the hell does that have to do with me, *mano*? You know I have no use for Indians or rangers," Lee replied in a low growl.

"Look, Velásquez, I know we got off to a bad start—" Jeremy began but Lee cut him off.

"We didn't get off to *any* start. I don't deal with rangers— or Indian agents," he added contemptuously.

"You have plenty of reasons to hate Indians and rangers," Jim interjected, "but you sure as hell ought to want to stop a full-blown Comanche uprising incited by a crooked ranger. Or do you want the wars of a generation ago to start up again?"

Lee's face was set in grim lines. "From what I've been hearing lately, they already have."

Patiently Jeremy replied, "The raids that have been increasing in the Bexar area are being instigated by a crooked trader who runs whiskey and guns to the renegades in return for stolen horses and cattle. The whole operation is being protected by Seth Walkman. That's why Houston and my superiors in the Interior Department picked me for this assignment. I'd been a militia volunteer in east Texas several years ago and I worked for the bureau." He paused a moment, then smiled coldly. "Surely you'd like to nail Walkman and Blaine, not to mention a murdering bastard like Buffalo Gall."

Lee looked straight ahead, digesting what Lawrence said. "So Walkman's dealing with renegades," he murmured, half to himself. Ever since he'd first run across the cold-eyed ranger, he'd known the man was especially dangerous. "Just exactly how do you know it's Walkman and Blaine who are dealing with Gall?"

Jim shifted nervously in the saddle and Jeremy cleared his throat uncomfortably. Jim spoke first. "Houston knew Blaine was getting big cash payments for bills at his post supposedly run up by Comanche chiefs. He's smelled a rat as far as Blaine's concerned for years. As to Walkman—"

"Your wife found out about his conversation with Blaine. That's what we were talking about that day in the restaurant," Jeremy interrupted.

"Melanie! How in the hell did she find out about Walkman?" Lee's eyes narrowed on Lawrence accusingly.

"It seems she's got a network of spies—small Indian children from that school the German priest runs," Jeremy answered, looking Lee in the eye straightforwardly.

Jim watched the exchange between the two men with growing unease. He had been sure it would be difficult to get Lee to trust a ranger, but there was more to this situation than Lee's hate for the rangers. Melanie was involved, and both men were walking around the issue like two dogs worrying a bone.

Lee recalled that Lame Deer had given Melanie information about Gall's raid. Her going after that story had led indirectly to their disastrous marriage. Once he had stopped her from following that Comanche at the creek, he'd thought no more about the raid. But then he'd had a lot of other things on his mind. Finally he said, "I told my wife when we married that Moses French's career was over. It seems she doesn't agree," he mused grimly.

"Look, Velásquez, I know how dangerous this is and I warned her to stay out of it when she gave me that information," Jeremy said defensively.

"What you tell her doesn't signify, Lawrence. I'm her husband, and she'll do as I say, if I have to lock her in her room," he finished with gritted teeth.

"I think we all agree Melanie isn't to be brought in on our plans to surprise Gall and his white friends," Jim said levelly, looking from Lee to Jeremy. "Now that we have that settled, shall we discuss how to stop a war?"

Lame Deer scurried through the brush, keeping low and out of sight as he watched Seth Walkman enter Blaine's trading post. As he crawled along the edge of a deep ravine, he forgot the bruises and cuts that covered his body. He must get near enough to overhear what the trader and the ranger were saying. He had left his burro, the one Father Gus let him borrow, behind a hill, tied in a cottonwood thicket. But how to get inside the big rickety log building to overhear the two men plotting? He was sure they spoke of Gall and his raiders, and he vowed to get the details for Melanie.

Just then a small band of women, mostly Kickapoo squaws, came into sight, trailing a gaggle of half-naked children with them as they trudged toward the post. They brought dressed buffalo hides to trade for iron cookpots and other implements. If he could only melt in with the other children, he could hang around the post while they browsed. No one would pay any attention to him if he acted as if he spoke no English.

Taking off the necklace and headband that marked him as a Lipan, he bundled them up in his shirt, which was far too new and clean. Clad only in worn buckskin pants and moccasins, he slipped in behind the last couple of small girls, unnoticed.

The post was dark inside, dank-smelling. The walls and aisles were piled high with goods—cooking implements, skinning knives, blankets. Brightly colored bolts of cheap calico were piled in a gaudy heap in one corner next to a large set of crude wooden boxes filled with mutlicolored loose beads. The pungent smell of tanned leather emanated from one corner where large stacks of tanned bison hides stood. Soft, glossy furs lay in a fluffy pile across one crude plank table that served as a work counter. A cash box and bookkeeping ledger sat next to the furs. Lame Deer knew how the trader kept everything written down, making the Indians sign their marks next to the lists of items purchased. He also knew the bills for a few handfuls of cheap beads and a moldy blanket often were presented to the Indian agents for a greatly inflated value.

A man in greasy buckskins and a coarse homespun shirt ambled over to the Kickapoo women and began to speak to them in a crude hodgepodge of Spanish and sign language. Lame Deer looked around, searching for the tall ranger and the fat Firehair, Blaine. Then he heard the low, growling tones of Walkman's voice coming from a back room. The conversation was muffled when Blaine appeared suddenly and slammed the door. Lame Deer swore to himself and then recalled how Father Gus would feel about his lapse. Quickly repenting the profanity, the child looked for a way around the back so he could eavesdrop. It only took a moment to find an old wooden barrel and shove it below the open window to Blaine's office.

"I tell ya, Seth, I don't like givin' them Comanch Brown Bess rifles. Better ta jist git 'em likkered up 'n' let 'em raid stock fer us. With them guns they's killin' too many settlers. Gittin' too bold. Afore yew know it, we'll have thet damn Neighbors down on us." Lucas Blaine's wheezing voice rose a bit as he finished speaking his piece and took a sip from a glass of clear liquid on the table in front of him.

Walkman watched with contempt as the other man folded his hands across his paunch. "Forget that fool Injun agent Neighbors. He's busy now up in Austin playin' at bein' a crusadin' reformer in the legislature. Tryin' to get the state to give the Injun Office land for reservations," he sneered.

"Some chance o' thet happenin'," Blaine agreed. "Still, if'n Gall 'n' his braves keep gettin' supplied with guns 'n' ammunition, th' army might git involved. Cud git real unhealthy for me out here in th' middle."

Walkman sneered again. "You're gettin' rich in the meanwhile—robbin' the Injun agents and them dumb redskins out there blind," he said, gesturing to the closed door, behind which the Kickapoo women made their purchases. "Sellin' whiskey's even more profitable, not to mention picking up them herds of prime beef and horseflesh. You want the money, you take your chances the same as me'n him."

Blaine's watery hazel eyes shifted away from Walkman's leaden ones, and he lifted his glass of whiskey again. "He's gettin' too greedy, Seth. Yew 'n' him been pushin' Gall ta raid too often. With them guns they's not jist takin' off stock—they's killin' folks—settlers, women and kids."

"You gettin' religion?" Walkman snickered.

"Jist makes me nervous, thet's all," Blaine said thickly, tossing off the last of his whiskey.

"Tell your pal Gall I got him a real sweet place to raid. I'm takin' my men on a patrol to the south for a few days. Up northwest a ways a fellow named Broughton has him a real fine corral full of mustangs, all broke and ready for sale to the army. I think Gall could pick them off real easy. Only the rancher 'n his family are there with half a dozen men. None of them got any guns better'n the Injuns."

Blaine nodded in resignation. He still didn't like it.

* * *

When Lame Deer returned to where his burro had been tied, the recalcitrant animal was nowhere to be seen. Francisco had a habit of pulling his reins free and taking off for home. But Lame Deer was miles from San Antonio and he had very urgent news to give Melanie. Those evil men must be stopped! Delaying only long enough to retrieve his shirt, headband, and necklace, he started out in a slow, dogged trot for town. With every step he cursed Francisco; with every other one he asked forgiveness. If he were lucky, he could make it to town by daybreak the next day. *Pray God I am in time!*

The sun was over the horizon when a sweat-soaked and panting Lame Deer staggered into town. His clothes were torn and his moccasins shredded. Impervious to his pain, he headed with single-minded purpose to the *Star*. Finding no one there, he crumpled tearfully against the locked door of the newspaper office, trying to decide on his next course of action. Exhaustion fogged his brain as he struggled to stay awake. Who else could he trust?

As if in answer to his question, a familiar big blue roan came loping up the street with Lee Velásquez seated on his back. Lame Deer struggled down from the *Star*'s porch and ran out into the street.

Before he could get enough wind to call out, Lee saw him and trotted his mount quickly to the boy. Dismounting, he grabbed the child angrily and asked, "Where the hell have you been? Your mother, Melanie, Father Gus, Wash Oakley—half of San Antonio's out searching for you! That burro came in late yesterday without you."

"Francisco ran off while I was at Blaine's trading post. I had to run back to town," the boy gasped out.

Looking at the child's feet, Lee could see the boy was telling the truth. "Why were you at Blaine's?"

"I was to tell Melanie, but I suppose since you are her husband, it is all right to tell you. . . ." he began uncertainly. At Lee's impatient nod, he spilled out the story of the raid on the Broughton ranch north of town while Walkman decoyed the rangers to the south.

Scooping up the exhausted, injured child, Lee swiftly

remounted Sangre and headed for Father Gus's school. First he must get some attention for the child, then find Jeremy Lawrence—if it wasn't already too late!

Chapter 19

After spending a terrifying morning searching in vain for Lame Deer, Melanie returned to town, praying that someone had located the lost boy. *If only I hadn't encouraged him to spy on Walkman and Blaine*, she berated herself. She had ridden all the way to the trading post, but there was no trace of the child. Forcing down her fears that the cutthroats might have killed the boy, she rode up to Father Gus's school.

As soon as she saw the beaming expression on the padre's face when he emerged from the adobe, she knew Lame Deer was all right. "Where is he? Oh, Father Gus, is he injured?" She leaped from her horse and flew past the priest, who followed her into the dim interior of the building.

"He is unharmed. Francisco was at fault, but fortunate we were that his rider could walk home—even if it took all the night. He sleeps now. The Abbess fed him enough to fill a man her husband's size," Father Gus said with a twinkle. Giving Obedience the nickname of "Abbess" seemed to amuse the young priest a great deal.

Quieting her overwrought emotions, Melanie tiptoed into the back room where the child slept on a small pallet. At once she saw the ugly bruises and cuts that disfigured his sweet face.

Gasping, she turned and whispered to Father Gus, "I thought you said he wasn't harmed! It looks as if someone beat him unmercifully."

After he escorted her from the room, he explained, "The marks you see he did not receive yesterday, but a couple of days earlier. They are healing well."

"Who did such a thing to this child?" she asked, fury rising at the bigotry she knew was responsible.

Father Gus threw up his hands in despair, "Felipe and Alfredo Rojas, I fear."

"They're older, not to mention twice his size!"

"That I pointed out to them when I gave them several days' worth of penance in church," he replied gravely. "Your husband it was who rescued the boy and brought him to me for care."

Her eyes blazed in recognition. "So that's why he sent those books to you the next day!"

"He has much bitterness in his heart for past wrongs done him, but he is a good man, Melanie," the priest said simply.

Her expression became guarded and she looked down, unable to meet his clear, penetrating gaze. "Well, I suppose even Lee Velásquez could show kindness to an Indian child." *But not a woman.*

"Yes, even more, he brought the boy to me this morning when he found him outside the *Star* office. I think the two of them will become friends. It is a good beginning, *ja?*"

"Where is Lee now, Father Gus?" Melanie's face reflected her puzzlement. If he had encountered the child at the *Star* before Clarence arrived, Lee must have returned to the ranch; yet she had not met him on the road.

Now it was his turn to evade her searching look. "Well, Lame Deer had some news about renegade Comanches. Lee and the ranger Jeremy Lawrence rode out with a group of volunteers about half an hour ago. It was after he left the child in my care."

"Where did they go?" she shot back, her reporter's instincts once more alerted.

Recalling the promise he'd made to Lee, Father Gus shrugged. "Hours have passed, and it is a very dangerous thing they do—going after raiding Comanches."

She sighed, realizing there was no way she could catch up

with them, even if she knew where they'd gone. It was well after noon now. All she could do was wait until they returned.

When her attempts to get Father Gus to divulge more details about the renegades failed, Melanie asked the priest to explain about the fight between Lame Deer and the Rojas boys.

Wanting to take her mind off more dangerous pursuits, the young priest described the incident, including his rather unsettling confrontation with the culprits at confession the next day. "Although they made an act of contrition, I fear they do not truly repent for attacking an Indian," he concluded sadly.

Melanie's eyes blazed contemptuously. "Of course not. They're the sons of an old aristocratic Hispanic family. Indians are just trash to them." *And to Lee.*

They were too late. Lee knew it as soon as he smelled the smoke, not hot and heavy as if still freshly burning, but faint and musty, from last night. He could detect those old familiar smells before any of the other men. *Why not? God knows, I saw enough butchering in the Apachería for ten lifetimes.*

When they crested a ridge and looked down at what had been the Broughton place, it was in ashes—house, barn, corrals. All the stock had been driven off. He knew what they'd find and he loathed seeing the carnage yet another time. With a sick knot of dread tightly coiled in his gut, Lee rode ahead of Lawrence and the others. Since Walkman had taken many of the more seasoned rangers on his decoy chase to the south, the men with Lawrence were mostly green. He hoped they wouldn't puke when they found the women. But he prayed they would find them. *If they're here, they died quicker.* If they had been taken by Gall and his raiders, Lee well knew what that meant and forced the thought from his mind.

The trail was useless to follow. Broughton's livestock had

been split into small bunches and driven in various directions, doubtless to rendezvous at some distant point, days
hence. Without spare horses and provisions, there was no
way the volunteers could pursue the killers.

"You see why Jim and I need your help, Velásquez?"
Jeremy asked in a tight voice as they watched two silent
men wrap Mrs. Broughton's remains in a blanket.

"Yeah, Lawrence, I see, and I said I'd do it," Lee
replied, turning sharply on his heel and reaching for Sangre's
reins.

On the ride back to San Antonio, Lee battled with
long-dead memories, forcing the savagery he'd just witnessed
from his mind, refusing to dwell on similar incidents committed again and again by reds and whites in New Mexico
and Chihuahua when he had ridden with Raoul Fouqué.
Unbidden, images of Melanie flashed into his mind as he
battled his ghosts silently: Melanie, with her hair spread like
a black satin mantle across her shoulders, her gold-coin eyes
wide and fathomless; Melanie, who had unearthed the
deadly link between Walkman and the savages. *Damn her
for endangering herself!*

It was nearly dusk when Lee and the others reached San
Antonio. If she'd gone home, he would check with Father
Gus about Lame Deer and then ride for Night Flower, but he
suspected Melanie was still in town waiting for the militia to
return. Did she fear for him—or for Lawrence?

As if he'd conjured her up, Melanie came flying down the
street as soon as the men reached the Main Plaza. A crowd
had gathered, hearing of the raid at the Broughton place. As
Jeremy's rangers and the other volunteers dismounted and
dispersed, talking with various townsmen, Melanie sought
out Lee.

Quickly scanning his closed, set features, she concluded
he was angry with her for remaining in town. "Lame Deer
told me all about Gall's raid when he awakened this afternoon. Were your rangers in time?" Her face was earnest as
she awaited a reply.

"They're not *my* rangers," he said, biting off each word.
"And, no, we weren't in time. Now let's go home." He

eached for her arm and tried to propel her away from the
angry, shouting crowd that had gathered to hear the grisly
ale of the volunteers.

"Let me go," she gritted, shaking free of his proprietary
grasp. "I intend to get the story for the *Star*. If you won't
give it to me, maybe Jeremy will."

If anything she said could have been more designed to
provoke him, he was damned if he could think what.
"Jeremy," he sneered, "is busy talking with the mayor. But
f you're so interested in the ghoulish details, let me recount
hem for you. Pity we already buried the poor bastards, but
suppose you'd even exhume them if you thought it would
get your name at the top of the story!"

"There's no need to be abusive, Lee. I want the facts for
he *Star*, not to satisfy some 'ghoulish' curiosity," she spat
back.

"You want the facts? I'll give you the facts. Seven people
were murdered. Three of them children, one a baby. Broughton
and his cowhands were killed pretty quick, by the looks of
t—before they could protect Mrs. Broughton and her children. The baby's head was smashed open on a rock. Their
twelve-year-old daughter was raped repeatedly before they
cut her throat. So was Mrs. Broughton, after they sliced off
her breasts—"

"Stop it," she hissed through clenched teeth. Her face
paled and the breath squeezed from her lungs in horror.
When she turned to stumble away from him, he caught up
with her in one long stride, turning her roughly around and
holding her at arm's length.

"You and your damn crusading over noble red men!
Maybe now you'll give up your stupid meddling and stay
home," he rasped out.

"Stay home and do what? At least here in town I have a
job. There's nothing for me at Night Flower, and you know
t, Lee!" she replied bitterly.

He released her just as Clarence Pemberton emerged from
he crowd, notebook in hand. Observing the exchange
between the young couple, the old editor walked purpose-
ully toward them. "I just talked with Jeremy Lawrence and

have the pertinent facts, Melanie. I daresay it's been a long day for you both, Velásquez. Why don't you take your bride home?'' At Melanie's murderous look, he continued unperturbed, ''I believe I have everything here under control until morning.'' With that curt dismissal, he turned and stalked toward another cluster of men who were discussing the militia's grisly report.

Melanie stomped toward the livery where she had stabled Liberator, her beloved stallion, brought by her parents on their ill-fated visit last month. Lee walked in angry counterstep leading Sangre. They rode home in silence, both grappling with their own particular demons. All she could think of was that he equated her with those renegades. Having Indian blood was a taint, a stain that placed an individual barely a step away from the savagery exhibited at the Broughton place last night.

By the time they arrived home and shared a light, cold repast in stony silence, Melanie was exhausted. After dinner she retired to her room, where she quickly slipped off her clothes and sank gratefully into the tub Genia had prepared for her. After almost falling asleep in the water, she roused herself enough to slip on a silk night rail and climb between the cool sheets in her lonely bed. There sleep claimed her at once.

Down the hall, Lee paced, unwilling to give in to the aching exhaustion and lie down. Visions of Melanie in her bath danced through his head. He heard the splash of water from her tub and Genia's low murmur as she bid the mistress good night. He could almost feel his wife's velvety skin, slick with bath oil, see her glistening and golden in the candlelight, smell the fragrance of night flowers that always seemed to cling to her. He felt unreasoningly angry with her for being involved in the dangerous tangle with Walkman and Blaine, but more than that, he was furiously jealous of her working on the project with Jeremy Lawrence. The young ranger's promise that he would no longer tell Melanie about their plans did little to reassure Lee. *She trusts him—likes him. And he's always treated her with kindness and respect.*

Lee sighed and ran his fingers through his hair in frustration. All she could think of was her damnable newspaper story—her crusade, never her husband. *Least of all her husband, who forced himself on her and then scorned her,* he admitted bitterly to himself for the first time. "Small wonder she turns to Lawrence and practically lives at the *Star* after the way I've handled things," he muttered aloud to the empty room. With a snarled oath he ripped off his clothes and rang for Kai to bring him bathwater. He must wash away the stink of death lingering from the Broughton place.

By the time he fell asleep it was past midnight. The moon was up, shining in on his long dark body as he tossed and turned in the throes of an old nightmare. He was back in the Apachería with McGordy's men. It was his first trip out as a scalper, a bitter twenty-two-year old boy riding with the others, screaming through the camp, shooting Apaches as they roused from drunken slumber. When his guns had all been fired, he used his knife and his feet, slashing and kicking at the warriors who threw themselves at him until he was covered with blood. So much blood. The bile rose in his throat; he thrashed across the big bed, reliving in his dreams the first time he had taken an Apache scalp.

Something awakened Melanie, a low keening cry, almost like an animal in unbearable pain. She sat up abruptly in bed, peering around the room and then out the window at the still, moon-bright night. There it was again, not outside but down the hall, coming from Lee's room! She threw the covers off and leaped from the bed, not even pausing to put on a robe as she dashed barefoot down the long hall.

When she shoved his door farther ajar, she could see him. Half enshrouded in the sheets, his body was dark against their moon-whitened sheen. He tossed and thrashed like a wild animal caught in the jaws of a cruel trap. Frightened and uncertain now, she slowly stepped into the room. It was large and forbidding, smelling of leather and tobacco, of male musk—his scent.

Once more Lee cried out, a sharp gasp of anguish, then subsided to unintelligible mutterings. He rolled over onto his stomach, clenching the pillow in his hands and burying his face in it as if to stifle his unconscious cries. Melanie felt compelled to move closer and closer to the big bed and the man writhing on it. He was slicked with perspiration and quite obviously naked beneath the thin sheet. She would have been tempted to admire his lean, well-muscled physique, outlined with such clarity in the moonlight, but just then he began to talk again—cry out, really. The anguish in his voice riveted her as a torrent of barely coherent Spanish poured out in whispered gasps.

"Blood, so damn much blood . . . the smell . . . God, I can't do it . . . I can't . . . you bastard, McGordy, you like it, don't you—don't you. . . ." He subsided for a minute, then resumed, "It's a woman, Blessed Virgin, a woman— no . . . don't—aaugh! Jesus, just pull it out, Fouqué . . . forget the barbs . . . it's got to come out or I'll bleed to death. . . ."

He's dreaming about his time as a scalper, she thought in dawning horror, now beginning to realize that his traumatic description of the Broughton atrocity was only one of many such savage scenes that he had witnessed in his years on the frontier. The intensity of his pain surged across the room and flowed over her in a tidal wave. Melanie knew she must end it for both of them by awakening him. She walked resolutely to the big bed and knelt on its edge. When she placed her hand on his back, the heat from his body scorched her palm. She could feel the hard muscles quiver beneath her cool fingers as she shook him.

"Lee, Lee, wake up. You're having a nightmare—it's only a dream. Wake up!" He knocked her hand away and rolled over onto his back in one rough motion, still crying out in the grip of the nightmare. Now the heat of his body was radiating along her thigh and belly as she sat on the edge of the bed, leaning over him. His darkly furred chest felt damp with sweat as she ran her fingers through the thick pelt, shaking and massaging him in an attempt to bring him out of the nightmare. "Wake up, Lee, please," she cried more loudly now, reaching up with the other hand to stroke his temple.

Suddenly one hand snaked up to encircle her slim wrist

and yank it away from his face. His eyes flew open and he stared at her in amazement and consternation. "What the hell are you doing here?" He levered himself up in bed and looked around the room, orienting himself, pulling back from the abyss that had once again enveloped him. His eyes glowed when he turned them on her, seeming to penetrate the sheer silk that barely concealed her lush curves.

"You—you were having a nightmare—a terrible dream. I heard you all the way down the hall, and I came to investigate. . . ." Her voice faded into a choked whisper as she realized the vulnerable position she was in now that she had awakened him.

He quirked one brow at her sardonically. "Always investigating, my little reporter." Gradually, as his mind cleared he realized what he had probably cried out. Eyes narrowed, he asked, "How well can you understand Spanish?"

Even before she replied, "I'm fluent in Spanish," he had been fairly certain. *Damn!*

Forcing herself to meet his accusing, angry gaze, she said, "I know you were reliving your experience in New Mexico. It must have been horrible. . . ." Once more her voice failed her and she looked down at his strong dark fingers clamped tightly over her tiny wrist. It throbbed wickedly and she pulled away. Sensing that he was hurting her, he loosened his hold but did not release her wrist.

"The Apachería was horrible—beyond anything you could imagine," he said tiredly. "Seeing the Broughton family must have triggered the dream. I haven't had it in months," he muttered darkly. When she tried to pull away again, he began to massage her aching wrist softly.

Melanie was certain he could hear her heart hammering. Surely he could see it pulsing through her thin night rail. "If you're all right now, I'll—"

"A minute ago you were investigating like a bold lady journalist. You're not going to turn and run now like a scared little rabbit, are you?" His voice held an odd teasing quality that excited and yet unnerved her.

"I'm not scared," she lied, "but you are hurting me." Her eyes refused to meet his, fixing on the imprisoned wrist. She couldn't help but notice the lean brown fingers that enwrapped it. *Damn, why do even his hands have to be beautiful!* Slowly he moved her hand up to his chest and pressed the small soft palm against his heart so she could feel its quickly pulsing rhythm. Of their own volition her fingers flexed into the thick, springy hair and her long nails raked through it. She could feel his heartbeat accelerate. He released his grip on her wrist and moved his hand deftly to her heart, touching her breast lightly with callused fingertips that grazed the sheer silk of her night rail. He was rewarded when her heart, too, sped erratically.

With a small smile he whispered, "Now we're even, little Night Flower."

"We'll never be even, Lee,' she replied on a choked sob. "Not in your eyes."

Angrily he pulled her to him, looping one long arm behind her back to hold her tightly against his chest. "Don't start your recriminations now, Mellie—you're my wife and you came to my room." He gave her no chance to reply but drew her quickly into a hot, searching kiss, tangling his other hand in the long straight hair that fell like satin down her back.

Melanie felt him savage her lips, demanding entry to her mouth while his fingers dug into her hair, twisting and pulling on it. She could hear the pounding of his heart and the rasp of his erratic breathing. His need was starkly revealed, making him vulnerable. First he was the trembling, sweating man gripped by a terrifying nightmare, then the harsh, demanding lover enslaved by passion—a passion which, God help her, she could never resist. With a low moan she opened her mouth and returned the kiss, her hot little tongue darting and entwining with his as he had taught her. He had taught her so much in so little time. *What will happen to me?* she thought in a flash of panic. Then his lips and hands gentled. The kiss became soft, experimental, his hold on her massaged instead of crushed. He pulled her small body close to him as he reclined on the bed until she lay full-length beside him. One small hand clung to his shoulder and the other wrapped around his neck, then inched upward into the curly hair of his head. She thought no more, only felt.

Lee felt a surge of white-hot exhilaration shoot through him when her rigid protest turned into melting surrender. Then, realizing how roughly he was using her, he brought his passion under control. He savored her mouth with his own, his tongue cunningly tasting, darting, flicking, feeling hers return the erotic exploration. Her breasts pillowed against his chest and her hips arched against his as she writhed in his arms while he ran his hands up and down her spine, feeling the silky perfection of her delicate little body through the night rail.

Slowly he broke the intensity of the kiss and moved his lips in a warm rush down her neck to feast on her slender throat and collarbone. As she arched her neck back to accommodate his caresses, her breasts thrust up, straining against the silk. Sitting up, he kicked the sheet from his lower body and then reached down and pulled up the hem of her night rail.

Understanding that he wanted the last sheer barrier between their bodies removed, she accommodated him, wriggling like a sylph until he pulled the gown over her head, fanning her hair out like spilled ink across the moon-drenched pillow. He tossed the flimsy silk on the floor and lowered his face over her arching, straining breasts. His slim long fingers teased and cupped one, then the other full, rounded globe and his breath warmed them until they tightened into hard rosy nubs.

Mellie wanted desperately to feel the heat of his mouth on her. She moaned and arched her aching breasts to meet his lips. He outlined one with the tip of his tongue, circling back and forth until she thought she'd go mad with the pleasure and the want. Then he switched abruptly to the other to repeat the process. Finally his hot, wet lips enveloped the nipple and suckled hard. She cried out in ecstasy, her hands gripping the curly hair of his head, pulling him closer.

Lee rolled over onto his back and lifted her above him so her breasts hung suspended like ripe, rounded melons begging to be tasted. When he opened his lips, she thrust an eager, hardened nipple into it, writhing and panting as he continued to suckle one, then the other.

She could feel his hot, hard phallus straining against the back of her thigh as she straddled his chest. While he continued to feast greedily on her breasts, she reached a hand behind her and stroked him delicately. Lee gasped and arched, nearly bucking her off his chest. Then his strong hands fitted over her small hipbones, lifting her up and lowering her down onto him, impaling her slowly on his rigid, pulsing shaft. As he felt her wet, sweet flesh envelop him, he watched her lush little body undulate, her heavy breasts thrust out as she arched her back in ecstasy. He slid his hands up to her tiny waist and held her as she fastened her thighs snugly around him. Eyes closed in a concentration of intense pleasure, she let her head fall back until the long mantle of her hair brushed his thighs.

Once she was fully seated, with his whole length buried inside her, he thrust upward and moved her lower body in a rotating motion with his hands. Melanie's eyes flew open as raw, electrifying pleasure shot through her. With passion-glazed eyes she looked down at him, then brought her clenched little fists around to his chest. Her hands opened and the fingers splayed through the thick pelt as she continued to follow his lead, rocking from side to side, then up and down, riding him in wilder, harder gyrations.

She was aflame. Her hips matched his in wild pounding rhythm. Lee reached up and pulled great fistfuls of her hair over her shoulders, drawing her face down to his for a long, fierce kiss. As Melanie returned the kiss, her lower body continued to move with a will of its own, unconsciously, instinctively, meeting his, drawing him into her, deeper, harder, until a low keening escaped her mouth through the kiss.

Lee felt the tight rippling waves begin deep inside her satin sheath and spread outward until her thighs and legs clamped against him. As she cried out and gave one last desperate arch in ecstatic climax, he joined her, his moans meeting hers deep in their fused mouths. He shuddered and exploded, deeply buried inside her, wanting never to be free again. His hands gripped her quivering thighs and held her tightly to him as she fell forward onto his chest.

They lay locked together in the still night air for several moments, trembling, breathless, disoriented. Gradually both began to regain their composure. Melanie kept her face buried against the curve of his neck, afraid to meet those glowing black eyes. They were wolf's eyes, predator's eyes, belonging to a man who ruthlessly took what he wanted regardless of the consequences. She crimsoned, recalling the shameless way she had impaled herself on him and ridden him. *No wonder he treats me like a* placée. *I act like one every time he puts his hands on me*, she thought bitterly.

Lee, too, was envisioning the picture of her with her hair flung back and breasts arched, straining to ride him like some pagan goddess on a wild stallion. Then he felt the stiff, still way she lay now that her passion had abated. Always it was the same—the irresistible melting into him when he reached out to her with his own fierce hunger, then the angry withdrawal after her body's needs had been assuaged. She used him in a far more dishonest way than her mother had used her father.

Slowly he raised her off of him and then rolled them both to their sides facing each other. But he did not release her. When she refused to meet his eyes in the dim white moonlight, he reached up and took her small chin in his fingers. Rather more roughly than he had intended, he raised her face to his. They were only inches apart.

"Regrets again, Night Flower?"

She forced herself to meet his eyes. "No more than you have, Lee."

"What the hell is that supposed to mean? You're the one who always freezes up and then turns on me afterward," he replied bitterly, angry at the vulnerability and hunger he always seemed to reveal to her.

"Can you honestly say you didn't regret it the first time, when all your plans for an annulment were destroyed?" Her eyes accused him.

"That's all over now," he evaded. "We're married,

Mellie, and we have to live together. It's inevitable that this happen, even though we sleep apart. A man and a woman who are attracted to each other like we are can't be under the same roof without making love," he argued reasonably, but he knew anger was creeping into his voice.

She shook her head and pulled away from him. "In other words, you want me, but you don't like it. Well, there's one simple solution to our dilemma." She rolled quickly out of his reach and scooped up her night rail as she moved across the floor toward the door. "If we don't live under the same roof, both of us should rest easier." She vanished down the hall with a slam of the door.

He flopped back angrily onto the bed and swore softly in Spanish.

Chapter 20

"I can't live this way, Obedience, I just can't," Melanie sobbed out as the big woman rocked her gently in her arms.

"Now don't take on so," Obedience said. "Let's git inside and set a spell 'n' yew kin tell me all 'bout it."

Leaving Liberator tied at the side of the boardinghouse, Melanie and Obedience walked arm in arm around to the kitchen door. It was just after dawn. Pink and mauve streaked the morning sky. Melanie had not slept at all last night when she returned to her lonely room. After restlessly pacing for several hours, she had thrown a few clothes in a bag and fled the ranch in the darkness, returning to the Oakleys' boardinghouse and the common sense and assurance she knew Obedience could provide.

"Now, I 'spect that young husband o' yourn'll come flyin' in here madder'n a scalded dog in a few minutes, so yew better talk fast.'' Obedience spoke as she began to make a giant pot of coffee. Even Sadie was not astir yet, and the usually busy kitchen seemed eerily quiet.

Melanie sat on the edge of a chair, fidgeting nervously with her skirt, looking like a wild bird ready to take flight. Her hair was in wild tangles down her back from the furious ride into the city, and her silk shirt was buttoned crookedly.

"I don't know where to begin," she whispered helplessly, splaying her fingers across her knees.

"How 'bout with last night?'' Obedience supplied shrewdly and was rewarded with a guilty red flush from the young woman. "He hurt yew?'' she asked incredulously, not really believing it herself.

"No, no—sometimes he frightens me, but . . . he's never hurt me."

Obedience nodded in dawning understanding. "He pleases yew too good, huh?''

More scarlet blushing and silence.

"Look, honey, what yew feel's right 'n' natural—ain't nothin' ta run from."

"It is if your husband's angry with you afterward," Melanie said in a sad, soft voice. "He wants me. As long as we're living under the same roof, he can't seem to help . . . well . . .'' She faded off in a misery of embarrassment.

Obedience gave a low, rich chuckle. " 'N' yew cain't seem to help it neither, which is jist 'zactly whut nature intended."

"But he doesn't love me! He was forced to marry me and never intended to consummate the marriage," Melanie blurted out. Once that shameful revelation was made, it was as if a dam burst inside her. She told Obedience everything, from their hateful agreement about the annulment that day in the orchard until their explosive confrontation the night of the ball.

"So you see, after it happened again last night and he acted the same way afterward, I just couldn't go on living like a prisoner, a—a whore. All he has to do is touch me and I can't help myself.'' She hung her head and big shiny tears spilled down her cheeks, splashing on her hands clenched in her lap.

From what Deborah had told her, Obedience knew that Melanie's illegitimacy and neurotic mother had left her with painful scars that she obviously still carried. A proud, pedigree-oriented *Tejano* like Lee Velásquez would just naturally do and say all the wrong things, unwittingly playing on her insecurity. But for all that, Obedience was certain they belonged together. If only the young fools could open up to one another and admit their fears and mistakes.

Before she could counsel any further, the sound of hoofbeats and flying gravel outside the kitchen door interrupted her. "If'n I don't miss my bet, thet's yore husband. Notice how glad he is ta be quit o' yew," she said with a wink as she ambled quickly toward the hall door, leaving Melanie to face Lee alone.

After taking the porch steps two at a time, he was at the door in a couple of long strides. Melanie stood up and balled her fists in her riding skirts, defiantly facing him as he slammed into the room, filling it with his menacing presence.

Furiously he threw the note she'd written him onto the kitchen table. "What the hell is that supposed to mean? We're married, lady, and moving back under Obedience's wing won't undo it."

"I won't live with you and be subjected to your lust and your scorn afterward," she replied, proud of her icy control.

"*My* lust, you damned little hypocrite! As if you don't return it! I've got to commend my sweet little bride—she's been a real apt pupil. With a few more lessons, I'm sure you could—"

"Could what?" she interrupted his hateful diatribe with a shriek. "Open my own bordello—or be placed on Rampart Street like my mother was?"

He ignored her outburst and reached for her bag, sitting forgotten on a chair near the door. "Come on, wife. We're going home."

"No. You don't want me for a wife. The only reason you

even came after me is because you're afraid of my father!'' she said spitefully.

He dropped the bag as if he were burned. Slowly he crossed his arms over his chest and stared at her contemptuously. ''Rafe Fleming be damned,'' was all he said, in a low clear voice. Then he turned and walked out the door.

Melanie remained at the boardinghouse, occupying her old room once more. For the next week she went to the *Star* each morning, saying nothing about her estrangement from her husband. If Clarence knew, he and Amos forbore mentioning the situation.

After riding Sangre furiously back to Night Flower, Lee spent the week breaking mustangs, a hot, dangerous, and dirty pastime better left to the *mestañeros* he had hired. But he needed to do something to burn off the killing rage that suffused his body. Each night, aching and exhausted, he lay in his bed, staring at the ceiling, thinking of the woman who no longer slept down the hall. *She's no farther away in San Antonio than she was under my roof, that's for damn sure.*

She was right about one thing. He could not make love to her if they lived apart. Still, the maddening desire for her did not abate. Finally, after a sleepless week, he went to San Antonio, not to be a supplicant at the boardinghouse once more, but to visit a discreet brothel on the outskirts of town.

Just as the first streaks of light were inching their hazy way across the dirty windowpane, Lee rubbed his eyes and looked around the room. Sunrise. It looked to be a cloudy day, but then if Clarice didn't clean her windows any better than she cleaned her room, it might be full sunshine outside. The place was a sty. Silk stockings and frilly underwear were tossed in artless abandon across the chairs and carpet. A dinner tray sat on a dust-coated walnut table alongside the horsehair sofa, its half-eaten meat and potatoes pooled in congealed gray grease with a steak bone protruding obscenely from beneath a linen napkin that had been hastily discarded. Ashtrays filled with cigars, cigarillos, and pipe ashes attested to the number and variety of customers Clarice had entertained in the past few days.

Dragging himself into a sitting position, he looked down at the woman sleeping next to him. The taffy color of her hair was betrayed by darker roots in the morning's merciless light, and her face, although youthful, was smeared with rouge and kohl. He had selected her last night because she did not yet have the hard, practiced airs of the older women. She seemed somehow vulnerable in such a gawdy pleasure palace.

Now as he stared at her, visions of his radiant ebony-haired wife flashed unbidden into his mind, her clear golden skin innocent of paint. He could almost smell her sweet, musky scent after making love. *But here I am sleeping with a pathetic doxy while she sleeps alone only a few blocks away.*

Angrily he threw back the sheet and swung his long legs over the edge of the bed. Clarice muttered something unintelligible in her sleep and rolled over. Lee dressed hastily and tossed a generous payment on the bed where he had lain. He quit the room without a backward glance.

The cool, cloudy day would be ideal for working stock. His men had just brought in a half-dozen really good mustangs culled from a large herd they'd captured to the west. He should ride quickly back to Night Flower and start breaking them. But something kept him in town. He walked slowly toward Simpson's Livery to reclaim Sangre, then changed his mind and strolled over to the secluded little park behind San Fernando Church. Larena had come to meet him here and tell him that she would not wait for him. Thinking it was a good thing she had been so sensible, he absently kicked a pebble with the toe of his boot. Obviously he would never be able to get an annulment to marry her now! But was she right about him and Melanie? Already he had betrayed his marriage vows with a brief and most unsatisfactory copulation in a whorehouse.

But his wife had made it abundantly clear that no matter how much she might respond to his touch, she wanted no part of a real marriage. She did not want to be his wife and bear his children. She wanted to crusade for the Indians and slaves, for women's suffrage and temperance. That last thought caused him to wince in guilt and massage his aching temples. He had drunk entirely too much whiskey last night.

But what do I want? he asked himself in confusion. Deep in thought, he did not see Father Gus come around the low-hanging cypress limbs along the path he was walking. The priest was on his way to the Indian school after saying an early morning mass in San Fernando's. They nearly collided before Father Gus reached out to steady himself as he sidestepped from the path.

"So early for you to be in town, Leandro," he said levelly, taking in the other man's rumpled clothes, unshaven face, and bloodshot eyes. The smell of cheap perfume and musky sheets clung to him. Knowing that Melanie had moved into town last week, Father Gus intuited where Lee had spent the night, and it was not in his wife's arms. He'd bet his burro Francisco on that!

Meeting the clear blue eyes of the priest, Lee sighed in resignation as a twisted grin spread unwillingly across his face. "Can't a man ever sin in private, Father?"

"*Ja.* He can. But does he want to live with it in private after it is done? That is the real question." The words were spoken with no recrimination.

They walked aimlessly through the tree-shaded park and out onto a side street, nearly deserted at such an early hour. Father Gus knew that if Lee wanted to unburden himself, he would do so; if not, no amount of lecturing or cajoling would make the private, self-contained *Tejano* unbend. He strove for a neutral topic they could discuss. "Our children conjugate Latin verbs from the grammar book you sent us. Also they read Chaucer and Cervantes. Even my poor English grows better each day as I study Mr. Keats and Father Newman. We all thank you for the wonderful books."

Lee shrugged dismissively. "They were gathering dust. I've already read them. Anyway, I have little time or need to conjugate Latin verbs or read poetry and essays these days. Melanie was amazed that I gave Uncle Alfonso's books to Indian children," he said in a voice laced with scorn and regret.

"How is your wife?" the priest asked gently. "I have not seen her this week. Lame Deer asks for her."

Lee stopped walking and faced Father Gus squarely. "I haven't seen her since she moved out of my house last week. Tell Lame Deer to visit her at Oakley's if he's all that worried about her."

"He's worried about you, too, my son. You know, Leandro, you've become quite a hero to him since you saved him from Felipe and Fredo."

"He's a good enough kid," Lee said gruffly.

"For an Indian?" Father Gus said, watching Lee's face.

"For *anybody's* kid. Hell, Father, you're beginning to sound like my wife," he said impatiently, once more beginning to walk.

The priest's much shorter legs had to churn to keep up with Velásquez's long stride. "Your wife, or your own conscience?" he asked, puffing.

"Sometimes I think God invented wives to be our consciences," Lee groused, half to himself.

"Then maybe it is you who should go to Oakley's and reclaim yours, before you go farther astray," the priest said with a twinkle.

Lee only grunted noncommittally and walked faster.

Stella Wolcott was a woman with a mission, and she looked the part. Tall and angularly thin, she had a determinedly set chin that was enhanced by a fierce underbite and penetrating gray eyes that could skewer a man to a chair at forty feet. Her thick graying hair was knotted inelegantly behind her neck, and she wore sensible shoes.

Clarence Pemberton detested her on sight. She reminded him of his stern New England mother, as grim and humorless as the rocky Maine coastline. The first time he'd met Melanie Fleming she had looked like a younger version of the harridan who now sat in his office. But Melanie had wit and spirit, a sense of life's infinite ironies. When she had metamorphosed into a beauty and married that young *Tejano* rancher, he had been secretly relieved. *Praise be, she won't end up like Marilla Pemberton—or Stella Wolcott!* Either of them was vicious enough to name an innocent son Vivian!

"Are you quite certain, madam, that I cannot help you? Mrs. Velásquez seems to have been detained this morning," he said to Stella, affixing her with his most forbidding glare over the top of his low-perched spectacles.

She matched him glare for glare. "No, thank you, Mr. Pemberton. I'll wait for Mrs. Velásquez. I have some important—" She stopped short when Melanie swished into the office. "Ah, there you are, my dear child."

Something in her solicitous tone alerted Clarence. It didn't fit. She had been after Melanie to write an exposé on the debauchery of the city's saloons and gambling halls. To date the girl had been too caught up with the Indian raids to work on it. Now the old harridan seemed to have a new card up her sleeve. When the two women exchanged hushed pleasantries and then she and Melanie left the office for a private interview, his reporter's instincts told him something was wrong.

Melanie was suspicious, too, when Stella began her preamble with unnatural motherly concern. "My dear," she said, taking Melanie's small hand in her large one, "you know how much I admire you and the work you've accomplished here in this wicked city."

"I thank you, Mrs. Wolcott," Melanie replied uneasily.

"But you know how much more there is to do. We must nail shut the door of every saloon and house of ill repute. Only then shall demon rum be vanquished. The evils of the flesh tempt men to saloons. Then when they're sodden with drink they perform heinous deeds—gambling their homes and fortunes away, betraying their noble wives with scarlet women."

Melanie felt the cold hand of dread squeeze her heart as she listened to Stella. She intuited where it was leading. "Are you trying to say that my husband was lured to one of these places?"

"The Gilded Cage," Stella spat with an air of righteous wrath. "He spent the night with a harlot named Clarice after drinking and gambling in the bar below! A lady such as you is fully vindicated in leaving such a debaucher. But, my child, you, of all women, are in a position to exact retribution. You wield a pen, and we all know the pen is mightier than the sword!''

Numbly Melanie let her rant about the Gilded Cage and other infamous places of similar ilk. All she could think of was Lee making love to a painted whore, waking up in a bordello bed with a slut named Clarice. As she vaguely fastened on what Stella said, she let the numbness dissipate, replacing it with a suffusing rage.

Finally she interrupted the temperance crusader. ''What would you say to a tour of the local saloons, Mrs. Wolcott? When I'm finished taking notes, I should have enough for quite a series of articles and you should be able to draw a sizable crowd to your next meeting—which should include just about every woman in San Antonio who can read, if I don't underestimate the power of *my* pen!''

Melanie stood in the middle of the *Star* office, facing her scowling editor, while Amos retreated behind the press to watch the fireworks. ''I tell you, Clarence, this story is fantastic!'' she pronounced doggedly, hands on her hips, feet braced apart for a fight. ''I know you don't like Stella Wolcott, but what I've written here is absolutely true. These places are sinkholes of corruption. I know of a small rancher who gambled away his whole herd of cattle on a turn of the cards last night and another whose family is living on rotten sweet potatoes while he drinks every night in a different saloon!''

''Alas, human frailty being what it is, these lamentable events have transpired since the dawn of civilization, Melanie. Neither you nor I, nor even your formidable Mrs. Wolcott, can close the saloons of San Antonio,'' Clarence said with world-weary tolerance.

''We can damn well try! At least look at it as a first step in awakening people's consciences to the worst abuses. If one man having an innocent drink sees his neighbor swilling down a whole bottle, maybe he'll take him home to his family before the sot drinks up a year's income,'' she pleaded. She played her final ace. 'It'll sell newspapers.''

"Run the first article on the crooked dealer at Caradines' place and we'll see how it goes," he replied consideringly. "And you're right—I *don't* like Mrs. Wolcott, so don't make this into a temperance crusade to drive the honest saloonkeepers out of the city. I'm one of their best customers," he added with pettish defiance.

Lame Deer gave Francisco another sharp kick in the ribs, but the fat old burro refused to move with any more dispatch. "What a slow, lazy fellow you are. Father Gus only keeps you out of Christian kindness," he complained to the burro. "I will tie you well this time," he promised grimly, thinking of that long trek back to town two weeks ago. The cuts and bruises on his feet still were not completely healed.

Lee was busy at the main corral, working with a promising new filly, when he saw the boy ride up on Father Gus's burro.

"You're a long way from town, *pequeño*. Playing hooky from school?" He grinned as he led the pretty pony from the corral.

"Oh, no, *Señor* Lee. It is Saturday and we have no lessons. Father Gus let me borrow this ugly one."

"Want to browse through my library? I expect you've read about all the books I sent to Father Gus by now," he said teasingly, noting how the boy's big dark eyes were transfixed on the little bay filly with the shiny coat and the white blaze on her face.

"Thank you, *Señor* Lee, but I still have one or two books to read at school," the boy said earnestly. "I only wondered how you were. You have not been in town during the day to visit our school for several weeks."

During the day. But he'd been in town plenty of nights. He looked at the guileless chocolate eyes with a guilty start. "As you can see, Lame Deer, I'm perfectly fine." *Liar.*

"So is Melanie," the boy replied airily, scooting over to rub the pony's nose gently.

So that was the lay of the land. "Did Father Gus send you to report on Melanie and check on me?" Lee asked with one brow arched in tolerant displeasure.

Unconcerned, the boy replied, "Not exactly. He wanted you to read the stories in the *Star* that she is writing, though." He walked over to Francisco and fished several crumpled newspapers from the saddlebag and handed them to Lee. "Why doesn't Melanie live here anymore? Aren't you still married?"

Lee decided he preferred the boy's Indian obliqueness to this newly acquired Anglo bluntness. "We're still married, but it's her choice to live in town," he muttered, quickly scanning the pages with their bold headlines:

CESSPOOL OF CORRUPTION
IN LOCAL GAMING ESTABLISHMENTS.

MAN SPENDS LIFE SAVINGS
ON DRINK WHILE FAMILY STARVES.

RANCHER ROBBED
IN HOUSE OF ILL REPUTE.

That last headline especially caught his eye, since the name of the Gilded Cage leaped from the body of print below it. Beneath the carefully orchestrated accounts of crooked faro dealers bilking customers, compulsive gamblers losing their life savings, and hapless bordello clients having their wallets lifted, a common theme pervaded: close down the saloons and legislate morality—especially sexual morality. Several of the younger women who worked at the Gilded Cage were even mentioned by name, including Clarice. It seemed, if the story were to be believed, they were poor unfortunates who were exploited by the saloon owners and forced into lives of fear and drudgery. His face darkened into a scowl, then a fierce grimace of disgust. Poor exploited Clarice! She'd run out on her husband and child in Houston two years ago because she was bored with being married to a shoe clerk! Obviously she'd told him one story and a nosy, gullible reporter another. He had no doubt about which was the truth.

Stella Wolcott's crusade was also a prominent news item. She had held several temperance rallies that were drawing increasingly large and rowdy crowds of participants who took the "pledge." He tossed the paper down in disgust. "And just what does Father Gus expect me to do about all this? Round up all these squawking women and stampede them out onto the Staked Plains like a herd of mustangs?"

The boy shrugged in perplexity. "He is worried about your *señora*. She and that *feote* vulture Wolcott spend much time together."

Lee had to laugh in spite of himself at the rather apt mixture of Spanish and English. "Hideous vulture! That fits old Stella, all right."

"*Señor* Pemberton calls her Madam Vulture, but I am not so polite," the boy agreed gravely, once more stroking the pony's nose. "Do you think you might come to town and see Melanie someday?" he asked wistfully.

"Maybe, *pequeño*. Do you borrow Father Gus's burro often?" Lee wanted to change the subject.

"Yes. Whenever I need to get somewhere far away. But the stupid fat one doesn't move much faster than I can walk," he replied dolefully.

"And you have many faraway places to go in a hurry," Lee said with a smile. "You aren't still spying on Blaine and his friends for Melanie, are you?" he asked suddenly, afraid for his wife and the boy.

"Oh, no, *Señor* Lee. I report to Ranger Lawrence now— or to you, if you wish," he added quickly, seeing the flash of anger in Lee's face.

"No, it's all right to talk to Lawrence. He's a lot closer in town, Lame Deer. But I don't want you taking any more dangerous chances hanging around Blaine or Walkman. Understand?"

The boy nodded. He *did* understand.

"You like her?" Lee asked, patting the filly's silky neck.

"Oh, yes. I bet she is as fast as the wind," he said with awe as he scratched the white blaze on her forehead.

"At least a lot faster than Francisco, here," Lee agreed, a slow smile spreading across his face. "Lame Deer, don' you think Father Gus might need Francisco sometimes when you're out riding him? After all, he is the only mount the good priest has."

The boy looked troubled. "Yes, I suppose that is true— and I've almost lost him several times. Of course, he' always come back to town, but . . ."

"If you had your own pony, then you could give Francisco back to Father Gus for good."

"But I don't have a pony," the boy replied sadly.

"I have several extra ponies from the last herd my hand captured. This pretty little girl is one of them. I've jus finished training her. I make her a gift to my friend, Lame Deer," Lee said gravely, offering the reins to the astonishe child.

Lame Deer's eyes grew enormous and positively glowed Suppressing the overpowering urge to shriek with glee, h nodded with grave politeness. "I thank you with all m heart, Señor Lee. I will take special care of her."

What god-awful racket was that awakening a body when she'd just gotten to sleep? Clarice thought irritably. Hadn' enough things gone wrong this night. First old Jake Barlow had refused to pay her until the two-hundred-pound barkeep belowstairs had persuaded him to reconsider. Then Lizzie had cajoled a wealthy cattle buyer away from her, and she had ended up with that fat, slobbering Whalen Simpson who always smelled of horses. And for the third night in a row Lee Velásquez hadn't shown up at all. Finally, she had retired early, leaving the customers of the Gilded Cage to her co-workers. The distant sounds of splintering wood and shattering glass mixed with feral cries of female voices Something was wrong. Tiredly she pulled on a blue satin wrapper and opened her door.

Several other of the girls at the Gilded Cage were already in the hall, in various stages of dishabille. Bare thighs encased in black lace hose rustled against open satin robes. Bounteous bosoms, replete with rouged nipples, spilled over high whalebone corsets. Interrupted while plying their trade, they were as confused as Clarice, who took the lead heading for the stairs.

"I bet it's that damn Wolcott bitch," Lizzie snarled.

"She's crazy mean. I heard she busted up a big place in Austin a couple months back," Gilda whispered fearfully.

"Shit, she wouldn't a got nowheres in Santone without that goddamn newspaper asshole writin' all that stuff. Hey, ain't she married to one o' yer regulars, Clarice?" Sandy Bateman asked.

"Do shut your mouth before one of those pesky horseflies hanging around the spittoon flits right in, Sandy," Clarice replied with acid sweetness.

Even Sandy Bateman's smile faded when she looked down the stairs at the havoc being wreaked below. Men were yelling and ducking as glasses and whiskey bottles flew in all directions, scattering lethal shards across the floor. Chairs were smashed and tables overturned. The big mirror behind the bar, Luce's pride and joy, was cracked clear across and hung precariously, attached to the wall only on one side now.

One tall, thin woman brandishing a hatchet seemed to be in charge of the brigade of sedately dressed matrons—the cream of San Antonio society! If their clothes proclaimed them ladies, their behavior certainly did not. As Stella Wolcott bellowed orders, they followed them with startling zeal, shrieking as they shoved tables over and used broken chairlegs to clear the long oak bar of all its bottles and glasses.

Melanie stood near the door, taking furtive notes, recording the mayhem going on around her. Clarence was going to flay her alive, but, hell, what a story! When Mrs. Wolcott had started her oration at the rally earlier that evening, Melanie knew the crusader had something special in mind. The crowd had been larger than usual, and many of the women responded with enthusiasm that bordered uncomfortably on fanaticism.

Stella had whipped the women into a frenzy with her speech on demon rum and its accompanying evil, gambling. Then she began a masterful diatribe on fallen women and their enticement of the poor sodden fools who frequented saloons—how they took fathers and husbands away from their families, stealing their money and inflicting disgusting diseases on them.

Although Melanie had not wanted to participate in a bar-smashing spree, she did want to yank one frizzy head of tan hair until its dark roots stood out. She suggested they use the Gilded Cage as an example to the rest of the saloon owners. Luce Grearden, the owner, was known for crooked card games and expensive whores. If his star doxy lost her job while he lost his saloon, so much the better.

When Melanie caught sight of the half-dressed prostitutes trooping into the fracas, she immediately recognized Clarice Lawton. Melanie had to admit grudgingly that she was young and rather pretty, with pale taffy-colored hair and wide blue eyes. Her ample curves were obvious beneath a clinging robe that matched her eyes.

Those eyes now hardened in anger as they swept across the room and fixed on the tiny raven-haired girl standing beside the bar with a reporter's notebook clutched in her hand. "You jealous little bitch—throw a gorgeous man like Velásquez out of your bed and then come here and bust up the place where he found a real woman!" Clarice shrieked, ignoring the clawing hands and swinging clubs of the reformers as she dodged across the room to get to Melanie.

Dropping her notebook, Melanie strode forward to accept the challenge. "A real woman," she mimicked, grabbing a hunk of tan hair, "doesn't have to dye her hair or paint her face to catch a man, you slut!" She yanked Clarice's hair viciously and the taller woman lurched forward. They both tumbled to the floor. Clarice had the advantage of height and several years of bordello brawling, but Melanie had fought her way through screaming antiabolitionist mobs in Boston and raced bareback on half-wild mustangs with her brothers at Renacimiento. She was small but squirrel-tough and blindly furious at the harlot's humiliating reference to her unfaithful husband.

Melanie shrieked every swear word she remembered her father's *vaqueros* using and added a few more the Boston longshoremen favored as she gouged and kicked at her nemesis. She was dressed in a heavy riding skirt and boots, significantly superior armor compared to Clarice's sheer robe, garter belt, and hose.

"When I'm through, I'll feed you those lacy stockings, garters and all," she promised through gritted teeth.

Clarice grabbed for a half-empty whiskey bottle, still miraculously intact, and yelled, "You prissy-assed, frigid, man-hating misfit! Let me show you how to apply rouge— *blood*-red rouge! I'll use yours!"

Melanie smashed a half-broken bar stool against an overturned table and parried with it. "Don't get ahead of yourself, you poor benighted clod. I can see how a man like Luce could lead you around by your crooked nose. You're too stupid to know when someone's going to break your neck!" She swung her club and the bottle went flying.

When the town marshal and a detachment of rangers arrived to break up the melee, Melanie was still standing. Her vanquished foe was sobbing on the floor with one eye darkened and several ribs cracked. Melanie had used the broken bar-stool leg to wicked advantage. The victor was not without scars, however. Her jaw ached from the lucky punch Clarice had landed, her shins and knees were kicked bloody by the whore's high-heeled slippers, and scarcely an inch of her body had escaped unscathed from Clarice's long nails.

Still, when Jeremy restrained her, Melanie had to give Clarice credit. The prostitute scrambled up and lunged for her again with a startlingly imaginative burst of profanity.

The marshal insisted they both be taken to jail to calm down, along with Stella Wolcott and two of the more militant whores. After an hour of glaring at each other across an aisle separated by iron bars, Melanie and Clarice had their attention diverted by Clarence Vivian Pemberton. The editor looked decidedly cross and rumpled, but his sardonically lifted eyebrows were faultlessly in place.

"I told you this carrion eater"—he gestured contemptuously at Melanie's cellmate—"would be your undoing, young lady. You're only fortunate I didn't refuse the call and summon your husband."

"You wouldn't—Clarence, you couldn't! Oh, damn! I have an unbelievable story," she said, bruised knuckles wrapped beseechingly around the bars as her gold eyes stared at him, dazed and glassy.

"Unbelievable, I'd believe," he said dryly. "As to what we can print, we shall see. Are you ready to face the formidable Mrs. Oakley? Your absent spouse will doubtless be along anon. . . ."

"I doubt it," both Melanie and Clarice responded simultaneously.

"If'n yew don't want yore man sleepin' with whores, warm his bed yoreself, yew young fool!" Obedience lectured sternly as she applied a buttermilk-and-aloe mixture to Melanie's abraded face and hands.

"Ooh! that stings. Damn, is there any part of me that doesn't ache? I should've given that slut one parting shot to the kidneys," she said with vehemence, ignoring Obedience's advice.

"It ain't thet hussy thet got yew riled 'n' yew know it. It's Lee. Yew stay here in town an' write stories 'bout th' places yew know he goes to—a damn foolish way ta git his attention, if'n yew ask me—'n' don't go sayin' yew ain't asked me, 'cause I'm tellin' yew anyways."

"I don't want his attention! Not if he's going to consort with painted tarts. And in case you haven't noticed, it's well past dawn and he's not exactly breaking his neck to see if I'm all right! More likely he's still at the ranch sulking because I've disgraced the grand Velásquez name yet again," she finished on a snort of derision. "He doesn't want me, Obedience. Now that he's got me out from under his roof—out of convenient arm's reach, he's well satisfied with the likes of Clarice Lawton. I bet if he comes to see if anyone's all right, it'll be her, not me." She turned disconsolately, still holding the buttermilk-soaked rag, and headed off to bed.

Chapter 21

For the next week Melanie nursed her wounds and brooded while Obedience fumed about the cussed stubbornness of young people. Melanie's article about the temperance ladies' "raid" on the Gilded Cage Saloon became the talk of San Antonio overnight. Clarence had Amos set her name at the top of the story, claiming that he wanted no harassment from the town's disgruntled men, nor did he wish to incur the disfavor of the local ladies of the evening. "One never knows when such a source might divulge some vital bit of information to me. I keep all channels of communication open."

Melanie wanted to reply with a vulgar Anglo-Saxonism but was too pleased about the story credit to do so. She did not see Lee all week. If Clarice did, Melanie knew the harlot had one hell of a shiner to show him!

Lame Deer was now acting as an apprentice matchmaker, coming to report to Melanie about Lee, and doubtless vice versa. After Lee had given him the lovely little bay filly, which the boy named Prancer, Lee had become Lame Deer's hero. First the bold *Tejano* had rescued him from the Rojas boys; then he had given him the most impressive gift of his impoverished lifetime. Small wonder Lame Deer wanted his Melanie to return to her princely husband.

Despite his loquaciousness in discussing Lee, Lame Deer had nothing to say lately about Blaine, Walkman, or the Comanche renegades. Melanie decided to stroll over to Father Gus's school that afternoon and have a casual chat with the priest's star pupil. If the boy had told Lee about that last raid, maybe his arrogant hero now had become the recipient of all Lame Deer's news tips.

Purposefully she set out from the *Star* across the plaza to the school. Just as she was about to step into the muddy street, she saw Seth Walkman dart into a back alley near the corner of Commerce and Winter streets.

How odd. He's alone and on foot, almost as if he doesn't want to be noticed, she mused to herself with a prickle of foreboding. Usually the loud, menacing ranger captain made his presence known wherever he went. Responding to her intuition, Melanie followed him at a distance as he strode down the narrow back street. Keeping up and remaining unseen at the same time were very difficult. She tried not to think what he would be capable of if he caught her spying on him. *But where is he going?*

As if in answer to her unspoken question, the man suddenly disappeared into the back entrance of a frame structure facing out onto Winter Street. It was one of a row of new buildings. She could not tell whose office Walkman had chosen. With utmost stealth she inched closer to the back door. Her teeth were chattering, but not from the cool fall weather. When she reached a window and inched up to listen, she was rewarded with silence. It was tightly closed. Cursing, she crept past the door and crossed to the other window. It was open! She could hear low, indistinct murmurs and strained to listen, even daring to raise her head for a few quick peeks over the sash.

Laban Greer admonished Seth Walkman, "I've told you I don't want you seen in this office, dammit." He ground out his expensive cigar and leaned back, waiting for the hard-faced gunman to speak.

"You need me, Greer. Don't you forget it. I'm the one who put you 'n' Blaine together, 'n' I'm the one takin' all the chances dealin' with that drunk old squaw man," Walkman said with contempt.

Laban Greer knew not to push too far with the dangerous, bitter ranger. "What do you have to tell me, Seth?" he asked.

"Just talked to Blaine. Seems him 'n' Gall got them a nice little passel of cash for Broughton's stock."

Greer snorted. "You mean Blaine got the cash and Gall took his share out in whiskey and bullets."

"That's what's puttin' a real burr 'neath Lucas's tail. He's whinin' somethin fierce 'bout sellin' guns 'n' ammunition to them Comanch. Seems to think he'll get caught someday 'tween the rangers 'n' the Injuns—right smack in the middle of a real war. Might even get hisself shot."

Greer's bulldog face reflected Walkman's venomous humor. "Wouldn't it be a pity? Convenient for us, however, to have a babbling drunk out of the way before he divulges our part in his illegal schemes. Just how many more massacres like Broughton's do you think it will take before the whole countryside goes up in flames?" Greer asked.

"Lots of folks herebouts talkin' right now 'bout sendin' out a big party of militia on a long scout—like Hays 'n' his boys did back in the forties," the ranger said. "Stay out there till every last Injun's dead er drove over the Red River."

"To do a job that thorough, we'd need the cooperation of the army," Greer responded thoughtfully. "Before federal troops can be requested by the governor, we'll have to have more civilian casualties. I'd just keep your rangers clear of Gall's renegades and let them do their job over the winter and into spring."

Walkman snickered. " 'N' every time another family gets burned out 'n' killed, you buy up their land real quiet like, for taxes. Hear any more from that fancy eastern feller who wants to sell sections to them foreigners?"

Greer shrugged. "In order to really begin such massive land dealing, we need the Comanche—indeed, all the tribes—cleaned out of Texas for good."

" 'N' you need your war to do that," Walkman said with fanatical hate in his voice.

"A war you want every bit as much as I, albeit for different reasons."

"Yeah, Greer, I want a war. Me 'n' my boys'll kill every Injun between here 'n' the Red River. I want me a state with nary a one o' them fuckin' red bastards left alive in it. They killed my whole family, all but me. Ain't no way I'll rest till I see Texas clean of 'em.''

Greer had heard Walkman's twisted ranting before, as well as Blaine's cowardly pleas. Busy and irritated at the interruption, he asked brusquely, ''I assume there is something more you wanted to discuss besides Blaine's usual whining lament?''

''I got a line on another good place for Gall to raid. Thought I'd have Zeb 'n' Pike check it out.''

''Whose place?'' Greer asked.

''That rich-ass greaser Velásquez. Got him a nice big herd of prime horses all set aside fer breedin', not to mention lots of saddle-broke mustangs 'n' beef cattle. Place is far 'nough from town so's not to attract much attention. Anyways, since he feels like he does 'bout rangers, my boys won't go near his place. Course, he ain't got no family at that big fancy ranch house since his little lady's done left him 'n's livin' in town,'' Walkman said with a sly snicker.

''That female reporter who writes gossip for the *Star*?''

''Yup. Feisty 'n' smart-mouthed for a gal. Reckon that's why that greaser got shut of her. Never could figger why a highfalutin type like him'd hitch up with a gal workin' for a newspaper.''

Laban Greer's face relaxed into a smile, wolfish and cold, but openly lustful. He recalled the night he'd danced with Melanie Velásquez. ''Madam Velásquez is a very beautiful woman, Seth. Just a bit too, er, unconventional to appeal to a man of your tastes.''

''Don't go gittin' smartass with me, Laban,'' Walkman retorted. ''I don't like bein' talked to like I'm some cur hangin' round your back porch.''

''As you said, Seth, we need each other to achieve our mutually complementary goals.''

Walkman unfolded his tall, gangly body from the chair and loomed over Greer's desk with his big hands planted on the polished walnut surface. ''Just don't you forget how much you need me. I ain't so easy got rid of like that drunk Blaine.'' With that he turned and strode toward the door.

Melanie scarcely had enough time to crouch behind a rain barrel before Walkman's boots crunched on the rocky ground as he passed within three feet of her. Once he had vanished around the corner, she stood up on wobbly legs. *They're going after Lee! I have to warn him!*

She walked as calmly as possible from the alley, headed for the livery stable to get Liberator, reviewing the incredible conversation she'd just overheard. No wonder Laban Greer's ranch prospered while he spent so much time in town at his small land office! "I wonder just how many murdered families' ranches he's bought up in the past year or two?" she muttered under her breath. As soon as she warned Lee, she'd go to the recorder's office and see what the public records showed. Formulating her plans, Melanie rounded the corner at Simpson's Livery when she saw Jeremy Lawrence.

He smiled warmly at her as she stopped abruptly in front of him. "Whoah, Melanie! You're out of breath. Where are you going in such a hurry?"

Looking around and seeing no one close by, she pulled the ranger into the dim interior of the livery and proceeded to relate what she had just heard.

Jeremy's face paled as he listened, realizing the danger she had been in. "You're certain neither of them saw you?"

"No. I left the alley after Walkman. Greer was still in his office."

"Let me walk you back to the *Star* office, Melanie. Then I'll ride out to Night Flower," he replied with relief in his voice.

"Forget me! Go to Night Flower and warn Lee! He could be killed, Jeremy—all so Laban Greer can get his land. Oh, it's monstrous—all those people butchered so brutally for revenge and money." She shuddered.

"Lee already knows he's being scouted," Jeremy said carefully, knowing he had to explain part of their scheme to Melanie or she'd stir up a hornet's nest and ruin everything. "Jim Slade and I talked your husband into helping us catch Blaine and Walkman. We didn't know about Greer, though.

Thanks for that invaluable piece of information. You are some reporter, lady.''

"Lee—working with you?" she asked incredulously.

He grinned wryly. "Believe me, it took some fancy talking from Jim to persuade him. But now, thanks to you, we know Walkman's taken the bait and sent his men to scout our carefully laid trap. We're prepared. But you have to keep quiet about this, Melanie—and stay out of it." He said the last with steel in his voice as he took her elbow, firmly propelling her toward the *Star* office.

As soon as Jeremy had ridden out of town, Melanie left the newspaper and headed to the recorder's office. Jarvis Phelps was the town recluse, perfectly suited to hiding behind stacks of rustling papers and keeping track of all land transactions in Bexar County. Small, bald, and emaciated, he lived alone in a room above the rickety frame office. Melanie wondered if Phelps might refuse her access to his precious records and mulled over her best approach. Entering the long musty room, she gave Jarvis a dazzling smile. "Good afternoon, Mr. Phelps. I have a problem and I surely do hope you can help me."

While Melanie was busy at the recorder's office, Jeremy Lawrence rode hard for Night Flower Ranch. He had some very interesting information to share with Lee Velásquez.

"She hid in the alley and eavesdropped on Greer and Walkman!" Lee's face darkened in a combination of anger and fright. Visions of what Seth Walkman could have done to his beautiful wife flashed before Lee's horrified eyes. He forced himself to concentrate on what Lawrence was saying.

"Laban Greer is apparently buying up the burned-out ranches after Gall and his renegades kill the owners. I haven't had time to check on the county records yet, but after what your wife overheard, I'm sure we can confirm it."

Lee's eyes narrowed. "If I know Mellie, she's already at Phelps's office going through every record book."

"I took her to the *Star* office and told her to stay out of this," Jeremy said defensively.

Lee smiled thinly. "If you can get my wife to do anything

sensible or safe, you'll be the first man in her life who could." He turned and began to pace, running his hands through his hair in nervous concentration. "We need to talk this over with Jim. He said Houston thought someone higher up with connections in the Indian Office had set Blaine up in business. Now we know who."

"Question is how do we stop Greer?" Jeremy asked in perplexity. "Catching Blaine and Walkman won't be hard if Walkman's already got his men scouting your herd. Jim's idea about rounding up that big batch of prize horses and corralling them at Oak Creek was good."

"I'll tell my foreman, Bill Ross, to alert those new *vaqueros* that Gall's getting ready to move." Lee paused a minute and looked warily at the ranger. "You're certain those Lipans won't be recognized as ranger scouts from Travis County?"

Jeremy Lawrence's expression came as near to being contemptuous as Lee had ever seen it. "You think men like Walkman can tell one Indian from another?" *Can you?*

Lee shrugged uneasily. "We need the Lipans if we're going to stop Blaine's Comanche renegades. That's for sure. Let's ride to Bluebonnet and see how Jim wants to deal with Greer."

"What about Melanie?" Jeremy asked, worrying about what the boldly curious newspaperwoman might do if left unattended.

"What about her, Lawrence?" Lee parried in a tight voice. "I'll see to my wife tonight," he said as he swung up on Sangre's back, leaving the ranger to follow in his dust.

After spending her dinner hour poring over a set of carefully recorded notes, Melanie locked them securely in the drawer of the big oak desk in Obedience's office. She had enough on Laban Greer's activities for quite a story. But it must wait until all the other pieces were in place. From now on she would watch Jeremy's comings and goings with a great deal of interest, not to mention that scamp Lame Deer, who was apparently in collusion with the men!

For now, she had a temperance meeting to report on, although she was certain the follow-up story about this gathering would be tame indeed compared to the riot at the Gilded Cage. In all the excitement of the past days' discoveries about Greer and Walkman's conspiracy and the trap Lee, Jim, and Jeremy were trying to spring on them, Melanie had little time to brood over her sundered relationship with her husband.

The meeting was slightly less crowded than it had been that evening before the saloon riot. *Probably some of the men kept their women under lock and key tonight*, Melanie thought disdainfully as she seated herself near the rear of the church to better observe the crowd while Stella spoke.

"Move over 'n' make room fer a body ta set," Obedience said to Melanie as she plunked her ample girth onto the groaning bench next to the amazed younger woman.

"What are *you* doing here? I thought you didn't hold with temperance ideas," Melanie said with raised eyebrows.

Obedience scanned the room, then looked back at Melanie. "Jist come ta see whut all the hullabaloo is 'bout, thet's all. 'Sides, Wash 'n' a couple o' his friends got them a red-hot poker game agoin' down at th' Red Dog Saloon."

Observing her friend's guileless expression, Melanie had a sudden sense of uneasiness. "Obedience, you wouldn't—"

A sharp rap of Stella Wolcott's gavel brought the whispering, tittering assembly to order. The Reverend Bixly, minister of Mount of Olives Methodist Church, opened the meeting with a prayer and several hymns. Then Stella took over, fixing the crowd with her piercing gray eyes. They glowed like banked charcoal, causing many of the men scattered through the audience to squirm uncomfortably. The audience was a motley assortment of San Antonians—well-dressed merchants in wool suits and elders in the Presbyterian Church sat next to farmers clad in homespun. Melanie's own simple blue linen suit looked elegant alongside the calico worn by many of the women. Store owners and clerks, ranchers and cowhands, but most of all, their wives, sisters, and mothers, filled the room.

Stella began by telling the story of a poor motherless family of six children whose drunken sot of a father spent every last cent he earned at the local saloon, leaving his fifteen-year-old son to support the younger siblings by scrubbing floors and emptying slops in that very establishment. The tale was probably apocryphal, but powerfully told, as if it were an Old Testament allegory mirroring the sins of all husbands and fathers, including those of San Antonio.

Melanie watched people shuffle in embarrassment, nod in agreement, or sob in regret as Stella ranted on. Finally Stella left the small speaker's lectern at the head of the room and began to march up the aisle. "Who will sign, sister? Brother? Come forward and sign the pledge. Not one drop more of demon rum!" She waved the sheets of paper and brandished the pen like a banner and sword as she began to collect signatures. "Take home a pledge for your husband or father, your brother or son to sign, ladies. It is your God-ordained duty." A number of stalwarts signed up and others nervously took copies of the pledge with vows to deliver them into the hands of their erring male relatives. Suddenly Stella stopped directly in front of Obedience Oakley.

"What about you, Sister Oakley? I understand that your man imbibes," she challenged.

Obedience had sat through the performance, passing a few backhanded asides to Melanie about the hypocrisy of some of the actors, but taking it quietly overall. Now she looked up into Stella's intimidating hatchet face, and her brown eyes squinted. Melanie knew that look.

"My man has a pretty considerable o' a thirst, yep. It fits h' rest o' him," she said proudly.

A few titters escaped around the room, and Melanie bent her head to take notes, hiding her smile.

"Then you should have him sign a pledge," Stella persisted.

"Whut fer?" Obedience asked reasonably.

"Why, to save him from the clutches of debauchery. To keep him from spending his income on whiskey and games of chance and wicked women!" Stella looked abashed at the big woman's density.

"Wal, as fer a snort o' good corn likker 'n' a turn o' th' cards, I guess I'll let Wash have hisself a time now 'n' thin. As fer th' other, I don't reckon I need ta worry, none," Obedience said dryly.

Stella drew herself up even more ramrod straight and stuck out her pointed chin. "Any man who gambles and drinks spirits will fall under the spell of those Jezebels. My late husband fell into the clutches of a painted hussy."

"Considerin' how yew treat th' men hereabouts, I reckon I kin see why he might jump headfirst inta her clutches," Obedience shot back with an expressive gesture of her big hamlike hands. Laughter bubbled up around the room, then subsided into nervous giggles.

Stella Wolcott's face suffused with wrath. "No decent man spends his money in saloons while his children go hungry."

"Yew keep yammerin' 'bout thet. Any woman worth her salt'd better settle with her man on whut's needed fer vittals 'n' sech afore he goes out fer a jug er a card game. All my husbands tuk care o' me 'n' our younguns jist fine. Now me 'n' Wash got us a good life. It's nobody's bizness whut we do with our money er whut we drink!" Obedience stood up as she finished her speech. It was obvious the zealot had ceased to amuse her.

Stella Wolcott was gauntly thin compared to Obedience's girth, but she matched the Tennesseean's height. Brown and gray eyes glared levelly at each other.

"Not all women, Mrs. Oakley, have your formidable weight to throw behind the decision of how a family's money will be spent," she spat with a vicious inspection of Obedience's hips.

"Yew ever hear of convincin' a man with a skillet twixt th' ears? Works wonders. Even a scrawny, dried-up old prune like yew cud handle it. 'Specially if'n she's got brains 'nough ta wait till her man's asleep." She paused for a beat as the laughter erupted in full force this time, then scratched her head consideringly. " 'Pears ta me it'd be even easier ta convince a feller if'n he wuz sleepin' with a leetle help from a jug. Might jist make this here scrap o' paper plumb unnecessary," she said, yanking the sheet from Stella Wolcott's clenched fist and balling it up. Her shrewd brown eyes were benignly calm as she waited to see what Stella was going to do.

Melanie was torn, wanting to let out the laughter she had suppressed, yet feeling sorry for the hapless crusader who had picked on the wrong adversary. Having seen the Tennesseean in action, she hoped Stella would curb any rash impulse toward physical violence. Obedience Oakley would shatter Stella Wolcott like a year-old buffalo chip!

The temperance lady seemed to sense that, for she balled up her hands in fists held impotently at her sides and spat her parting sally, "You and your husband are bound straight for hell."

"Long as yew'll be headin' th' other direction, suits me jist fine!"

"First a riot in the Gilded Cage, then a riot in a Methodist Church!" Melanie shook her head in consternation as she sat beside Obedience's big oak desk in the boardinghouse library.

"Thet woman's plumb dangerous, that's all. Crazy, unnatural ideas. Good Lord gave us spirits. Even th' Good Book says Noah got drunk. Wouldn't surprise me none if'n St. Peter 'n' a few others didn't tetch a drop now 'n' then, too."

"When did you become such a biblical authority?" Melanie asked, a smile curving her lips in spite of her chagrin over the riotous outcome of the meeting.

"I read th' Good Book 'n' I go ta church—leastways when I kin heer me a good hellfire 'n' brimstone Baptist preacher. Thet Bixly feller's a mewler 'n' pewler."

"But Mrs. Wolcott isn't, though, is she? Obedience, honestly, you baited her something awful," Melanie scolded. "Why did you come to that meeting anyway?"

The big woman walked carefully over to the cabinet across the room. She opened it and removed two delicate glasses and a bottle of clear white liquid. "This here stuff is th' best me 'n' Wash ever tasted. Them fancy leetle cups belonged ta my sister-in-law, God rest her soul. Mebbee they'll make it taste better ta yew." She poured two shots, full to the brim, and handed one to Melanie.

"Obedience! I've taken the pledge. You know I'm temperance."

"Harumph! Temperance means moderate—not goin' ta extremes, don' it?"

"Well, literally, I suppose that's true," Melanie said, equivocating as Obedience forced the crystal glass into her hand.

"Then one sip ain't gonna kill ya!"

They drank. Melanie was surprised at the silky smooth taste of the drink—indeed, it had virtually no taste at all, just a slight warmth as it coiled downward into her stomach. "This is nice, Obedience. It doesn't smell or taste like the vile stuff they drink in the saloons at all," she said with a grin. "Now, tell me why you came to that meeting."

Taking another drink and making sure Melanie followed suit, Obedience began, "Take a look at thet dried-up, hatchet-faced ole woman, Melanie. Drove her man away, lives alone, 'n' travels from town ta town, stirrin' up grief. Yew wanna end up like thet?" Obedience asked brutally.

Melanie jumped up angrily. "That's monstrously unfair! I left Lee because he doesn't want me. I'm not like Stella Wolcott!"

"No, yew shore ain't. And I aim ta see yew don't end up like her neither! Set yerself down 'n' finish yore drink. I got me a piece ta speak 'n' I'm gonna speak it." Slowly, like a wilting flower, Melanie sank back in the chair and allowed her friend and mentor to refill her glass.

Chapter 22

Lee and Jeremy met Jim Slade at Bluebonnet and shared their new information about Walkman and Greer. Charlee insisted Lee stay for supper, although Jeremy Lawrence begged off the invitation and departed after their strategy meeting with Jim. When the meal was over, Jim excused himself and took the children out for a late evening ride, leaving Charlee and Lee alone. Lee wanted to unburden himself about his separation from Melanie. He and Charlee talked for several hours. He explained the series of confrontations and fiascoes that had led to Melanie's flight from Night Flower.

"When she accused me of only wanting her back because I was afraid of her father, I left her in town," he finished bitterly.

"You, of course, never thought of telling her you wanted her back because you love her," Charlee said gently. Her bright green eyes met his startled black ones.

Lee swallowed convulsively. "I never told her that because I don't love her!"

Charlee leaned her chair back and studied the scowling, angry man across from her. "You don't love her—don't care for her the least little bit, but you can't keep your hands off her when she's around, can't stop thinking about her when she's not around, and break your neck riding to town after her when she leaves you. Just what would you call it?"

He put his head in his hands and leaned his elbows on the kitchen table. "Damned if I know," he muttered, then said in a hoarse, pained whisper, "Whatever I feel for her, she's made it clear what she feels for me. Everytime I touch her she responds—loses herself just like I do. But as soon as it's over she freezes up, as if she hated herself for giving in—and hated me for seeing her weakness. She doesn't want to be my wife. Hell, she doesn't want to be a woman!''

"Partly you're right—she is afraid of being a woman and a wife.''

Lee flashed her a look of surprise and dismay, but said nothing.

"Didn't you ever think about why?''

"She'd rather be out marching with Stella Wolcott or risking her neck for a newspaper story than tending to a home and family,'' he replied angrily.

"Her causes are symptoms of her problem, Lee, not solutions to it. She wants to uplift the downtrodden because she's identified with them all her life. For the first twelve years of her childhood she was shuttled back and forth between St. Louis and New Orleans. Rafe wasn't around to be a real father to her, and his mistress certainly wasn't a fit mother. She's afraid to show you how much she cares because you, my proud, mule-headed *criollo*, have made her feel pretty damned unworthy. Or do I miss my guess?''

At his dawning look of guilt, she went on, "Throwing her mixed blood and her crusading career at you is her way of protecting herself from more hurt and rejection.''

Lee's dark brows rose sardonically. "And you think she loves me?'' The way he asked the question spoke volumes.

"Yes, I do,'' Charlee replied simply.

As he rode into town late that evening, Lee mulled over what Charlee had said. He admitted to himself that he'd hidden his real feelings from Melanie. Perhaps she had done the same. The only way to find out was to confront her. Since Jeremy Lawrence had told him about her latest dangerous escapade, Lee had a legitimate excuse to stop at the boardinghouse and talk with her.

When he reined in Sangre, it was quite late. The realization struck him that she might already be asleep. But if she were asleep and he awakened her, she just might be disoriented enough to tell him the truth. He headed for the side porch entry to the kitchen, thinking to slip up to her room undetected. Then he saw the dim light from the study. Peering through the lace-curtained window, he saw Obedience and Melanie seated on opposite sides of the desk. They were sipping something from fancy etched crystal glasses. Obedience poured another refill of clear liquid. *No, it couldn't be!* But it was. Wash's incredibly potent white lightning. How well he remembered his confessions when the Oakleys had plied him with the smooth brew last year. Grinning to himself, he walked to the side door and entered the long dark hall.

Hearing soft, murmuring voices emanating from the study, he opened the door and peered inside. Obedience sat behind the desk while Melanie leaned limply to one side in an overstuffed chair. His tiny wife looked like an arrestingly innocent waif swallowed up in the large chair.

"Can an interloper join the party?" he asked with a smile, letting himself in.

Obedience's broad face split in a wide grin and she stood up, stretching her Amazonian frame and yawning. "Jist th' feller I wanted ta see. Me 'n' th' leetle gal here been drinkin'—temperately, now mind yew. But I'm plumb tuckered 'n' I'd admire if'n yew'd see yore wife gits ta sleep all right." With a wink she scooted past him and out the door, moving with surprising speed and grace for one of such bulk.

Melanie sat with her head swimming, only half paying attention to Obedience's lecture about Lee, when the subject of their argument sauntered into the room as if conjured up.

"Obedience, did you plan thish—this?" Melanie tried to stand and reach out to her hastily departing drinking companion, but the big woman was too quick for her.

Lee towered over her, surveying her wrinkled blue linen suit and tousled hair. Self-consciously she ran her fingers through the loose hair, remembering how she had taken it down because the pins had felt uncomfortable. Melanie could feel Lee looking at her as he stood, hat pushed casually back on his head, fingers hooked arrogantly in his belt. She refused to meet his glowing jet eyes.

"Well, my little Night Flower, looks like you've been dipped in ninety-proof dew," he whispered, sniffing from the delicate glass she had deposited on the table. "Your petals must be all curled up."

She stood in affronted dignity. "I am not crilled—curled up," she said carefully, angry because her mouth refused to obey her brain.

"Your tongue sure seems to be," he said with a small laugh, reaching to steady her as she teetered precariously to the right.

"Don't touch me, Lee," she said in a small, plaintive voice.

He held on to her despite her plea, for the first time not angered by her apparent rejection. "Why not, Night Flower? Don't you like it when I touch you?" he whispered.

"No—yes—I don't know. I do at first, but afterward it's always the same. You never—" She was babbling!

When he saw that she had forced herself to stop talking, he drew her closer into his arms and began to rain soft, light kisses across her forehead, temples, eyelids, and cheeks, nuzzling her neck and then gently tipping her chin up so she faced him with lips breathlessly parted. He could feel her body melting into his, her arms stealing around his waist, her mouth expectantly waiting for his kiss.

"Open those golden eyes, my beautiful little Night Flower. Look at me." He held her chin, willing her to comply. When the thick dark lashes fluttered unwillingly open, what he saw in her eyes took his breath away. And he knew the same emotion was mirrored in his own.

Very slowly he lowered his mouth to hers, experimenting, savoring. She tasted sweet and he recognized the faint hot glow of the moonshine. It warmed his tongue as he twined it with hers in a delicate dance of desire.

"Mellie, oh Mellie, what fools we've both been," he murmured against her silky hair. She pressed against him like a small soft kitten, purring deeply in her throat, the liquor loosening all her inhibitions. Lee reached down and scooped her up into his arms. "I think it's time Mrs. Velásquez went to bed." Obediently she slid her arms around his neck as he carried her from the office and up the long stairs at the end of the hall.

When he reached her room, he opened the door and carried her inside to the bed, where he deposited her. It was rather small but would serve, he decided as he turned and quickly closed the door, sliding the bolt against any unexpected intrusion.

Melanie sat on the edge of her bed, watching the movements of his lean, pantherish body avidly, making no attempt to conceal her interest. When she began to unfasten the buttons of her blouse with unsteady fingers, he brushed them aside, saying, "Here, let me."

Slowly Lee unbuttoned the silk blouse, peeling the sheer fabric back to reveal the rich swell of her golden breasts, barely shielded by a lacy camisole. He slipped his fingertips inside and teased the dark rosy crests until they hardened into points. Her breath caught at the tingling pleasure and she gasped, arching into his caress. When he pulled the open jacket and blouse off, she helped him, shrugging them carelessly from her shoulders, languorously baring her flesh for his hands and lips.

"Raise your legs—one at a time, Mellie," he commanded as he knelt by the side of the bed and removed her delicate kid slippers and silk stockings. Then he pulled her up to stand in his arms so he could unfasten her suit skirt and the tapes to her petticoats. She wrapped her arms around his neck and kissed him ardently while his fingers worked deftly until the whole weight of her skirts slithered to the floor.

Lee stood back and spanned her tiny waist with his hands. "So perfect, so delicate, like a small, golden figurine," he breathed as he slid his fingers up and unhooked her camisole, freeing her breasts. Hefting one in each hand, he lowered his head and suckled, alternating between them until she cried out her pleasure in a wordless, incoherent moan. Then he laid her back on the bed to watch him as he stripped.

He seemed to shimmer before her eyes like a bronzed god, lean corded muscles flexing as he shrugged off his shirt and reached to unfasten his trousers. With her eyes she traced the intricate symmetry of his curly black body hair, longing to feel the crisp, springy texture of it rubbing against her skin. When he kicked off his boots and peeled down fitted buckskin breeches from his long hard legs, she stared unashamedly at the swollen proof of his desire, feeling a quivering response between her legs.

"Lee," she breathed softly as he sank down alongside her on the narrow bed. He quickly unfastened her pantalets and pulled them down her sleek little legs. She raised her buttocks and helped him free her of the unwanted encumbrance of clothing. Then his hand fastened around one delicately slim ankle. He raised it and leaned over to kiss the arch of her foot, trailing soft nibbling kisses along the curve of her calf, over the back of her knees, then up the inside of her thigh.

His fingers grazed the soft inky curls between her legs. "You're wet and sweet with passion, Night Flower," he breathed as he lowered his mouth to kiss and caress where his hands had just been. She arched up in frenzied pleasure, her head tossing from side to side in wild abandon. His tongue flicked and teased at the sweet, silky core of her until he could feel the pulsating waves of her orgasm. He raised his head and watched her writhe and quiver in ecstasy, then kissed a scorching trail up her belly to her breasts as he positioned himself between her legs.

Still in a haze from the aftershock of intense pleasure, Melanie opened to him as he plunged into her with a harsh, rasping cry, betraying the cost of holding back his own release. He stroked frantically for a moment, then gradually regained control of his desperate hunger, slowing his pace to long, languorous caresses. She arched to meet him and her nails dug into his biceps, pulling him down to her eager, open mouth.

The cool night air was heavy with the heady, dizzying scent of their lovemaking. It intoxicated her even more than Obedience's liquor had. Melanie felt him tense and shiver with the aching need to spill his seed. Crying out his name from deep in her throat, she kissed him fiercely and tightened her legs around his hips for a last hard, long explosion. *Again, again.* She never knew if she spoke the words aloud or not, but she could feel his swelling, pulsing climax as he joined her in surfeit, collapsing on top of her soft, small body.

They clung to each other in the quiet of the night, sweat-soaked and panting. Finally he rolled his greater weight from her and pulled her to curl against his side. She sighed and fell instantly asleep. For a long while he watched her in the moon-drenched silence of the small room before drifting off to sleep.

When the bright rays of autumn sunlight filtered across the bed, Lee opened his eyes and blinked. It was well past dawn. Raising himself up carefully on one elbow, he looked down at her small, beautiful face, so serene and youthful in repose. Quickly he thought of the headache she'd have upon arising. Perhaps explanations were better left until after this mess was settled with Walkman and Blaine. Still, he couldn't just leave her without a word. Softly he kissed her eyelids, cheeks, lips, feathering light kisses across her face until she opened her eyes.

Melanie looked up at her husband's smiling face, darkened by a bristling shadow of beard. "You look like a bandit," she said. Her voice surprised her with its raspy edge. Then, when she turned her head and tried to rise, she plopped abruptly back down. "Ooh! God, what was in that stuff! Stella Wolcott is right! I'll never again drink anything stronger than coffee!"

She could feel the bed rock from his laughter, and it added to her aching misery. Melanie struggled to remember what had happened last night after the first two drinks of that wicked brew Obedience fed her. She had a shadowy recollection of Lee's arrival and Obedience's abrupt departure. After that, he had spoken to her in the office and she had told him—what? Gingerly she rubbed her aching head, but could not remember. She did remember their wildly abandoned loving, his tenderness. Something more niggled at the periphery of her consciousness, but she could not dredge it up. Then she felt his fingertips graze her cheek and turn her chin so that she was forced to look into his eyes.

"Mellie, last night I learned some things," he began

hesitantly, uncertain of how to phrase what he wanted to say. Seeing the wary, withdrawing expression that began to shutter her eyes, he leaned down and kissed her lightly on the lips. "Don't pull away from me again. I know now—"

Just then a sharp knock sounded on the door. Swearing under his breath, Lee tossed back the covers and reached over to the crumpled heap of his buckskin breeches, which had been tossed in a corner. The whole room was strewn with their hastily discarded clothing. As he donned his pants, the rap sounded again. Barefoot and bare-chested, he strode across the room and slid the bolt on the door. He was greeted by the grim-visaged face of Jeremy Lawrence. "What the hell are you doing here?" Lee demanded furiously as he noted the tall ranger's eyes traveling past him to the bed where Melanie sat with the covers pulled up to her neck.

Lawrence shifted his gaze quickly back to the scowling, furious man in front of him. "I figured you'd be here since you said you were coming to town when I left you at Bluebonnet yesterday afternoon. One of my scouts just came to get me. Seems he spotted Zeb Brocker and a couple of Gall's braves creeping around your herd. He thinks they might hit tonight. We need to get the men lined up and alert Slade."

"I'll be right down. You ride to get Jim. I'll head for Night Flower and check with my men to see what they know." Lee quickly closed the door as Lawrence turned and departed. Looking at Melanie's wide-eyed fright and confusion, he cursed the rotten turn of events. They had laid out the bait for Walkman and had waited for weeks. *Of all the miserable timing—now the bastard comes after it!*

"Jeremy told me you were working together to catch Blaine and Walkman, but he wouldn't say anything specific. What's going on, Lee?" She leaped from the bed, ignoring her usual modesty and the pounding in her head. Walking over to a small chest, she opened a drawer and began to pull out some lacy underwear.

"You're staying here," he said flatly, ignoring her question as he pulled on shirt and boots. His face bore a hard, shuttered look that she recognized immediately.

"Why should I? I've been waiting for this story for weeks," she replied angrily as she slid her riding skirt on and reached for a blouse.

"You *are* staying here, Mellie, because I'm your husband and I say so. It's going to be dangerous and no reporter—male or female—is going to get in the way before the trap is sprung," he added, struggling for patience.

"I could at least wait at the ranch," Melanie retorted.

He reached over and whirled her around, holding her tightly by her shoulders. "You stay here." He bit off each word.

"What will you do if I refuse, Lee? Lock me in a closet?"

He gritted his teeth in fury. "I'm considering it. What do you think you can do—shoot Comanches?"

"I don't want to shoot anyone. I just want to get the story." *I want to be with you and see that you're safe*, she suddenly realized.

Lee was already out the door, calling over his shoulder, "Stay in town. Moses French has retired!"

"The hell you say," she muttered under her breath. Did he really want her to stay here out of concern for her safety? Or did he just want her out of the way, not complicating his life now that their lovemaking idyll of last night had ended? If only Jeremy hadn't interrupted when he did. She knew Lee had been about to say something revealing to her. But what?

Pushing aside her brooding, confused thoughts, she finished dressing and raced down to the stables to get Liberator.

Gradually Melanie calmed down and began to think more logically about a plan of action. Jeremy hadn't said where the herd was that they were using as bait. Night Flower was an enormous ranch. She could ride around for hours and not find the right location, or worse yet, blunder onto the Comanche and get herself killed or captured. Now that Lee was gone, she was left with a cold trail. But Jeremy had gone to Bluebonnet to warn Jim. Maybe Charlee knew something about what was going on! At least it was a lead.

As she rode briskly through the deserted streets in the early morning light, Melanie did not know the cold gray eyes of Seth Walkman watched her from behind the window of his hotel room. "Where the hell is that little bitch going this time of the morning?" he muttered to himself as he stretched and scratched his bare chest. Too bad she wouldn't be at her husband's ranch tonight. Gall would enjoy her. He chuckled mirthlessly to himself as he dressed.

Jarvis Phelps was nervous. He fidgeted with his glasses, polishing and repolishing them as he watched Laban Greer go through the deeds—those very same land titles that shameless female reporter had asked to see yesterday. Should he tell Mr. Greer or not? Phelps was afraid to meddle in the powerful speculator's business. He was also smart enough to figure that the business wasn't altogether legal, but that was not his affair. Still, he didn't like meddlesome females, especially ones who were Indian lovers and temperance crusaders to boot.

"Er, Mr. Greer." Phelps cleared his throat uncertainly. "There's something I think you might want to know. . . ."

Within five minutes Greer had located Seth Walkman at the Golden Nugget Saloon, hunched over a breakfast of greasy fried potatoes and silty black coffee. Looking around to see if they were observed, he noted with satisfaction that the fat old Mexican cook had returned to the kitchen out back and the Irish bartender was more interested in swatting flies with his dish towel than in drying the glasses from last night's business.

"What you want at this piss-ass hour?" Walkman snarled, knowing whatever it was that brought Laban Greer to town this early could bode no good for either of them.

"That damnable female reporter, Melanie Velásquez, has been snooping around the land office, asking to see the title transfers for Ryan's and Broughton's places, among others that I've acquired in the past several years," Greer said levelly.

Walkman's eyes narrowed. "'N' we got Blaine and his Injuns fixin' to raid her husband's place tonight. I don't like it, Laban."

Greer scratched his jaw slowly. "They're estranged. I've heard rumors that the marriage was a shotgun affair. She's lived and worked here in town while he's running his ranch. This may just be a coincidence, especially considering her penchant for crusades, but it's best not to take a chance. Deal with her as soon as you can find a clean chance when she's alone."

Walkman's gray eyes glowed ferally. "Now, that might just be real easy. Not half hour ago I seen her ride out of town—alone."

Melanie paced Liberator steadily as she rode toward Bluebonnet, turning over and over last night's events in her mind. Her head was finally beginning to clear from the effects of the alcohol as she breathed in the cool, crisp fall air. She reviewed every word Lee had spoken, every nuance of his behavior, trying to decide what he had been preparing to tell her when they were interrupted. *Do I dare hope that he loves me? Or am I just reading meanings into his words and actions?* She scoffed to herself, realizing how Stella Wolcott would castigate her for last night's debauch. "I wonder if poor Stella's ever been in love," she murmured aloud to Liberator.

Just then her reverie was interrupted by a crashing sound in the heavy brush at the side of the trail. Melanie turned in the saddle and was horrified to see the forbidding figure of Seth Walkman emerge with a Walker Colt aimed at Liberator's head. When she attempted to pull her Allen and Thurber pepperbox from her pocket, she could hear the distinct hammer click of his Colt.

"Now, Miss Prissybritches, just cool down 'n' rein that black devil in," he rasped. "I'll take that fancy little gun you got stashed in that skirt, too."

Melanie forced herself to stop trembling as she handed over the gun. He stopped both horses in the middle of the road. *I can't outrun him in the open. Wait and see what he plans to do.*

He grinned at her. "Sensible for a female, aintcha?"

"I couldn't get far if you shot Liberator, could I?" she replied, proud of how steady her voice sounded. "What do you want, Mr. Walkman?"

"Question is, reporter lady, what do you want with them land-office records about Laban Greer's property?" He observed the way her hand tightened on the saddle pommel and grinned again. "Nothin' to say, huh? I bet ole Gall will get you to talk—scream your fool head off. Him 'n' your greaser husband got them a date tonight. He expects to get the Velásquez horses. And you'll just be an extra little bonus, yes sir. . . ."

Chapter 23

When they drew in sight of Blaine's trading post, Melanie's heart felt leaden in her chest. On the long ride from where he had accosted her near Bluebonnet, she had racked her brains for a means of escape. At first she was terrified that the reptilian Walkman might drag her into the bushes to rape and murder her, but he seemed to have no interest at all in her as a woman, only a perverse eagerness to deliver her into the hands of Gall and his renegades.

Walkman spoke little and kept a tight rein on Liberator, telling her only that they were going to meet Blaine, who always acted as his contact with the savages. "I don't get no nearer them stinkin' Injuns than I got to. That's what we got that squaw man Blaine for," he said contemptuously.

Melanie recalled his words to Greer that day in town about Comanches killing his family. His obsessive hate of

Indians was scarcely that rare in Texas, but few men would turn a white woman over to them. Casting about desperately for some way to forestall her terrifying fate, Melanie asked, "If you hate murdering savages like Gall, why are you willing to give me—one of your own people—to him? Surely the women in your own family must have—"

He struck her a wicked blow to the face with Liberator's reins, causing the big stallion to rear up, nearly throwing her. "The women in my family's dead! There ain't no more worth botherin' with, least of all the likes of you! Stirrin' up folks to take pity on them poor starvin' redskins with them goddamn newspaper stories! You 'n' that greaser husband of yours'll help me get my revenge. His fancy ranch'll be burned 'n' all his stock drove off 'n' then you turn up dead. After Gall 'n' his boys is finished with you—all Bexar County'll be screamin' for rangers to kill every one of them bastards." He fixed her with his lead-colored eyes and paused, then said, "You'll do *my* cause a lot of good, reporter lady, but only if you're raped, tortured, and stone-cold dead!"

Melanie shivered, knowing that his twisted mind would in no way be amenable to any kind of pleading. She rubbed her stinging cheek. An evil welt was forming, but no cut had been opened. Just then she felt Liberator's gait become slightly irregular. He was favoring his right rear foot. "My horse is lame," she said tersely, realizing the stallion must have picked up a stone in his shoe.

"We're almost at Blaine's. I expect he can give you another pony. That big black devil oughta bring me a pretty penny with horse traders up north a ways. I'll take real good care of him," he said in a cruel, taunting drawl.

As they rode slowly the last few hundred yards into Blaine's big corral, a pair of wide black eyes followed their progress. Lame Deer was crouched in the shadows of a century plant. He had been riding Prancer out in the general direction of the post every day, scouting to see what men, red and white, visited Blaine's lair. Several times when a Comanchero or a Comanche renegade had come to the place, he informed Jeremy Lawrence. But now Walkman had Melanie!

The hateful *rinche* pulled her roughly from Liberator's back and dragged her into the dim interior of the log structure. Hoping the conspirators would use that same back room again, the boy stealthily slipped around the back of the building. Oddly, the place appeared deserted. Something important and dangerous was about to happen. Lame Deer knew he must find out what it was and rescue Melanie quickly. Climbing up on a pile of crates against the rough log wall, he clung precariously beneath the window and listened to the conversation inside.

"You take her to Gall. Call it a present from me," Walkman said with an ugly laugh.

"I don't like it, Seth. It's too dangerous. Whut if someone saw yew bring her here? They'd string me up faster 'n I cud spit. If'n Greer wants her dead, let *him* kill her," Blaine said.

"Greer don't do his own dirty work. He ain't got the stomach for it. *I* do. 'N' I want her worked over by them Injuns so's everyone in Santone will know they done it!" The menace in his voice cut through the still air like a whiplash.

Standing between them, Melanie took in the argument in silence, as her mind churned furiously, turning over one possibility, then another. They didn't know Gall was riding into a trap, but she might still be dead before all the shooting was over. Yet it was at least a chance. If they took her to Lee's herd, Jeremy and Jim should be waiting, too. But Blaine's next words froze that hope.

"While Gall's raiders pick off thet herd, a few o' my men 'n' his braves er goin' ta torch thet greaser's ranch. I reckon I cud git one o' them ta take her off from there 'n' head out ta their camp. Kinda keep her fer Gall till he kin git back."

They can't burn Lee's home—not again, for the third time! a voice inside her screamed. With a speed born of desperate fear and fury, she darted past Walkman and snatched a whiskey bottle from Blaine's filthy desk. Smashing it over the chair she slashed with its jagged edge at Walkman's arm as he lunged for her.

Blaine backed off with a bleat of surprise, and the big ranger swore and grabbed his arm as a crimson ooze was blotted up by his coarse cotton shirtsleeve.

"Bitch!" He advanced on the small cornered woman who once more swiped at him with her deadly weapon, this time narrowly missing his abdomen while she ducked agilely past him. By this time Blaine had recovered his wits sufficiently to pull a heavy .44-caliber Colt pistol from his belt and club her quickly from the side. The glancing blow to her temple was just hard enough to daze her and knock her backward into Walkman's none too gentle grasp. The broken bottle crashed in shards on the hard-packed dirt floor.

"Tie her up hand 'n' foot. I want her full awake to think 'bout what Gall's gonna do to her," Walkman grated out at his companion.

Blaine shakily replaced the gun in his belt and walked over to his desk. He pulled a drawer open and yanked thin strips of crude rawhide from inside it. "Shit, Seth, she coulda laid one o' us open so bad we bled ta death," he said in awe. "Shore is mean fer sech a little bitty thing."

Walkman grunted as he grabbed a piece of the rawhide from Blaine and tied her feet roughly. "I expect Gall'll teach her who's boss quick enough."

"Whut th'—fire!" Blaine bellowed as he coughed and peered frantically through the door to his big main store-room. Thick black smoke billowed into the office from the crowded trading warehouse. He gave the cord on Melanie's wrist another hard yank and dropped her semiconscious body back onto the floor.

Lame Deer had set a torch to several piles of dried buffalo hides after quickly dousing them with some of Blaine's cheap whiskey. They flared into a stinking, smoldering fire that quickly filled the overstocked room with black smoke.

While Blaine fought his way to the hides and began to beat out the flames, Walkmen rushed past him and out the door, yelling for several of the half-breeds who worked at the post. Lame Deer frantically raced back to the rear of the

store and climbed through the window. In a flash he had the
bonds cut from Melanie's hands and feet and was back to
the window, helping her climb out.

She was still dazed from the blow to her head, but fought
down the surge of dizziness as she whispered, "Liberator's
lame. I can't ride him."

"I know. Prancer is very fast, and I have her tied over in
that thicket. Come quickly," the boy replied as he jumped
from the window ledge with the lithe grace of a small cat.

"But we can't both ride her. They'll catch us," she
replied as they dashed for the bushes. In truth, she was
afraid if Walkman shot at her he might hit the boy by
mistake. "Lame Deer, you run and hide down by the
arroyo. Wait until the men follow me. Then steal a horse
from the corral and ride as fast as you can to my ranch
house. Tell Kai the raiders are coming to burn him out.
He'll know what to do."

"But what of you? If they see you ride away, they'll
shoot at you." When they arrived at the thicket, he reached
for the pony's reins, undecided.

The yells coming from the post and Seth Walkman's
looming form as he cursed and scanned the surrounding area
made the decision for them. Before the boy could react,
Melanie grabbed him and shook him. "It's me they want.
I'm going to Lee for help! Hide yourself and then find help
with Kai!" With that, she leaped on the little horse and sped
down the arroyo, out of view but not earshot of the men at
the post.

When she came into sight as she rode over the far ridge of
the gully, shots erupted, kicking up dust around her. None
seemed to hit the speeding rider or horse. Lame Deer let out
a whistling breath of relief and quickly vanished into the
spiny underbrush of the gully. Walkman and Blaine came
thundering past his hiding place in pursuit.

Melanie had not ridden bareback since she was a girl at
Renacimiento, but she'd had lots of practice then, with
Cherokee Joe as her teacher. Now she was immensely
grateful that she could hang on to the small fleet pony. Her
slight weight and the absence of a heavy saddle would give

her an edge over the two large men chasing her. She knew she would need it.

The twilight air was briskly cool, but sweat trickled down Lee's back. He looked over at Slade and saw that his friend was also nervous. "How much longer, damn their eyes?" he muttered.

"Jeremy's scouts said they'd seen Gall and twenty braves fording the creek at sunset. We can't get too close without spooking them," Jim replied. "Don't worry. His Lipans know what they're doing."

Lee grunted and looked over at Bill Ross, who sat crouched against an outcropping of rocks in the narrow ravine where they waited with a dozen men, experienced Indian fighters from Night Flower and Bluebonnet ranches. They were heavily armed with rifles, knives, and handguns, all superbly mounted and ready to ride at the prearranged signal from Johnny Gray Arrow, one of Jeremy's Lipan scouts. The ranger and another twenty men were waiting across the creek on the far side of the low, wide valley that narrowed into a steep-walled opening to the north. When the Comanche swooped down on the unattended herd of horses neatly bunched together near the stream in the natural corral of the valley, two forces of heavily armed men would be ready for them.

"You keep your head with Lawrence, *mano*. I know the two of you have tangled over Melanie, but—"

"Let it rest, Jim, and leave my wife out of it," Lee snapped. "I'll resist the temptation to shoot that damn anger in the melee. Good enough?"

"I reckon that'll have to do," Slade replied with a wolfish grin.

Just then a figure slipped into the ravine, silent as a summer breeze. He was a small, thickly built man in buckskin leggings, shirt, and moccasins, with shoulder-length straight black hair. *One of Lawrence's tame Indians*, Lee thought, oddly without rancor.

"They come, maybe five minutes, maybe less," he reported tersely.

Each man checked his weapons once again, ready to ride. At the first cries of *Aaa-hey! Aaa-hey!* the trap would be sprung.

As Jim and Lee mounted up, Jim said uneasily, "I hope your Kanaka friend has enough men to keep the house and corrals safe. Those bastards want you burned out and killed so Greer can buy up your ranch."

Lee smiled grimly. "Kai will take care of the ranch house. He has a crew of special recruits who know how to handle hostiles, believe me."

"Now let Gall lead us to Blaine," Jeremy whispered, half to the Lipan scout next to him, half to himself. His men and Slade's across the valley would trail at a good distance, splitting up into smaller groups to follow the pattern of the raiders, tracking them until they all met with the whiskey runner.

The Comanche did just as expected, dividing the herd of prime horses into smaller groups and scattering with them. Somewhere to the north, probably by moonrise, they'd rendezvous with Blaine and a band of his men.

While Jeremy, Jim, and Lee stalked the raiders, Walkman and Blaine pursued Melanie. "She's keepin' a good lead on us, but we've got her headin' away from town," Walkman said. "Sooner or later that pony'll tire out or she'll break its leg or lame it. Then I'll have her."

"It's gotten on to dark 'n' my men er waitin' fer me, Seth. I gotta be there ta handle Gall 'n' his braves," Blaine whined nervously, scanning the brushy landscape around them. "Yew shore she ain't got a gun?"

Walkman's cold gray eyes didn't waver from his tracking, but his voice was contemptuous as he replied, "Head for your meet with Gall 'n' take care of that herd. See to the ranch buildin's bein' burned, too. I can handle that little bitch by myself. When I get through with her, they'll think it was Comanche that done for her!"

Melanie was scratched, bruised, and aching from the

hours she had spent clinging to the back of her small mount. Her head ached from the blow Blaine had given her, and she was faint from thirst, not to mention hunger, but her life depended on escaping her pursuers. She must also keep them from heading near Lee's ranch house. Lame Deer probably had had time to warn Kai by now. Lee might even have posted extra men to protect the house before he and Jeremy went after Gall. But she could not be certain and had to divert her pursuers long enough for the trap to be sprung. "If only I can stay alive long enough," she rasped hoarsely to Prancer. Lame Deer's pony was small and young, without the stamina of her larger stallion.

After several hours, Melanie was thoroughly lost, having left familiar trails to ride in circles through brushy, boulder-strewn country in an attempt to elude Walkman and Blaine. *God! Don't let me stumble onto those Comanche in the dark,* she prayed silently as the dusk thickened. She struggled to get her bearings, hoping for some familiar landmark that would enable her to take an indirect route back to San Antonio. The main road was far too open. It would be easy for Walkman to ride her down or ambush her.

One stand of scrub pine looked like a familiar configuration. Was it on the northernmost boundary of Night Flower? As she mulled that over, a dim sound of gunfire echoed from beyond the low, jagged hills ahead of her. Could it be Lee's men and the raiders? She decided to take the desperate chance. Exhausted, hurting, and disoriented, she could not evade a skillful tracker like Seth Walkman much longer. She headed toward the sounds of conflict.

Lucas Blaine lay flattened to the ground, pinned in a crossfire between his men and a force of militia volunteers, Lipan scouts, and that damnable new ranger, Lawrence. He'd even seen Velásquez at one point. The whole thing had been a trap, and his renegade friends had led the lawmen right to him and his men! Luckily, when the shooting had begun, he'd been near an outcropping of rock where he could take cover. He'd crawled from there on his belly through prickly pear and Spanish dagger until his clothes were torn and his skin raw, but he was pulling away from

the screeching yells of the surrounded Comanche, who
fought like cornered demons. They were mostly afoot, the
worst thing that could happen to Comanche warriors, but
they would never surrender. Of course, given what they had
done in the past years, it was unlikely they'd be given the
option of surrendering anyway. But Blaine vowed not to be
caught. Somehow he'd get away and get to Laban Greer's
ranch. Greer owed him—at least a couple of fresh horses
and enough gold to get across the Red River to Indian
Territory.

He raised himself up just enough to observe the carnage
as rangers and their Lipan allies clubbed and shot Gall's
braves and his own Comanchero friends. The raiders were
only slightly outnumbered, but the lawmen had such an
element of surprise on their side that the battle's outcome
was inevitable. If only he could get to a horse.

Melanie could see better as the moon rose full and
dazzlingly bright. Terrified horses neighed and raced hither
and yon as Comanche and Texian hacked at each other
between their flailing hooves. Everything was chaos. Where
was Lee? She must find him before Walkman found her. At
one point she caught sight of a group of Lipans and Jeremy
Lawrence with them. *Oh, please let Lee be safe*, she prayed
as she pulled Prancer behind a boulder to wait.

Walkman, too, had heard the shooting and come to
investigate, reasoning it would draw the woman. Once he
observed the fight, he could see the trap laid for Blaine and
Gall. Swearing, he considered. If he could find Blaine and
kill him before the blubbering old drunk told Velásquez
about him and Greer, the situation might yet be redeem-
able. He scanned the battle, awaiting his opening as he
pulled a Sharps rifle from his scabbard.

Melanie finally caught sight of her husband wrestling on
the ground with a Comanche. They were only a few
hundred feet from her. She watched in horrified fascination
as Lee rolled on top of the savage and slashed his throat in
one quick, clean motion. Instantly he was up, bloody knife
in hand, turning to face another foe. *He needs a gun*, she
thought frantically, realizing his Dragoon Colt must be out

of ammunition. Close to her hiding place a dead Lipan lay sprawled grotesquely, his body partially concealing a rifle.

Looking to left and right, Melanie made a dash for the gun. She knew how to shoot and would cover Lee.

Blaine saw a flash of waist-length, gleaming black hair and a white shirt. Velásquez's woman here! Of course the bitch knew about the trap and had come to help her husband! She was close by but obviously unaware of his hiding place. He'd grab her and use her as a hostage to get away from here. Slade and Lawrence wouldn't shoot a woman, and she was that greaser's wife—a perfect shield. He could see she was trying to get to the rifle beneath that dead scout. Quickly he scurried down between the rocks, pulling his pistol from his belt.

Melanie struggled with the dead weight of the Lipan and almost had the rifle free when an arm grabbed her in a choke hold from behind. "Drop th' rifle, little squaw," Blaine hissed, tightening his cruel grip on her windpipe until she complied. He held a gun to her head and began to back toward the rocks. "Now, let's jist find us yore horse 'n' git outta. here."

Walkman watched from his vantage point across the clearing, sighting his rifle on the fool Blaine, whose usefulness to him was ended, and the meddling woman who had earned his undying hate. He could kill them both and get free of here in a trice!

"I wouldn't, Walkman," Jeremy Lawrence's voice said in a low growl that cut through all the screams and shots around them. A .44-caliber Walker Colt was pointed at his captain's back. He had seen Walkman and had dismounted to sneak around and catch him from behind. Walkman gestured over to Blaine and Melanie as he lowered the rifle. "My friend there has some business with the pretty lady."

Seeing Melanie struggle as Blaine dragged her off, Jeremy's face whitened in shock. "My God, how did she—you bastard!"

In the split second Lawrence's eyes took in the struggle, Walkman struck like a rattler, swinging his rifle up and firing at the other ranger. The shot went wild as Lawrence deflected the barrel, but his own shot also missed its mark when he fired at Walkman. He lunged at the renegade ranger and the two men went down in a thrashing tangle, rolling across the rocky ground, punching and gouging.

Lee was drowning in blood once again as the battle raged furiously around him. He had shot, stabbed, and clubbed countless Comanche until he was covered with gore and sickened by it. Despite the clear autumn air, the earth stank of death in the cold, dead moonlight. Slowly he hacked his way across the melee to where Sangre waited. The Comanche who had dragged him from the horse was dead, and the superbly trained stallion would let no one but Lee ride him. The big blue roan shied and danced as his master dispatched another Comanche with his knife and then mounted up.

Lee had hoped to catch Blaine but had not seen him yet. Then he saw Jeremy Lawrence lunge at Seth Walkman. A piece of real luck to find him here! Surely his whiskey-dealing *compadre* must be nearby. He kicked the roan into a trot and headed to help Lawrence. Just as he drew near, Walkman pulled a small pistol free from his boot and shot Jeremy in the side. Before he could aim the deadly little weapon for another more accurate shot, Lee leaped from Sangre and landed on the renegade, knocking him clear of his victim. The gun clattered uselessly out of reach across the rocky ground.

"So, the greaser who set this trap," he grinned evilly, as if he knew something Lee did not.

Lee already had his knife poised as he rolled onto his feet. So did Walkman. The two men circled, ignoring the unconscious form of Lawrence. "This is one greaser you won't walk away from, *rinche*," Lee gritted out as he parried a wicked thrust.

"You're already so bloodied I can scarce figger where to stick you," Walkman panted as he dodged several exceedingly close thrusts.

"You're pretty chewed up yourself, Comanchero," Lee said scathingly, indicating Walkman's lacerated arm.

The bigger man grinned again. "Got this from your woman this afternoon, greaser." He paused, sensing the coiled tension in Velásquez. Then he continued, ''I caught her 'n' took her to Blaine's post. She used a broken bottle—tried to gut me, but all I got was this little scratch.''

''Where is she, Walkman? You've never seen what the Mescalero do to their captives, but I have—and I swear, I'll do it to you until you tell me. Ever peel a man's eyelids off? Put live coals beneath his fingernails? Take his cock and...''

Walkman lunged and struck Lee a glancing blow across his ribs. The renegade's tale about Melanie filled him with a terrified rage. Deflecting what he knew could have been a deadly thrust, Lee forced himself to calm. He was too angry, and as his foe well knew, angry men made careless mistakes. He knew he must win and he must keep Walkman alive to tell him about Melanie. He kept up a steady stream of taunts, describing in sickening detail what he had witnessed in the Apachería, meanwhile opening several seeping wounds in Walkman's neck, arm, and thigh, wounds designed to weaken him and slow him down through blood loss without killing him.

Just when Lee was about to make his move on the glazed-eyed renegade ranger, a shot rang out and Walkman pitched forward into Lee's arms. Bill Ross rushed over with a smoking Colt in his hand.

''Are you hurt, boss? Jesus, I thought he had you—you're covered with blood!''

Lee ignored his would-be savior and bent over the inert form of Walkman, shaking him furiously. ''Walkman, you son of a bitch, you can't be dead! Damn you! Where is she? Where is Melanie?'' He turned pain-glazed eyes up to his foreman, who looked down with dawning horror in his face.

''He has Miss Melanie?''

Jeremy Lawrence groaned and called out weakly, ''Blaine— Blaine took her away.''

Lee dropped Walkman's body and quickly moved over to the fallen ranger. ''Melanie was here in the fight? You saw her?'' He raised Jeremy up slightly while Ross checked the wounded man's injuries. ''Over there, by those rocks—'' When he tried to point, he coughed and nearly blacked out with the pain.

Lee's eyes followed to where Jeremy had indicated. "If Blaine took her off as a hostage, there's only one place left for him to go—Greer!"

Without looking at Ross or giving any further instructions, he lay the unconscious ranger back and reached for Lawrence's Walker Colt. Within seconds Lee had swung up on Sangre and spurred the stallion into a gallop toward Laban Greer's ranch.

Mellie, oh, Night Flower, if they've hurt you . . . Lee forced his mind into a cold blankness in order to save his sanity. He must remain in control of his wits to save his love. Heedless of the battle din he was leaving behind, Lee rode alone into the still night at breakneck speed. The cold brilliance of the Texas moon lit his way on a mission of rescue and of death.

Chapter 24

"You goddamn fool! Why the hell did you come here and drag her with you?" Laban Greer was dressed only in hastily donned trousers and slippers, having been awakened from a sound sleep by the pounding on his door. His face purpled in rage as he looked past Lucas Blaine's shoulder at the quiet moonlit landscape. Nothing stirred.

"I wasn't followed, Greer. Them militia wuz so busy cuttin' up Gall's braves they never seen me," Blaine replied as he supported Melanie's dazed, semiconscious body. When he had slipped up on her in the thick of the fighting, Blaine had struck her a blow to the jaw, dumped her across a horse and fled. By the time her captor brought her into Greer's front hall, she was struggling to focus her eyes and to overcome the rubbery weakness in her legs. She listened to the two men discuss her fate.

"You never should have let her get away from your trading post. Walkman's as goddamn incompetent as you."

"But th' fire—" Blaine protested.

"Set by someone else who's probably alerted half of San Antonio by now," Greer interrupted with a hiss of impatient disgust. He began to pace, stroking his jaw in consideration. He looked at Melanie's drooping head, her face covered by the curtain of ebony hair. With one thick hand he raised her chin and inspected her face.

Gold eyes met pale blue ones defiantly. "So, still as feisty and beautiful as ever, champion of the redmen. Too bad you stumbled onto my land deals. You know I'll have to kill you now that Seth has failed me. A respectable rancher and businessman like me—"

"Everyone knows about your conspiracy with the renegades— Walkman and Blaine's deals with you, your buying up Broughton's and Ryan's ranches—even your plans to burn my husband's ranch and get it, too. Jim Slade, Jeremy Lawrence, and my husband all were in on this trap to catch Gall and Blaine so this fool here would confess and lead them to Walkman and you. It worked," she finished with grim satisfaction. "You can kill me, but it won't help you, Greer—it'll only make things worse for you. My story is already in print," she added with a bluff of cool bravado.

Melanie was rewarded by a shadow of doubt flickering in Greer's eyes. "She may be lying about the news story, but judging from the trap you escaped, Blaine, I don't doubt that someone higher up knows about our plans," he said consideringly.

"Try someone as high up as Sam Houston," Melanie shot back.

Now Greer swore in earnest at Blaine. "And you brought her to my ranch to cement his case! You crack-brained, fucking moron!"

Blaine whitened, both at the mention of the senator's name and at Greer's unleashed fury. "We kin git away, Mr. Greer. I know lots o' real important fellers up in Injun

Territory. With this here leetle gal as pertection, we kin cross th' Red without th' rangers botherin' us."

The veins in Greer's bull neck stood out as he ground his teeth. "I do not intend to pass the rest of my life living in filthy shacks with your half-breed cronies." He reached for Melanie and yanked her roughly out of Blaine's grasp.

"Watch it, Greer. She's quick 'n' mean as a snake. She nearly got Seth 'n' me at th' post with a busted bottle," Blaine cried as Melanie twisted suddenly free from Greer and darted toward the nearest open door. It led to his study.

The gun racks on the wall were instantly in her line of vision and she dashed for a .54-caliber Sharps rifle. She yanked it off its pins and turned to aim it at Greer, who burst through the door with Blaine behind him. Greer was unarmed; Blaine was not. Using the thick, muscular body of the rancher as a shield, the whiskey runner fired at his small target with his pistol, hitting her before she could fire the heavy long arm. It clattered to the floor as she was propelled backward by the impact of the slug.

A cry as fearsome as any uttered by a Comanche raider echoed down the hallway as Lee burst into the house, shooting Blaine at point-blank range with Lawrence's Colt. The .44 slug ripped into Blaine's fat gut from the left side, splattering the blue silk wallpaper behind him with red gore as he pitched headlong down the hall, dead before he landed.

Greer vanished into the study, intent on getting the rifle from Melanie, but Lee was on him before he could free it. Fearful of hitting his fallen wife if he fired, Lee tossed his gun behind him and yanked Greer away from her, rolling him across the wide floor until the two of them hit the large oak desk with a solid whack. Although shorter than Lee, Laban Greer was muscular and thickset, built like a bulldog, with all the strength and tenacity of the breed. He reached for Lee's throat, intent on gaining a choke hold. Lee pummeled and gouged his antagonist, breaking the deadly grip only when he pressed his thumb into Greer's right eye.

Dazed from the near strangulation, Lee shook his head to clear it as he struggled to his feet. After they broke apart,

Greer reached inside a desk drawer behind him and extracted a knife. "Now, you greaser son of a bitch," he snarled and lunged at Lee.

Lee had his own knife freed instantly in a reflex action. "Walkman and Blaine are already dead, Greer," he rasped. "I'd like you to die slower, but I don't . . . have . . . time," he said with seemingly methodical detachment as he feinted low, parried Greer's slower thrust, and then brought his own blade up to slice the squat thick neck cleanly across with surgical precision. Greer's eyes glazed over and large bubbles of red frothed from his mouth. He slid down the desk and sat flat on the floor, his head lolling at a bizarre angle in death.

Lee whirled and raced to Melanie. He knelt and gently stretched out her crumpled body to examine the extent of her injuries. His hands were trembling as he peeled the silk shirt away from her blood-soaked side.

Melanie moaned as she fought her way back to consciousness. Sharp pain stabbed at her side, but a low, soothing voice comforted her, Lee's voice, her husband, her love.

"Shh, Night Flower, be still. I have to stop this bleeding. You'll be all right, darling," he crooned softly as he worked, tearing his shirt into strips for bandages.

"Blaine—Greer—I heard shots," she whispered in confusion.

"Don't worry. They're dead, sweetheart. They can't hurt you anymore." His callused fingertips stroked her face with tender reassurance.

Suddenly his words of endearment registered—"darling," "sweetheart." She struggled to focus her pain-darkened eyes on the harsh, angular planes of his face. Now it had lost all traces of forbidding anger or sarcastic scowl. It blazed with love and fear for her.

Before she could puruse that thought further, Lee's voice again broke in. "I have to move you, Mellie—carry you out to Sangre and get you to town to the doctor."

With surprising strength she raised one small hand and pressed the palm against the rapid pounding of his heart. His naked chest felt warm and hard, reassuring to her. "No,

not town. Take me home, Lee—home to Night Flower.
Kai's better with bullet wounds than Dr. Westin, anyway. I
want to go home . . . please," she entreated.

"Oh, Mellie, I love you. Whatever you want," he
whispered in a stricken voice. *She'll be all right. She can't
die.* "Come on, darling, I'm taking my wife home," he
said softly as he gently scooped her up and strode from the
room.

Lee paced Sangre as smoothly as possible, trying not to
jar his injured wife any more than necessary. He had no
more than cleared a few hundred yards when Jim Slade's
big buckskin skidded to a halt in front of him, followed by
half a dozen other riders kicking up dust and pebbles.

"Jeremy told us what happened," Slade said tersely.
"Melanie?"

"She's been shot in the side just below her ribs. I can't
tell more, but I'm taking her to Night Flower. Send someone to town for Doc Westin," Lee said quickly and kneed
Sangre forward with no more ado, calling over his shoulder,
"Blaine and Greer are dead in the house."

By the time Dr. Westin arrived, it was well past sunrise.
A careworn but calm Father Gus accompanied him. Kai
already had Melanie's wound cleaned, disinfected, and
wrapped. The bullet had entered and exited her side cleanly.
Despite having treated numerous bullet wounds, the Kanaka
was uncertain of whether any vital organs had been dam-
aged. He was also uncertain the doctor could do anything
more than he could, even if that were the case. Nevertheless, he had left the final stitching to the physician and
simply wrapped the injury with great care.

The old physician, too, had tended many bullet wounds
and knew when he unwrapped Melanie's side that it was
serious. He looked up at Lee and Kai. "How much has she
bled?"

"I packed the wound tight before I rode home with her,"
Lee said anxiously, turning to Kai.

The big man's expression was grave. "He kept her from

bleeding bad. Before I cleaned the wound I applied more packing. Seemed to slow it, but she's such a little thing. . . ."

"She's young and strong. Since shock's not set in yet, I think she has a good chance. No vital organs hit," he concluded, then checked her pulse. Westin issued orders to Genia, who stood in the background wringing her hands, to bring more clean linens. He instructed Kai to assist him by holding Melanie in case she came to while he stitched.

Lee nodded for the big Kanaka to move away and he sat down beside his wife, taking a position on the edge of the bed. "I'll hold her, Doc. Just get it done while she's out."

Westin assessed the set features and calm hands. "Yep, reckon you can handle it. Some men haven't the stomach— especially when it's someone they love."

Someone they love. The words accused him. Did it take a bullet to convince him? He knew so surely now that he loved her, wanted her for his wife, was proud of her and everything she was and did. *And she may die never knowing it. No! I won't let you, Mellie, my Night Flower, my love.* She moaned in his arms, in an unconscious stupor, as the doctor worked deftly. Lee stroked her cheek softly with one hand while his other arm held her shoulders firmly. All the while he murmured soft reassurances in her ear, willing her to fight for her life.

When the doctor finished, the priest took him quietly aside and ushered him outside the door. "Is there any need for me to give her last rites, Doctor? I do not want to upset her husband, but I am not sure . . ."

The doctor shook his head. "No, Padre. I don't think you have to do that now. The next twenty-four hours will tell the tale."

Mercifully Melanie did not awaken during the course of the day. Lee kept a tense vigil by her bedside, listening to her moans and simply watching her laudanum-induced sleep. By noon Charlee Slade arrived and stalked into the room, where she took one look at Lee's unshaven face, bloodshot eyes, and generally exhausted appearance. She ordered Kai to draw Lee a bath and turn down his bed.

"You get some rest and have those cuts and scrapes

tended. You'll do your wife no good if you frighten her into shock with your haggard looks when she wakes up, which Doc Westin assures me won't be for another twelve hours, at least. How long since you've slept?" she queried, giving him no chance to debate her commands.

Lee thought dazedly over the past thirty hours since he'd left Melanie in her room at the boardinghouse. "Early yesterday morning," he replied vaguely. "But I have to talk to her when she wakes up," he added with despair in his voice. *If she wakes up*. He forced that thought aside.

Charlee was slight, but she could be formidable when she chose to be. "Your wife is going to be all right, Lee. But with all the laudanum the doc gave her, she won't wake up for hours. Get some rest so you'll be clearheaded and know what to say to her when she does come around," she said patiently, as if talking to one of her children.

"You'll have the rest of your lives—long lives together— to tell her everything."

"Whar is thet child! Jeehosaphat, turn my back one minute 'n' she's off agin gettin' in a fix," Obedience's voice boomed from the front hall.

Even Lee managed a half smile at that, and Charlee said with a grin, "Now, with the two of us watching over her, you can rest easy for a few hours—in the next room. Father Gus is here too. We won't let her down, Lee."

Melanie slept as the doctor had predicted. Late that evening a roomful of fretful people took turns sponging her brow—Charlee, Obedience, Kai, and Genia. Lame Deer waited outside, praying for his beloved Melanie with Father Gus.

"She seems warm, Doc," Charlee said worriedly to the doctor.

Westin nodded. "I was afraid she might get a fever. The first battle is the shock of the wound and blood loss, and she survived that miraculously well. The next is a slower-moving danger—fever. Don't let her take a chill. Sometimes it's best to sweat a fever out, but—"

"Jeehosaphat! Child's already burnin' up," Obedience interrupted forcefully. "I pulled many a youngun includin' my own Joseph, outa fevers—use cool sheets 'n' keep changin' em.'' She arose and virtually seized Genia, instructing her to bring a tub of springwater and ignoring the spluttering doctor.

"Yes, well, I was going to say, Mrs. Oakley, that the other school of medical opinion favors your methods," Westin added pettishly, realizing that, surrounded by three hostile females and a towering Kanaka, he would not carry the day, even if he were so rash as to contradict Obedience Oakley.

Just then, Lee burst into the room from the adjacent one, where he had awakened from a fitful but exhausted sleep. "What's this about a fever?" Without waiting for the doctor or anyone else to answer, he rushed to Melanie's side and removed the compress Charlee had just placed there. "She's on fire!"

"No," Charlee replied calmly. "She has a fever, but we all agree it isn't that bad."

"We'll git it down quick 'nough," Obedience added as she and Genia left the room, intent on their project.

After carefully checking the wounds for signs of inflammation or fresh bleeding, the doctor rebandaged her side and departed, promising to return early in the morning.

In the next twenty-four hours, Lee more than once thanked heaven and Charlee Slade that he had taken her advice and gotten the few hours of desperately needed sleep and medical attention she insisted upon. Melanie's fever raged, and he, Kai, and the three women soaked sheets with cool water and placed them on her heat-racked body. Even the priest and young boy fetched springwater and wrung out sheets.

Delirious and semiconscious as the laudanum wore off, Melanie talked. At first she rambled in incoherent whispers. Then, as her strength seemed to return, she cried out, reliving all the pain and fear of her childhood as the unwanted daughter of a neurotic *placée*. Even though Lee knew the superficial facts, hearing it pouring from her in this totally uninhibited and frightening way tore at him.

When she began to murmur about her first encounter with Leandro Velásquez on the Galveston waterfront when he was a handsome eighteen-year-old and she an impressionable girl of twelve, Charlee shrewdly ushered everyone from the room. Some things between a man and woman were too personal for anyone else to overhear.

But Lee listened and relived with her those long-ago days in Galveston and four years later in Austin. This time he saw them from her perspective. She also spoke of their encounter on the hillside and the forced marriage that followed it.

"Oh, Night Flower, Charlee was right and I've been such an arrogant, self-centered fool," he whispered brokenly, kissing her glowing cheek as he sponged her.

Later, when she had quieted, Lee called Charlee back into the room, asking for fresh water and linens. Although she could see on his face the ravages of reddened eyes and tear stains, she appeared not to notice and quickly went off to do as he asked.

The fever had broken by the time Doc Westin returned the next morning, and Melanie fell into a deep, healing sleep. By that evening Obedience pronounced her young charge on the road to recovery, and everyone but Lee breathed a sigh of relief. Until those wide, beautiful eyes once more looked at him with love, he would know no peace.

Melanie felt as though she had just been thrown from Liberator at a hard gallop—no, make that thrown into a pile of jagged rocks—then trampled by a herd of longhorns! She turned her head slightly and opened her eyes. It was dusk. The room was dimly lit by the fading sun, but she recognized it—the master bedroom—Lee's room. She was in her husband's bed and he was standing across the room from her. His face was darkened by a beard and lined from exhaustion. His wrinkled clothes and tousled hair also betrayed his long bedside vigil.

As he turned to look at her, she quickly closed her eyes and feigned sleep, struggling to gather her scattered thoughts before confronting him. His tenderness and words of love when he had rescued her from Blaine and Greer returned to her in a confused jumble. *Does he just feel guilty because I was shot? Or could he love me?*

Experimentally she tried to roll over, and a sudden burst of agony caused her eyes to fly open in shocked surprise. The gasp brought Lee instantly to her side.

"Mellie? Are you awake? Does it hurt, darling?" He gently pushed her back into the pillows, flat on her back.

She moaned, unable to stifle the complaint of her screaming side. Then, sucking in her breath, she gritted out, "Yes. Damn, yes, it hurts like—ooh, God, Father Gus would faint if he heard me say what it hurts like. Did Blaine—Greer—"

"They're both dead. Forget them," Lee interrupted impatiently. "You've had a fever in addition to having had a bullet rip through your side. I thought I told you Moses French had retired," he said with mock sternness, but the obvious happiness in his face belied the scolding.

"What a story I'll have for Clarence—once you fill me in on all the rest of the facts."

Now it was his turn to groan.

Hearing voices, Charlee opened the door and entered the room, a huge smile wreathing her face. "At last Obedience can bring you some of that chicken soup she's been simmering in Kai's kitchen for the past two days. He's in a real snit because she took over his domain."

Picturing the battle of wills between those two fearsome giants, Melanie laughed, then gasped in pain again.

"There are several people outside who have been driving us crazy waiting to see you, Night Flower," Lee said.

As if on cue, Charlee opened the door and Lame Deer fairly flew in at her summons, followed by a scurrying Father Gus and an amblingly nonchalant Clarence Pemberton.

"Melanie! You—you are awake!" The boy could scarcely restrain the impulse to leap on the bed and hug his princess. But when she patted a place alongside her on the mattress, he eagerly sat down and gave her a gentle hug. "Are you going to be all right?"

"Yes. Just weak and sore now. Tell me what happened to you," she asked, knowing the boy was about to burst with his tale.

"When you left with those bad men chasing you, I stole a pony and rode very fast for here. Kai was ready with many men and guns. Then the Comanche came and it was a terrible fight, but they did not burn your house," he finished, expelling an exuberantly breathless squeak.

"I'm very grateful to everyone," Melanie replied gravely. "And as soon as someone brings me a pencil and paper, I'll write quite a story," she said, casting a suspicious glance at Clarence, who had turned slightly pink.

"Well, perhaps you'd better wait until you've regained more strength and until you've read what I've already written. Alas, Melanie, news is news—"

"—only until it's passed around by word of mouth," she finished the old newspaper axiom. "I suppose you talked to everyone from Jeremy to Lame Deer and then wrote the biggest action story since the Council House fight of 1840!" she accused with blazing eyes.

One shaggy white brow arched. "You *were* unconscious, dear child." With a flourish he thrust a copy of the *Star* at her. "Once you've read it and, er, recovered all your objectivity, I'm sure you'll find a good deal that I've left out." A flicker of a smile played around his lips. "When you write your first-person account of the grand finale, I'll even have Amos print your name at the head of the column," he said magnanimously.

"Moses French?" she asked with a nervous glance toward Lee, whose face remained unreadable.

"Your husband has informed me in no uncertain terms Moses French is dead. No, I rather expect it should bear the name Melanie Velásquez. Has a ring of authenticity, don't you think?" With that startling piece of news, Clarence Vivian Pemberton actually winked at her, nodded to Lee, and then turned to leave the room with a jaunty stride. "See you at the *Star*—and don't be too long sending in that story. No one wants stale news." With that, he was gone.

Melanie looked up at Lee with a mixture of joy and confusion on her face. "Why, that old—" She caught herself just in time and looked guiltily over to Father Gus.

Lame Deer, who often caught himself in just such lapses in front of the holy father, muffled a giggle.

The young priest laughed jovially. "It would seem, my dear, all our prayers have been answered."

"I think so, Father," Lee replied, his eyes never leaving his wife's face.

"'Nough o' news stories 'n' prayin'," Obedience interrupted. "I got this here ailin' youngun some fine vittles to put a bloom back in them peaked cheeks. Now, shoo, all o' yew! She needs food 'n' sleep."

Melanie ate obediently and almost immediately fell into a sound sleep. Lee made a pallet on the floor and spent the night beside her bed. Over the next few days they arranged a routine. Every morning when Melanie awakened, Genia brought her a special breakfast, carefully prepared by Kai. Lee's pallet was always carefully folded up and resting on the chest in the corner. Looking at it, she felt oddly warmed to know he watched over her with such devotion each night. But he was gone before she awakened. Of course, he had a big ranch to run, and he did come to her room to share dinner each evening, keeping her posted on what had happened in town and at the ranch.

Jeremy Lawrence was recovering from injuries suffered in his fight with Walkman. Gall had been killed along with most of his followers and the rest driven off and scattered. With Blaine's trading post closed and Greer out of business, savage depredations on a large scale were over.

One evening at dinner, as she carefully balanced her tray and cut her steak, Melanie asked, "Who is replacing Seth Walkman now?"

"Lawrence," was the terse reply.

His curt tone of voice caused her to look up in surprise. They had been getting on so amicably during her recuperation, even if they did only discuss superficial things. Still, he harbored an intense dislike of Jeremy Lawrence. "He's a good man for the job, Lee," she said noncommittally. Surely he didn't still think she and Jeremy were in any way involved?

Wanting to change the subject, she said, "I've been

working on my story for the *Star*—my personal account of all I found out about Walkman and Greer, then of being abducted and taken hostage. I've almost finished. Lame Deer has filled me in on most of the details I missed.'' She hesitated and looked at him. ''You did mean what you said about letting me write for Clarence and using my own name . . . ?''

He tossed down his napkin, still unsettled by her mention of Lawrence. ''Why should you ask my permission to write your story? You never have before.'' Seeing the surprised hurt in her eyes, he immediately relented. ''Mellie, I'm sorry. I did talk to Clarence when the old curmudgeon came out to see how you were, and we agreed about the story— when you were strong enough to do it.'' He did not add that it was he who had suggested his wife be allowed to use her own name on the news piece.

''I'm getting stronger each day, Lee,'' she said softly, with a hint of challenge to her voice. ''Once my health's returned, do we go back to the way things were before?'' The minute the words were out she regretted them. *Fool! Don't ask questions when you're afraid of the answers!*

He stood up and walked across to her bed, where he carefully removed her tray, setting it on the bedside table. Then he sat down on the side of the bed and placed one slim hand on the side of her face caressingly. ''No, Night Flower, we don't. You asked me to bring you here, and here you stay. You're my wife and I love you. I want to build a life together.'' He looked deeply into her expressive golden eyes, willing a response from her, yet afraid of what it might be.

''Then why—why haven't you told me until now? It's as if I have to wring a confession of love out of you.'' She hated the accusatory sound of her own voice, but seemed unable to stop herself. ''You had to marry me, and maybe you do love me—at least you desire me.'' She reddened in mortification. ''But—but you don't *want* to love me. I'm not your proper Hispanic ideal like Larena Sandoval . . . or Dulcia.'' There, she had said it, mentioned her rivals.

Larena was alive and Melanie could fight her, but dead, Dulcia was the greater threat.

Lee dropped his hand from her as if burned and stood up. All his thoughts were so crazily jumbled up. He must not botch this now. Sighing, he began to pace and run his hands through his hair. "As to waiting to tell you I love you, there's so much to be said and explained. I wanted to let you recover your strength . . . and give myself time to think this through.

"While you were delirious with the fever, you told me lots of things, Mellie." He saw a wary, frightened look flare in her eyes. *Damn, I'm messing this up!*

"What things?" she asked in a low voice.

"The things that gave you nightmares. Remember all the ugly things I confessed to you when I awakened you with my nightmare?" At her wide-eyed nod, he went on, "Well, your confessions weren't that heinous. It wasn't what you'd done, darling, but what had been done *to* you—by Lily, by Rafe's desertion and your grandmother's death." At her stricken look, he quickly went over and sat down beside her, taking her in his arms.

"Oh, Mellie, I was a fool, a bloody cruel monster for all the rotten things I said to you about being a *placée*'s daughter. You grew up to be Deborah Fleming's daughter, and she and everyone else—including me—is proud of you."

"But I'm still of that blood—African and Indian," she whispered in a muffled voice, not wanting to abandon the comfort of his embrace, yet unwilling to let the issue be unresolved between them.

"I don't care. No, that's not true—I *do* care. If you share the blood of people like Lame Deer and Amos Johnston, I'd be a fool not to be proud of you. You're bright and lovely and good," he said, stroking her shiny ebony hair. "You also talked about when we met in Austin." He felt her stiffen in his arms.

"I was so hurt that you were married. Oh, Lee, she was the kind of wife you wanted."

"I was eaten alive with guilt ever since Austin, Mellie. I

guess that's why I took such a perverse delight in acting like a bastard every time I met you since then," he said soberly.

Melanie looked up into his face in confusion. "Guilt? I don't understand."

"Don't you see, love? You've been jealous and afraid of shadows all this time. I was a naive boy of twenty-one when I married Dulcia. By the time we got to Texas, I realized it had been a mistake. She was a hothouse flower, prim and delicate. She hated the land of my birth, hated the ranch. Even worse, she hated my touch. She did her duty," he said with sad irony in his voice. "When I left her in San Antonio and went to Austin, I met this vision in a mustard silk shirt and indecently split riding skirts—Rafe Fleming's spoiled little darling all grown up—and I wanted you." His eyes bored into hers, angry with himself, yet pleading for her understanding.

"And you sensed the same thing in me—that I wanted you. But you were already married to the right girl; I was the wrong girl. . . ." Her voice trailed off in quiet amazement. So many things made sense now.

"When I told Charlee I still wanted to marry Larena, she told me how much better suited you'd be for me than Dulcia or Larena. Then Larena told me the same thing. They both were a lot smarter than I was," he added ruefully.

At that last remark, Melanie's eyes lit up. "In spite of being hatefully jealous of Larena, I always knew she was a woman of rare common sense." Suddenly her heart took flight, as if freed from the constriction of iron fetters that had manacled it for long months—perhaps all of her life. She framed her husband's handsome face with her hands and said joyously, "I love you, Leandro Angel Velásquez. I have loved you since I was twelve years old. . . ." She kissed him softly on the lips. "Oh, Lee, I've always been afraid—afraid to love a man, to trust my life to a husband, someone who would own me body and soul, but with you I'm not afraid anymore."

"Why should you be? Can't you see, Night Flower, you own me too—body and soul?" He kissed her softly, gently, as if afraid she'd break.

Melanie, however, had just spent a week recuperating and felt a great deal less fragile than her husband imagined. She returned his careful caress with abandoned ardor, pulling him tightly to her and wrapping her arms around his waist. When he felt her hot, searching mouth open in invitation, he responded instinctively, kissing her back passionately as their tongues eagerly entwined and their breathing accelerated. Only when he began to run his splayed fingers down her throat and lower, cupping a breast and fondling it, did he feel the thick bandaging below it that reminded him of her injury. Slowly he gentled their passion, raining light butterfly kisses across her cheek and neck, onto her throat. Then he drew one arm from around his waist and pulled it in front of him so he could kiss the soft bend of the elbow and inner wrist, then the palm.

"You are a passionate little creature, aren't you?" he teased softly. When she stiffened, he gave her no chance to speak but pressed his fingertips to her lips. "Don't start with more hurt and guilt. I just told you I wanted my wife to love my touch, not shrink from it. Oh, Night Flower, I need your passion, but you're not recovered yet."

To prove his point, he reached down very carefully and touched the thick packing around her waist. When she let out an involuntary gasp of startled pain, he immediately kissed her lips softly, saying, "See. You're still in pain, but just wait, Mrs. Velásquez, until Doc Westin pronounces you recovered. I think I owe you a honeymoon, and I intend to pay my debt—with interest."

She blushed beneath the teasing scrutiny of his hot black eyes, but stared back into them boldly and said, "I shall do my very best to follow doctor's orders to make a full recovery—very, very soon."

Chapter 25

Melanie's story was printed on the front page of the *Star* the first of the week, and a beaming Amos Johnston brought a page proof out to the ranch to show her early that day.

That afternoon Father Gus came to bring her the sacrament and regale her with the latest tales about the antics of the children at school.

"Lame Deer, is he still at the head of his class?" she asked with a small frown. "He's been here so much, I feared he was neglecting his schoolwork."

"Ach, not to worry. That young rascal is very bright. And now that his mama works in the Abbess's kitchen, the family has enough food and money so he need not resort to, er, undesirable means of earning money," the young priest said with a twinkle in his blue eyes.

"Lee's given him some simple chores at the corral. Mostly I think it's an excuse to keep him out of here long enough for me to get a few catnaps during the afternoons, and it also gives him the chance to ride Prancer and learn skills from the *vaqueros*. Lee says he's becoming quite a horseman."

Noting the way her eyes lit up when she talked of her husband, Father Gus could not resist teasing, "A lesson in faith it is—the way my earnest prayers—and the good Baptist ones of the Abbess—were answered."

Melanie looked at him in perplexity. "You prayed for Lame Deer?"

He threw back his head and chuckled. "When he stole my burro and a few times after that, *ja*, but that is not what

I meant just now. Do you remember the day I married you and Lee? Your eyes flashing defiance and his dark sullen look. Ach! I see you do. It is not that way any longer. Maybe by next year this time we baptize a new little Velásquez, *ja?*''

Melanie mulled over what the priest had said to her after he left that afternoon. *A new little Velásquez.* She dearly wished for children. For the first time, instead of dreading the physical confinement of pregnancy and with it the increased dependency on her husband, she actually welcomed the thought.

But what of Lee? He had said he loved her and accepted her mixed blood. He wanted a passionate, responsive wife. That must inevitably lead to children. Heirs for Night Flower Ranch.

''There are a great many things we've never been able to talk about before,'' she murmured aloud to herself. ''Now we can.''

That evening was to be her first meal in the dining room. At last she was free of the confinement of eating in the bedroom! Melanie ran her hands over the gowns in her wardrobe, once again grateful to Charlee Slade for talking her into abandoning ''sensible clothes.'' What she planned to wear tonight was certainly not sensible in the least!

When she walked into the dining room that night, the vision in a froth of pale pink looked far more appealing to Lee than Kai's elaborate banquet. Her gown was all lace, yards and yards of it in a softly swaying full skirt that accented her tiny waistline. The long fitted sleeves had lace cuffs that spilled daintily onto her delicate wrists. Her only adornment was a cluster of pale pink roses pinned in her upswept jet hair.

''You are a vision,'' Lee said simply. He walked across the room to kiss her very carefully, making certain he did nothing foolish to inflame the passion he had been struggling to control during her convalescence. The very innocence of the delicately hued lace gown added to her aura of ethereal sensuality.

She inspected his white stock and the silk shirt tha
stretched across his broad shoulders, then let her eyes trave
down the immaculately tailored brown suit jacket to the
tightly molded pants that encased his long legs. Remembering
the last time she had dressed elaborately for dinner and
found him in casual attire, she appreciated the care he had
taken and was touched by the importance he, too, placed on
this evening.

"I might say, *Don* Leandro, that you look like a vision
yourself—tempting a poor woman's soul to perdition. I'll
have to ask Father Gus to pray for me," she teased.

"No, you won't. We're married—it's all right to be
tempted now." He grinned and added, "Anyway, after as
long as it took us to see the light, I suspect the good father's
knees are pretty worn out by now."

She laughed and placed her left hand on his arm. "Escort
me to dinner, husband?"

"First I have something for you—to match that," he
said, running his fingertips lightly over her heavy ruby-and-
gold wedding ring. "While I was in New Mexico, Jim and
Charlee saved all my family's personal belongings—the
things I left behind in the old house before it was burned
out. What I didn't know until the day of our wedding was
that Charlee had found another trunk stored by old Will
Slade at Bluebonnet, filled with things he had salvaged from
the Comanche raid when my family was killed."

"That's where my wedding ring came from," she said
quietly.

He raised her hand and kissed the ring finger lingeringly.
"It was Charlee's idea to surprise me with it and have Jim
hand it to me in church. . . ."

"Where you couldn't back out and had to give it to me."

He smiled sadly and said, "They knew better than I did,
sweetheart. But my mother's ring wasn't the only thing in
the trunk. With it came these." He pulled a slim velvet box
from his jacket pocket and handed it to her. The fabric cover
was very old and brittle, embossed with an old coat of arms
probably dating from the days when Velásquez men served
the Spanish kings.

She opened it reverently. Inside lay a necklace and earring set that matched her ruby-and-gold wedding band. She gasped in awe at the intricate workmanship of the gold filigree and flawless perfection of the gems. "They're exquisite, Lee—and so old—family heirlooms from generations ago." She lifted the necklace out and held it up in the candlelight, unable to say more, her throat closed with emotion.

"Here, let me." He took the necklace and fastened it about her slender throat. The graduated rubies dropped gracefully so the largest one nestled in her cleavage. With trembling hands, she put the long, delicately tapered drop earrings in her ears. "If I'd selected your gown to match the jewelry, I couldn't have chosen better. This was my greatgrandfather Velásquez's betrothal gift to his wife. Each generation it's passed on, traveling from the Old World to the new land of Texas."

Melanie concentrated on her recovery, doing stretching and bending exercises in secret and riding Liberator each afternoon for a brief stint while she was certain Lee was busy elsewhere.

Another week passed and Melanie's restlessness was matched by Lee's. *If we don't get that long-promised honeymoon soon, we'll be at one another's throats like caged wildcats*, she thought one morning after another night of tossing and turning, with him in one room, her in the other. But he was so fearful of hurting her, so guilty because she'd been shot in the first place, that he'd insisted they wait a while longer.

Doc Westin was a fussy old maid who still advised she not overdo, even though he had removed all the bandages and admitted the wound was nicely healed. Somehow she could not bring herself to ask him if it was all right to resume marital relations with her husband. She had far fewer qualms about asking Obedience Oakley. Obedience had not ridden to the ranch for a couple of days. After seeing her charge mending so well, she had trusted Kai and Genia to tend Melanie.

Today Melanie decided it was time for Muhammed to go

to the mountain, since the mountain hadn't been inclined to come to the ranch. Of course, if Lee knew she was up on horseback, he'd skin her, but then, that might not be so bad, she giggled to herself. The ride to town was tiring, she admitted, but as luck would have it, not completely necessary. She was about halfway there when the familiar old buckboard wagon and its Amazonian driver pulled into view.

"Jeehosaphat! Lee know yew 'n' thet big devil er out gaddin' round?" She observed Melanie's pallor and was well prepared to scold until the girl revealed her plight and plan to the older woman.

"Look, Doc took all the bandages away, but he's too fussy and Lee's too overprotective and I'm . . . well, randy as a she-cat in heat to have my husband back in my bed!" she finished on a note of bravado.

Obedience slapped her thigh with a hamlike hand and let out a loud guffaw. "Yer ma wouldn't a never said it so open—but Charlee would! Bless me, child, if'n I don't think her 'n' me been a real unladylike influence on yew!"

"Then you'll ride back to the ranch with me and deliver a personal report to my husband about how fit I am?"

"Huumph! Do better 'n' thet. We'll show him! Let's git goin'. Time's awastin'. I'll jist take this here lunch ta Lee out at th' corral—'n' happen ta mention seein' yew out fer yer usual mornin' ride."

At Melanie's look of alarm, Obedience added with a wink, "*After* I tell th' young jackass yore fit as th' day he married yew!" She was off, calling over her shoulder, "Jist ride near th' ranch house round back by th' creek 'n' thet pond."

Within half an hour, as she sat sponging her neck with cool water from the pool out behind the house, she heard Sangre's hoofbeats pounding down on her. The big blue's hooves kicked up pebbles and sprayed them into the clear water as his irate rider stopped the horse by the edge of the pool.

"A few more feet and you'd be very wet," she teased, getting up to face his thunderous face as he dismounted.

"What the hell are you doing riding without my permission?" He took her by her shoulders and almost shook her before reason reasserted itself and he dropped his hands into clenched fists.

"I've been riding every day for the past week," she replied oversweetly, "and what's this tiresome stuff about *permission* again? I thought we had that settled. I can scarcely track you down on this big ranch every time I need *permission* to cover a story for Clarence, now can I?" She watched his mounting fury and danced just out of his reach, luring him away from Sangre as she neared where Liberator was standing.

"Mellie, I'm warning you. You—you and Obedience cooked this up, didn't you?" By the time he finished the rhetorical question, his agile little wife had swung up on her big black and sped away toward the ranch house, calling back to him, "Catch me if you can!"

He did. She had made a circle around the willow copse and was heading toward the nearest corral when Sangre pulled abreast of Liberator. A strong arm reached out and snatched her from Liberator's back, depositing her in front of him, held fast to his body. Her arms quickly wrapped around his waist, and she buried her face against his shoulder as he slowed the furious gallop and turned Sangre back to the house.

"See how fit I am?" she whispered in his ear as he dismounted and pulled her down after him.

"I'm not so sure—I just beat you in a horse race," he said with a smile tugging at the corners of his mouth. He carried her inside, straight past the *sala*, and down the hall to the big master bedroom.

"That first day, after our wedding, when Kai brought my things to this room and you made him take them down the hall—"

"I was a fool who spent a sleepless night regretting that I hadn't let him proceed on his very reasonable assumptions," he murmured in her ear. "We're not dressed like a bride and groom today, but I think we can improvise."

Slowly he let her small body slide to the ground while holding her close to him. She kept her fingers locked behind his neck, nipping and kissing at his throat, her small tongue tasting the faint salty tang of male sweat and musk. She could feel his hands roam up her hips to her waist, then glide higher to cup her breasts and fondle them through the sheer silk of her gold shirt.

When he reached over and began to unbutton the blouse, he murmured, "Mustard yellow, just like the one you wore that day in Austin. God, I wanted to do this then." With that he slipped the shirt from her shoulders and she helped him, shrugging it off. Then he unhooked her lacy camisole and freed her breasts, taking one hard-pointed nipple in each hand, rolling the dusky tips around with his fingers until she moaned in pleasure, thrusting them into his palms. He lowered his mouth to trail wet, soft kisses from her throat, down her collarbone to one breast, then the other.

Melanie arched in bliss at his slowly savoring caresses as her own hands unbuckled his belt and unbuttoned his shirt. She slid the simple blue homespun from his shoulders and ran exploring fingers down his biceps as she peeled off the shirt.

"Now what? There's only one boot jack in this room, and we both have to get rid of our gear unless we want Genia to scream about the sheets," he said, teasing his impatient little wife.

She whispered an unladylike oath and reached up to kiss him thoroughly, her hot, sweet tongue making him forget their boots for a moment as they explored each other's upper bodies with tantalizing slowness while their hips rotated together insistently. Suddenly he scooped her up once more and strode quickly to the bed. "Ladies first." With that, he dropped her gently onto the bed and pulled one leg up into his arms. First one, then the other small boot was discarded carelessly. Then, rolling her onto her back in the center of the bed, he began to pull down her split riding skirt, whispering in a passion-roughened voice, "When I first saw you in one of these, I heartily disapproved."

"And now?" she prompted with a wicked wiggle of her hips as she slithered out of the garment.

"I still disapprove—only because it keeps me from this." He ran his hands up her legs and over her flared hips, centering one hand over the small mound at the juncture of her legs. He quickly untied her pantalets and inched the lacy undergarments down her hips, kissing and caressing with his tongue while she writhed and moaned, her fingers tangling and pulling in the curly black hair of his head. Then he paused at the top of her thighs and began to kiss between them.

Quickly her legs opened and she found her body instinctively arching to let him work his wondrous magic on her once again. The sensations began like low, warm throbs with each flick of his tongue and built gradually. She bucked and arched madly, her hands holding on to his head until he raised himself up and whispered, "I was trying to keep you from injuring yourself, woman, but I see there's no use." He stilled her thrashing hips and rolled, catlike, to the edge of the bed, where he quickly pulled off his boots and hose, then stood and shed his pants.

In a haze of need she watched him strip, devouring him with her eyes, her dark, beautiful *Tejano*. When he knelt on the bed, she reached out and grasped one hand and pulled it to her now healed side. "See—all healed. You won't hurt me—just love me, any way, every way, please!"

"Anything to oblige my bride," he whispered hoarsely, rolling down beside her and taking her in his arms for a long, savoring kiss while his hand tangled in the skein of her long glossy hair.

She could feel the sensuous texture of his body as it pressed against hers. It was now familiar and yet so exciting as she felt his hairy chest gently abrade her sensitive nipples and that hard, velvety shaft probe between her legs. Opening her thighs, she trapped it between them and squeezed until he growled with desire. Letting out a low chuckle, she said, "Now you know how I felt a moment ago when you stopped—for my own good."

"Witch—oh, you little, teasing—" He abandoned all attempts at coherent speech and rolled her backward while he carefully raised himself over her and thrust in the sweet, wet core of her flesh, knowing she wanted this as desperately as he did.

"Slow, Night Flower, easy," he whispered as he slid in and out in fluid, graceful motions.

She followed his lead, whispering between kisses, "Slow and easy—for my own good." And magically, for the first time secure in love, they did go very slowly, savoring each moment, murmuring sweet endearments, sharing soft laughter and small gasps and startled moans of pleasure, twisting and arching like two dancers in perfect sync, body, mind, and soul. Then it happened, so quietly, slowly, differently from the times before, that she did not expect it until it seized her in rapturous rhythm. Her eyes widened in amazement and he looked down at her in gentle awe, keeping up the firm, even thrusts, prolonging the incredibly sweet, slow completion for her until he, too, was taken unawares by an explosion in his loins. He joined her, pulsing his seed in long, full, convulsive shudders deeply inside her. Then he grew still, as did she, each holding tightly to the other until he caught his breath long enough to roll them gently over so she lay on top of him.

"Are you all right?" he whispered, his hand straying to the small scars on her side.

She put her fingertips on his lips and smiled a wobbly smile. "If you mean that, yes. I never even felt it . . . but the other . . . I don't know what to say. It was so . . ."

He kissed her nose, eyelids, brows, and cheeks softly while he struggled with how to express the wonder of what they had just shared. "It's never been like that before for me, either, Night Flower. I love you, Mellie, with everything in me, and I *want* to love you, not because we're married or had to get married, but because you're you.

"Did I ever tell you the story of how I named this ranch?" he asked as she propped one elbow up on his chest and looked down at his beloved face.

"You said you found those evening primroses growing by the edge of the stream the night before I came out to interview you. It was an omen of some sort, to begin over again and rebuild on this site."

He reached one hand up and caressed her softly flushed cheek. "That's what I tried to tell myself. But I was only fooling myself, Mellie. Even that long ago, those flowers reminded me of you—with your eyes and sun-kissed golden skin—a Texas girl on the brink of womanhood in a mustard-yellow silk shirt.''

"Like the one I wore today?" she asked softly.

"Yeah. Like the one you wore today," he replied with a chuckle.

"Some things are just fated to be, I guess," she said, kissing him again. "Maybe that's why I wore those flowers in my hair for Senator Houston's dance. I loved it when you called me your Night Flower, and I really wanted to seduce you even then—only I didn't know how."

He laughed ruefully. "You knew how to make me crazy jealous, that's for sure. And every move you made, everything about you made me desire you. Just like now," he said and began to kiss her again.

"Lee. . . ."

"Mmm?" He rolled them on their sides and continued working magic with his hands and lips.

"What you were doing to me earlier . . . do you think we could try it again sometime?"

He smothered a laugh as he lowered his mouth, nibbling toward her navel and then lower. "We can try it right now," he whispered. "In fact, there are several variations I haven't shown you yet, and every good reporter deserves to have all her questions answered," he teased.

"Aah! Even if she . . . can't . . . print the story," she gasped in ecstasy when his lips found her.

He teased and suckled her for a moment, then gently shifted his position until he had reversed it so that his long body was lying opposite hers. Quickly she realized his intention and reached for his once more hardened phallus with one soft little hand. His sudden gasp of pleasure told her to continue. When he resumed his nuzzling caresses of her, she slowly moved her mouth to envelop him. It seemed so natural to love him this way, and if it felt as good to him as his caresses did to her . . . At her first stroke, his reaction convinced her it did.

Once more they made languorously slow, gentle love,

lying side by side, each giving and receiving intense, prolonged pleasure. When he felt her stiffen and the tiny rippling contractions begin, he joined her in sweet release, more sudden and sharp this way, yet exquisite for all that.

Planting a kiss on her curly mound, he raised his head and swung about to take her in his arms. "See, I told you there were variations. That's one...."

"You mean there are more?"

The awe in her voice brought more laughter. "Still the inquiring newspaper reporter? Oh, wife, I love you."

"And I love you, husband." The simple declaration seemed so natural now, and she knew she would repeat it often in the years to come.

He pulled a sheet over them and instructed her to rest. Exhausted from her exertions, she did and fell into a sound, sated sleep. When she awakened, Lee was standing in the door, clad in a robe with a heavy dinner tray in his hands.

"Going to sleep all night? Kai has outdone himself with a special restorative dinner for my worn-out wife."

She snorted scornfully and got up to fetch her robe from a nearby chair while he set the feast on the bedside table. It consisted mostly of simple foods, cheeses and fresh fruits, small hand pies filled with meat, and a bottle of cool white wine. They sat on the big rumpled bed and fed each other, laughing and talking as they ate.

Suddenly she stopped and looked into his eyes, saying softly, "Who ever would have dreamed we'd be sitting here talking like this after the way we started out?"

He smiled. "Oh, Charlee, Obedience, Lame Deer, and Father Gus—he's a man of infinite faith, you know."

"He said he hoped we'd have a baby for him to baptize by next year. Do you think—" She got no farther before he kissed her. "If we don't, it won't be for lack of effort, Night Flower. We'll fill this house with the laughter of children. My father's dream will come true." Then he stopped and stroked her jaw gently. "That is, if you want lots of babies . . . or, if you want to keep busy at the *Star*, we could only have one or two." He looked into her eyes, earnestly asking her opinion, insisting on no male prerogative.

"My arrogant *Tejano*, willing to settle for a wife with a job and only one heir? Oh, Lee, if nothing else had convinced me of your love, this alone would! But I want your children—lots of them. Clarence and the *Star* will just have to settle for what spare time I have left over."

He grinned. "Considering what Charlee's managed to get into while raising her brood, I bet that'll still be plenty. Now, as to the matter of making babies . . ."

Epilogue

August 1853

San Fernando's high vaulted roof echoed with the surprised shrieks of the newborn infant as the cool baptismal water touched the dark curls on her head. Having often heard the same serenade, Father Gus remained unperturbed as he continued the sacramental ritual. Glancing around the crowd gathered at the baptismal font, he found it difficult to believe the difference in their demeanor since the last time they had all assembled for the marriage of Lee and Melanie Velásquez. Rafe Fleming's forbidding countenance now beamed with the joy of being a grandfather, and his beautiful wife positively glowed with grandmotherly pride. Obedience, his Abbess, and her husband, Wash, were grinning like possums while the godparents, Jim and Charlee Slade, could scarcely keep their eyes off the wiggly bundle Charlee held so lovingly as the infant was sanctified. The Fleming and Slade children were exuberant as usual.

Most of all, the priest felt his prayers answered because of the young parents standing before him. They had such obvious love for each other and for their offspring shining from their eyes. "I baptize thee Marie Deborah Charlene

Velásquez. . . .'' The squalls almost drowned out the ancient intonation.

Lee bent down and whispered to his wife, "I told you she'd be the one. Jimmy will be stoic like a *Tejano*. She's the contrary one—just like her mother." He grinned and looked from the red squalling face of his daughter to the beatific calm of his son, James Alexander Thomas Velásquez, her fraternal twin, held securely in his mother's arms.

Melanie smiled serenely and whispered back, "Just wait." When it was Jimmy's turn, Charlee and Melanie exchanged babies and the ritual was repeated. Again the startled squall, this time emanating from the twin. Marie fell blissfully asleep in her mother's arms while Jimmy squirmed and cried. Melanie looked up at her tall husband with a self-satisfied smirk.

When the baptisms were completed, Father Gus dismissed his little flock with a joyous blessing. By the time they had all emerged into the warm August air outside the cathedral, both twins were dozing contentedly, Marie in her father's arms, Jimmy in his mother's.

"You and Charlee planned this," Lee accused, and his wife stifled a giggle.

"How could we? Neither of them like getting their heads wet, that's all," Melanie explained patiently.

"Surely you can't fault my experience holding babies, Lee," Charlee asked with a laugh, patting her protuberant belly. The proud godparents were expecting their fourth child within two months.

Everyone laughed, even the usually pompous and solemn Clarence Pemberton. He and Amos were present for the family celebration, as were all the children from Father Gus's school. Lame Deer, an honorary godfather, hovered between the two babies, in awe of such tiny bits of humanity and half afraid of them, although he would never admit as much.

Above the babble of children's laughter and adult conversation, a special guest of honor offered his opinion of the occasion. His orator's voice rang out sonorously across the plaza as he addressed Lee. "May I offer my sincere felicitations and commend you, Lee, on beginning with the odds even. Alas, I fear I have become sadly outnumbered since Mrs. Houston has presented me with four sisters for young Sam. You have a fighting chance with a boy and a girl at the onset."

"Well, Senator, when you wait until you're twenty-three to have your first baby, you might as well not do it by halves. That's why we decided on twins," Melanie replied with a twinkle.

"Considering what your Grandfather Manchester endured during your crusading years, dear heart, he's the one who's overjoyed most of all," Deborah said fondly.

Rafe placed his arm around his eldest daughter and a smile lit his harshly chiseled face. "He's waiting in Boston, broken leg and all, for you to bring his first great-grandson and -daughter for a visit, princess."

"We've already booked passage, Papa." Melanie assured her father.

"Yes, the *Star* waited for its best reporter during two months' maternity hiatus, and now she takes off for an extended visit to Massachusetts," Clarence interjected testily. "Adam Manchester is no older than I. Tell him to come to Texas as I did."

"Jeehosaphat! Yew old goat, Mr. Manchester's got hisself a broke lag—'n' if'n yew don't quit yore bellyachin' he won't be th' onliest one afflicted that way," Obedience warned the editor, who edged away from her warily while everyone else, including Amos, laughed.

Viewing the assembly of beloved friends and family, Lee felt his heart overflowing. "Looking forward to the trip, Night Flower?" he asked his wife.

"Oh, yes. Grandfather will be so thrilled to meet you and Jimmy and Marie! I'll even introduce you to William Lloyd Garrison and Lucretia Mott."

Lee rolled his eyes and exchanged a look of mock martyrdom with Jim Slade and Wash Oakley.

"I have every faith in this young woman," Houston boomed out. "Having frequently made the arduous trek to the citadel of eastern power, I have learned that nothing is so sweet as to set foot once again on Texas soil."

"I heartily agree, Senator," Melanie said simply, reaching out to squeeze Lee's hand.

Lee looked down at their children and then at the small beautiful face of his wife, "My parents came to Texas with a dream." Then raising his eyes to the assembled multitude filled with so many beloved faces—Hispanic, German, and Anglo, black and red—he said, "Through all of us, their dream will live on."

Author's Note

In terms of research, *Night Flower* proved to be the most troublesome, yet fascinating, of the Gone to Texas Trilogy. Originally we had conceived of a story in which the good guys were ranchers and rangers, and the bad guys were stereotypical Indian agents of B western lore. As with Carol's research into Texas horticulture, my research into Texas history destroyed our preconceived notions. Far from being the villains so often portrayed, Texas Indian agents, such as Robert S. Neighbors, who was an actual historical figure, were mostly unsung heroes who faced corrupt whiskey dealers and land-hungry settlers. Men like Neighbors struggled and often sacrificed their own lives to save Native Americans from extinction.

I also found that a number of Texas rangers like Seth Walkman were far from being the fearless champions of law and order described by Walter Prescott Webb. Such men may well have outnumbered noble rangers like Jeremy Lawrence. As to the Comanche and other smaller tribes beleaguered in blood feuds with the Texians, they, as all other races, produced people as good as Lame Deer and as corrupt as Buffalo Gall. Somewhere between the noble red man of Robert Trennert and the contemptible savage of Walter Prescott Webb, the truth about Texian-Indian relations must lie. My research indicates that neither side was blameless.

For those wishing to investigate these topics further, I would suggest several sources cited previously in the trilogy: John Henry Brown's *History of Texas*, Volume II, Walter Prescott Webb's *Texas Rangers* and Lesley Byrd Simpson's *Many Mexicos*, all standard reference works. For a more detailed and documented chronicle of the unsuccessful attempts to establish federal Indian reservations in Texas—the only state to enter the Union as a sovereign nation—I highly recommend *Alternative to Extinction* by Robert A. Trennert, Jr. *United States-Comanche Relations* by William T. Hagen moves beyond the time frame of our story to the tragic conclusion of one of the longest and bloodiest race wars in history, as do *The Comanche* and *Lone Star* by T. R. Fehrenbach. Both Fehrenbach's books are standard reference works mentioned earlier, superbly evenhanded and insightful in their treatment of this controversial issue.

As in *Cactus Flower* and *Moon Flower*, Sam Houston again makes a cameo appearance in *Night Flower*, now as a United States senator and the proud father of one boy and four girls. (The Houstons were later blessed with three more boys!) *Sam Houston's Wife, A Biography of Margaret Lea Houston* by William Seale is interesting and written from a point of view different from that of standard biographies of the great man already cited. I must beg pardon for taking a liberty with historical events, in that I placed Senator Houston in San Antonio in the fall of 1852, when in fact he was in Washington at that time, not even home in Texas. For the purposes of my plot, his presence as guest of honor for the gala ball was essential, and he did relish such political and social events. Additionally, I might add that although the details about the Blaine, Walkman, and Greer conspiracy were fictional, Houston's unpopular concern for the plight of the Indians has been well-documented. His

involvement with Lawrence would have been in keeping
with his character.

A fascinating, well-documented, and bloodcurdling description of an adventurer's life in the old Southwest,
Savage Scene, the Life and Times of James Kirker, by
William Cochran McGaw, provided me with ample and
grisly details for Lee's nightmares. The diary of Susan
Shelby Magoffin, *Down the Santa Fe Trail and into Mexico*,
gives excellent insights into how women fared on the
frontier and describes politics, social customs, and daily life
in superb detail.

As in the first two books of the trilogy, *Night Flower* is
the weaving of a rich historical tapestry peopled by real-life
and fictional characters. I hope their heroism and villainy,
their humor and courage entertain you and deepen your
appreciation of the complex and wonderful land of Texas.

Shirl loves to hear from
her readers. You can write
to her at:

P.O. Box 72
Adrian, Michigan 49221
(Please enclose SASE.)

Smoldering Shirl Henke

Surrender yourself to these rapturous
tales of love by the award-winning
author *Romantic Times* hails as
"a new rising star of historicals."

GOLDEN LADY

LOVE UNWILLING

CAPTURE THE SUN

CACTUS FLOWER

MOON FLOWER

WARNER BOOKS

AVAILABLE AT YOUR LOCAL BOOKSTORE